George Henry Lewes

**Collection of british authors: The Physiology of Common Life**

Volume: I.

George Henry Lewes

**Collection of british authors: The Physiology of Common Life**
*Volume: I.*

ISBN/EAN: 9783742830975

Manufactured in Europe, USA, Canada, Australia, Japa

Cover: Foto ©Andreas Hilbeck / pixelio.de

Manufactured and distributed by brebook publishing software
(www.brebook.com)

George Henry Lewes

**Collection of british authors: The Physiology of Common Life**

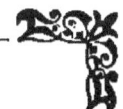

# COLLECTION

## OF

# BRITISH AUTHORS

## TAUCHNITZ EDITION.

VOL. 518.

THE PHYSIOLOGY OF COMMON LIFE BY LEWES

IN TWO VOLUMES.

VOL. 1.

LEIPZIG: BERNHARD TAUCHNITZ.

PARIS: C. REINWALD & Cᵉ, 15, RUE DES SAINTS PÈRES.

# ˙JCHNITZ EDITION.

*Each volume ¹/₂ Thlr.*

ADAMS: Sacred Allegories 1 v.
‚UILAR: Home Influence 2 v. The
.ecompense 2 v.
llia 1 v. Carr of Carrlyon 2 v. The
: v. In that State of Life 1 v.
OBTH: Windsor Castle 1 v. Saint
. v. Jack Sheppard (w. portr.) 1 v. The
olreWitches 1v. The Star-Chamber 2v.
ltoh of Bacon 1 v. The Spendthrift 1 v.
Mervyn Clitheroe 2 v. Ovingdean Grange 1 v.
The Constable of the Tower 1v. The Lord Mayor
of London 2v. Cardinal Pole 2v. John Law 2v.
The Spanish Match 2v. The Constable de Bour-
bon 2 v. Old Court 2v. Myddleton Pomfret 2 v.
South-Sea Bubble 2v. Hilary St. Ives 2v. Talbot
Harland 1 v. Tower Hill 1 v.
ALL FOR GREED 1 v. Love the Avenger 2 v.
MISS AUSTEN: Sense and Sensibility 1 v.
Mansfield Park 1 v. Pride and Prejudice 1 v.
NINA BALATKA 1 v.
REV. R. H. BAYNES: Lyra Anglicana 1 v.
CURRER BELL: Jane Eyre 2 v. Shirley
2 v. Villette 2 v. The Professor 1 v.
E. & A. BELL: Wuthering Heights, and
Agnes Grey 2 v.
LADY BLESSINGTON: Meredith 1 v.
Strathern 2 v. Memoirs of a Femme de
Chambre 1 v. Marmaduke Herbert 2 v. Coun-
try Quarters (w. portr.) 2 v.
BRADDON: LadyAudley's Secret 2v. Aurora
Floyd 2v. Eleanor s Victory 2v. Marchmont's
Legacy 2v. Henry Dunbar 2v. Doctor's Wife 2v.
Only a Clod 2v. Sir Jasper's Tenant 2 v. Lady's
Mile 2v. Rupert Godwin 2v. Dead-Sea Fruit 2v.
Run to Earth 2 v. Fenton's Quest 2 v.
BROOKS: The Silver Cord 3 v. Sooner or
Later 3 v.
BROWN: Rab and his Friends 1 v.
TOM BROWN'S School Days 1 v.
BULWER (LORD LYTTON): Pelham (w.
portr.)1 v. Eugene Aram 1v. Paul Clifford 1 v.
Zanoni 1 v. Pompeii 1 v. The Disowned 1 v.
Ernest Maltravers 1 v. Alice 1 v. Eva, and the
Pilgrims of the Rhine 1v. Devereux 1v.Godol-
phin and Falkland 1 v. Rienzi 1 v. Night and
Morning 1v. The Last of the Barons 2v. Athens
2 v. Poems of Schiller 1v. Lucretia 2 v. Harold
2 v. King Arthur 2 v. The New Timon; Saint
Stephen's 1 v. The Caxtons 2 v. My Novel 4 v.
What will he do with it? 4 v. Dramatic Works
2 v. A Strange Story 2 v. Caxtoniana 2v. The
Lost Tales of Miletus 1 v. Miscellaneous Prose
Works 4 v. The Odes and Epodes of Horace 2 v.
SIR HENRY LYTTON BULWER: His-
torical Characters 2 v. Life of Palmerston 2 v.
BUNYAN: The Pilgrim's Progress 1 v.
BURIED ALONE 1 v.
MISS BURNEY: Evelina 1 v.
BURNS: Poetical Works (w. portr.) 1 v.
BYRON: The Works (w. portr.)compl. 5 v.
T. CARLYLE: The French Revolution 3 v.
Frederick the Great 13v. Oliver Cromwell 4v.

# COLLECTION

OF

# BRITISH AUTHORS.

## VOL. 518.

---

THE PHYSIOLOGY OF COMMON LIFE BY G. H. LEWES.

IN TWO VOLUMES.

VOL. I.

# THE

# PHYSIOLOGY OF COMMON LIFE.

BY

## GEORGE HENRY LEWES,

AUTHOR OF "SEASIDE STUDIES," "RANTHORPE," &C.

WITH NUMEROUS WOODCUTS.

*COPYRIGHT EDITION.*

TWO VOLUMES.

VOL. I.

LEIPZIG

BERNHARD TAUCHNITZ

1860.

# PREFACE.

----

THE object of the following Work differs from that of all other works on popular science in its attempt to meet the wants of the Student, while meeting those of the general reader, who is supposed to be wholly unacquainted with anatomy and physiology. The many excellent Treatises which exist are only suited to the advanced student; they assume a knowledge, and a facility of apprehension, which can only issue from a practical familiarity with the subjects.

The remembrance of my own wants and difficulties led me, many years ago, to the belief that the work which was really the most suitable for general culture, would also be of material assistance to the Student. Accordingly, although there are many topics, interesting and important to the physiologist, which find no place in this work, because they are without the range of general culture, I have done my best to render the exposition, of all the topics selected, on a level with the science of our day.

In pursuance of this object I have been forced to depart very widely from the practice of other popular writers, who consider themselves bound to act as "middlemen" between scientific authorities and the public, and to expound facts and doctrines as they find them. I could not adopt this easy and convenient plan. I could not bring myself to publish, on the authority of respected names, statements which I knew to be false, and opinions which I believed to be erroneous. After having laboured earnestly to get at the truth, it would have been disloyal to contribute in any way to the spread of what I believed to be error. All that I felt bound to do, was to state impartially the facts and opinions current among physiologists; and, when those opinions seemed inadmissible, to state the reasons for their rejection. There is therefore a great deal of criticism, and much original matter in this work.

It is in the chapters on the Nervous System that the greatest amount of dissent from current opinions will be found; and it is there that the reader will most probably feel the greatest difficulty in agreeing with me, especially if he be versed in the doctrines of the schools, and not very familiar with the subjects through direct observation and experiment. I can only say that the views there put forth are the result of very considerable research, embracing molluscs, bees, beetles, spiders, locusts, crabs, fishes, frogs, tritons, lizards, chickens, moles, mice, rats, cats, dogs, sheep, pigs, calves, oxen, and men.

The literature of each subject has been given with as much fulness as seemed useful; and never at secondhand, unless specially acknowledged. The deficiencies in this respect will be found greatest in the English department; the reason of which is that my purse is not long enough to command the Transactions, Journals, and Reviews in which my countrymen have recorded their labours; and I have not the advantage of commanding a public library. It has been my desire to render every one his due; but of course a great many claims have been passed over in ignorance.

*March* 1860.

# CONTENTS

## OF VOLUME I.

---

### CHAPTER II.

#### FOOD AND DRINK.

##### SECTION I. — ON THE NATURE OF FOOD.

Varieties of food — The eaters of clay — The chemical and physiological methods of investigation — "One man's meat another man's poison," illustrated — A caution to parents — Wholesome and unwholesome food — Relation of food to the organism — Vital process incapable of chemical

## CHAPTER III.

### DIGESTION AND INDIGESTION.

## CHAPTER IV.

### THE STRUCTURE AND USES OF OUR BLOOD.

## CHAPTER V.

### CIRCULATION OF THE BLOOD: ITS HISTORY, COURSE, AND CAUSES.

## CHAPTER VI.

### RESPIRATION AND SUFFOCATION.

## CHAPTER VII.

### WHY WE ARE WARM, AND HOW WE KEEP SO.

XIICONTENTS OF VOLUME I.

# THE PHYSIOLOGY OF COMMON LIFE.

## VOL. I.

---

## CHAPTER I.

### HUNGER AND THIRST.

Incentives to action — Cause of hunger: waste and repair of the body — Periodicity of hunger — Comparison of the organism with a steam-engine Inaccurate — The blood of starving men — Starvation — Cases of prolonged fasting in animals — Fabulous stories of long fasting in men and women — Aspects of starvation — The parts of the body which first disappear in starvation — Sleeplessness of starving men — Agonies of starvation — Pathetic stories — The sensation of hunger, and its cause — Hunger as a general, and as a local, sensation — Thirst as a sensation — Cause of thirst — Necessity of water in the organism, and consequences of deficiency — Thirst as a mode of torture — Story of the Black Hole of Calcutta — How to quench thirst — The drink of animals — Effects of thirst.

HUNGER is one of the beneficent and terrible instincts. It is, indeed, the very fire of life, underlying all impulses to labour, and moving man to noble activities by its imperious demands. Look where we may, we see it as the motive power which sets the vast army of human machinery in action.

It is Hunger which brings these stalwart navvies together in orderly gangs to cut paths through mountains, to throw bridges across rivers, to intersect the land with the great iron ways which bring city into daily communication with city. Hunger is the invisible overseer of the men who are erecting palaces, prison-houses, barracks, and villas. Hunger sits at the loom, which with stealthy power is weaving the wondrous fabrics of cotton and silk. Hunger labours at the furnace and the plough, coercing the native indolence of man into strenuous and incessant activity. Let food be abundant and easy of access, and civilisation becomes impossible: so indissolubly dependent are our higher efforts on our lower impulses. Nothing but the necessities of food will force man to that labour which he hates, and will always avoid when he can. And although this seems obvious only when applied to the labouring classes, it is equally though less obviously true when applied to all other classes, for the money we all labour to gain is nothing but food, and the surplus of food, which will buy other men's labour.

Hunger, although beneficent, is no less terrible. When its progress is unchecked, it becomes a devouring flame, destroying all that is most noble in man. Hunger is a stimulus to crime, no less than to honest labour. It wanders through dark alleys, whispering desperate thoughts into eager ears; and it maddens the shipwrecked crew till they cast away all shame, all pity, all desire of respect, and perpetrate deeds which cannot be mentioned without horror. Hunger subjugates the humanity in man, and makes the brute predominate. Impelled by this ferocious instinct, men have eaten their companions, and women have even eaten their own children. Hunger has thus a twofold character: beside the picture of the activities it inspires, we must also contemplate the picture of the ferocities it evokes.

What is this Hunger — what its causes and effects?

In one sense we may all be said to know what Hunger is; in another sense no man can enlighten us; we have all felt it, but Science as yet has been unable to furnish any sufficient explanation of it. Between the gentle and agreeable stimulus known as Appetite, and the agony of Starvation, there are infinite gradations. The early stages are familiar even to the wealthy; but only the very poor, or those who have undergone exceptional calamities, such as shipwreck and the like, know anything of the later stages. We all know what it is to be hungry, even *very* hungry; but the terrible approaches of protracted hunger are exceptional experiences. From materials furnished by sad experiences, both familiar and exceptional, I will endeavour to state the capital phenomena and their causes.

And first we must explain what is meant by a *tissue*, as the word will be of constant recurrence in these pages. Previous to the time of Bichât, who may be called the founder of philosophical anatomy, the body was considered 'as made up of various parts or organs; when these parts had been enumerated, the task of description was over. Bichât flashed light upon the science when he showed that the organs themselves were made up of various tissues, or elementary structures, each of which preserved its characteristic properties in whatever part of the body it might be found. Thus the heart, for instance, is an organ constructed out of muscular tissue, connective tissue, nervous tissue, and adipose tissue — each of these tissues manifesting the same properties in the heart which it manifests in every other organ; just as the various substances out of which a ship is constructed — wood, hemp, copper, iron, tar, &c. — preserve their characteristic properties, though the wood may be rudder, deck, or mast, and the iron anchor, nail, or cable.

The tissues are the elementary portions of the animal fabric; and a distinct branch of the science is devoted to their study under the name of *Histology*, also called *General* Anatomy. The organism is composed of organs, and the organs of tissues.

I. THE CAUSE OF HUNGER. — In every living organism there is an incessant and reciprocal activity of *waste* and *repair*. The living fabric, in the very actions which constitute its life, is momently yielding up its particles to destruction, like the coal which is burned in the furnace: so much coal to so much heat, so much waste of tissue to so much vital activity. You cannot wink your eye, move your finger, or think a thought, but some minute particle of your substance must be sacrificed in doing so. Unless the coal which is burning be from time to time replaced, the fire soon smoulders, and finally goes out; unless the substance of your body, which is wasting, be from time to time furnished with fresh food, Life flickers, and at length becomes extinct.

Hunger is the instinct which teaches us to replenish the empty furnace.

But although the want of food, necessary to repair the waste of life, is the primary cause of Hunger, it does not, as is often erroneously stated, in itself constitute Hunger. The absence of necessary food causes the sensation, but it is not itself the sensa-

1*

tion.   Food may be absent without any sensation, such as we express by the word Hunger, being felt: insane people frequently
subject themselves to prolonged abstinence from food, without
any hungry cravings; and, in a lesser degree, it is familiar to us
all how any violent emotion of grief or joy will completely destroy, not only the sense of Hunger, but our possibility of even
swallowing the food which an hour before was cravingly desired.
Further, it is known that the feeling of Hunger may be allayed
by opium, tobacco, or even by inorganic substances introduced
into the stomach, although none of these can supply the deficiency of food.   Want of food is therefore the *primary*, but not
the *proximate*, cause of Hunger.   I am using the word Hunger
in its popular sense here, as indicating that specific sensation
which impels us to eat; when the subject has been more fully
unfolded, the reader will see how far this popular sense of the
word is applicable to all the phenomena.

We can now understand why Hunger should recur periodi-
cally, and with a frequency in proportion to the demands of
nutrition.   Young animals demand food more frequently than
the adult; birds and mammalia more frequently than reptiles
and fishes.   A lethargic boa-constrictor will only feed about
once a-month, a lively rabbit twenty times a-day.   Temperature
has also its influence on the frequency of the recurrence: cold
excites the appetite of warm-blooded animals, but diminishes
that of the cold-blooded, the majority of which cease to take any
food at the temperature of freezing.   Those warm-blooded animals which present the curious phenomenon of "winter sleep,"
resemble the cold-blooded animals in this respect; during hybernation they need no food, because almost all the vital actions are
suspended.   It is found that, at the temperature of freezing, even
digestion is suspended.   Hunter fed lizards at the commencement of winter, and from time to time opened them, without
perceiving any indications of digestion having gone on; and
when spring returned, those lizards which were still living,
vomited the food which they had retained undigested in their
stomachs during the whole winter.*

Besides the usual conditions of recurring appetite, there are

* HUNTER: *Observations on Certain Parts of the Animal Economy.*

some unusual conditions, depending on peculiarities in the individual, or on certain states of the organism. Thus during convalescence after some maladies, especially fevers, the appetite is almost incessant; and Admiral Byron relates that, after suffering from a month's starvation during a shipwreck, he and his companions, when on shore, were not content with gorging themselves while at table, but filled their pockets that they might eat during the intervals of meals. In certain diseases there is a craving for food which no supplies allay; but of this we need not speak here.

The animal body is often compared with a steam-engine, of which the *food* is the *fuel* in the furnace, furnishing the motor-power. As an illustration, this may be acceptable enough, but, like many other illustrations, it is often accepted for a real analogy, a true expression of the facts. As an analogy, its failure is conspicuous. No engine burns its *own substance* as fuel: its motor-power is all derived from the coke which is burning in the furnace, and is in direct proportion to the amount of coke consumed; when the coke is exhausted, the engine stops. But every organism consumes its own body: it does not burn food, but tissue. The fervid wheels of Life were made out of food, and in their action motor-power is evolved.

The difference between the organism and the mechanism is this: the production of heat in the organism is not the *cause* of its activity, but the *result* of it; whereas in the mechanism, the activity originates in, and is sustained by, the heat. Remove the coals which generate the steam, and you immediately arrest the action of the mechanism; but long after all the food has disappeared, and become transformed into the solids and liquids of the living fabric, the organism continues to manifest all the powers which it manifested before.

There is of course a limit to this continuance, inasmuch as vital activity is dependent on the destruction of tissue. The man who takes no food, lives, like a spendthrift, on his capital, and cannot survive his capital. He is observed to get thin, pale, and feeble, because he is spending without replenishing his coffers; he is gradually *impoverishing* himself, because Life is waste.

11. The Effects of Hunger. — In a future chapter we shall inquire minutely into the structure and composition of the Blood;

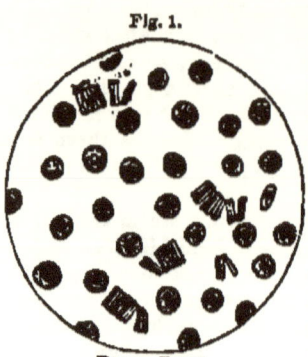

Fig. 1.

Blood-Discs.

for the present, it must suffice to say that the Blood carries in its current certain bodies called blood-discs, which perform the chief part in nutrition. They are of two kinds, the red and the colourless. Here is the figure of the red discs, as seen under the microscope.

If we examine the blood of a starving man, we shall find its elementary composition to be precisely similar to that of the same man in his healthy state, but the *proportions* of that composition will be greatly altered; the discs — which have been denominated the nutritive solids of the blood — are much diminished in quantity, and all its inorganic constituents, which are the products of destroyed tissues, are much increased. In fact, these inorganic products, like the pawn-tickets found in the spendthrift's desk, are significant of the extravagance and the poverty which point to ruin.

We cannot say how long such a spendthrift life may continue, because Time has no definite relation to the phenomena of starvation; these phenomena depend on certain specific changes going on in the body, which may occur with indefinite rapidity. Within the same period of time the *whole cycle of change* necessary for destruction may have completed itself, or *only a few of the stages* in this cycle may have been gone through: a man under certain conditions will not survive six days' fasting, and under other conditions he will survive six weeks'.

But if we cannot with any precision say *how long* starvation will be in effecting its fatal end, we can say *how much* waste is fatal. From the celebrated experiments of Chossat on Inanition,[*] it appears that death arrives whenever the waste reaches

_____
[*] Chossat: *Recherches Expérimentales sur l'Inanition.* 1843.

an average proportion of two-fifths. That is to say, supposing
an animal to weigh 100 lb., it will succumb when its weight is
reduced to 60 lb. Life may of course cease before that point
is reached, but cannot, in ordinary circumstances, be prolonged
after it.

The average loss which can be sustained is 40 per cent;
sometimes the loss is greater, especially if the animal be very
fat: thus in the *Transactions of the Linnæan Society*, a case is reported of a fat pig which was buried under thirty feet of chalk
for one hundred and sixty days; his weight fell in that period
no less than 75 per cent. Curiously enough, as an illustration of
what was just said respecting Time not being an index of the
amount of change, fishes and reptiles were found by Chossat to
perish at precisely the same limit of *weight* as that at which
warm-blooded animals perished, but they required a period
three-and-twenty times as long to reach it in: thus if the experiment be performed of starving a bird and a frog during the
warm weather, although both will perish when their loss of
weight reaches 40 per cent, the one will not survive a week, the
other will survive three-and-twenty weeks.

It appears from Chossat's observations that the animal body
daily wastes one twenty-fourth of its entire weight; and this ac-
cords very closely with the experiments of Bidder and Schmidt,
which show that the animal requires at least one twenty-third of
its entire weight in daily assimilable food, otherwise it will lose
in substance.*

III. PROLONGED FASTING. — Having clearly fixed these principles, we may proceed to consider the many remarkable cases
of *prolonged fasting* which appeal to the credulity of the public,
and which find a place even in very grave treatises, as well as in
the less critical columns of newspapers. Are we to believe these
marvels, or reject them? and on what grounds are we justified
in rejecting them? Such questions the reader will frequently be
called upon to answer; and as a contribution towards the formation of a definite and philosophical judgment, here are some of

* BIDDER u. SCHMIDT: *Die Verdauungssäfte und der Stoffwechsel*, 1852.

the most striking cases on record, and the physiological principles implied in them.

The human body is in many respects so different from that of animals, especially in its complexity, that we can draw no very accurate conclusion from *their* powers of enduring abstinence; but after all, the differences will only be differences of degree, and the same physiological laws must regulate both, so that we may be certain of the effect of abstinence on man not being *essentially* dissimilar to that on all other warm-blooded animals.

Let us therefore first see how the case stands with animals. The experiments of Pommer establish that carnivorous animals resist starvation longer than the herbivorous; birds of prey longer than birds feeding on seeds and fruits.

I think we might *a priori* have deduced this conclusion from the known differences in the *intervals* of recurring Hunger, and in the different quantities of food eaten by the two classes. The carnivorous animal eats voraciously when food is within reach, but having satisfied his appetite, he remains several hours before again feeling hungry; and in a state of nature the intervals between his meals are necessarily variable, and often much prolonged, because his food is neither abundant nor easy of access. The herbivorous animal, on the other hand, has his food constantly within reach, and is almost always eating, because an enormous amount of vegetable food is needed to furnish him with sustenance. The lion, or the cat, becomes inured to long abstinence; the rabbit or the cow scarcely knows the feeling. It is clear, therefore, that the one will better endure long fasting than the other.

Chossat's experiments on eight-and-forty birds and animals, show that the average duration of life exceeded nine days and a half—the maximum being twenty days and a half, the minimum a little more than two days.

The young always die first, the adult before the aged; this is true of men as of animals.

Some of the simpler animals exhibit remarkable powers of endurance. Latreille pinned a spider to a cork, and after four months found it still alive. Baker kept a stag-beetle three years in a box without food, and at the end of that period it flew away. Müller relates that a scorpion not only survived the voyage from Africa to Holland, but continued without food for nine months afterwards. Rondelet kept a fish three years without food, and Rudolphi a *Proteus anguineus* five years! Snakes, we know, live for many months without eating; and Redi found that a scal lived, out of water and without food, four weeks.

In all these cases, except that of the fish kept by Rondelet, the animals were quiescent, and did not waste their substance by the ordinary activities; and with regard to the fish, some doubts may be entertained whether it did not find worms and larvæ in the water.

Passing from animals to man, we find that death arrives on the fifth or sixth day of total abstinence from food and drink. But this is a general statement to which various exceptions may be named. Much depends on the peculiar constitution of the individual, his age, health, and other conditions. Some die on the second and third days; others survive till the tenth, eleventh, and even sixteenth days. Again, considerable differences will result from the different situations in which the men are placed — such as those of quiescence or activity, of temperature, moisture, &c.

The examples of protracted fasting recorded are, as usual, deficient for the most part in that rigorous authenticity which is demanded by science; many of them are obviously fabulous exaggerations. M. Bérard has borrowed the following from Haller, adding some cases which came under his own knowledge. I give them as specimens — not as data.

"A young girl, ashamed to confess her poverty, went without food for seventy-eight days, during which she only sucked lemons.

"Another woman of the same place remained four months without food, and another fasted a whole year.

"Haller reports two other cases of fasting for three and four years.

"Mackenzie reports in the *Philosophical Transactions* the story of a young girl who had lockjaw for eighteen years, and had taken no food during four years.

"A Scotchwoman is reported in the *Philosophical Transactions*, vol. lxvii., to have lived eight years without taking anything except a little water on one or two occasions.

"A case of fasting for ten years is celebrated in many works. Fabrice de Hilden, who took precautions against deception, says that Eva Flegen neither ate nor drank during six years.

"But all these stories are surpassed by that of a woman who remained fifty years without food; it is added, however, that she sometimes took skimmed milk."

"Admitting," says M. Bérard, "that there has been deception in some of these cases, and that the love of the marvellous has presided over the narration of others, we cannot refuse to believe that some are authentic. Every year such cases are registered. In 1836, M. Lavigne invited me to visit a woman of fifty-two, who, after having reduced herself to a glass of milk daily during eighteen months, had taken nothing in the shape of food or drink during the last five months. In 1839, M. Parizot communicated to me the fact of a girl at Marcilly who had taken no solid nutriment for six years, and for the last five years no liquid or solid. In 1838, M. Plongeau wrote to me to say that he had seen a woman at Ayrens, aged eight-and-forty, who during the last eight years had received no nourishment whatever."*

It is rather startling to find so learned a physiologist as M. Bérard recording such cases, and trying to explain them. The possibility of deception and exaggeration is so great, that we are tempted to reject almost every one of these cases rather than reject all physiological teaching.

The following is one of the most extraordinary of the cases which are repeated by modern writers with confidence. Janet M'Leod, after epilepsy, and fever, remained five years in bed, *seldom speaking*, and receiving food only by constraint. At length she obstinately refused all sustenance, her jaws became locked, and in attempting to force them open two of her teeth were broken. A small quantity of liquid was introduced by the aperture, none of which she swallowed, and dough made of oatmeal was likewise rejected. *She slept much*, and her head was bent down on her breast. In this deplorable state she continued

---

* BÉRARD: *Cours de Physiologie*, 1848, I. 538.

four years, without her relatives being aware of her receiving any aliment except a little water; but after a longer interval she revived, and subsisted on crumbs of bread with milk, or water sucked from her hand.

Attention is called to the two facts of Janet's seldom speaking and sleeping much, because, supposing the case to be true, they materially affect the question. In a state of such quiescence as is here implied, the waste of the body would be reduced to a minimum, consequently the need of food would be minimised. Nevertheless, in the present state of Physiology, I think we are justified in asserting that some deception or exaggeration, not now ascertainable, is at the bottom of this as of all similar cases; and until a case free from all suspicion shall have been produced for the satisfaction of Science, we are bound to deny the probability of such stories; since that which all our knowledge shows to be in itself contradictory, must necessarily have the highest improbability, and can only be accepted on the most rigorous evidence. Either we must give up our Physiology altogether, or we must reject these stories.

For observe, on the one hand, several of the reported cases of long fasting have been subsequently proved to be impostures, and this naturally throws a suspicion over all similar cases. On the other hand, physiological laws, established by induction from thousands of facts tested by every variety of method, pronounce these cases to be not possible; and we are called upon to decide whether it is more probable that these inductions should be wrong, or that some imposture or exaggeration should lie at the bottom of the narrated marvels. There cannot be a moment's hesitation as to which alternative we must accept; but the reader will naturally desire a clear conception of the physiological contradictions which I have asserted to be implied in these marvellous narratives — the more so as many professed physiologists do not seem to be fully aware of them.

Supposing the *waste* of the body to be reduced to a minimum by the perfect quiescence in which the patients remained, we must still bear in mind that this *diminution* is not *total arrest* of waste. The patient scarcely moves, seldom speaks, and sleeps

much.  Very little destruction of tissue will take place, compared with the amount destroyed by the same person in ordinary
activity, and very little food will be needed to repair such waste;
but although *comparatively* small, the amount of waste will be
*absolutely* large; we cannot say how large it will be, we can only
say that it must be large.

Let us fix our attention on only two sources of this waste, and
the proof will be evident.  The production of animal heat is only
possible through a large amount of chemical change going on in
the organism; it is produced by "direct combustion" (according
to the chemical school of physiologists), by "the disengagement
of heat in chemical compositions and decompositions" (according
to another school), and according to all schools the high temperature of the body depends on organic processes, which necessarily imply waste of tissue.  The warmth of the bed in which the
patient lies is not sufficient to preserve her temperature at its
proper height; she must burn her own substance to keep up her
animal heat; and when we think of the high degree of temperature maintained during a period of four years, solely by the combustion of the body itself, we shall see at once that it is utterly
*impossible* any organism, during so long a period, could sustain
such waste without repair.

Here, then, is the dilemma: either Janet M'Leod *did* maintain the ordinary temperature of the body during these four
years, in which case she must have destroyed more tissue to produce that heat than the body could lose without cessation of life;
or she did *not* maintain the ordinary temperature, in which case
she would have died from the very want of this animal heat, since
all organisms perish when their normal temperature is considerably lowered.

Let us now consider the second source of waste.  Janet
breathed during these four years; gently, we may suppose, and
with no deep inspirations, yet constantly, day and night without
interruption.  Now, what does this breathing depend on?  It
depends on the constant interchange between carbonic acid in
the blood, and oxygen in the air.  Unless there were carbonic
acid in the blood, no exchange could take place, no breathing

could be effected.* Every moment, therefore, some small portion of carbonic acid must be separated from the blood, and replaced by oxygen. Whence came this carbonic acid? From destruction of tissue. Directly, or indirectly, carbonic acid was produced in the act of waste. Its presence implies waste, and the act of breathing implies a continuous supply of such waste.

That this is no hypothesis, but the simple expression of the facts, every physiologist knows. It may be rendered generally intelligible by referring to what is observed with the hybernating animals. The dormouse begins its winter sleep well clothed with fat. It never moves for months; its respiration is slow and feeble, but it does breathe, and the waste of its tissues which this breathing causes is very noticeable at the close of winter. Now, if we suppose Janet to have been in a state of "suspended vitality" analogous to that of the dormouse, we shall still have to admit that her breathing alone would gradually waste her substance; and however slow that waste may be supposed, it cannot have been such that four years would not have exhausted the whole amount of available material. Every time she moved in bed, every time she spoke, every time she raised her hand, the rate of waste would be accelerated.

It is found that a slug kept without food loses one-eleventh of its weight in six weeks. We cannot admit that, even in a bedridden girl, the vital activity would be slower than in a slug; and we know from Chossat's experiments that the loss of two-fifths of their weight destroys all animals.

From these general considerations, which might be multiplied, I affirm that, unless all Physiology is a delusion, the marvellous stories of your years' fasting, and the like, are impostures; and this affirmation is strengthened by all the cases in which the motive and possibility of deception are eliminated. Thus when men have voluntarily starved themselves to death, they have never survived three months. Granié, who murdered his wife, starved himself in the prison of Toulouse, and expired on the sixty-third day, during which time he drank water, and occasionally ate a little. The religious enthusiast, whom Dr. Willan

* This will be shown further on in the Chapter on RESPIRATION and SUFFOCATION.

refers to, lived only two months, although he occasionally sucked an orange.

These men only survived thus long, because in abstaining from solid food, they did not also abstain from liquid. Life is considerably prolonged if liquid be taken. Redi found that birds kept without water as well as food lived only nine days; those to whom he gave water lived twenty days.* I cannot, however, agree with those physiologists who, like Burdach and Bérard attribute this sustaining power of water to the organic particles suspended in it, because such an amount must necessarily be quite inadequate to supply the loss of an organism whose waste is rapid; and we must remember that an animal dies of *Thirst* even more rapidly than of Hunger; so that when water is withheld, the death is hastened by the complication of two causes. Now Janet M'Leod, and other persons said to have lived without food or drink, were under the pressure of these two causes, and sustained that pressure, we are told, four years!

We are thus forced to reject all narratives of absolute fasting prolonged over three months.

Having considered the effects of total abstinence, we may now inquire into the effects of partial abstinence.

An animal deprived of food perishes whenever its loss of weight reaches a certain point; and, curiously enough, *insufficiency of food* causes death at precisely the same point as total want of food, *i. e.* as soon as the original weight is reduced to six-tenths. Men, therefore, reduced to an insufficient allowance, whether from famine, shipwreck, or siege, will inevitably perish unless the allowance be increased; it will be as if they had received no food at all, only they will be longer before they succumb. An important lesson is contained in this fact, and one which should never be forgotten in the management of prisons, schools, or workhouses.

IV. Aspects of Starvation. — Terrible are the aspects of starving men; and it is well that we should know these aspects, lest we be the dupes of impostors, or confound the truly wretched with the professional mendicant. The first noticeable point is

* Redi: *Osservazioni intorno agli animali viventi;* quoted by Burdach.

the excessive thinness of starving men, which is not the leanness of lean men, but manifests itself as unmistakable emaciation. The face is always lividly pale, the cheeks are sunken, the eyes —what an expression in the eyes! never to be forgotten by those who have once seen it: all the vitality of the body seems centred there, in feverish brightness; the pupil is dilated, and the eye is fixed in a wild stare, which is never veiled by the winking lids. All movements of the body are slow and difficult: the hand trembles; the voice is feeble; intelligence seems gone; the wretched sufferers, when asked what they feel, have but one answer, "We are hungry."

There is one remarkable fact with reference to starvation which may here be noted, and that is the resistance opposed by the nervous substance to the effects of emaciation. Instead of being the first to suffer from deficient food, as its complexity and the lateness of its appearance in the animal series would lead us to suppose, the nervous tissue is the last to be affected. From the experiments of Chossat we learn that, in every 100 parts of *each* of the following substances, 93 are lost of the fat, 52 of the liver, 42 of the muscles, 16 of the bones, and only 2 of the nerve-substance, by the time starvation has terminated in death. The idea of our solid bones, principally composed of inorganic matter, losing eight times as much as our semi-liquid nerves, which are so predominantly organic in their structure, will seem very paradoxical; and the paradox is increased when we learn that, in spite of fat being beyond all proportion the most destructible tissue in the body, Von Bibra finds the fat in the brain scarcely affected in starvation, although the fat in the muscles has been greatly wasted.*

It is this which enables us hypothetically to explain the sleeplessness of men and animals suffering from hunger. A starving man has been known to remain seven days and nights without sleep. This nervous excitability, which often manifests itself as delirium, probably arises from the disengagement of the brain from those organic activities which in the normal state call so largely on its energies; for the energies of the brain are not expended only on intelligence and emotion, but likewise, and to a

* CANSTATT: *Jahresbericht*, 1854, p. 119.

great extent, on the functions of nutrition and locomotion. Considering the nervous system as a centre or fountain of influence, we may detect three streams in which the influence flows — a nutritive stream, a locomotive stream, and a sensitive stream. If the demand from the nutritive stream be large, the supply to the sensitive and locomotive streams will be proportionately reduced. Deep thought, or anxiety, disturbs the digestion and circulation; violent and protracted exercise, amounting to fatigue, incapacitates for thinking: the habitually trained athlete is nearly an idiot, the over-eater little better. When, therefore, a man is starving, the amount of nervous activity usually expended on his nutritive system is disengaged; and as his feebleness diminishes his muscular activity, the amount of nervous influence usually expended on locomotion is reduced, leaving the brain, with all this surplus activity, to prey upon itself: sleeplessness and madness naturally result from this over-excitement.

V. AGONIES OF STARVATION.— Respecting the agonies endured by starving men, we have little accurate information. When those who have undergone the horrors of starvation are preserved, and attempt to recount them, they cannot do more than give vague indications; for there is nothing more difficult to describe than the sensations of the digestive organs, even during the continuance of the sensation; and how difficult it is to describe them when past, may be conceived by any one who attempts to do so in his own case. Most of the narratives we have are recorded by men little accustomed to analyse their sensations, and we must be content to fix our attention on the general characteristics of these narratives. From these cases two may be selected.

Goldsmith says that the captain of a wrecked vessel told him that "he was the only person who had not lost his senses when they received accidental relief. He assured me his pains at first were so great that he was often tempted to eat a part of the men who died, and which the rest of his crew actually lived upon. He said that, during the continuance of this paroxysm, he found his pains insupportable, and was desirous at one time of anticipating that death which he thought inevitable. But *his pains gradually* *ceased after the sixth day* (for they had water in the ship, which kept them alive so long), and then he was in a state rather of languor than desire; nor did he much wish for food except when he saw others eating. The latter part of the time, when his health was almost destroyed, a thousand strange images rose upon his mind, and every one of his senses began to bring him wrong information. When he was presented with food by the ship's company that took him up, he could not help looking at it with loathing instead of desire; and it was not till after four days that his stomach was brought to its natural tone, when the violence of his appetite returned with a sort of canine eagerness."*

It will doubtless seem very strange to the uninitiated that a man after prolonged fasting, when his system is in such need of food and his appetite so keen, should be nevertheless in no proper condition to eat that food, and can only arrive at the proper condition by degrees, by eating a little at a time. The fact is, however, that, like all other organs, the stomach suffers for want of regular work. In fasting, the glands no longer secrete; the blood quits the stomach; the regular activity is interrupted; and when food again calls upon the stomach to do its old work, there is not the old vigour at command. Gradually the stimulus of food recalls the vigour of the secreting glands, and then appetite may be safely indulged.

The next case is peculiarly valuable, as being the daily record of a man who voluntarily starved himself. He was a merchant, whose losses so preyed upon his mind that he resolved on suicide; and after roaming about the country from the 12th to the 15th of September 1818, he dug himself a grave in the wood, and remained there till the 3d of October, when he was found, still living, by an innkeeper. Hufeland, who records the case, says that, after an abstinence of eighteen days, the man still breathed, but expired immediately after a little soup had been forced down his throat. On his person they found a diary, written in pencil, from which the following are extracts: —

"*Sept.* 16. — The generous philanthropist who may find my corpse is requested to bury it, and to repay himself for the

* *History of the Earth,* II. 126.

trouble by my clothes, my purse, my pocket-book, and knife.
I have not committed suicide, but I die of starvation because
bad men have deprived me of my fortune, and I do not choose to
be a burden on my friends. It is unnecessary to open my body,
since I have said I die of starvation.

"*Sept.* 17. — What a night I have passed! It has rained; I
am wet through. I have been so cold.

"*Sept.* 18. — The cold and rain forced me to get up and
walk; my walk was very feeble. Thirst made me lick up the
water which still rested on the mushrooms. How nasty that
water was!

"*Sept.* 19. — The cold, the length of the nights, the slightness
of my clothing, which makes me feel the cold more keenly, have
given me great suffering.

"*Sept.* 20. — In my stomach there is terrible commotion;
hunger, and, above all, thirst, become more and more frightful.
For three days there has been no rain. Would that I could lick
up the water from the mushrooms now!

"*Sept.* 21. — Unable to endure the tortures of thirst, I crawled
with great labour to an inn, where I bought a bottle of beer,
which did not quench my thirst. In the evening I drank some
water from the pump, near the inn where I bought the beer.

"*Sept.* 23. — Yesterday I could scarcely move, much less
write. To-day thirst made me go to the pump; the water was
icy cold, and made me sick. I had convulsions until evening;
nevertheless, I returned to the pump.

"*Sept.* 26. — My legs seem dead. For three days I have been
unable to go to the pump. Thirst increases. My weakness is
such that I could scarcely trace these lines to-day.

"*Sept.* 29. — I have been unable to move. It has rained.
My clothes are not dry. No one would believe how much I suffer.
During the rain some drops fell into my mouth, which did not
quench my thirst. Yesterday I saw a peasant about ten yards
from me. I bowed to him. He returned my salutation. It is with
great regret I die. Weakness and convulsions prevent my wri-
ting more. I feel this is the last time....."

This pathetic case illustrates, as indeed all other cases do,
the truth that Thirst is far more terrible than Hunger. The

man's resolution was not strong enough to resist the desire for drink, yet he never seems to have faltered in his determination to refrain from food. It will be further noticed that he ceases to complain of the cold when thirst sets in fiercely, because then fever had also supervened.

VI. THE SENSATION OF HUNGER. — The sensation of Hunger is at first rather agreeable, but it quickly becomes unpleasant if prolonged. The sense of keen appetite is delightful, but that "sinking in the stomach" which ensues, quickly passes from an uneasy sensation into positive pain. The pain soon becomes acute; and if food be still withheld, we feel as if the stomach were being torn by pincers. This is followed by a state of general exhaustion, feverishness, headache, light-headedness, often flaming into madness. The whole being seems possessed by one desire, before which even the energetic instinct of maternity has been known to give way, and mothers have actually disputed with their companions for the flesh of their dead children.

But let us avert our eyes from such scenes, and turn them on that of the eight colliers, who were shut up in a pit for one hundred and thirty-six hours.* The first day they shared between them half a pound of bread, a morsel of cheese, and two mugs of wine, which one of them had brought into the mine, and refused to keep for himself alone. Two of the men had eaten before descending into the mine, and they generously declared that they should not die sooner than the others, and would not share the small supply of food. It is very remarkable that these men, who for five days had no nourishment whatever, declared, when they were rescued; that their abstinence had not greatly inconvenienced them. If we knew more of the circumstances, we might perhaps explain this now inexplicable fact.

What causes the sensation of Hunger?

It has been seen that the absence of food needed to repair the waste of tissue is the primary cause; but it has also been seen that this primary cause may exist without the existence of that sensation known to us as Hunger. All animals need food, but we have no ground for supposing that polypes, jelly-fish,

* This case is quoted by LONGET in his *Traité de Physiologie*, 1857.

and other simpler animals destitute of a nervous system, feel the *sensation* of Hunger; we must therefore seek for some more proximate cause of this sensation.

The popular notion is that Hunger arises from emptiness of the stomach, which emptiness, according to some physiologists, allows the walls of the stomach to rub against each other, and then the friction causes the sensation.

It is easy to show the inaccuracy of this hypothesis, but two facts will suffice here: first, the stomach is always empty some time before Hunger is felt; secondly, it may be empty for days together — in illness — without the slightest sensation of Hunger being felt.

Another notion is that the gastric juice accumulates in the stomach, and attacks its walls. Such a cause would certainly be ample for the effect, and I know but of one objection to our accepting it, namely, that the fact on which the explanation rests is unfortunately a fiction; the gastric juice does *not* accumulate in the empty stomach, but is only secreted after the stimulus of food.

A more ingenious explanation has been propounded by Dr. Beaumont, whose name is always cited when Digestion is under discussion, because he was enabled to enrich science with many valuable observations made on a patient who had a hole in his stomach, produced by a gunshot wound. "During the hours of fasting," says Dr. Beaumont, "the gastric juice is slowly being secreted in the follicles* and retained in their tubes, thereby distending them: this distension, when moderate, produces the sensation of Appetite; when more powerful, of Hunger."

There are several analogies which give colour to this explanation. Thus, milk is slowly accumulated in the breast, and the sense of fulness, if unrelieved, soon passes into that of pain. But ingenious as the explanation is, a closer scrutiny causes us to reject it.

Out of many arguments which might be urged, I will mention only two — one anatomical, and one physiological. If the

---

* The *follicles* are small secreting glands in the lining membrane of the stomach. They will be described and figured in the chapter on DIGESTION and INDIGESTION, fig. 5.

gastric juice were accumulated in the tubes, there is no anatomical obstruction to its immediate passage into the stomach, and the distension would at once be obviated (see Fig. 5). Nor have we any good ground for supposing that an accumulation does take place; for Dr. Beaumont's argument that it *must* take place, because it flows so abundantly on the introduction of food into the stomach, would equally prove that tears must be accumulated in advance, because they gush forth so copiously on the first stimulus of grief; or that saliva must be accumulated, because it flows so freely whenever a stimulus is presented.

While Dr. Beaumont's explanation wants an anatomical basis, it is still more directly at variance with the physiological fact, that when food is injected into the veins or the intestines, the sensation of Hunger disappears, although the stomach is as empty as it was before, and the tubes as distended as they were before.

The fact last named would dispose us to believe that want of food was, after all, the proximate as well as the primary cause of Hunger, did we not know that tobacco, opium, and even inorganic substances, introduced into the stomach, will remove the sensation. In a succeeding chapter (see FOOD and DRINK) we shall learn that there are nations who eat clay to allay their hunger; and we all know how the first mouthful of food takes away the sharpness of the sensation, although two or three hours must elapse before the food will really have *entered* the body. For we must remember that food in the stomach is as much *outside* the organism as if it were in the hand. The digestive canal is nothing but a folding-in of the general envelope, like the inverted finger of a glove; and until the absorbent vessels carry the food from the stomach *into* the circulating system, the food remains *outside.*

Here, then, are two noticeable facts: we may relieve the sensation of Hunger without directly acting on the stomach, the mere supply of food to the blood sufficing; and we may relieve the sensation simply by acting on the stomach, the want of food being as great as before. Do not these facts indicate that Hunger must be related to the *general* state of the system, and to the *particular* state of the stomach? If we once regard the subject in this light, we shall be easily led to perceive that although the general state of the system, under deficiency of food, is the *primary cause* of Hunger, it is only so in as far as it produces a certain *condition of the stomach;* and this condition of the stomach is the *proximate cause* of the sensation.

I think this mode of viewing it will extricate us from the difficulties which have been brought forward in the many discussions as to whether the stomach, or one part of the nervous system, is the *seat* of Hunger. The stomach is the seat of the sensation, just as the eyes are the seat of the sensation of sleepiness: the general state of exhaustion causes the eyes to droop heavily, and the general state of the system causes the stomach to produce the sensation of hunger; and as in sleepiness we may relieve the sensation by bathing the eyes with cold water, yet this will not relieve the general exhaustion; so in hunger, we may relieve the sensation by opium, or even clay, but this will not relieve that general state of the system which produced the sensation.

It is evident that the general state of the system must be felt, and to it we owe those daily variations in comfort which we express in the terms "vigour," "gladness," "lassitude," "depression," &c.; nevertheless physiologists have not assigned a name to such sensations.

In a future chapter (FEELING and THINKING) I shall enter more fully into these, which I propose to call *Systemic* Sensations, because they arise in the system at large, or are not localised by consciousness in any one organ. But for the purpose of this chapter, current terms must be accepted; and although, therefore, strict accuracy would lead us to say that Hunger, as a Systemic Sensation, is caused by want of food to repair the waste of tissue, and, as a Local Sensation, is caused by a specific condition of the stomach; yet, following popular language, we must say that Hunger is a sensation having its seat in the stomach; and all the arguments or experiments which attempt to prove that its seat must be elsewhere, have reference to the general state of the system, but not to the specific sensation known to us as Hunger.

If we examine the stomach of a fasting animal, we shall find it pale, and in a condition of obvious *atony.* The blood has retreated from the smaller vessels, and circulates only in the larger channels. But no sooner is the organ stimulated by the introduction of food, or any irritant substance, than this pale surface becomes visibly congested, turgescent, and its secretions pour forth abundantly. With this rush of blood to the stomach the sensation of uneasiness is carried away. Hence we may conclude that Hunger is in some way dependent on the state of the circulation in the stomach.

VII. THIRST closely resembles Hunger in being a general or Systemic sensation, although it is usually considered only as a local sensation, arising from the dryness of the mouth and throat. This dryness of the throat and mouth, so familiar to us all, is produced by a deficiency of liquid in the body; but it may be, and often is, produced when there is no deficiency in the general system, nothing but a local disturbance, this disturbance producing a local sensation. Wines, coffee, and spices create a strong feeling of thirst, yet the two first increase the quantity of liquid instead of diminishing it. And we know how ineffectual liquid in any quantity is to quench the feeling of Thirst under some conditions, especially after long suffering.

Andersson, in his travels in Africa, describes the sufferings of his men and cattle, adding, "even when the thirsty men and animals were let loose in the water, although they drank to repletion, the water seemed to have lost its property, for our best endeavours to slake our thirst proved unavailing." * The long continuance of Thirst had produced a certain feverish condition which could not be immediately relieved when the system received its necessary supply of liquid; this shows that although deficiency of liquid is the *primary* cause of Thirst, the *proximate* cause must be some local affection which has been induced.

On the other hand, this local sensation is so dependent on the system, that if water be injected into the veins or the intestines, Thirst disappears, although the mouth and throat have not been touched. A humid atmosphere prevents Thirst; a bath relieves it, because the water is absorbed through the skin.

On this principle, Franklin grounds his advice to men who are exposed to scarcity of drink : they should bathe themselves in tubs

* ANDERSSON: *Lake Ngami*, p. 38.

of salt water, he says. This would undoubtedly relieve their thirst, but it is a plan which would be excessively dangerous in ship-wrecks, unless food were abundant, since the abstraction of so much heat as would follow a bath, would in all probability be fatal.

VIII. CAUSE OF THIRST. — As deficiency of food to supply the waste of tissue is the primary cause of Hunger, so deficiency of water to supply the waste which goes on incessantly in the ex-cretions, respiration, and perspiration, is the primary cause of Thirst.

Fig. 2.

Every time we breathe we throw from our lungs a quantity of water in the form of va-pour. We are made sensible of this when the breath condenses on the colder surface of glass or steel, and when, as in winter, the atmosphere is sufficiently cold to condense the vapour on its issuing from our mouths.

This is only one source of the waste of water: a more important source is that of perspiration, which in hot weather, or during violent exercise, causes the water to roll down our skins with obtrusive copiousness. But even when we are perfectly quiescent, the loss of water, although not obvious, is con-siderable.

To render this intelligible, let attention be fixed on the following diagram, which represents one of the glands that secrete this perspiration. It represents the vertical section of the sole of the foot (after Todd and Bowman).

The gland at *d* is seen to possess a twisted duct, which passes upwards to the surface. From this tube comes the perspira-tion, sensible and insensible.

It is calculated that there are no less than twenty-eight miles of this tubing on

SWEAT-GLAND.

*a* is the cuticle or scarfskin (epidermis), the deeper layers, dark in colour, being the *rete mucosum; b* are the pa-pillæ; *c* the cutis or true skin (derma); *d* the sweat-gland, in a cavi-ty of oily globules.

the surface of the human body, from which the water will escape as *insensible perspiration;* and although the amount of water which is thus evaporated from the surface must necessarily vary with the clothing, the activity, and even the peculiar constitution of the individual, an average estimate has been attained which shows that from *two to three pounds of water* are daily evaporated from the skin. From the lungs it is ascertained that every minute we throw off from four to seven grains of water, from the skin eleven grains. To these must be added the quantity abstracted by the kidneys, a variable but important element in the sum.

It may not at first be clear to the reader why an abstraction of water daily should profoundly affect the organism unless an equivalent be restored. What can it matter that the body should lose a little water as vapour? Is water an essential part of the body? Is it indispensable to life?

Not only is water an essential part of the body, it might be called the *most* essential, if pre-eminence could be given where all are indispensable. In quantity, water has an enormous preponderance over all other constituents: it forms 70 per cent of the whole weight! There is not a single tissue in the body — not even that of bone, not even the enamel of the teeth — into the composition of which water does not enter as a necessary ingredient. In some of the tissues, and those the most active, it forms the chief ingredient. In the nervous tissue 800 parts out of every 1000 are of water; in the lungs 830; in the pancreas 871; in the retina no less than 927.

Commensurate with this anatomical preponderance, is the physiological importance of water. It is the carrier of the food, the vehicle of waste. It holds gases in solution, dissolves solids, helps to give every tissue its physical character, and is the indispensable condition of that ceaseless change of Composition and Decomposition on which the continuance of life depends.

From the elaborate experiments of Bidder and Schmidt, it is clear that the changes which go on in the organism are far more concerned with its water than with its solids. In the digestive fluids, for example, one-fifth to one-fourth of the water contained in the body will be found passing and repassing; whereas only one-sixtieth or one-seventieth of the solids of the body pass into them. *

Such being the part played by water in the organism, we can understand how the oscillations of so important a fluid must necessarily bring with it oscillations in our feelings of comfort and discomfort, and how any unusual abstraction of it must produce that disturbance of the general system which is known under the name of Raging Thirst — a disturbance far more terrible than that of Starvation, and for this reason: During abstinence from food, the organism can still live upon its own substance, which furnishes all the necessary material; but during abstinence from liquid, the organism has no such source of supply within itself.

Men have been known to endure absolute privation of food for some weeks, but three days of absolute privation of drink (unless in a moist atmosphere) is perhaps the limit of endurance. Thirst is the most atrocious torture ever invented by Oriental tyrants. It is that which most effectually tames animals. Mr. Astley, when he had a refractory horse, always used thirst as the most effective power of coercion, giving a little water as the reward for every act of obedience. The histories of shipwreck paint fearful pictures of the sufferings endured from thirst; and one of the most appalling cases known is the celebrated imprisonment of one hundred and forty-six men in the Black Hole at Calcutta — a case frequently alluded to, but which must be cited here at some length on account of its physiological bearing: —

The Governor of Fort-William at Calcutta having imprisoned a merchant — the well-known Omychund, — the infamous Nabob of Bengal, Surajah Dowlah, on the look-out for a pretext, marched against Fort-William with a considerable force, besieged and took it, and imprisoned the surviving part of the garrison in the barrack-room named the Black Hole. The letter in which Mr. Holwell, the officer in command, describes the horrors of this imprisonment is printed in the *Annual Register* for 1758, and from it the following extracts are made: —

"Figure to yourself the situation of a hundred and forty-six wretches, exhausted by continual fatigue and action, crammed

* BIDDER and SCHMIDT: *Die Verdauungssäfte,* p. 267.

together in a cube of eighteen feet, in a close sultry night in
Bengal, shut up to the eastward and southward (the only quarter
whence air could reach us) by dead walls, and by a wall and door
to the north, open only to the westward by two windows strongly
barred with iron, from which we could receive scarce any the
least circulation of fresh air. . . . We had been but a few
minutes confined before every one fell into a perspiration so
profuse, you can form no idea of it. This brought on a raging
thirst, which increased in proportion as the body was drained
of its moisture. Various expedients were thought of to give
more room and air. To gain the former it was moved to put off
their clothes; this was approved as a happy motion, and in a
few moments every one was stripped — myself, Mr. Court, and
the two young gentlemen by me, excepted. For a little while
they flattered themselves with having gained a mighty advantage; every hat was put in motion to gain a circulation of
air, and Mr. Baillie proposed that every man should sit down on
his hams. This expedient was several times put in practice, and
at each time many of the poor creatures, whose natural strength
was less than that of others, or who had been more exhausted,
and could not immediately recover their legs when the word was
given to rise — fell to rise no more, for they were instantly trod
to death or suffocated. When the whole body sat down, they
were so closely wedged together that they were obliged to use
many efforts before they could get up again. Before nine o'clock
every man's thirst grew intolerable, and respiration difficult.
Efforts were made to force the door, but in vain. Many insults
were used to the guard to provoke them to fire on us. For my
own part, I hitherto felt little pain or uneasiness, but what re-
sulted from my anxiety for the sufferings of those within. By
keeping my face close between two of the bars I obtained air
enough to give my lungs easy play, though my perspiration was
excessive, and thirst commencing. At this period so strong a
urinous volatile effluvia came from the prison that I was not able
to turn my head that way for more than a few seconds at a time.

"Now everybody, except those situated in and near the
windows, began to grow outrageous, and many delirious. *Water!
water!* became the general cry. An old Jemmantdaar, taking

pity on us, ordered the people to bring us some skins of water. This was what I dreaded. I foresaw it would prove the ruin of the small chance left us, and essayed many times to speak to him privately to forbid it being brought; but the clamour was so loud it became impossible. The water appeared. Words cannot paint the universal agitation and raving the sight of it threw us into. I flattered myself that some, by preserving an equal temper of mind, might outlive the night; but now the reflection which gave me the greatest pain was, that I saw no possibility of one escaping to tell the dismal tale. *Until the water came I had not myself suffered much from thirst, which instantly grew excessive.* We had no means of conveying it into the prison but by hats forced through the bars; and thus myself, and Coles, and Scott supplied them as fast as possible. But those who have experienced intense thirst, or are acquainted with the cause and nature of this appetite, will be sufficiently sensible it could receive no more than a momentary alleviation: the cause still subsisted. Though we brought full hats through the bars, there ensued such violent struggles and frequent contests to get it, that before it reached the lips of any one, there would be scarcely a small tea-cupful left in them. These supplies, like sprinkling water on fire, only seemed to feed the flame. Oh! my dear sir, how shall I give you a just conception of what I felt at the cries and cravings of those in the remoter parts of the prison, who could not entertain a probable hope of obtaining a drop, yet could not divest themselves of expectation, however unavailing, calling on me by the tender considerations of affection and friendship. The confusion now became general and horrid. Several quitted the other window (the only chance they had for life) to force their way to the water, and the throng and press upon the window was beyond bearing; many, forcing their way from the further part of the room, pressed down those in their passage who had less strength, and trampled them to death.

"From about nine to eleven I sustained this cruel scene, still supplying them with water, though my legs were almost broke with the weight against them. By this time I myself was near pressed to death, and my two companions, with Mr. Parker, who had forced himself to the window, were really so. At last I be-

came so pressed and wedged up, I was deprived of all motion.
Determined now to give everything up, I called to them, and
begged them, as a last instance of their regard, that they would
relieve the pressure upon me, and permit me to retire out of the
window to die in quiet. They gave way, and with much difficulty I forced a passage into the centre of the prison, where the
throng was less by the many dead, amounting to one-third, and
the numbers who flocked to the windows; for by this time they
had water also at the other window. . . . I laid myself down on
some of the dead, and, recommending myself to Heaven, had
the comfort of thinking my sufferings could have no long duration. My thirst now grew insupportable, and the difficulty of
breathing much increased; and I had not remained in this situation ten minutes before I was seized with a pain in my breast,
and palpitation of heart, both to the most exquisite degree.
These obliged me to get up again, but still the pain, palpitation,
and difficulty of breathing increased. I retained my senses notwithstanding, and had the grief to see death not so near me as I
had hoped, but could no longer bear the pains I suffered without
attempting a relief, which I knew fresh air would and could only
give me. I instantly determined to push for the window opposite
to me, and by an effort of double the strength I ever before possessed, gained the third rank at it — with one hand seized a
bar, and by that means gained a second, though I think there
were at least six or seven ranks between me and the window. *In
a few moments the pain, palpitation, and difficulty of breathing
ceased,* but the thirst continued intolerable. I called aloud
' *Water for God's sake!*' I had been concluded dead; but as
soon as the men found me amongst them, they still had the respect and tenderness for me to cry out, ' *Give him water!*' nor
would one of them at the window attempt to touch it till I had
drunk. *But from the water I had no relief; my thirst was rather
increased by it;* so I determined to drink no more, but, patiently
wait the event. I kept my mouth moist from time to time by
sucking the perspiration out of my shirt-sleeves, and catching
the drops as they fell like heavy rain from my head and face;
you can hardly imagine how unhappy I was if any of them escaped my mouth. . . . I was observed by one of my com-

panions on the right in the expedient of allaying my thirst by
sucking my shirt-sleeve. He took the hint, and robbed me from
time to time of a considerable part of my store, though, after I
detected him, I had the address to begin on that sleeve first when
I thought my reservoirs were sufficiently replenished, and our
mouths and noses often met in contact. This man was one of
the few who escaped death, and he has since paid me the com-
pliment of assuring me he believed he owed his life to the many
comfortable draughts he had from my sleeves. No Bristol water
could be more soft or pleasant than what arose from perspiration.

"By half-past eleven the much greater number of those
living were in an outrageous delirium, and others quite un-
governable; few retaining any calmness but the ranks near the
windows. They now all found that water, instead of relieving
their uneasiness, rather heightened it, and Air! air! was the
general cry. Every insult that could be devised against the
guard was repeated to provoke them to fire on us, every man
that could, rushing tumultuously towards the windows with eager
hopes of meeting the first shot. But these failing, they whose
strength and spirits were quite exhausted laid themselves down,
and quietly expired upon their fellows; others who had yet some
strength and vigour left, made a last effort for the windows, and
several succeeded by leaping and scrambling over the backs and
heads of those in the first ranks; and got hold of the bars, from
which there was no removing them. Many to the right and left
sunk with the violent pressure, and were soon suffocated; for
now a steam arose from the living and the dead, which affected
us in all its circumstances, as if we were forcibly held by our
heads over a bowl of strong volatile spirit of hartshorn until
suffocated; nor could the effluvia of the one be distinguished
from the other. I need not ask your commiseration when I tell
you that in this plight, from half an hour after eleven till two in
the morning, I sustained the weight of a heavy man with his
knees on my back, and the pressure of his whole body on my
head; a Dutch sergeant who had taken his seat on my left
shoulder, and a black soldier bearing on my right: all which
nothing would have enabled me to support but the props and
pressure equally sustaining me all round. The two latter I fre-

quently dislodged by shifting my hold on the bars, and driving my knuckles into their ribs; but my friend above stuck fast, and, as he held by two bars, was immovable. The repeated trials I made to dislodge this insufferable encumbrance upon me, at last quite exhausted me, and towards two o'clock, finding I must quit the window or sink where I was, I resolved on the former, having borne truly, for the sake of others, infinitely more for life than the best of it is worth.

"I was at this time sensible of no pain and little uneasiness. I found a stupor coming on apace, and laid myself down by that gallant old man, the reverend Jervas Bellamy, who lay dead with his son, the lieutenant, hand in hand, near the southernmost wall of the prison. Of what passed in the interval, to the time of resurrection from this hole of horrors, I can give you no account."

At six in the morning the door was opened, when only three-and-twenty out of the hundred and forty-six still breathed. These were subsequently revived.

Although the principal cause of this mortality must be ascribed to the vitiated atmosphere rather than to Thirst, we nevertheless see some of the frightful phenomena of Thirst exemplified in this narrative. Death by asphyxia (from vitiated air) is generally peaceful, and not at all such as is described in the foregoing. Attention is moreover called to certain passages in italics. These show that the sensation of Thirst is not merely a sensation dependent on a deficiency of liquid in the system, but a local sensation dependent on a local disturbance: the more water these men drank, the more dreadful seemed their thirst; and the mere sight of water rendered the sensation, which before was endurable, quite intolerable. The *increase* of the sensation following a *supply* of water, would be wholly inexplicable to those who maintain that the proximate cause of Thirst is deficiency of liquid; but is not wholly inexplicable, if we regard the deficiency as the primary, not the proximate cause; for this primary cause having set up a feverish condition in the mouth and throat, that condition would continue after the original cause had ceased to exist. The stimulus of cold water is only a momentary relief in this case, and exaggerates the sensation by stimulating a greater flow of blood to the parts. If, instead of cold water, a little lukewarm tea, or milk-and-water, had been drunk, permanent relief would have been attained; or if, instead of cold water, a lump of ice had been taken into the mouth, and allowed to melt there, the effect would have been very different — a transitory application of cold increasing the flow. of blood, a continuous application driving it away.

If, therefore, the reader is ever suffering from intense thirst, let him remember that tepid drinks are better than cold drinks, ice is better than water.

We must not, however, forget that although, where a deficiency of liquid has occasioned a feverish condition of the mouth and throat, no supply of cold liquid will at once remove that condition, the relief of the Systemic sensation not immediately producing relief of the local sensation, nevertheless, so long as the system is in need of liquid, the feeling of thirst must continue. Claude Bernard observed that a dog which had an opening in its stomach drank unceasingly, because the water ran out as fast as it was swallowed; in vain the water moistened mouth and throat on its way to the stomach, Thirst was not appeased because the water was not absorbed. The dog drank till fatigue forced it to pause, and a few minutes afterwards recommenced the same hopeless toil; but no sooner was the opening closed, and the water retained in the stomach, from whence it was absorbed into the system, than thirst quickly vanished.*

After learning the physiological importance of water, and remembering how the water is continually being removed from the body in respiration, perspiration, and the various excretions, we are greatly puzzled by the great variations which animals exhibit in the quantity they drink. The difficulty is not explained by a reference to the food of the animals, for some vegetable feeders require large quantities of water, while others subsist for months without drinking, the supply they receive in the vegetables they eat being sufficient for their wants.

Dr. Livingstone found the elands on the Kalahari Desert, although in places where water was perfectly inaccessible, with

* CLAUDE BERNARD: *Leçons de Physiologie Expérimentale*, II. 51.

every indication of being in splendid condition, and their stomachs actually contained considerable quantities of water. "I examined carefully the whole alimentary canal," he says, "in order to see if there were any peculiarity which might account for the fact that these animals can subsist for months together without drinking, but found nothing. Other animals, such as the düiker (*Cephalopus mergens*), the steinbuck (*Tragulus rupestris*), the gemsbuck (*Oryx capensis*), and the porcupine, are all able to subsist for many months at a time by living on bulbs and tubers containing moisture. Some animals, on the other hand, are never seen but in the vicinity of water. The presence of the rhinoceros, buffalo, and gnu, of the giraffe, zebra, and pallah (*Antilope melampus*), is always a certain indication of water being within seven or eight miles." *

The only solution of the difficulty which presents itself to my mind is, that animals which can subsist long without drinking, do not lose more water by evaporation and excretion than can be replaced by their vegetable food, since that they *require* the same amount of water as other animals for the performance of all their functions is physiologically certain. It has been observed that, in persons who voluntarily abstain from drinking, the excretions were diminished to a minimum. Sauvages, in his *Nosologia Medica*, mentions the case of a member of the University of Toulouse who never knew what thirst was, and passed several months, even in the heat of summer, without drinking. Another case is cited by the same author of a woman who took no liquid for forty days. M. Bérard thinks that the marvellousness of these facts disappears when we remember how much liquid is contained in all food; ** but I am rather disposed to doubt the accuracy of the facts than to accept such an explanation: at any rate, they are facts so very exceptional as to have little bearing on our general argument.

The effects of Thirst are first a dryness of the mouth, palate, and throat; the secretions become less copious; the mouth is covered with a thick mucus, the tongue cleaves to the palate, the voice becomes hoarse. Then the eyes flash fire, the breath-

* LIVINGSTONE: *Missionary Travels in South Africa*, p. 56.
** BÉRARD, *Cours de Physiologie*, vol. II. p. 501.

ing becomes difficult, a feverish excitement, often passing into delirium, comes on.* Sleep is fitful, and distressed by dreams akin to the torments of Tantalus. The men shipwrecked in the "Medusa" dreamt constantly of shady woods and running streams.

It is to be noticed that the sensation of Thirst is never agreeable, no matter how slight it may be, and in this respect is unlike Hunger, which, in its incipient state of Appetite, is decidedly agreeable. The bodies of those who have perished from Thirst show a general dryness of all the tissues, a thickening of the humours, a certain degree of coagulation of the blood, numberless indications of inflammation, and sometimes gangrene of the principal viscera. According to Longet, Thirst kills by an inflammatory fever, Hunger by a putrid fever.**

Such are Hunger and Thirst, two mighty impulses, beneficent and terrible, monitors ever vigilant, warning us of the need there is for Food and Drink — sources of exquisite pleasure and of exquisite pains, motives to strenuous endeavour, and servants to our higher aims. We are all familiar with them in their gentler aspects; may we never know them in their dreadful importunities!

---

* From some experiments by Professor E. HARLESS, in Munich, at which I assisted, it appeared that the nerves gain an extraordinary *increase* in their excitability as their proportion of water decreases. (For a fuller account of this remarkable fact, see BIRKNER, *Das Wasser der Nerven*, 1858.) The nervous excitability, delirium, and sleeplessness, occasioned by Thirst, may be greatly owing to this cause.

** LONGET: *Traité de Physiologie.*

# CHAPTER II.

## FOOD AND DRINK.

### SECTION I. — ON THE NATURE OF FOOD.

An Irish peasant, in a windowless hut, dining off a meal of potatoes and skimmed milk, flavoured by the aroma of a lively imagination as each mouthful is "pointed" at the side of bacon hanging against the wall, and a London Alderman seated at a Guildhall feast, are two figures presenting an impressive contrast of the varieties of Food with which, in the restless activity of life, the human organism repairs its incessant waste. Potatoes and skimmed milk, and it may be a little sea-weed, supply the wants of the one; before the other there is spread a wasteful profusion of turtle captured on the North American coasts, of turkey reared in quiet farmyards, of mutton grazed upon the downs of Sussex, of beef fed on the rich pasture-lands of Herefordshire, of pheasants shot in a nobleman's preserves, of turbot from the Atlantic Ocean, and salmon from the Scotch and Irish rivers, of cheese from France and Switzerland, oil from Italy, spices from the East, and wines from Portugal, Germany, and France — a gathering from all nations, assorted with exquisite

3*

culinary skill. Yet, in spite of these differences in the things consumed by the two men, the dinner of the one and the dinner of the other become transmuted by vital processes into similar flesh and blood, into the same organic substance and organic force.

However various the articles of Food and Drink may be, it is clear that there must be a process by which all differences are annulled, and a similar result attained. Whatever characters these substances may have *outside* the organism, must be altered shortly after their entrance *into* it, specific differences must vanish, and all varieties be merged in a vital unity.

The hunter on the Pampas subsists on buffalo beef, with scarcely a particle of vegetable food to vary his diet. The Hindoo is content with rice and rancid butter, and cannot be induced to eat flesh. The Greenlander gorges himself with whale oil, and animal fats of any kind he can secure; the moderate Arab has his bag of dates, his lotos-bread, and dhourra. On the coast of Malabar we find men regarding with religious horror every species of animal food; while the native of New Holland has not a single edible fruit larger than a cherry on the whole surface of his vast island. The Englishman considers himself ignominiously treated by fortune if he cannot get his beef or bacon; the peasant of the Apennines is cheerful with his meal of chestnuts.

Besides varieties in the staple articles of Food, there are the infinite varieties of fancy. Our Chinese friends make delicacies of rats and of birds' nests; our French allies are epicurean over the hind-legs of frogs. The ancients, who carried epicureanism to lengths never dreamed of by Guildhall, thought the hedgehog a titbit, and had a word to say in favour of the donkey, which they placed on an equality with the ox; dogs they considered equal to chickens; and even cats were not to be despised. The pork, which we eat with great confidence, they considered, and not untruly, the least digestible of animal meats, fit only for artisans and athletes. They ate snails, at which we shudder, with the gusto we acknowledge in eating oysters. It would be difficult to persuade the British stomach to dine, in full consciousness, off a "sirloin of donkey," flanked by "ribs of dog, with fried toadstools." Is this repugnance only prejudice, or were Greek dogs and donkeys more succulent than ours?

*The Clay-eaters.* — The varieties just rehearsed are at any rate easily accepted as probable aliments, but what will the render say on hearing that in many parts of the world even clay is a respectable and respected food? Travellers, who see strange things, are very positive in their assertions on this head. Humboldt, a man whose word justly carries with it European authority, confirms the statement of Gumilla, that the Otomacs of South America, during the periods of the floods, subsist entirely on a fat and ferruginous clay, of which each man eats daily a pound or more. The well-known botanist and explorer, Martius, informed me that the Indians of the Amazon eat a kind of loam, even when other food is abundant. Molina says the Peruvians frequently eat a sweet-smelling clay; and Ehrenberg has analysed the edible clay sold in the markets of Bolivia, which he finds to be a mixture of talc and mica. The inhabitants of Guiana mingle clay with their bread; and the negroes in Jamaica are said to eat earth when other food is deficient. According to Labillardière, the inhabitants of New Caledonia appease their hunger with a white friable earth, said by Vauquelin to be composed of magnesia, silica, oxide of iron, and chalk. The same writer asserts that at Java a cake is made of ferruginous clay which is much sought for by women in their pregnancy. To conclude this list we must add Siam, Siberia, and Kamtschatka as countries of clay-eaters. *

This is rather a staggering accumulation of assertions, which we cannot dismiss altogether, even if we suppose a large allowance of scepticism justifiable. Granting the fact that certain kinds of earth are really nutritious — and it is difficult to escape such a conclusion — we are completely at a loss for an adequate explanation of it. Little light is thrown on it by the assumption, probable enough, that the earth must contain organic matters; because we should imagine that in ten pounds of such earth there could scarcely be contained sufficient organic matter to supply the demands of an adult.

* BURDACH: *Traité de Physiologie*, ix. 200.

Nor will it get rid of the difficulty to say that the earth only appeases hunger without nourishing the system; because, in the first place, Humboldt's testimony is that the Otomacs *subsist* on the clay at periods when other food is deficient; and, in the second place, although the *local* sensation of Hunger may be appeased by introducing substances into the stomach, the more imperious *systemic* sensation of Hunger is not thus to be appeased.*

We must, therefore, be content, at present, with accepting the fact, which the science of a future day may possibly explain.

Omitting clay, as not explicable for the present, we propose to take the reader with us in an inquiry, having for its object to ascertain what Science can tell us positively respecting the relation of alimentary substances and the organism — to see what is known respecting Food and its varieties. If in the course of this survey we detain the reader to consider certain generalities, when he is impatient to arrive at the details, let him be assured that these generalities, seemingly too abstract and remote for immediate practical objects, are essential to a right comprehension of the details; and that our most practical and pressing objects, whether of feeding cattle, or feeding ourselves, do inevitably rest upon abstract philosophic principles, and are determined by scientific hypotheses. We promise him abundant detail, but must ask him to approach the question through such avenues as we shall open, and not to try any short cut of his own.

1. How to Investigate Food. — Assured as we are that all alimentary substances must be transformed into the organic unity we name Blood, and assured also that the substances so transformed are really various in kind, specifically distinct *before* they have undergone this transformation, it is clear that our chief attention should be withdrawn from the alimentary *substances* to fall with greater emphasis on the alimentary *process;* that is to say, we must less consider what the Foods are in themselves, than *what relation* they bear to the organism which they nourish.

* See the Chapter on HUNGER AND THIRST.

Obvious as this may seem, it has generally been disregarded, especially of late years. The researches into the nature of Food have been extensive and minute, but they have been almost exclusively confined to alimentary substances, which have been analysed, weighed, and tabulated with great labour, and in a chemical point of view with considerable results; but in a physiological point of view — the only one really implicated — with scarcely any results at all. No one doubts that Food is a physiological question, inasmuch as it relates to an organism. Nevertheless, it has fallen into the hands of the chemists; and our treatises, text-books, and popular works, have been encumbered by hypotheses which may amuse speculative ingenuity, but furnish very little positive result.

Against this vice of Method, and this misdirection of valuable labour, a voice should energetically be raised. The error is not a speculative error, simply; it is one carrying important consequences; it either leads physicians and farmers into serious mistakes, or leads them to throw up scientific guidance in disgust, because the hypothesis, so convincing on paper, turns out stubbornly irreconcilable with fact.

Let us not, however, be misunderstood. In declaring the chemical hypothesis on the subject of Food to which Liebig, Dumas, Boussingault, Payen, and others, have given the sanc-. tion of their names, to be more of an encumbrance than an illumination, we have not the remotest intention of undervaluing their labours. All real work is important, no genuine research is unworthy of our gratitude; but it is one thing to reverence power, and respect the work achieved, another thing to assign the nature and position of that work. With regard to the vast chemical researches into the subject of Food which have occupied a quarter of a century, it seems to me that their value has been almost exclusively *chemical*, and only in an indirect and limited degree *physiological*. Hence, in spite of the unanimity and apparent precision observable in the analyses and hypotheses offered by chemists, no important practical results have been attained, scarcely a single alimentary problem has been solved by them.

There may be readers who, failing to see the ground of this

distinction between chemical and physiological investigations, will not understand the importance I attach to it; but they will perhaps come round to my point of view before this chapter reaches its close. The chemists, whatever we may think of them, will continue their labours, analysing, weighing, experimenting, and propounding hypotheses; and it is right they should do so: all honour and success to them! But if the question of Food is to receive any practical solution, it must no longer be left in their hands; or only such details of it left in their hands as properly belong to them. It must be taken up by physiologists, who, while availing themselves of every chemical results, will carry these into another sphere and test them by another Method. Not a step can the physiologist advance without the assistance of the chemist; but he must employ Chemistry as a means of *exploration*, not of *deduction* — as a pillar, not a pinnacle — an instrument, not an aim. The chemist may analyse fat for him; but he, on receiving this analysis, will request the chemist *not* to trouble him with hypotheses respecting the part played by fat in the organism; for although the chemist may accurately estimate the heat evolved in the oxidation of so much fat, the physiologist has to do with a vital laboratory, extremely unlike that in which the chemist works, and he has to ascertain how the fat comports itself *there*.

Alimentary substances are substances which serve as nourishment; but a great mistake is made when it is imagined that their nutritive value can chiefly reside in the amounts of carbon, nitrogen, hydrogen, oxygen, and salts, which they contain; it resides in the relation which the several substances bear to the organism they are to nourish.

Music is not harmonious to the deaf, nor is colour splendid to the blind. The substance which nourishes one animal affords no nourishment to another, nor will any table of "nutritive equivalents," however precise, convince us that a substance ought to nourish, in virtue of its composition, when experience tells us that it does *not* nourish, in virtue of some defective relation between it and the organism.

That "one man's meat is another man's poison" is a proverb of strict veracity. There are persons, even in Europe, to whom

a mutton-chop would be poisonous.  The celebrated case of the
Abbé de Villedieu is a rare, put not unparalleled example of
animal food being poisonous: from his earliest years his repugnance to it was so decided, that neither the entreaties of his
parents nor the menaces of his tutors could induce him to overcome it.  After reaching the age of thirty on a regimen of vegetable food, he was over-persuaded, and tried the effect of meat
soups, which led to his eating both mutton and beef; but the
change was fatal: plethora and sleepiness supervened, and he
died of cerebral inflammation.*

In 1844, a French soldier was forced to quit the service because he could not overcome his violent repugnance and disgust
towards animal food.

Dr. Prout, whose testimony will be more convincing to English readers than that just cited, knew a person on whom mutton
acted as a poison: "He could not eat mutton in any form.  The
peculiarity was supposed to be owing to caprice, but the mutton
was repeatedly disguised and given to him unknown; but uniformly with the same result of producing violent vomiting and
diarrhœa.  And from the severity of the effects, which were in
fact those of a virulent poison, there can be little doubt that if
the use of mutton had been persisted in, it would soon have
destroyed the life of the individual."  Dr. Pereira, who quotes
this passage,** adds, "I know a gentleman who has repeatedly
had an attack of indigestion after the use of roast mutton."

Some persons, it is known, cannot take coffee without vomiting; others are thrown into a general inflammation if they
eat cherries or gooseberries.  Hahn relates of himself that seven
or eight strawberries would produce convulsions in him.  Tissot
says he could never swallow sugar without vomiting.  Many persons are unable to eat eggs; and cakes or puddings having eggs
in their composition, produce serious disturbances in such persons: if they are induced to eat them under false assurances of
no eggs having been employed, they are soon undeceived by the
unmistakable effects.

* *Journal de Médicine.*  Août 1769, quoted by LUCAS, *De l'Hérédité*, who
is the authority for the next statement.
** PEREIRA: *Treatise on Food and Diet*, p. 242.

Under less striking forms this difference in the assimilating power of different human beings is familiar to us all; we see our friends freely indulging, with benefit instead of harm, in kinds of food which, experience too painfully assures us, we can eat only with certain injury.

To this fact the attention of parents and guardians should seriously be given, that by it they may learn to avoid the petty tyranny and folly of insisting on children eating food for which they manifest repugnance. It is too common to treat the child's repugnance as mere caprice, to condemn it as "stuff and non-sense," when he refuses to eat fat, or eggs, or certain vege-tables, and "wholesome" puddings. Now, even a caprice in such matters should not be altogether slighted, especially when it takes the form of refusal; because this caprice is probably nothing less than the expression of a particular and temporary state of his organism, which we should do wrong to disregard. And whenever a refusal is constant, it indicates a positive un-fitness in the Food.

Only gross ignorance of Physiology, an ignorance unhappily too widely spread, can argue that because a certain article is wholesome to many, it must necessarily be wholesome to all. Each individual organism is specifically different from every other. However much it may resemble others, it necessarily in some points differs from them; and the amount of these differ-ences is often considerable. If the same wave of air striking upon the tympanum of two different men will produce sounds to the one which to the other are inappreciable — if the same wave of light will affect the vision of one man as that of red colour, while to the vision of another it is no colour at all, how unrea-sonable is it to expect that the same substance will bear precisely the same relation to the alimentary system of one man as to that of another! Experience tells us that it is not so.

A glance at the animal kingdom reveals the striking differ-ences manifested by two closely allied organisms in their capa-bility of assimilating the same substance. There are two species of Rhinoceros, the black and the white. The black species feeds on the graceful, but deadly, plant, *Euphorbia candelabrum*, and converts it into its own substance; but if the white species happen to eat thereof, it is inevitably poisoned. The Herbivora are divided into two classes, the first subsisting on a variety of plants, the second on one kind only. But even the various feeders will not touch certain plants eagerly devoured by others: thus the horse passes over almost all the cruciferæ; the ox all the labiates; goats, oxen, and lambs refuse almost all the solaneæ. The poisons are food to many; the rabbit devouring belladonna, the goat hemlock, and the horse aconite. The dog will feed on bread, or biscuit, which his ancestor the wolf would starve rather than touch. The cat, although preferring animal food, will eat bread and milk, which the tiger will not look at.

We have brought these facts forward for the sake of giving distinct relief to the importance which must inevitably belong to physiological considerations in every question of Food; and to indicate the necessity of fixing our attention on the *organism to be nourished*, rather than on the *chemical composition of the substances* which nourish it.

When we are building a bridge, or making a machine, we can accurately guide ourselves by estimates of the strength of the wood and iron, because these substances do not lose their properties under new arrangements; but in building the mysterious fabric of the body, we have little or no guidance from our estimates of the properties of substances *out* of the body, because the body itself is an important factor in the sum, acting on the substances as well as being acted on by them, annulling or exalting their ordinary properties in a way quite peculiar to itself. And it is because this has been overlooked, or not sufficiently estimated, that our text-books are at once so precise, and so erroneous. Open almost any work on Physiology or Organic Chemistry, and you will meet with expositions of the theory of Food, and the nutritive value of various aliments, which are so precise and so unhesitating in their formulæ, that you will scarcely listen to me with patience when I assert that the precision is fallacious, and the doctrines demonstrably erroneous. Nevertheless I hope, before concluding, to convince you that Chemistry is itself in too imperfect a condition to give clear and satisfactory answers to its own questions in this direction — as

Mulder and Lehmann frankly avow* — and further, that Chemistry, even supposing it to be perfect, must ever be incompetent to solve physiological problems, to which, indeed, it must
always afford indispensable *aid*, without hope of doing more.

Vital processes depend on-chemical processes, but are not
themselves chemical, and cannot, therefore, be explained by
Chemistry. There is something *special* in vital phenomena which
necessarily transcends chemical investigation. We need not pretend to settle *what* vitality is, or on what the speciality of its
phenomena ultimately rests, to be assured that it is something
different from what goes on in laboratories, and demands other
tests than those furnished by Chemistry. The philosophic poet
warns us —

> "From higher judgment-seats make no appeal
>     To lower;"

and such appeal, from higher to lower, is the appeal of Physiology to Chemistry. No analysis of a nerve will ever throw light
on Sensibility; no arrangement of chemical formulæ will explain
the form and properties of a cell. You may take a mechanism to
pieces, and explain by physical laws the action and interaction
of each wheel and chain; but you cannot take an organism to
pieces, and explain its properties by chemical laws, such as are
revealed in the laboratory. If an overwhelming illustration of
this obvious truth be needed, we find it in the egg of an animal:
here is a microscopic sphere, composed of substances well known
to chemists, which contains potentially an animal, and which
will reproduce not only the form, features, stature, and specific
attributes of the parent animals, but also many of their acquired
habits, tendencies, and tricks; has Chemistry, in the whole extent of its domain, anything analogous to this? Can Chemistry
furnish us with even an approach to an explanation of it? Chemical analysis may conduct us to the threshold of Life, but at
the threshold all its guidance ceases. There, a new order of
complications intervenes, a new series of laws has to be elicited.
Chemistry confesses its inability to construct complex organic
substances, or even to say *how* they are constructed; it can, at

* MULDER: *Versuch einer Physiol. Chemie.* LEHMANN: *Lehrbuch der
Physiol. Chemie,* 2d edit.

present, only say *of what* they are constructed. This being so, it is clear that every attempt to explain chemically the nutritive value of any aliment by an enumeration of its constituents, must belong to what Berzelius admirably styles "the physiology of probabilities."

There is one cardinal rule which can never be violated with impunity, and which is, nevertheless, perpetually violated in our gropings towards the light. It is this: *Never attempt to solve the problems of one science by the order of conceptions peculiar to another.*

There is an order of conceptions peculiar to Physics, another peculiar to Chemistry, a third peculiar to Physiology, a fourth peculiar to Psychology, a fifth peculiar to Social Science. While all these sciences are intimately related, each has its sphere of independence which must be respected. Thus Chemistry presupposes Physics, and Physiology presupposes Chemistry; but physical laws will not alone explain chemical phenomena, chemical laws will not alone explain vital phenomena; nor, conversely, will Chemistry solve physical problems, nor Physiology solve chemical problems. In every vital process physical and chemical laws are implied, and the knowledge of these becomes indispensable; but over and above these laws, there are the specific laws of Life, which cannot be deduced from Physics and Chemistry.*

An illustration drawn from social science may serve to render this canon intelligible, and at the same time to uproot a widespread fallacy. Few errors have gained more general acceptance than that which declares the Family to be the perfect type of the State. This fallacy would have us regulate polity by domestic rules. A paternal government, in which the monarch is the head of the family; and a social government, in which all men are united as brothers, are the ideals of absolutists and socialists, who are pitiless in scorn of all other political schemes. When we see how a well-conducted household is harmoniously governed, each member fulfilling his proper office, and each assisting all; when we see how the farmer administers his affairs without any

---

* What is said in the text is by no means to be interpreted as indicating belief in the so-called "Vital force;" but the question will be fully discussed in the final chapter of this work.

one to question his absolute will; the idea of so managing a nation naturally suggests itself; for, What is a nation but an extension of the family? ask the theorists.

I answer, the Family is specifically different from the Nation: it is no type of the State, because, not to mention other points, it has the bond of personal affection, and the bond of personal interest, which two puissant influences can never operate to anything like the same extent on the State. The father dearly loves his children, and his despotism may be absolute because it is truly paternal: his tender vigilance and forgiving love will soften all the harshness of absolute rule. But no philanthropist will be romantic enough to expect that king or kaiser can by any possibility feel this affection for his subjects; and thus one *essential* element of the family disappears. Again, the father's personal interest is bound up with his administration (as the farmer's is), and every false step he makes will be made feelingly evident to him. But the sovereign's personal interest is not in any such manner directly bound up with the goodness of his administration; if he can keep secure upon his throne, if neither revolutions nor assassins are provoked, it can make little difference to his welfare that the streets are filled with lamentations, and the battle-field with corpses. And even supposing him to be tender-hearted and conscientious, really desirous of the good of his subjects, yet his own personal interest is not so directly and obviously bound up with theirs as that of the father is with his household. Thus, on the supposition that the despot is the best and wisest of men, and his subjects are really desirous of universal brotherhood (two rather extraordinary assumptions always quietly made), the Family could offer no proper type of the State, because the two most puissant elements in the Family must be wanting in the State.

The application of the canon just laid down is easily seen: while, on the one hand, the Family must necessarily enter into the State, which is in truth an aggregation of families, it can never furnish the typical laws for the State, because the actions of *individual* men cannot be the standard for the actions of *masses*, and the mere aggregation of families brings about such a complication of interests, passions, and opinions, that a totally new set of relations is evolved.

Thus precisely as Polity presupposes Domesticity, but is not embraced by it — precisely as the State is dependent on the Family, and is, nevertheless, belonging to a higher jurisdiction, so does Physiology presuppose Chemistry, but is not included in it, cannot be wholly regulated by its laws. Domestic life furnishes the basis for political life, as chemical actions furnish the basis for vital actions.

Whatever the future progress of Chemistry may effect in the way of simplifying physiological problems (and no one doubts that it must greatly aid us), there is one radical distinction which must ever keep the two sciences separate. It is this: Chemical laws are *quantitative*, because chemical actions are *definite* combinations; whereas physiological laws can never become quantitative, but only *qualitative*, because vital substances are *indefinite* in composition; that is to say, while chemical substances are formed by combinations of unvarying quantities, never more, never less — so much acid to so much base always forming the same salt, so many atoms of one substance always uniting with so many of another to form a third; the substances on which vital actions specially depend are never precisely and accurately definite: they vary in different individuals, and at different ages of the same individual; and as every variation in composition necessarily affects the properties of each substance, it is impossible that physiological actions can be reduced to those exact quantitative formulæ on which Chemistry is founded. Chloride of sodium is the same substance, having precisely the same composition and properties, whether taken from the sea, from the earth, from the plant, or manufactured in the laboratory. But nerve-tissue is never *precisely* the same in two men; the blood of two men is never precisely alike; the milk of two women is never identical in composition — they vary (within certain limits), and sometimes the variation is considerable. It is on this that depends what we call the difference of "temperament," which makes one twin so unlike his brother, and makes the great variety of the human race.

If in this digression the reader's assent has been gained, he will see that, from the radical incompetence of Chemistry to settle any true physiological question whatever, all the laborious efforts of later years have been barren, or nearly so, as regards the important subject of Food, because they have been only chemical reasonings on Physiology. Plausible and brilliant as some of the theories have been, they are all at fault when reduced to practice. They have gained general acceptance, because of the simplicity with which they *seemed* to solve abstruse problems; and the human mind is so eager to have explanations, that any logical plausibility is sure to captivate it.

II. LIEBIG'S CLASSIFICATION OF FOOD. — Of all current hypotheses on this subject, none claims a closer scrutiny than that which Liebig has made familiar to all Europe, and which, winged by the two qualities of simplicity and plausibility, has been carried into the lecture-room and study, where it continues to hold its place, in spite of the growing conviction that it is untenable.

To render the classification intelligible to those unfamiliar with chemistry, it is needful to premise that organic substances are chiefly composed of the four elements: oxygen, hydrogen, carbon, and nitrogen. Some few of these substances — such as the essential oils — contain only carbon and hydrogen. A far greater number, including the fixed oils, starch, sugars, vinegar, and alcohol, contain oxygen as well as carbon and hydrogen. One of the chemical peculiarities of the starchy, or saccharine, group is, that these substances all contain oxygen and hydrogen in exactly the proportions which would form water; and, although it is not supposed that these elements exist under the form of water in these substances, the chemists have named this group the *hydrates of carbon*, or *carbo-hydrates*. Besides these two classes there is a third, which contains nitrogen, in addition to the oxygen, hydrogen, and carbon. This group includes the seeds of plants and the tissues of animals. The amount of nitrogen in these substances is small compared with the amount of carbon: nevertheless the mere presence of nitrogen has caused them to be distinguished 'as the *nitro-*

*genous* group; while the other classes are placed together as the *non-nitrogenous*, or *carbonaceous*, group.

Bearing this in mind, we shall understand Liebig's division of Food into two classes:

The first is *Plastic*, or tissue-making, and comprises those organic substances into the composition of which nitrogen enters largely. These *nitrogenous* substances are — 1°, *Vegetable* Albumen, Fibrine, and Caseine; and, 2°, *Animal* Flesh and Blood. They are said to be plastic, or tissue-making, because they are capable of being converted into Blood; and from the Blood all the tissues are formed. According to this hypothesis, no other substance has any *nutritive* value; but inasmuch as many other substances are employed for Food, there must be some purpose served by them. Liebig groups them together in his

Second class: the *non-nitrogenous* or *heat-making* substances. These substances are the Fats, Gums, Sugars, Starch, Pectine, Bassorine, Wines, Beers, and Spirits. They are all assumed to be incapable of forming Blood, or of entering into the composition of any tissue, consequently they cannot nourish, or build up the body. But they are all capable of being "burned" in the body, and thus they furnish the needful animal heat, without which no organic function could be performed. When these substances are said to be "burned," we are to understand that burning here means simply *oxidation* — or the union of the oxygen derived from the atmosphere during Respiration, with one of these non-nitrogenous substances in the blood. The oxidation (rusting) of iron, and the burning of a candle, are one and the same process, differing only in degree. The union of oxygen with fat, is, in like manner, said to *burn* it. And because this oxygen is furnished in Respiration, all the articles of food which are burned by it are called *Respiratory*, i. e., supporters of the respiratory process; and because in their burning they evolve heat, they are called heat-making.

Besides these two main classes of nitrogenous, or nutritive, and non-nitrogenous, or heat-making, there is also a class of *inorganic substances*, such as Water, Salts, Iron, &c., which we shall hereafter see to be truly entitled to rank as Food.

The classification just expounded is certainly a brilliant effort of genius, and has given an immense impulsion to science. Indeed *that* may be said of all Liebig's views: right or wrong, they have agitated Europe, and inspired laborious research. It is not wonderful that he should have missed the truth on this subject, for the subject is far too complex to be embraced by any chemical hypothesis; but the gratitude of Europe is due to him (and is freely given) for having rendered the solution of the problem possible. There where he found a wilderness, he has left a pathway. On this pathway thousands of explorers are now hurrying; he has made it easy for them to find new ways.

Neque ego illi detrahere ausim,<br>
Hærentem capiti cum multa laude coronam. *

In rendering this tribute to Liebig's services, I must also explicitly declare that the classification he has proposed seems to me founded on a misconception. It has been much criticised,** sometimes with more asperity than befits the calm heights of science. It has made the tour of Europe, and become stereotyped in lectures and text-books. It has caused a vast amount of experimental research, which would have been more valuable had it been better directed. And it is now, more or less explicitly, relinquished by all advanced physiologists.

"It is indeed upon the assumption of this broad and fundamental classification of the constituents of food," write Messrs. Lawes and Gilbert, "according to their varied offices in the animal economy, that a vast series of analyses of foods have of late years been made and published; whilst, founded upon the results of these analyses, numerous tables have been constructed, professing to arrange the current articles of diet both of man and other animals, according to their comparative values as such."***

The question is one of very great importance, and the

---

* HORACE.
** See MULDER: *Physiologische Chemie.* MOLESCHOTT: *Kreislauf des Lebens;* and ROBIN et VERDEIL, *Traité de Chimie Anatomique.*
*** *Report on Foods in Relation to Respiration and Feeding,* in *Reports of Brit. Assoc.* 1852.

reader's patience is requested for an examination of it. So long
as we place ourselves at the *chemical* point of view, Liebig
carries us along with him; but no sooner do we perceive that we
are dealing with a vital problem, not a chemical problem, than
the necessity of abandoning the chemical and taking up the *physiological* point of view is at once evident, and we then quit our
ingenious guide.

Let us state the question. Man requires food which is both
tissue-making and heat-making, to repair the fabric, and sustain
the temperature of his body. This much is true. But it is demonstrable that nitrogenous substances are *not* the only plastic
materials, not even the chief materials, whereas they *are* also
heat-producing. Conversely, it is demonstrable that non-nitrogenous substances *are* tissue-making as well as heat-producing;
so that any distinction between them, founded on their supposed
offices nutritive and respiratory, falls to the ground; not to
mention that it rests on the assumption of Respiration being the
source of Animal Heat — an hypothesis we shall hereafter have
to consider.*

The division of Food into Nitrogenous and Non-Nitrogenous
is a chemical division to which no objection need be made, for it
expresses a chemical fact. But when the fact that albuminous
substances form a necessary proportion of organised tissues, is
made the ground for specially distinguishing them as plastic;
and when the presence of nitrogen in these substances is made
the ground for specially distinguishing nitrogen as *the* plastic
element, the per-centage of which is to afford the standard
of nutritive value, we see a striking example of chemical reasonings applied to Physiology, which a confrontation with nature suffices to upset. For observe: while it is true that "albumen is the foundation, the starting-point of the whole series
of peculiar tissues which are the seat of vital actions" (LIEBIG) —
while it is true that the *peculiar* characteristic of organised
tissues is that they contain albuminous substances as necessary
ingredients; not less is it true that the *other* substances, thus ar-
bitrarily excluded from the rank of tissue-makers—namely, the
fats, oils, and salts, all destitute of nitrogen — are *as essential*

* See the Chapter WHY WE ARE WARM, AND HOW WE KEEP SO.

4*

as albumen itself. *Not a cell, not a fibre can be formed, nor can subsist, without a certain amount of fat and salts.* Not a tissue can come into being, nor continue its functions, without a large proportion of non-nitrogenous materials — a proportion greatly *exceeding* that of the nitrogenous.

This is an anatomical fact which must surely discredit the idea of selecting one element out of several, all indispensable, and assigning to it alone the character of nutritive. If tissues were composed of albumen, or any other nitrogenous substance, *without* the admixture of fats, water, and salts; and if albumen did not likewise disengage heat in its transformations, Liebig's classification would be strictly accurate; but in the face of anatomical evidence which shows that *no* such tissue exists, and in the face of physiological evidence that even albumen undergoes chemical changes accompanied by the disengagement of heat, the classification must be rejected. Indeed the anatomist must ask with surprise, whether what he calls the adipose tissue is, or is not, chiefly composed of fat? Is the fat which exists in the muscles, cartilages, and bones an accident — a thing not worthy of being taken into account? The answer cannot be dubious. In 100 parts of muscle there are only 25.55 parts solid matter, and of these no less than 4.25 are fat. In 100 parts of the white substance of the brain, fat bears the large proportion of 13.9, whereas albumen is only 9.9; in the grey substance of the brain, the proportion of fat is 4.7 to albumen 7.5. If after this it be said that fat does not help to form tissue, is not an essential integral element of tissue, and consequently *plastic*, in the most rigorous sense of the word, the anatomist must confess that he fails to understand the language employed.

The reader need not be informed that Liebig is fully aware of the facts which can be brought against him, and that if he errs it is from theoretic bias. He is a chemist, and views these questions in their chemical light. To the chemist muscle is not a compound substance; for all those substances over and above albumen which he finds in it, he regards as mere *accessories;* the essential and characteristic element for him is the albuminous substance. But to the anatomist *all* the substances are essential, because it is by their *united* properties that the muscle performs its peculiar offices. A muscle deprived of its water will no longer act *as* a muscle: the anatomist therefore regards water as *essential* to the muscle; the chemist regards it as an accessory. In the laboratory the water may be disregarded: it will not interfere with chemical reactions. In the organism, the water is just as essential to the functional activity of the muscle as the albumen itself. Liebig, however, regards water and fat as having only a physical influence: —

"Many of the physical properties of organs, or tissues, depend on the presence of their non-nitrogenous constituents — namely, of water and fat. These bodies assist in the changes and processes by which the organised structures are formed. Fat has a share in the formation of cells; and on water depends the fluidity of the blood, and of all other juices. So also the milk-white colour of cartilage, the transparency of the cornea (of the eye), the softness, plasticity, flexibility, and elasticity of muscular fibre and of membranes, all depend on a fixed proportion of water in each case. Fat is a never-failing constituent of the substance of the brain and nerves; hair, horn, claws, teeth, and bones, always contain a certain amount of water and fat. But in these parts water and fat are only mechanically absorbed, as in a sponge, or enclosed in drops, as fat is in cells, and they may be removed by mechanical pressure, or by solvents, *without in the least affecting the structure of the parts*. They never have an organised form peculiar to themselves, but always take that of the parts, the pores of which they fill. They do not therefore belong to the plastic constituents of the body or of the food." [*] A little further on he repeats the statement that "they take no direct share by their elements in the formation of organs," and that they have "no vital properties."

By these expressions it is clear that, in his view, organs are not formed out of fat and water, *as well as* out of albumen; but that these substances are merely accessory, and afford the re-

* LIEBIG: *Chemical Letters*, 1851, p. 346; ed. 1859, p. 379. As these sheets are passing through the press, a fourth edition of the *Chemical Letters* has appeared, but without any modification of its views on the subject having been produced by the criticisms to which they have been subjected. For convenience of readers I shall give double references.

quisite physical conditions; just as, when wo use chloride of
potassium, the water in which the salt is dissolved counts for nothing in the chemical agency of the salt. And from several con-
versations I had with this distinguished philosopher, in which he
stated his point of view, I am persuaded that this is the explanation of all the differences which exist between him and those
physiologists who oppose his hypothesis. My answer then was,
what it is now — namely, that to the anatomist, nerve-tissue
without fat is no longer vital nerve; and blood without water is
no longer vital blood. To suppose that water simply gives
fluidity to blood, when in truth it is as much an integral constituent of blood as albumen itself, is equivalent to saying that heat
only gives expansion to steam — steam itself being, as all know,
the product of the operation of heat on water. If fat has no vital
properties in itself, neither has albumen in itself. To say that
fat and water are "mechanically absorbed," is to contradict anatomical evidence, which shows them to be *structurally combined*,
and always in constant quantities, varying within very small
limits.

A classification of Food, more or less imperfect, would not
trouble us did it not lead to important errors, as in the present
case. No sooner do we accept the idea of nitrogenous food being
*the* plastic material, than we are landed on the proposition that
"only those substances are in a strict sense nutritious articles of
food, which either contain albumen, or a substance capable of
being converted into albumen"* — a proposition elsewhere expressed in even a cruder form: "Only nitrogenous substances
are capable of conversion into blood."** Such passages as these
are only intelligible, coming from so eminent a writer, when we
remember that the chemical point of view dictates them. To the
chemist, indeed, only nitrogenous substances are capable of conversion into Blood; but to the anatomist every substance which
enters into the normal structure of Blood must be reckoned among
those capable of conversion into it. He cannot separate one
part of the Blood from another, as the chemist does — He must
take the whole structure as he finds it, for it is with the whole

---

* LIEBIG: *Chemical Letters*, 1851, p. 346; ed. 1859. p. 371.
** Ibid., p. 497; ed. 1859, p. 506.

structure that the functions are performed. Now what does he find? Examination of the structure of the Blood shows that, so far from being composed exclusively of nitrogenous substances, it is composed of a variety of substances, among which the nitrogenous albumen and fibrine amount to less than 80 in 1000 parts, including what must be added for the globulin and hæmatin of the blood-discs: that is *all* the nitrogen in the blood said to be composed solely of nitrogenous substances. No one knows this better than Liebig himself; yet his argument entirely overlooks it.

Let it not be supposed that this discussion is without a practical bearing: the whole question of Food depends on its decision. The chemical point of view is incapable of directing us to a single rule in practice: and to show how entirely it fails we may be content with one fact: The very substances said to be alone capable of conversion into blood — the only "strictly nutritious substances," are, when taken alone, utterly unable to nourish.

"Muscular flesh," says Majendie, in the celebrated Report of the Gelatine Commission, "in which gelatine, albumen, and fibrine are combined, according to the laws of organic nature, *and where they are associated with other matters, such as fats, salts,* &c., suffices, even in very small quantity, for complete and prolonged nutrition. Thus dogs fed for 120 days solely on raw meat, from sheep's heads, preserved their health and weight during this period, the daily consumption never exceeding 300 grammes, and often less. But 1000 grammes of isolated fibrine, with the addition of some hundred grammes of gelatine and albumen, were insufficient to support life. What, then, is this peculiar principle which renders meat so perfect an aliment? Is it the odorous and sapid matter which has this function, as seems probable? Do the salts, the trace of iron, the fatty matters and the lactic acid, contribute to the nutritive effect, notwithstanding that they constitute so minute a portion of meat?"[*]

The minuteness in quantity would be no argument against their potency of influence; but far more important will be the state of combination of the various elements. "The albumen of

* Quoted by PEREIRA: *Treatise on Food and Diet,* p. 211.

egg, and the fibrine separated from the blood, may to the chemist be identical with the fibrine and albumen which concur in the formation of muscle, incorporated there by a process of nutrition; but they are not the same for the organism which has to assimilate them, and which requires that they should be in a special state of elaboration, which they have undergone in another organism; it is muscular flesh which the organism demands, and not the elements of which flesh is composed: it needs aliments not chemical products."*

It has been found that dogs perish of starvation when liberally supplied with albumen, or with white of egg, or with fibrine, or with mixtures of albumen and fibrine — if these substitutes constitute their sole diet — whereas they flourish when fed on gluten alone, although, according to the chemists, gluten is identical with albumen and fibrine: a sufficient proof that the nutritive value of a substance cannot be determined by its chemical composition.

But this kind of proof awaits us on all sides. While Chemistry determines the nutritive value of foods according to their percentage of nitrogen, experience flatly contradicts the application of such a standard, for it shows us that wheat contains only 2.3 per cent of nitrogen, whereas beans contain as much as 5.5 per cent, lentils 4.4, and peas 4.3; and yet, with this remarkable inferiority in its per-centage of nitrogen, wheat is remarkably superior in nutritive value to beans, lentils, or peas. The discrepancy here is so glaring that Liebig has attempted to explain it. "The small quantity of phosphates which the seeds of the lentils, beans, and peas contain *must* be the cause of their small value as articles of nourishment, *since* they surpass all other vegetable food in the quantity of nitrogen which enters into their composition. But as the component parts of the bones (phosphate of lime and magnesia) are absent, they satisfy the appetite without increasing the strength."** The argument might be reversed, and the whole nutritive value assigned to the phosphates with equal justice. If nitrogen is *the* plastic element, and its per-centage afford the true nutritive standard, the presence or ab-

* LEVY: *Traité d'Hygiène*, II. 85, quoted by LONGET, *Physiologie*.
** LIEBIG: *Chemistry in its Application to Agriculture and Physiology*, p. 147.

sence of the phosphates can have nothing to do with it; and if their presence or absence is all-important, then we are certain that nutritive value does not admit of being estimated by the percentage of nitrogen, but by the conjunction of nitrogen with other substances.

It is noticeable that when Liebig has to explain the nutritive inferiority of beans and peas, he finds the cause to lie in the absence of phosphates, which, as he truly says, are component parts of the bones; whereas, when denying any nutritive quality to fat, he refused to admit that it was a component part of tissues. Into such contradictions he is forced by his theory of nitrogenous substances being the only plastic materials — a theory incessantly at variance with fact.

Messrs. Lawes and Gilbert call especial attention to one series of their experiments, in which sheep fed on succulent unripe turnips "lost weight notwithstanding the *very high* per-centage of nitrogen;"[*] and, without laying any stress on the fact that vegetable poisons are highly nitrogenous, let us ask the dispassionate reader to reflect on the chaotic condition of a doctrine which, while proclaiming nitrogen to be the true standard of nutritive value, declares that gelatine, a substance richer in nitrogen than even flesh or blood, has no nutritive value at all. We do not, indeed, attach much credit to this opinion, which we shall examine by-and-by, but it is certainly in flagrant contradiction with the chemical hypothesis of nutritive values.

In spite, therefore, of what is so confidently asserted, we have the admission of chemists themselves that nitrogen is only nutritive in peculiar combinations. The consequence is inevitable. We must direct our attention towards substances which *do* nourish, and disregard the chemical formulæ which proclaim what substances *ought* to nourish. Inquiries so directed yield little that is satisfactory to the chemical hypothesis.

We find, for example, thousands of Irish subsisting chiefly on potatoes and skimmed milk; and millions of Hindoos subsisting chiefly on rice and rancid butter — substances which, in a chemical analysis, exhibit very little of the so-called plastic material. Payen gives the following proportions in 100 parts of rice: —

* *Report*, p. 336.

Starch, 89.15; Nitrogenous matters, 7.05; Dextrine, &c. 1.; Fats, 0.80; Cellulose, 1.10; Mineral matters, 0.90.  And Liebig himself calculates the proportion of plastic to non-plastic material in rice, as only 10 to 123; whereas in beef it is 10 to 17, and in veal 10 to 1.

Respecting the rice-eating Hindoos, it may be observed that although Dr. Forbes Watson's elaborate investigations have dispelled the very general notion of rice forming the *entire* bulk of the diet of the inhabitants of the East, they also give an unequivocal refutation of the chemical theory of Food.

In the work on the "Food Grains of India," which is at this moment passing through the press, Dr. Watson remarks that "the stomach of the poor Ryot, large as it is, could not with impunity take in and digest the quantity of rice which would be sufficient day by day to supply the wants of his system."*  In a private communication he informs me that where rice is cheap, as at the deltas of rivers and in other water-abounding situations, it forms the *chief* food of the inhabitants; although disease ensues unless a certain proportion — say ¼ to ½ of *pulse*, or dried fish, be added to supply the required nitrogenous elements.  In some parts where rice forms almost the entire food of the population, "pot bellies" and the results of starvation are visible in every direction.  In all cases rice, when procurable, forms two-thirds of the food, and may therefore be considered the staple food of a considerable population.  "Nature, however, has taught the native to add pulses, or flesh, to his rice — just as she has suggested to the Irishman the free use of buttermilk to his potatoes."                                                          .

The facts are important.  While admitting the proved nutritive quality of nitrogenous food, such as the pulses, I am far from clear that the Hindoo is forced to mix them with his rice merely on account of the nitrogen they contain.  The fact that rice alone is insufficient to the effective sustainment of the organism, and that "pot bellies," diseases, and even signs of starvation are the consequences of its exclusive employment, is only one among a series of facts which prove that man cannot flourish on *one* kind of food.  Pulses are even worse than rice when eaten alone.

* WATSON: *The Food-Grains of India*, 1859, p. 25.

Albumen itself, nay, milk itself, would not suffice alone. We are justified, therefore, in assigning this effect to some other cause than the mere deficiency in nitrogen; and wo are at all events certain that rice suffices to sustain the waste and repair of the organism, if not in a very admirable manner. And Dr. Watson further informs me that the other grains of the Hindoos are all highly carbonaceous; although the native, as a rule, combines these, *when he can*, so as to make a food which contains about eight or nine parts of carbon to one of nitrogen — which Dr. Watson regards 'as the proper standard for tropical *as well* as temperate climates.[*]

Now let us observe the bearing of these facts on the chemical theory of Food. Rice is confessedly extremely deficient in plastic, nitrogenous, elements; abundant in heat-making, carbonaceous, elements. Rice is therefore among the very substances which, on the chemical hypothesis, the Hindoos would seem least to require.

We are told that non-nitrogenous matters are incapable of entering into the composition of tissues, or of furnishing plastic material: "they only serve to keep up the temperature of the body, being rapidly burnt in the body." We are further told that the demand for such substances is necessarily much greater in cold than in hot countries, because of the greater amount of heat required to keep the body at its proper point.

"In winter, when we take exercise in a cold atmosphere, and when, consequently, the amount of inspired oxygen increases, the necessity for food containing carbon and hydrogen increases in the same ratio; and by gratifying the appetite thus excited, we obtain the most efficient protection against the most piercing cold. The oxygen taken into the system is given out again in the same form, both in summer and winter: we expire more carbon at a low than at a high temperature, and require more or less carbon in our food in the same proportion; and consequently more is respired in Sweden than in Sicily; and in our own

[*] Liebig's calculation of a standard food is four parts of non-nitrogenous to one part of nitrogenous matter. — *Chemical Letters*, 1859, p. 391. Dr. Watson finds the heat-making elements double this quantity — and in a hot climate too.

country, an eighth more in winter than in summer. If an equal weight of food is consumed in hot and cold climates, Infinite Wisdom has ordained that very unequal proportions of carbon shall be taken in it. The fruits used by the inhabitants of southern climes, do not contain, in a fresh state, more than 12 per cent of carbon, while the blubber and train-oil which feed the inhabitants of the polar regions, contain 66 to 80 per cent of that element."[*]

Considering the importance of the idea, one cannot but be struck with the singular meagreness of these illustrations. That fruits are eaten in southern climates which are less heat-producing, because they contain much less carbon, than the train-oil eaten in polar regions, would be a tolerable argument, if *only* fruits were eaten in the South; but the Sicilian and Neapolitan eat more oil than the Swede, and their macaroni is a highly carbonised substance; and the Hindoo often subsists on rice and butter — substances highly carbonised, and classed as chiefly Respiratory, furnishing in superabundance that very heat which his climate renders so undesirable.

According to *theory*, the Hindoo should eat very little non-nitrogenous food, and be content with plastic substances, since he wastes his tissues in daily labour, but does not stand in need of any surplus heat; whereas, according to *fact*, he eats very little nitrogenous food, and a great deal of "heat-making" food.

It is remarkable that such a contradiction to the chemical theory should have been overlooked, especially by those who laid so much stress on the large consumption of nitrogenous food by the inhabitants of cold countries — a consumption said to be caused by the need of rapid combustion to sustain the animal heat. For my own part I see no reason whatever to believe in the current hypothesis that food is "burned" in the organism; and elsewhere (see chapter on "Why we are Warm"), will give reasons for that dissent, and for believing that it is the tissues which are burned (if burning there be) and not the food itself. Waiving this objection, however, for the present, let us consider merely the important conclusion to which Dr. Watson's researches have led him, namely, that the proper standard, chemically speaking, is the same for tropical and for temperate climates.

* LIEBIG: *Chemical Letters*, 1851, p. 320; ed. 1859, p. 347.

And this damaging fact is brought into even greater relief by the experiments of Messrs. Lawes and Gilbert, as thus recorded by them: "The weather, during part of the period of this second series of experiments, was exceedingly hot; from this several of the animals suffered considerably; and some, either from this or other causes, became quite ill, and died, or were 'killed to save their lives.' Nevertheless it is seen that there was upon the whole *a larger amount of respiratory food consumed* in relation to weight in this series than in the previous one, during the cooler season."[*] Against such evidence as this, the respiratory nature of non-nitrogenous food is more than equivocal.

It is a fact that, in cold countries, fat and oil are greedily devoured; and it is the most striking fact that can be adduced in favour of the hypothesis now under discussion. But we have yet to learn that fat is simply so much "combustible" material. The demand for fat in cold countries may arise out of various conditions. Increase of cold causes increased activity of respiration, and increased activity of muscular exertion. These cause a greater waste of tissue; consequently increased repair is needed; and as fat is indispensable to such repair, we can therein see one source of the demand for fat.

The reader will bear in mind, that we are not in *this* place disputing the position that fat is burned in the body, or that it is not one important source of animal heat; the point disputed is, whether fat is *only* a heat-producer, and the demand for it in cold countries *only* a demand for combustible material. On this point it is well worthy of remark, that Schmidt's researches prove *fat to be less easily combustible in the organism than the carbohydrates, and even than albuminates;*[**] so that the Hindoo, in his rice, eats a substance more easily oxidisable in the organism than the tallow eaten by the Esquimaux.

What has been already said will perhaps suffice to show how untenable a position is that which denies nutritive value to fats, sugars, starch, water, &c., throwing the whole burden of nutrition

---

[*] *Report*, p. 840.

[**] See on this point BIDDER and SCHMIDT, *Die Verdauungssäfte*, p. 360-63, and LEHMANN, *Lehrbuch der Physiol. Chemie*, 2d edit. vol. III. pp. 203, 386.

on the albuminous substances; it may complete the overthrow of
that position if I now show that, while the fats are tissue-makers
and heat-producers, the albuminates are heat-producers and
tissue-makers.

No one doubts that heat is evolved in the chemical changes
which albuminates undergo; the doubt raised can only be as to
the amount. Liebig says: "If the combustible elements of the
plastic constituents of food served for the production of heat, the
whole amount of the substances consumed by the horse in his hay
and oats, by the pig in its potatoes, could only suffice to support
their respiratory process, and consequently their animal heat, in
the horse for 4½ hours daily, in the pig for 4 hours daily; or if
confined to plastic food, they would require to consume five or
six times as much of it. But even in this last case it is exceedingly
doubtful whether these substances, considering their properties,
would in the circumstances under which they are presented to
oxygen in the organism produce the necessary temperature of the
body and compensate for the loss of heat; for of all organic compounds, the plastic constituents of food are those which possess
in the lowest degree the properties of combustibility, and or
developing heat by their oxidation." *

Every chemist would echo this statement, because Chemistry
teaches that of all the elements of the animal body nitrogen has
perhaps the feeblest attraction for oxygen; not only so, but it
even deprives other substances, with which it combines, of their
tendency to unite with oxygen. Phosphorus, for example, has an
eager affinity for oxygen, as we know from its ready combustibility in atmospheric air at ordinary temperatures; but
when combined with nitrogen its combustibility is so difficult
that it can only be effected at red heat and in oxygen gas. Liebig
hence concludes, and from the chemical point of view is justified
in concluding, that precisely the same relations are preserved in
the blood. The albuminous (nitrogenous) bodies have, he says,
but a very slight affinity for oxygen. "If the albumen of the
blood, which is derived from the plastic portion of the food, possessed in a higher degree the power of supporting respiration, it
would be utterly unfit for the process of nutrition. Were albumen

* LIEBIG: *Chemical Letters*, p. 372; ed. 1859, p. 394.

as such destructible, or liable to be altered in the circulation, by the inhaled oxygen, the relatively small quantity of it, daily supplied to the blood by the digestive organs, would quickly disappear. As long as the blood contains, besides albumen, other substances which surpass it in attraction for oxygen, so long will the oxygen be unable to exert a destructive action on this the chief constituent of the blood; and the significance of the non-nitrogenous food is thus made clear."

It is not surprising that a theory so logical should have gained general acceptance; and as a specimen of chemical reasoning on physiological problems it is very brilliant. Nevertheless, when we study what takes place in the organism, we find direct and unequivocal contradiction given to each separate clause of the theory. We find races of men living always on vegetable food, containing little nitrogen, and in climates where a superabundance of animal heat is not needed; so that to them non-nitrogenous food must be sufficient for the chief supply of nutrition.

And not only do numerous facts overpower the chemical hypothesis, but even Chemistry itself, when interrogating the facts of organic life, discovers that, however weak the affinity of albuminates for oxygen, *out* of the organism, their affinity, *in* the organism, surpasses that of fat. Schmidt, to whose experiments science is so deeply indebted, found that on feeding cats now with flesh alone, and now with fat alone, or with much fat and little flesh, the *albuminates were always more rapidly destroyed than the fat*, which was at first stored up in the body to be afterwards gradually oxidised;* and these experiments are confirmed by those of Persoz in fattening geese with maize: the blood of the fattened geese was very rich in fat, but notably impoverished in albumen; the quantity of muscular substance was much diminished, and when the fattening was rapid the weight of the whole body was absolutely diminished. It is therefore an error to say that if albumen were liable to oxidation, life would be impossible. Experiment proves it to be more liable than fat.

To the chemist these results will be paradoxical, if not inconceivable, and he will doubtless point to the well-ascertained fact that in starvation it is the fat which disappears first, the

* BIDDER and SCHMIDT, p. 363.

muscles only yielding up their elements to destruction when most of the fat has been oxidised. This point has already been dwelt on by us when treating of Hunger and Thirst. All that can here be said is, that it needs to be reconciled with the seemingly contradictory facts. How slow we should be in drawing conclusions from what takes place out of the organism, as to what takes place in it, is taught us in a hundred physiological facts: thus the fat which can be decomposed into fatty acid and glycerine by means only of the most energetic acids and alkalis in the laboratory, is changed in the organism by the pancreatic juice, which has but feeble chemical properties, but which brings about the result by means of an organic substance acting as a ferment.[*]

We might multiply to a great extent the objections which present themselves to the chemical classification of Food; but those already stated are sufficient to show that it is erroneous in every particular, in spite of its logical dependence and plausibility.

The only extensive series of experiments on feeding, with which we are acquainted, as immediately serviceable, are those instituted by Messrs. Lawes and Gilbert, and to them the reader is referred; because, although they are by no means such as, from the nature of the experiments, can give Physiology any accurate data, they are valuable as practical results. They show among other things, that "although pigs were satisfied to eat a smaller proportion of food in relation to their weight, in those pens where the proportion of nitrogen was comparatively large, yet the proportion of increase to the food consumed was *less* than where the amount of *non*-nitrogenous food consumed was greater." And further, that "whilst the non-nitrogenous substance consumed to produce 100 lb. increase in weight is *very nearly equal* in the two series; yet that of the nitrogenous constituents varies in the proportion of from three to two!" Again: "In the fourth pen, where there was by far the *largest amount of nitrogen* consumed, the animals *lost weight;* and in the other three pens, the productiveness of the food is in the *inverse order of the amounts of nitrogen* taken in the food. Indeed, we believe that an unusually

---

[*] CLAUDE BERNARD: *Leçons de Physiologie Expérimentale. Cours de* 1854-55, p. 391.

high per-centage of nitrogen in succulent produce is frequently a pretty sure indication of immaturity and innutritious qualities." Summing up the results of their whole series of experiments, the largest yet instituted, they declare that it is "their available non-nitrogenous constituents, rather than their richness in nitrogenous ones, that measure both the amount consumed to a given weight of animal, in a given time, and the increase in weight obtained."* And they refer to the instinctive preference given by the under-fed labouring classes to fat meat, such as pork, over those meats which are leaner and more nitrogenous.

Long as we have tarried over this part of our subject, the time will not have been misspent if it have clearly impressed the conviction that nitrogenous food is *not* the exclusively plastic food, and that per-centages of nitrogen afford *no* nutritive standard — the conviction that Liebig's classification, except in a chemical point of view, is erroneous — and the conviction that Chemistry is incompetent to solve the problem of Food.

III. INORGANIC FOOD.— As soon as we relinquish the seductive notion of physiological deduction from chemical laws, and place ourselves at the proper point of view, namely, that of the organism to be nourished, our classification of Food speedily falls under two main divisions — Inorganic and Organic substances; and, doubtless to the reader's surprise, the Inorganic turns out to be the *more* important of the two, supposing always that a question of degree can lawfully be entertained where both kinds are indispensable.

We are not, indeed, accustomed to consider minerals as food, or water as highly nutritious; but that is because we are not accustomed to consider the subject with the needful accuracy. Tell the first man you meet that water is on the whole more nutritious than roast-beef, and that common salt, or bone-ash, is as much an edible as the white of egg, and it is probable that he will throw anxious glances across the streets to assure himself that your keeper is at hand. Make the same statements to the first man of science you meet, and the chances are, that he will think

* *Report*, p. 344. Compare also their *Report on the Equivalency of Starch and Sugar in Food.* British Assoc., 1851.

*The Physiology of Common Life.* 1. 5

you very ignorant of organic chemistry, or that you are playing with a paradox.* Nevertheless, it is demonstrably true, and never would have worn the air of a paradox, if men had steadily conceived the nature of an alimentary substance.

*That* is an aliment, which nourishes; whatever we find in the organism, as a constant and integral element, either forming part of its structure, or one of the conditions of vital processes, that, and that only, deserves the name of aliment.

But men have been seduced from this simple conception, partly by vain endeavours to ascertain in analysis of food and excreta what are the truly nutritive substances, and partly by misconceptions of the processes of Nutrition.

*Nutrition in Plants and Animals.* — Of these misconceptions there is one, widely spread, which declares, that while Plants are able to nourish themselves directly by inorganic materials furnished them in the air, earth, and water, Animals are incapable of thus drawing nourishment from inorganic materials, but depend solely on the organic materials prepared for them by Plants. The Plants feed on minerals, the Herbivora feed on Plants, and the Carnivora on the Herbivora. The cycle is complete, the symmetry of nature seems perfect.

One feels a kind of pity in having to disturb so elegant a formula; yet the truth must be told, and the truth is, that not a single statement so expressed is altogether correct. Certain it is that Plants can, and do, convert inorganic substances into organic, but it is not less certain that this power is very limited, all except the simplest (perhaps not even these) needing organic principles to be yielded by the soil in which they grow. This destroys the distinction between Plants and Animals, by showing that both, more or less, depend on organic substances. It is this inability in Plants to dispense with organic matter, that renders manure necessary.**

---

* "Minerals are not in the least alimentary, although many animals often eat them mixed with or combined with their food." — TIEDEMANN: *Physiologie*, i. 230.

** VERDEIL and RISLET have ascertained that all fertile soils contain a soluble organic substance resulting from the decomposition of vegetable matter. — *Comptes Rendus de la Société de Biologie*, iv. 111, 112.

While so much is certain, the general assumption is, that Animals are altogether incapable of converting any inorganic materials into organic; and are rigorously dependent on Plants for every organic substance met with in their bodies. This assumption seems to me wholly unwarranted by any decisive knowledge yet obtained. The main argument on which it rests, namely, that unless organic substances be given in the food, and in certain proportions, the animal perishes of starvation, has no longer any coercive force when we reflect that starvation as inevitably follows if inorganic substances be withheld.* Organic substances — of a low order it is true — have been manufactured by the chemist out of inorganic substances; and if urea, alcohol, and camphor are already capable of being made in the laboratory, I see no reason for supposing that even more complex substances may not be made in the vital organism, which is the seat of such incessant chemical transformations.**

Be this as it may, the distinction between Animals and Plants falls to the ground when we see that Plants *do* require organic substances, and that Animals *do* nourish themselves with inorganic substances taken directly from earth, air, and water. We hew salt from the quarry to cast it in handfuls upon our stews and soups, or in pinches on our meat and potatoes. We draw water from the spring to drink; and, like the plants, we draw gases (oxygen, perhaps also nitrogen) from the air, to enter into those various combinations without which no life is possible.

It may be unusual to call these nutritive principles, but if unusual, it is not unscientific. If "to nourish the body" mean to *sustain its force* and *repair its waste* — if food enters into the living structure — and if all the integral constituents of that structure are derived from food — there can be nothing improper in designating as nutritious, substances which have an enormous preponderance among the integral constituents. People who think it paradoxical to call water Food, will cease their surprise on learning that water forms two-thirds of the living body; and

---

* The necessity for organic food will be better understood when we come to speak of Digestion, and the action of nitrogenous substances as ferments.

** LEHMANN is of the same opinion. — *Physiol. Chemie*, III. 180.

they will perhaps cease to marvel at the nutritive value here attributed to minerals, on learning that when all the water is eliminated, and the solids which form the remaining one-third are analysed, they are found to contain no less than one-third of mineral substances which remain as ashes. Nor must the presence of these mineral substances be regarded as accidental or unimportant. They are constant, constituent, essential. Blood is not blood without its salts and iron; bone is not bone without its phosphates; muscle is not muscle without its salts.

Let us glance at one or two of these inorganic elements; and, first, at *phosphate of lime.* There is not a single humour, nor a single tissue in the body, which is without a certain proportion of this salt. By removing it, the integrity of the tissue is destroyed, and all characteristic properties are as infallibly altered as if the organic elements were removed. If the needful quantity be withheld or withdrawn, the bones become weakened, as we see in pregnant women, whose fractured limbs are with difficulty healed (sometimes not at all), simply because their phosphate of lime has been diminished by the demands of the child.

A similar effect is noticeable in infants during teething, a period when the "rickets" often make their dreaded appearance.

But still more fatal is the effect of withholding this salt from the food, as we learn in the striking experiments of Chossat, who withheld it from pigeons, allowing them to eat no more than was contained in the grain and water on which he fed them: they all perished miserably, after attacks of diarrhœa and softening of the bones. *

. The absolute necessity of a supply of inorganic materials in Food is further illustrated in one of the experiments of Messrs. Lawes and Gilbert, who note that "the pigs in the pen, where Indian meal alone was given, had become affected with large tumours breaking out on their necks, their breathing and swallowing becoming at the same time difficult. We, in order to test the question as to whether this arose from the defect of nitrogen

* Von Bibra found that the quantity of phosphate of lime contained in the bones was determined by their ratio of work; those of the legs and feet containing more than the arms and hands, and both these more than the ribs or the passive bones.

or from other causes, supplied them with a trough of *mineral substances:* they soon recovered from their complaint, and eventually proved to be among the fattest and best of the entire series of pigs; at least a dealer in pork, with a practised eye, purchased, by preference, one of these animals from among the whole set of carcasses. The mineral mixture supplied to them was composed of twenty parts coal-ashes, four parts common salt, and one part superphosphate of lime; and for it they seemed to exhibit considerable relish."*

The point is forcibly put by Liebig: — "In the two preceding letters, there has been ascribed to certain constituents of seeds, tubers, roots, herbs, fruits, and flesh, the power of supporting the processes of nutrition and respiration; and it will appear as a very striking contradiction when it is stated, that no one of these substances by itself, neither caseine alone, nor the substance of muscular fibre, nor the albumen of eggs or of the blood, nor the corresponding vegetable products, are able to support the plastic or formative processes; that neither starch, sugar, nor fat, can sustain the process of respiration. Nay, it may excite still greater astonishment to add, that these substances, even when mixed, no matter in what proportions, are destitute of the property of digestibility without the presence of certain other substances; so much so, indeed, that if these other conditions be excluded, the above-named compounds are utterly unable to effect the continuance of life and the vital phenomena."**

He then proceeds to explain that these matters are the salts of the blood, and examines, with his usual acuteness when dealing with chemical phenomena, the part played by the alkalis in the nutritive process.

We must remark, however, that even here the absence of the true anatomical point of view renders his teaching incomplete; for he only takes into account the part played by the inorganic substances as *conditions* of vital phenomena (such as promoting digestibility and nutrition), entirely overlooking their part as integral *elements of tissue,* on which many of the properties of tissues depend.

* *Report,* p. 339.
** *Chemical Letters,* 1851, p. 382; ed. 1859, p. 404.

It is from this mistaken view, we imagine, that he omits *water* from the list; yet anatomy assures us that water is an essential element of tissue; and its enormous preponderance in quantity is the expression of its pre-eminence in nutritive quality, and explains the paradox of water being, *longo intervallo*, the most sustaining of all articles. Life, we know, may be prolonged for weeks without any organic food being taken, if water be freely supplied; but life will not continue many days when water is withheld. If, therefore, the purpose of Food be to sustain the organism, that article which sustains it longest, and can with least immunity be withheld, must be the most nutritive of all; and thus water claims pre-eminence over beef.

Water is so abundant around us, and it passes in and out of the system with such freedom, that we are naturally disposed to overlook the fact of its forming a *constituent*, tolerably constant in amount. Many of its uses are accurately known. It dissolves gases, without which Respiration would be impossible; and gives the tissues their elasticity, the humours their fluidity. It is the great vehicle of chemical change. If the lungs were formed precisely as they are, with the single exception of having no moisture on their surfaces, Respiration could not be effected; as we see when the fish is taken out of water, and its gills become dry by evaporation. The cornea of the eye owes its transparency to water, and the removal of that small quantity would render vision a mere perception of a local change in temperature.

But it is unnecessary to rehearse the manifold properties of water in the vital organism; we have said enough to show its eminence as Food.

*Common Salt* (chloride of sodium) is another constant and universal substance which claims rank as Food. It forms an essential part of all the organic fluids and solids, except the enamel of the teeth;* a statement to which attention is called, because Liebig, in one passage,** seems to deny that it forms

---

* ROBIN and VERDEIL: *Traité de Chimie Anatomique*, II. 175; and LEH-MANN, II. 404; III. 60.
** *Chemical Letters*, 1851, pp. 405, 406; ed. 1859, p. 426. That this statement should be left unmodified is the more surprising since it relates to a purely chemical question. Was it overlooked by Liebig in his revision of the Letters, or does he maintain his original opinion in spite of the analyses made

part of the tissues, declaring that in muscle chloride of potassium is abundant, but no chloride of sodium exists; but the analyses of Von Bibra, Barral, and others, declare the existence of this salt in muscle.

Common salt is always found in the blood, in quantities which vary within extremely narrow limits, forming less than a half per cent (0.421) of the entire mass, water included, and as much as 75 per cent of the ashes of the blood. This quantity is wholly independent of any surplus contained in food; for the surplus is either not absorbed, or is carried away in the excretions and perspiration;* and this shows salt to be an anatomical constituent, not an accident. If too little salt be taken in the food, instinct forces every animal to supply the deficiency by eating it separately. "The wild buffalo frequents the salt licks of North-Western America; the wild animals in the central parts of Southern Africa are a sure prey to the hunter who conceals himself beside a salt spring; and our domestic cattle run peacefully to the hand that offers them a taste of this luxury. From time immemorial it has been known that without salt man would miserably perish; and among horrible punishments, entailing certain death, that of feeding culprits on saltless food is said to have prevailed in barbarous times."**

When Cook and Forster landed in Otaheite they astonished the natives who saw them eating white powder with every morsel of meat; and every one remembers Man Friday's expressive repudiation of salt. But the savages who ate no "white powder," ate fish; and cooked their flesh in sea-water, rich in salt. In several parts of Africa men are sold for salt; and on the Gold Coast it is the most precious of all commodities. On the coast of Sierra Leone a man will sell his sister, his wife, or his child, for salt, not having learned the art of distilling it from the sea.

The properties of salt are manifold. It forms one of the essential conditions of vital processes. It renders albumen

by others? Enough for us that the latest authorities — to which may be added Professor MILLER: *Elements of Chemistry*, 1857, iii. 691 — proclaim the existance of chloride of sodium in muscle as well as other tissues.

  * DE BLAINVILLE has noticed that people living on the coast, or eating salted meats, have a decided increase of salt in their perspiration.

  ** JOHNSTON: *Chemistry of Common Life*, p. 400.

soluble, and is necessary for digestion, being decomposed in the stomach into hydrochloric acid for the gastric process, and soda for the bile.

*Law of Endosmosis.*—Salt has also a most important property, namely, that of aiding to effect the interchange of fluids through the walls of the vessels, in accordance with that law of *endosmosis*, on which so many vital processes depend — a law which we must pause for a moment to consider, since we shall hereafter have frequent occasion to invoke it. If a bladder be filled with alcohol, or any other liquid, and placed in an empty glass vessel, none of the alcohol will pass through the bladder into the vessel. If we pour alcohol into the vessel — or if we pour any other liquid into it having the same density as the liquid contained in the bladder — none will pass from the vessel into the bladder, nor from the bladder into the vessel. We say the bladder is "impermeable" by fluids; and because of this impermeability, we employ it to hold fluids. Nevertheless we make a great mistake in saying so. The bladder is perfectly permeable, and will allow fluids to pass in or pass out, provided the conditions be slightly changed. Thus, if we place this bladder of alcohol in a vessel of water, the water being a liquid of *different density* from the alcohol, a surprising phenomenon occurs — the water penetrates rapidly into the bladder, and a little of the alcohol passes into the vessel. This action goes on till a complete equality of density is established between the fluid in the bladder and that in the

Fig. 3.

ENDOSMOMETER.

vessel. This *rushing in of the water* is called *endosmosis;* this *rushing out of the alcohol* is called *exosmosis.* The following figure represents the endosmometer of Dutrochet, the discoverer of this surprising law.

The small bladder *a* is tied to a glass-tube *d*, open at both ends, one of which is bent, *c*. The bladder is filled with alcohol till it reaches the point of the tube *d;* it is then placed in a vessel of water *e;* and almost at once the alcohol, having its volume increased by the water which has penetrated the bladder, will be seen rising in the tube and falling drop by drop into the glass *b*. This continues till the alcohol and water are completely mixed in bladder and vessel.

We must not enter further upon this subject, interesting though it is. Enough if we bear in mind that *whenever an animal membrane separates two fluids of different densities, a mutual interchange between those fluids will take place.* Thus although the minute blood-vessels, called capillaries, are closed tubes, and would keep the blood in them as a bladder holds water, they suffer gases and liquids to pass through their walls *from them*, and *into them*, whenever the gas or liquid outside is of a different density to that inside.

We may now return from our digression to the consideration of Salt, which, by increasing the density of the fluids into which it enters, is one of the many agents in endosmosis. Indeed, so great are the services of salt, that we may confidently accept the statement of Dr. Bence Jones, that it is "a substance as essential to life as nitrogenous food, or non-nitrogenous food and water;"[*] and if so essential, then assuredly Food.

It would lead us too far, and the excursion would be unnecessary, to examine separately all the inorganic substances taken as Food; enough has already been said to justify the classification, which places the inorganic beside the organic substances, as one of the two great divisions into which the subject naturally falls. If we do not dine off minerals, nor find ourselves pleasantly munching a lump of chalk, as we should munch a lump of bread; if, as a general rule, we eat mineral substances only in combination with organic substances, and not separately; the rule is absolute which forces us to eat organic substances in combination with inorganic, because in fact no pure organic substance can be found. It may seem absurd to talk of eating inorganic food, because we rarely eat it separately; but in that sense it is absurd to talk of eating organic food, because organic substance, free from all admixture of the inorganic, has never been eaten by any man.

[*] BENCE JONES: *On Gravel, Calculus, and Gout*, p. 40.

# CHAPTER II.

### (Continued.)

#### FOOD AND DRINK.

##### SECTION II. — ALIMENTARY PRINCIPLES.

Effect of different conditions in substances — Life interferes to disturb
ordinary chemical actions — Effect of Form — Food considered chemically
and physiologically — Blood as a standard of food — Milk as a standard —
Albumen — Fibrine — Caseine — The protein bodies — Gluten — Gelatine,
is it nutritious? — History of the inquiry — Fats and oils; their digestibility
in various conditions — Starch as food — Sugar — Does sugar injure the
teeth? — Alcohol as food — Teetotalism — Iron as food — Acids, do they
prevent scurvy? — Does vinegar keep people thin?

HAVING in the preceding section argued some of the general
questions relative to food, we must now review, in a brief manner,
the various Alimentary Principles of which food is composed;
and then we may pass on to the various articles of food consumed
by man.

1. *Effect of different conditions.* — The water which drowns
us as a fluent stream, can be walked upon as ice. The bullet
which, when fired from a musket, carries death, will be harmless
if ground to dust before being fired. The crystallised part of the
oil of roses, so grateful in its fragrance — a solid at ordinary temperatures, though readily volatile — is a compound substance
containing exactly the same elements, and in exactly the same
proportions, as the gas with which we light our streets. The tea
which we daily drink, with benefit and pleasure, produces palpi-
tations, nervous tremblings, and even paralysis, if taken in excess; yet the peculiar organic agent — called theine — to which
tea owes its qualities, may be taken by itself (as theine, not as
tea) without any appreciable effect.* The water which will allay

* SCHLEIDEN: *Die Pflanze*, 1858, p. 205.

our burning thirst, augments it when congealed into snow; so that Captain Ross declares the natives of the Arctic regions "prefer enduring the utmost extremity of thirst rather than attempt to remove it by eating snow."* Yet if the snow be melted, it becomes drinkable water; and it *is* melted in the mouth. Nevertheless, although, if melted before entering the mouth, it assuages thirst like other water, when melted *in* the mouth it has the opposite effect. To render this paradox more striking, we have only to remember that ice, which melts more slowly in the mouth, is very efficient in allaying thirst.

These facts point to an important consideration, which has been little regarded by the majority of those who have written on Food: the consideration of the profound differences which may result from simple differences in the *state* of substances. The chemist, in his elementary analysis, necessarily gives no clue to such differences. He tells us *of* what elements an article of Food is composed; but he cannot tell us *how* those elements are combined, nor in what state the substance is. Even when he has ascertained the real composition and properties of any substance, he has still to ask the physiologist what are the *conditions* presented by the organism in which this substance is to undergo chemical transformation.

We know that a change in the conditions will cause a change in the manifestation of a force; so that often what ordinarily takes place in the laboratory will not at all take place in the organism. Chlorine and hydrogen are gases having a powerful affinity for each other—that is to say, they will unite when brought together in the daylight; but if we change the conditions — if we bring them together in the dark — their affinity is never manifested; and thus, while in the sunlight they rush together with explosive force, producing an intense acid, they will remain quiescent in the darkness, and there for all eternity would form no combination. Again, this same chlorine decomposes water in the sun's rays; but in darkness it has no such power.

If such are the effects of so simple a change in the *conditions*, it is easy to imagine how various must be the differences between the phenomena which occur in the laboratory, and those which

* Ross: *Narrative of Second Voyage*, p. 366.

the same substances present under the *complex conditions of the organism.*

2. *Interference of Life.* — The chemist employs vessels of glass, in which he isolates the substances he examines, keeping them free from the interference of other substances, because he knows that, unless such interference be avoided, his experiment will be nullified. He knows, for example, that a drop of water which, if poured into a red-hot crucible, flies up into his face as *steam*, will rapidly pass into *ice* if a little liquid sulphurous acid happen to be present. He knows, in short, that the stronger affinity prevents the action of the weaker affinity; and, to be sure of his experiment, he must isolate his substances.

But in the vital laboratory no such isolation is possible. The organism has no glass vessels, no air-tight cylinders. Vital processes go on in tissues which, so far from isolating the substance introduced — so far from protecting it against interference, do inevitably interfere, and are *themselves involved* in the very changes undergone by the substance. Thus, while it is true that an alkali will neutralise an acid out of the organism, we must be cautious in applying such a chemical principle in the administration of drugs, because the alkali may stimulate a greater secretion of the gastric acid; so that, over and above the amount neutralised, there will be a surplus of acid free, owing to the interference of the organism in which the process takes place.

Besides the complications which occur from the inevitable interference of the organism itself, and from the differences resulting from differences in the state of bodies, there are other complications arising from causes peculiarly vital. In Biology, questions of Form are scarcely less important than questions of Composition. Spread out a cell into a layer, and you will find, that in ceasing to be a cell, it has ceased to act as such — it has lost all the properties which distinguished it as a cell.

Thus, the green cells of the plant decompose carbonic acid. Even the torn leaf will equally fix the carbon and liberate the oxygen, provided its cells are preserved in their integrity of form. But if these cells are crushed, or otherwise injured, this vital property ceases, because the cell alone is capable of manifesting it. [*]

Under the influence of yeast, sugar is decomposed into alcohol and carbonic acid; but if the yeast-cells be crushed and disorganised, their action on the sugar is said to be quite different: instead of converting it into alcohol and carbonic acid, they convert it into lactic acid.

We must ackowledge, then, that when certain combinations of carbon, oxygen, hydrogen, nitrogen, and salts, assume the form of a cell, the phenomena manifested are no longer simply chemical, but assume the speciality of vital action.

Such considerations need all our attention in dealing with so complex a question as that of Food. They show the radical incompetence of chemical laws alone to solve the questions of Physiology, and urge us to reject, as misdirected labour, all attempts at establishing anything more than chemical facts in the "Chemistry of Food."

It was undoubtedly a great discovery which Mulder made in 1838, that the albumen of plants was identical, or nearly so, with the albumen of animals; and consequently, that, when the ox ate grass, and the lion ate the ox, both derived their nutriment from the same chemical substance. A great discovery; but I cannot agree with Moleschott [**] in thinking this discovery first settled the basis of a science of Food. It was a chemical triumph, fruitful in results to chemistry; but its physiological bearing has been greatly exaggerated, and has given increased impetus to that chemical investigation of Food, which, as we have seen, cannot, in the nature of things, be other than misleading. And although Mulder has shown the inaccuracy of the notion, that vegetable albumen is *identical* with the fibrine of the blood, and vegetable caseine with the caseine of the blood [***] — although he energetically repudiates, as unphilosophical, the idea of a chemical analysis furnishing any true standard of nutritive value — yet even he has not clearly stated what the true method of investigation must be.

* MULDER: *Versuch einer Physiol. Chemie*, I. 193. LEHMANN: *Lahrbuch der Physiol. Chemie*, III. 170.
** MOLESCHOTT: *Kreislauf des Lebens*, 1857, p. 101.
*** MULDER: *Physiol. Chemie*, p. 917.

To the chemist there may be little or no difference between plant and flesh, as Food; to the physiologist the difference is profound: he sees the lion perishing miserably of inanition in presence of abundant herbage, which to the elephant or buffalo furnishes all that is needful. The ox eats the grass, and the tiger eats the ox, but will not touch the grass. The flesh of the ox may contain little that is not wholly derived from the grass; and the chemist, analysing the flesh of both, may point out their identity; but the physiological question is not: What are the chemical constituents of nutritive substances? it is: What are the substances which will nourish the organism? If the animal will not eat, — or, having eaten, cannot assimilate, — a certain substance, that substance is no food for that animal, be its chemical composition what it may.*

We thus see that *digestibility* is an important element in the estimate of Food: unless the substance can be digested, it cannot be assimilated, cannot nourish; although, perhaps, *if assimilated*, the substance might have a high value. A pound of beefsteak contains an enormous superiority of tissue-making substance over that contained in a pound of cabbage; yet to the rabbit the cabbage is the superior food, while to the dog the cabbage is no food at all.

3. *The Blood as a standard of Food.* — When we consider the part played by Food, as furnishing the materials out of which the organic fabric is constructed, and its actions facilitated, it seems natural to assume that the Blood is the proper standard we should have in view; and that we should designate those substances as Aliments which, directly or indirectly, go towards the formation of Blood.

Yet, on a deeper scrutiny, this is seen to lead us a very little way. An analysis of Blood will neither give us a complete list of alimentary substances, nor indicate the alimentary value of each special substance. True it is that all the tissues are formed from the Blood, and that all alimentary substances, in their final state previous to assimilation, make their way into it. But we

---

* It is curious that carnivora feed chiefly, sometimes exclusively, on herbivora, and not on carnivora, whose flesh most resembles their own.

will briefly point out why, in spite of all this, the Blood can never furnish us with the desired standard.

In the first place, while Blood is truly the vehicle of nutrition, it is at the same time the vehicle of many products of decay and disintegration. It carries in its torrent the materials for the use of to-day and to-morrow, but it also carries the materials which were vital yesterday, and are effete to-day, unfit to be retained, and hurrying to the various issues of excretion.* Blood is thus at once purveyor-general and general sewer, carrying life and carrying death. We shall therefore always find in it substances which are not alimentary, mingled with those which are; and we cannot separate these, so as to make our analysis of use.

In the second place, among the substances normally current in the circulation we do not find several which are notoriously serviceable as aliments. Some of these, as theine, caffeine, alcohol, &c., are not present in the blood; and others, as fats and sugars, are present in quantities obviously too small for the amounts consumed as food.

Finally, although substances are nutritive, or bloodmaking, in proportion to their resemblance to blood, yet this resemblance must exist *after*, not before, the substances have gone through the process of digestion; since no sooner is any substance taken into the stomach than a series of changes occurs — changes indispensable for its admission into the circulation, but which impress on it a very different character from the one it bore on its entrance. A beefsteak is assuredly more nearly allied in composition to the blood of an ox than is the dewy grass of the meadow; yet the beefsteak will form no blood for the ox, because it cannot be properly digested, whereas the grass becomes converted into blood in the course of the changes impressed on it during digestion; and what was thus *unlike* becomes *like*, or, as we say, *assimilated.*

* See on this point JOHN SIMON, *Lectures on Pathology*, p. 23 : — "Mentally we can separate these three kinds of blood, but experimentally we cannot. They are mixed together — past, present, and future — the blood of yesterday, the blood of to-day, and the blood of to-morrow — and we have no method of separating them."

The experiments of Claude Bernard are highly suggestive on this point. He found that if sugar, or albumen, were injected into the veins, it was not assimilated, but was eliminated, unchanged, by the kidneys; whereas, if either substance were injected into the veins together with a little gastric juice, assimilation was complete. In another experiment he found that if sugar and albumen were injected into the portal vein (which would carry them through the liver, where certain changes are always impressed on them), they would be assimilated; but if he injected them into the jugular vein, by which they would reach the lungs without passing through the liver, no assimilation would take place.

We here once more see the necessity of taking into account the organism and its vital acts, whenever we would attempt an explanation of Food.

The general considerations which *a priori* caused us to relinquish the idea of finding a proper standard in the composition of the Blood, are fully confirmed by the results of Payen's experiments, which show that Blood is not a good aliment. He fed pigs on equal proportions of flesh and blood, and found that they exhibited all the signs of starvation; whereas, when fed under similar conditions, except that blood was replaced by an equal amount of flesh, they fattened and grew strong.[*]

4. *Milk as a standard of Food.* — The Blood, then, must be given up. Shall we try Milk? Others have done so before us, making it the standard of Food, because it is itself an aliment which contains all the substances necessary for the nourishment of an organism during the most rapid period of growth. Out of milk, and milk alone, the young elephant, the young lion, or the young child, extracts the various substances which furnish muscles, nerves, bones, hair, claws, &c.; milk furnishes these in such abundance, that the increase of growth is far greater during the period when the animal is fed exclusively on it, than at any subsequent period of its career. "In milk," says Prout, "we should expect to find a model of what an alimentary substance ought to be — a kind of prototype, as it were, of nutritious elements in general."

The idea was so plausible that its acceptance was general.

* PAYEN: *Des Substances Alimentaires*, p. 45.

Nevertheless nothing is more certain than that milk is not this model food, since, however it may suit the young lion, or the young child, we cannot feed the adult lion, or the adult man on milk alone: we can feed the lion on bones and water, and the man on bread and water, but not on milk. A model food for the young, it ceases to be so for the adult; that relation which existed between the Food and the Organism in the one case, no longer exists in the other.

If milk does not furnish us with an absolute standard (except for the young), it furnishes an approximative standard of great value. Its composition points out the proportions of inorganic and organic substances necessary in the food of the juvenile organism, and of course approximatively in that of the adult. In 1000 parts, milk contains —

| | |
|---|---|
| Water, . . . . . | 873 |
| Caseine (nitrogenous matter), | 48 |
| Sugar of milk, . . . . | 44 |
| Butter, . . . . . | 30 |
| Phosphate of lime, . . . | 2.30 |
| Other salts, . . . | 2.70 |
| | 1000 |

The reader may remark with some surprise, that in an aliment so notoriously high in nutritive value as milk, the proportion of nitrogenous matter is so very insignificant (48 in 1000) as to render the hypothesis of nitrogenous matters being pre-eminently *the* nutritive matters somewhat perplexing.

The foregoing analysis of milk aids our investigation, by proving the necessity of four distinct classes of principles in Food. These four classes are, —

$1^0$. The Inorganic principles.

$2^0$. The Albuminous principles.

$3^0$. The Oils and Fats.

$4^0$. The Sugars.

The proportions of these substances requisite will, of course, vary with the needs of the various organisms, as modified by race, age, climate, activity, and so forth; but Nutrition will be imperfect unless all four are present, either *as such*, or else under

82          FOOD AND DRINK.

conditions of possible formation — thus fats and sugars can, we
know, be formed in the organism with a proper allowance of
materials; and I am strongly disposed to think that albuminous
substances can also be formed, though not unless some albumen
be present to act as a leaven.

We are thus, by the principle of exclusion, reduced to the
one method of investigation which remains, and that is to inter-
rogate the organism, not the laboratory.

"Experience, daily fixing our regards
On Nature's wants,"

must guide us in the search.  To ascertain what substances are
nutritious, we must ascertain those which really nourish; and
the relative value of these can only be ascertained by extensive
and elaborate experiments on the feeding of animals, conducted
on rigorously scientific principles.  In other words, we must
adopt that very method which common sense has from time immemorial pursued; with this important difference, that instead
of allowing it to be, as hitherto, wholly empirical, we must subject it to the rigour, caution, and precision which characterise
Science.

And even when Science shall have established laws on this
point, such as may accurately express the general value of each
substance as food, there will always remain considerable difficulty in applying those laws, owing to that peculiarity of the
vital organism, previously noticed — namely, that the differences among individuals are so numerous, and often so profound,
as to justify the adage, "one man's meat is another man's
poison."

Thus, while experience plainly enough indicates that, in
Europe at least, meat is more nutritious than vegetables, those
who eat largely of meat being stronger and more enduring than
those who eat little or none; we must be cautious in the application of such a principle.  Difference of climate may, and difference of temperament certainly does, modify this question.
The Sepoy, who lives chiefly on rice, would, it is said, outrun,
knock down, or in any other way prove superiority in strength
over the Gaucho of the Pampas, who lives on flesh.  And not

only are some organisms ill adapted to a flesh diet, as we have seen; but Andersson says, that the strongest man he ever knew scarcely ever touched animal food: this was a Dane, who could walk from spot to spot carrying a stone, which was so heavy that it required ten men to lift it on to his shoulders; his chief diet was gallons of thick sour milk, tea, and coffee;* a diet which no ordinary man could support with success.

Having discussed the chief topics relating to Food in general, we may now ascertain what Science can tell us respecting the various Articles employed as nourishment by man. Our inquiry falls naturally under two heads — first, the Alimentary Principles, considered separately; and next, the Compound Aliments, or those articles of Food and Drink which make up the wondrous variety of human nourishment.

1. *Albumen.* — This substance, familiar to all as the white of an egg, constitutes an important element in Food. It exists as a liquid in the blood, as a solid in flesh. When raw, or lightly boiled, it is readily digested; less so when boiled hard, or fried. Majendie has observed that the white of eggs combines many conditions favourable to digestion, for it is alkaline, contains saline matters, especially common salt, in large proportions, and it is very nearly allied to the albumen found in the chyle and blood. It is liquid, but is coagulated by the acids of the stomach, forming flocculi having slight cohesion, and rendered easily soluble again by the intestinal juices.

Many people imagine that white of egg is injurious, or innutritious, and they only eat the yolk. To some this may be so; and when experience proves it to be so, white of egg should not, of course, be eaten; but as a general rule, white of egg is agreeable and nutritious. Nevertheless, if given *alone*, neither white of egg nor albumen will continue to be eaten by animals; they soon cease to eat it, and, during the period in which it is taken, they show unmistakable signs of starvation.

Albumen, then, is highly nutritious; and if we estimated the nutritive value of various articles *solely* according to their amounts of albumen, we should place caviare, ox-liver, and

* ANDERSSON: *Lake Ngami*, p. 58.

G *

sweetbread at the top of the list, leaving the muscle of beef very
far below them.  The following table shows the proportions of
albumen in 100 parts of various articles of food: —

| Caviare, | | | | | | | 31.00 |
| Ox-liver, | | | | | | | 20.19 |
| Sweetbread, | | | | | | | 14.00 |
| Muscle of pigeon, | | | | | | 4.05 |
| „ of veal, | | | | | | 3.02 |
| „ of chicken, | | | | | | 3.00 |
| „ of beef, | | | | | | 2.02 |

This table is very instructive, as showing the vanity of attempting by a chemical analysis to assign the nutritive value of any
food.  Beef is considered the most nutritive of all these articles,
which, according to this analysis, should be least so.  This
discrepancy is lessened, but not removed, when we take into
account the quantity of fibrine contained in these articles,
namely —

| Sweetbread, | | | | | | 8 |
| Veal (muscle), | | | | | | 19 |
| Chicken (muscle), | | | | | 20 |
| Beef (muscle), | | | | | | 20 |

2. *Fibrine* is liquid in the serum of the blood, and is very
closely allied to albumen — indeed, for a long while was supposed to be identical with it and with the fibrine of muscle, which
is now more accurately called *musculine* (by Lehmann *syntonin*).

When the blood is drawn from the body, fibrine passes from
the liquid to the solid state, and coagulates into what is called
the *clot*, which is nothing but solid fibrine enclosing some of the
red corpuscles.* It was formerly supposed that this solidification
was all that took place when blood-fibrine passed into muscular
fibre; but recent investigations have shown that muscle-fibrine
is really a different substance, allied to, but not identical with,
blood-fibrine.

Albumen and fibrine are found abundantly in vegetables —
the former being most abundant in wheat, rye, barley, oats,
maize, and rice.  Albumen is found also in the oily seeds, such

* See the chapter on THE STRUCTURE AND USES OF THE BLOOD for details
respecting the serum, the fibrine, and the clot.

as almonds, nuts, &c.; iu the juices of carrots, turnips, cauli-
flowers, asparagus, &c.* Fibrine is also abundant in the
cereals, grape-juice, and the juice of other vegetables.

Although closely allied to animal albumen and fibrine, vegetable albumen and fibrine are not identical with these substances, differing from them both in composition and properties;
but the differences are so slight, that vegetable albumen easily
passes into animal albumen in the process of digestion.

3. *Caseine* is another of the albuminous substances, and may
be regarded as a modification of albumen, into which it readily
passes. It forms the *curd*, or coagulable matter of milk. Unlike
albumen, it does not coagulate by heat. If heated in an open
vessel, an insoluble pellicle is formed on the surface, as we often
see in the milk-jug brought up with our coffee; but this effect is
produced by the action of the oxygen of the atmosphere.

The proportion of caseine in different kinds of milk is as
follows: —

| | | | | |
|---|---|---|---|---|
| Cow's milk, | . | . | . | 4.48 |
| Ewe's milk, | . | . | . | 4.50 |
| Goat's milk, | . | . | . | 4.02 |
| Asses' milk, | . | . | . | 1.82 |
| Human milk, | . | . | . | 1.52 |

It thus appears, we hope without derogation to human dignity,
that asses' milk is considerably more like that on which we were
suckled, than any other milk. Asses' milk may be given to infants with safety; but goat's or cow's milk must be diluted — as
all experienced nurses know.

Caseine forms the chief ingredient of cheese. It is an important element of food, as we see by its presence in milk. "The
young animal receives, in the form of caseine, the chief constituent of the mother's blood. To convert caseine into blood,
no foreign substance is required; and in the conversion of the
mother's blood into caseine, no elements of the constituents of
blood have been separated. When chemically examined, caseine
is found to contain a much larger proportion of the earth of

* Albumen forms three compounds — basic, acid, and neutral. In the
white of egg, and in the serum of blood, it is a basic albuminate of soda. In
certain diseases it is a neutral albuminate in the blood.

bones than blood does, and that in a very soluble form, capable of reaching every part of the body. Thus, even in the earliest period of its life, the development of the organs in which vitality resides is, in the carnivorous animal, dependent on the supply of a substance identical in organic composition with the chief constituents of blood."[*]

Caseine is also found in beans, peas, lentils, almonds, nuts, and perhaps in all vegetable juices.

These three bodies — albumen, fibrine, and caseine — from the readiness with which they are transformed into each other, are not inaptly designated "protein-bodies," even now that Mulder's idea of an organic radical, named by him "protein," has been given up by all the leading chemists.

In the egg we see caseine arise from albumen, and in digestion caseine passes back again into albumen.

Fibrine, again, appears to be only albumen with an addition of oxygen; and it may be easily reconverted into albumen by nitrate of potash. It differs from albumen in assuming something of definite structure when coagulated: it forms itself into delicate fibres, which albumen never does.

There are many unexplained facts known respecting fibrine, which, when explained, may clear away other obscurities. Lehmann found, by experiments on himself, that animal diet produced more fibrine in his blood than was produced by vegetable diet — a fact seemingly at variance with another fact, namely, that, during starvation, the quantity of fibrine is increased, as it is also during acute inflammations. Thus, animal diet, known to be nutritious, produces one result known to be characteristic of inflammation and starvation.

Nor does the difficulty cease here: the blood of the vegetable feeders, among animals, has more fibrine than that of the flesh-feeders; yet the carnivorous dog has *less* fibrine when fed on vegetable food, than when his diet has been exclusively animal. Finally, although herbivora have more fibrine than carnivora, birds have more than both.

4. *Gluten* is not found in animals, but exists abundantly in vegetables, and is the most important of all the nitrogenous sub-

* Liebig: *Animal Chemistry*, p. 58.

stances, because, as we have seen, it is capable of supporting
life when given alone. "It is the presence of gluten in wheaten
flour that renders it pre-eminently nutritious; and its viscidity
or tenacity confers upon that species of flour its peculiar excellence for the manufacture of macaroni, vermicelli, and similar pastes, which are made by a kind of wiredrawing, and for
which the wheat of the south of Europe is peculiarly adapted."[*]
The following table, which is selected from Dr. Pereira's
work, gives the proportions of gluten in 100 parts of various
vegetables:

| | | |
|---|---|---:|
| Wheat, Middlesex (average crop), | . . | 19. 0 |
| „ Spring | . . . . . . | 24. 0 |
| „ Thick-skinned Sicilian, | . . . | 23. 0 |
| „ Polish, | . . . . . . | 20. 0 |
| „ North American, | . . . . | 22. 5 |
| Barley, Norfolk, | . . . . . . | 6. 0 |
| Oats, Scotland, | . . . . . . | 8. 7 |
| Rye, Yorkshire, | . . . . . . | 10. 9 |
| Rice, Carolina, | . . . . . | 3.60 |
| „ Piedmont, | . . . . . . | 3.60 |
| Maize, | . . . . . . . | 5.75 |
| Beans, | . . . . . . . | 10. 3 |
| Peas, | . . . . . . . | 3. 5 |
| Potatoes, | . . . . . . | 4. 0 |
| Turnips, | . . . . . . . | 0. 1 |
| Cabbage, | . . . . . . . | 0. 8 |

These four albuminoid[**] substances, namely albumen, fibrine,
caseine, and gluten, are remarkable among other things for
their extreme *instability*, — the readiness with which they are
transformed, or decomposed. It is this alterability which renders
them peculiarly apt to act as *ferments*, and to induce chemical
changes in the substances with which they come in contact. It is
on this alterability that their great value in nutrition depends.
Further, we must remark that, no matter what is the form in

---

[*] BRANDE'S *Chemistry*, quoted by PERKIRA. On this subject see the
chapter "The Bread we eat," in JOHNSTON'S *Chemistry of Common Life.*
[**] *Albuminoid* means having the character of albumen.

which they are eaten, whether as white of egg, fibrine, caseine, or gluten, these substances are all reduced by the digestive process to substances named *peptones*, under which forms only are they assimilabe.\*

5. *Gelatine.*—There is perhaps no substance on our list which more interestingly illustrates the want of a true scientific doctrine presiding over the investigations into Food, than Gelatine: a substance richer in nitrogen than any of the albuminoid substances, yet denied a place among the plastic elements: a substance which, under the forms of jellies and soups, is largely given to convalescents, who get strong upon it, yet which, we are emphatically assured, has "no nutritive value whatever." Mulder says that no physician, who has had experience, could doubt the nutritive value of gelatine; and we may be pretty sure that common usage, in such cases, is founded upon some solid ground, and that no substance is largely used as food which has not a nutritive value.

Common usage, or what is called "common sense," must not indeed be the arbiter of a scientific question; but it has a right to be heard when it unequivocally contradicts the conclusions of Science; and it can only be put out of court on a clear exposition of the source of its error. In the present case, the savans pretend that Gelatine *cannot* be nutritive, common sense asserts that it *does* nourish; and unless the fact can be proved against common sense, it will be reasonable to suppose that the savans are arguing on false premises. False, indeed, are the premises, and false the conclusion. But let us see what has been the course of inquiry.

In 1682 the celebrated Papin discovered that bones contained organic matter; and he invented a method of extraction of this matter, which subsequently occupied the chemists and savans, in the early days of the French Revolution, with the laudable desire of furnishing food to the famished people. A pound of bones was said to yield as much broth as six pounds of beef, and, with the true fervour of inventors, the savans declared bone-soup to be better than meat-soup.

\* See the ensuing chapter on DIGESTION AND INDIGESTION.

In 1817, M. d'Arcet applied steam on a grand scale to the preparation of this gelatine from bones, promising to make four oxen yield the alimentary value of five, as usually employed.

Great was the excitement, vast the preparations. In hospitals and poorhouses, machines were erected which made an enormous quantity of Gelatine. Unfortunately the soup thus obtained was found to be far from nutritious; moreover, it occasioned thirst, digestive troubles, and finally diarrhœa. The savans heard this with great equanimity. They were not the men to give up a theory on the bidding of vulgar experience. Diarrhœa was doubtless distressing, but science was not implicated in *that*. The fault must lie in the preparation of the soup; might not the fault be attributable to the soup-eaters? One thing only was positive — that the fault was *not* in the Gelatine.

In this high and unshaken confidence, the savans pursued their course. Thousands of rations were daily distributed; but fortunately these rations were not confined to the bone-soup, or else the mortality would have been terrific. Few men of science had any doubts until M. Donné positively assured the Academy that experiments on himself, and on dogs, proved Gelatine, thus prepared, to be scarcely, if at all, nutritious.

He found that employing a notable quantity in his own diet caused him rapidly to lose weight, and that during the whole experiment he was tormented with hunger and occasional faintness. A cup of chocolate and two rolls nourished him more effectually than two litres and a half of bone-soup accompanied by 80 to 100 grammes of bread. *

These statements were confirmed by other experimenters; and the confidence in Gelatine was rudely shaken, and would have been ignominiously overthrown, had not Edwards and Balzac published their remarkable memoir (1833), in which experiments conducted with great care and scientific rigour established the fact that although Gelatine is *insufficient* to support life, it has nevertheless nutritive value. Dogs fed on gelatine and bread became gradually thinner and feebler; but when fed on the same amount of bread alone, their loss was far more rapid.

* A *litre* is a trifle more than a pint and a half; a *gramme* is about 15¼ grains.

At this period it became necessary to have the question definitively settled, and the French Academy appointed a Comision to report on it. This is the celebrated "Gelatine Commission" so often referred to. The report appeared in 1841. It showed that dogs perished from starvation in presence of the Gelatine extracted from bones, after having eaten of it only a few times. When, instead of this insipid Gelatine, the agreeable jelly which pork-butchers prepare from a decoction of different parts of the pig was given them, they ate it with relish at first, then ceased to eat it, and died on the twentieth day, of inanition; when bread, or meat, in small quantities, was given, the dogs lived a longer time, but grew gradually thinner, and all finally perished. A striking difference was observed between bone-soup and meat-soup: the animals starved on the first, and flourished on the second.

The conclusion generally drawn from this Report is, that Gelatine is *not* a nutritive substance. But all that is really proved by the experiments is that Gelatine *alone* is insufficient for nutrition; a conclusion which is equally true of albumen, fibrine, or any other single substance. For perfect nutrition there must be a mixture of inorganic and organic substances: salts, fats, sugars, and albuminates.

When animals are fed on albumen alone, or white of egg alone, with water as the single inorganic element, they perish; but they live perfectly well on raw bones and water— the reason being that bones contain salts and small proportions of albumen and fats, to supplement the Gelatine, and *they contain these in the state of organic combination*, not in the state of chemical products.

The paramount importance of this last condition may be gathered from the experiments mentioned in the Gelatine Report — namely, that boiling the bones, or digesting them in hydrochloric acid, and thus resolving their cartilaginous tissue into Gelatine, *destroyed* this nutritive quality. The very bones which, when raw, supported life, failed utterly when boiled. This seems to show that Gelatine is so altered by heat as to lose its power of fermenting, and so passing through the transformation necessary to assimilation.

Attention is called to the fact of the very small proportions of Albumen which exist in the bones, as strikingly confirming my hypothesis respecting the power of the organism to form Albumen for itself, if a small amount be present to act as a sort of leaven. Moleschott also maintains, on other grounds, that Gelatine must be converted into Albumen, since the amount of Albumen in bones is in itself utterly insufficient for the demands of the tissues;[*] and Mulder points to the fact that, when an animal is fed on Gelatine, we never find this substance passing away in the excreta: a sufficient proof that it must in some way have been incorporated with the organism, or decomposed in it, to subserve the purposes of nutrition.[**]

Physiologists who admit *some* nutritive quality in Gelatine, have suggested that it is confined to the formation of the gelatinous tissues. This is one of those hypotheses which seduce by their plausibility; and accordingly it has been frequently adopted, although physiological scrutiny detects that this is precisely one of the uses to which Gelatine can *not* be turned. For on the one hand we see that the herbivora have gelatinous tissues, although they eat *no* Gelatine; and, on the other hand, we see that even the carnivora, who do obtain it in their ordinary food, cannot form their gelatinous tissues out of it, because Gelatine is never found in their blood, from which all their tissues are formed.

Bernard has shown that part of the Gelatine is converted into sugar; and sugar, we know, is necessary to the organism. It may also be converted into fat; and, as has been said, there is much evidence to show that it may be converted into Albumen, among the complex processes of vital chemistry; but whatever may be the decision respecting this point, there can be no legitimate reason for denying that Gelatine ranks among nutritive principles.

6. *Fats and Oils.* — These are various and important, including suet, lard, marrow, butter, and fixed oils. Vegetables also yield a great variety of oils, fixed, and volatile or essential.

[*] MOLESCHOTT, *Kreislauf des Lebens*, p. 135,
[**] MULDER, *Physiol. Chemie*, p. 637,

The quantity procurable from 100 parts of vegetable and animal substances is as follows: —

| | |
|---|---:|
| Filberts, . . . . . . . | 60 |
| Olive seeds, . . . . . . | 64 |
| Cocoa-nut, . . . . . . | 47 |
| Almonds, . . . . . . | 46 |
| White mustard, . . . . . | 36 |
| Linseed, . . . . . . . | 22 |
| Maize, . . . . . . . | 9 |
| Yolk of Eggs, . . . . . . | 28.75 |
| Ordinary meat, . . - . . . | 14. 3 |
| Caviare, . . . . . . . | 4. 3 |
| Ox-liver, . . . . . . . | 3.89 |
| Milk, Cows', . . . . . . | 3.13 |
|    ,,    Women's, . . . . . | 3.55 |
| Milk, Asses', . . . . . . | 0.11 |
|    ,,    Goats', . . . . . | 3.32 |
|    ,,    Ewes' . . . . . . | 4.20 |
| Bones of sheep's feet, . . . . | 5.55 |
|    ,,    of ox-head, . . . . . | 11.54 * |

Fats and oils are all difficult of digestion — more so, indeed, than most other principles; but the degree in which they are digestible is very much a matter of individual peculiarity, some men digesting large quantities with ease, others being unable to digest even small quantities.

M. Berthé instituted an elaborate series of experiments on his own person, with the view of ascertaining the comparative digestibility of various fats and oils.** The following classification of his results is all we can find space for.

First class, comprising those difficult of digestion: Olive oil, almond oil, poppy-seed oil.

Second class, comprising those easy of digestion: Whale oil, butter and animal fats, colourless liver-oil.

Third class, comprising those very easy of digestion: Pure liver-oil.

* PEREIRA: *Treatise on Diet*, p. 167.
** BERTHÉ: *Moniteur des Hôpiteaux*, 1856, No. 69. CARSTATT: *Jahresbericht*, 1856, p. 69-72.

It should be remembered that great differences are observable according to the state in which oils are eaten. If taken by themselves, they are scarcely affected by the digestive process, and act as laxatives; but if taken mingled with other substances, they may be reduced to an emulsion, and so absorbed.

Thus we eat olive oil with salad, or butter with bread, and the greater part is absorbed; but the same amount of olive oil administered alone would act as a purge. It is owing, moreover, to the minute state of subdivision and mixture of the oils in all vegetable substances that they are so much more digestible than animal fats.

Dr. Pereira quotes the statement of Dr. Beaumont, that "bile is seldom found in the stomach, except under peculiar circumstances. I have observed that when the use of fat or oily food has been persevered in for some time, there is generally a presence of bile in the gastric fluids." Upon which Dr. Pereira remarks that the popular notion of oily or fatty foods "causing bile" is not so groundless as medical men have generally supposed. The reason of fat being indigestible is thus suggested: "In many dyspeptic individuals, fat does not become properly chymified. It floats on the contents of the stomach in the form of an oily pellicle, becoming odorous, and sometimes highly rancid, and in this state excites heartburn, nausea, and eructations, or at times actual vomiting. It appears to me that the greater tendency which some oily substances have than others to disturb the stomach, depends on the greater facility with which they evolve volatile fatty acids, which are for the most part exceedingly acrid and irritating. The unpleasant and distressing feelings excited in many dyspeptics by the ingestion of mutton-fat, butter, and fish-oils, are in this way readily accounted for, since all these substances contain each one or more volatile acids to which they owe their odour. Thus mutton-fat contains hircic acid; butter, no less than three volatile acids — viz. butyric, capric, and caproic acids; while train-oil contains phocenic acid." *

The effect of a high temperature on fat is to render it still more unsuitable to the stomach; and all persons troubled with

* PEREIRA, p. 171.

an awful consciousness of what Digestion is, and not living in that happy eupeptic ignorance which only knows Digestion as a name, should avoid food in the cooking of which much fat or oil has been subjected to a high temperature — as in frying in butter or lard. Melted butter, buttered toast, pastry, suet-puddings, fat hashes and stews, are afflictions to the dyspeptic; and although the oil which is eaten with salad does not assist the digestion of the salad, as many writers and most salad-eaters maintain, it is assuredly far more digestible than any fat or oil which has been cooked, probably because it contains no free volatile acid.

Besides the fats and *fixed* oils, there are certain volatile (essential) oils employed as condiments. These are contained in the leaves and seeds of sage, mint, thyme, marjoram, fennel, parsley, anise, and caraway; to which may be added, mustard, horse-radish, water-cress, onions, leeks, and various spices. The volatile oil contained in each of these substances stimulates but does not incorporate itself with the organism, and is soon ejected, retaining its characteristic odour.

7. *Starch.* — The gentle housewife, familiar with starch only in its relations to the wash-tub, will be probably surprised at meeting with it among articles of food; yet under the various names of amylum, fecula, farinaceous matter, and starch, this substance, widely distributed over the vegetable kingdom, ranks as an important alimentary principle. It must, however, be cooked before it can be eaten. It is never found in the blood, nor in the tissues, so that we are certain it is transformed during the digestive process; and some of these transformations have been detected: first, as it passes into dextrine, and thence into sugar, and most probably fat.

The various starchy substances — sago, tapioca, arrowroot, and *tous les mois*, have been so amply treated of by Professor Johnston in his admirable *Chemistry of Common Life*, that our readers need only be directed to his pages.

8. *Sugar.* — Sugar exists abundantly in vegetables, and in some animal substances, notably milk and liver. Dr. Pereira has compiled the following table, which exhibits the proportion of sugar in 100 parts: —

| Barley-meal, | | | | | | | 5.21 |
| Oatmeal, | | | | | | | 8.25 |
| Wheat-flour, | | | | | | | 8.48 |
| Wheat-bread, | | | | | | | 3. 6 |
| Rye-meal, | | | | | | | 3.28 |
| Maize, | | | | | | | 1.45 |
| Rice, | | | | | | | 0.29 |
| Pease, | | | | | | | 2. 0 |
| Figs, | | | | | | | 62. 5 |
| Greengages, | | | | | | | 11.61 |
| Fresh ripe pears, | | | | | | | 6.45 |
| Gooseberries, | | | | | | | 6.24 |
| Cherries, | | | | | | | 18.12 |
| Apricot, | | | | | | | 11.61 |
| Peach, | | | | | | | 16.48 |
| Beet-root, | | | | | | | 9. 0 |

That sugar is nutritious no one doubts. Although easily digested, there are persons with whom it disagrees, and in some dyspeptics it produces flatulency and acidity. There is no tissue into the composition of which it enters as a constituent, unless we make an exception in favour of muscle, in which Scherer has discovered a substance, by him named *inosite*, having the chemical composition of sugar ($C^{12} H^{12} O^{12}$), but having none of its characteristic properties, and existing, moreover, in extremely minute quantities.

The sugar we find in the blood and milk is not derived from the sugar we eat; *that* is transformed into fat, lactic acid, and other substances. The sugar of the blood is formed partly from the starchy substances of our food during the process of digestion; the rest is formed *by* the liver, and is formed *from* albuminous substances in their passage through the liver; the quantity being wholly independent of any amount of sugar taken in the food, and being the same in amount when *none* is taken in the food. *

* CLAUDE BERNARD's discovery of this sugar-forming function of the liver has been attacked by FIGUIER, LONGET, and others; but the discussion, after exciting considerable sensation, may now be said to be finally closed in BERNARD's favour. See his masterly *Leçons de Physiol. Expérimentale*, 1854-55;

Because sugar forms part of no tissue, and is a carbo-hydrate, it is classed by Liebig's school among heat-making foods. But we not only saw ample reason for rejecting such an idea when we considered the general question — we must even more peremptorily reject it, now that we come to grapple with the details. Against the supposition of sugar having no plastic property, it is enough to oppose the fact that many insects feed solely on sugar and saccharine juices; and in them, therefore, it is clear that something more than heat is evolved from sugar. Lehmann also bids us remember that in the egg a small quantity of sugar exists, and this quantity increases, instead of diminishing, as the development of the chick proceeds; whereas, if sugar only served for purposes of oxidation, it would be oxidised and disappear as development advanced.

In the *Chemistry of Common Life*, the subject of sugar is treated in detail, which renders repetition here superfluous. Two questions only need be touched on. Is sugar injurious to the teeth? Is it injurious to the stomach?

To answer the first, we have only to point to the Negroes, who eat more sugar than any other human beings, and whose teeth are of enviable splendour and strength.

To answer the second is not so easy; yet, when we learn the many important offices which sugar fulfils in the organism, we may be certain that, if injurious at all, it is only so in excess. The lactic acid formed from sugar dissolves phosphate of lime, and this, as we know, is the principal ingredient of bones and teeth. By its dissolution it becomes accessible to the bones and teeth; and as sugar effects this, its utility is vindicated. But a surer argument is founded on the instinct of mankind. If we all so eagerly eat sugar, it is because there is a natural relation between it and our organism.

Timid parents may therefore check their alarm at the sight of juvenile forays on the sugar-basin when not excessive; may cease to vex children by forbidding moderate commercial transactions with the lollypop merchant, and cease to frustrate their desires for

and the *Mémoires* on both sides in the *Annales de Sciences Naturelles*, 1854-6; and the Report of the Commission appointed by the Académie de Médicine, reprinted in Brown Séquard's *Journal de la Physiologie*, i. 549.

barley-sugar by the never-appreciated pretext, that the interdict is "for their good."

9. *Alcohol.* — If it astonished the reader to see water and salts classed as alimentary principles, if it puzzled the housewife to see starch placed on the same list, it will we fear exasperate the members of Temperance Societies to see alcohol elevated to that rank. They are accustomed to call alcohol a *poison*, to preach against it as poisonous in large doses or small, concentrated or diluted. Nevertheless, in compliance with the dictates of Physiology, and, let me add, in compliance also with the custom of physiologists, we are forced to call alcohol food, and very efficient food too. If it be not food, then neither is sugar food, nor starch, nor any of those manifold substances employed by man which do not enter into the composition of his tissues. That it produces poisonous effects when concentrated and taken in large doses, is perfectly true; but that similar effects follow when *diluted*, and taken in small doses, is manifestly false, as proved by daily experience.

Every person practically acquainted with the subject knows that concentrated alcohol has, among other effects, that of depriving the mucus membrane of the stomach of all its water — *i. e.* of hardening it, and destroying its powers of secretion; whereas diluted alcohol does nothing of the kind, but *increases* the secretion by the stimulus it gives to the circulation. The alcohol is always much diluted which is taken in wines or spirits.

An instructive illustration of the difference between a concentrated and diluted dose is seen in Bardeleben's experiment on dogs. He found that forty-five grains of common salt, introduced at once into the stomach through an opening, occasioned a secretion of mucus, followed by vomitings; whereas five times that amount of salt in *solution* produced neither of these effects. The explanation is simple, and will be understood by any one who has seen the salt, which was sprinkled over a round of beef, converted into brine, owing to the attraction exercised by the salt on the water in the beef: this attraction is incalculably smaller when the salt is in solution, and the salt is already saturated.

We might multiply examples of the differences which result from the use of *concentrated* and *diluted* agents, or from differences in the quantities employed; as when a certain amount of acid assists digestion, but, if increased, arrests it.  But the demonstration of such a position is unnecessary, since no well-informed physiologist will deny it.  The fallacy of concluding that whatever is true of a large quantity of concentrated alcohol is equally true, in a proportionate degree, of a small quantity of diluted alcohol, lies indeed at the basis of the Total Abstinence doctrine.  But we need scarcely tell the student that the difference of effect is absolute: a difference in *kind*, and not simply in degree.

Another fallacy in the Teetotal argument, and one constantly invoked, is this: You must abstain altogether from alcoholic drinks, since, unless you abstain, you are certain to end in excess.  Moderation necessarily becomes excess, because the frame gets habituated to stimulants; and thus, to produce the original effect, you must gradually increase the dose: according to Dr. Carpenter, that which was "at first sufficient to whet the appetite and increase the digestive power, being no longer found adequate."

I have elsewhere* answered this, as well as the other fallacies of Teetotalism, and will venture to repeat a few sentences here: "He who drinks will drink again, and Moderation, we know, oils the hinges of the gate leading to Excess. Nobody doubts the danger.  The only absolute preservative against taking too much, is to take none.  But to suppose there is any necessary connection between moderation and excess, is to ignore physiology, and fly in the face of evidence. . . . . Men take their pint of beer, or pint of wine daily, for a series of years. This dose daily produces its effect; and if at any time thirst or social seduction makes them drink a quart in lieu of a pint, they are at once made aware of the excess.  Men drink one or two cups of tea or coffee at breakfast with unvarying regularity, for a whole lifetime; but who ever felt the necessity of gradually increasing the

---

* *Westminster Review.* New Series, vol. viii.  Art. *The Physiological Errors of Teetotalism.*  Compare, also, CHAMBERS' *Digestion and its Derangements,* p. 526-29, where some of the arguments are refuted.

amount to three, four, or five cups? Yet we know what a stimulant tea is; we know that treble the amount of our daily consumption would soon produce paralysis — why are we not irresistibly led to this fatal excess? Every time fresh oil is poured on fresh burning coal, the same phenomenon presents itself; every time an eel is skinned, he wriggles with ancestral vigour, and will *not* become 'used to it.' In like manner, every time a fresh stimulus is applied to fresh nerve tissue, the original effect ensues. For we must not forget this: the tissue burnt to-day is not the tissue that was burnt yesterday; the nerve particles stimulated by alcohol to-day will not be living to-morrow, when fresh stimulus is applied. Change — incessant change, is the law of our being. Fresh food renews fresh tissue for fresh stimulants to act upon. The basket is always wriggling with eels; but the eels are strangers, and can't get used to skinning."

On the other hand, it is needless to dwell on the dangers which unhappily surround the use of alcohol. Terrible is the power of this "tricksy spirit:" and when acting in conjunction with ignorance and sensuality, its effects are appalling. So serious an influence does it exercise on human welfare, that we may readily extenuate the too frequent exaggerations of those zealous men who have engaged in a league for its total suppression. So glaring are the evils of intemperance, that we must always respect the motives of Temperance Societies, even when we most regret their exaggerations. They are fighting against a hideous vice, and we must the more regret when zeal for the cause leads them, as it generally leads partisans, to make sweeping charges, which common sense is forced to reject. All honour for the brave and sincere; all scorn for the noisy shallow quacks who make a trade of the cause!

No real gain can be achieved by any cause when it eludes or perverts the truth; and whatever temporary effect, in speeches or writings, may arise from the iteration of the statement that alcohol is poison — a poison in small quantities, as in large — always and everywhere poisonous — the cause must permanently lose ground, because daily experience repudiates such a statement as manifestly false. Alcohol *replaces* a given amount of

7*

ordinary food. Liebig tells us that, in Temperance families where beer was withheld and money given in compensation, it was soon found that the monthly consumption of bread was so strikingly increased, that the beer was twice paid for, once in money, and a second time in bread. He also reports the experience of the landlord of the Hôtel de Russie, at Frankfort, during the Peace Congress: the members of this Congress were mostly teetotallers, and a regular deficiency was observed every day in certain dishes, especially farinaceous dishes, puddings, &c. So unheard-of a deficiency, in an establishment where for years the amount of dishes for a given number of persons had so well been known, excited the landlord's astonishment. It was found that men made up in pudding what they neglected in wine. Every one knows how little the drunkard eats: to him alcohol replaces a given amount of food.

The general opinion among physiologists is, that alcohol is only heat-producing food, and that it thereby saves the consumption of tissue. Moleschott says that, although forming none of the constituents of blood, alcohol limits the combustion of those constituents, and in this way is equivalent to so much blood. "He who has little can give but little, if he wish to retain as much as one who is prodigal of his wealth. Alcohol is the savings' bank of the tissues. He who eats little, and drinks alcohol in moderation, retains as much in his blood and tissues as he who eats more, and drinks no alcohol."[*] But the physiological action of alcohol is still unexplained; we know that it does sustain and increase the force of the body; we know that it supplies the place of a certain quantity of food; but *how* it does this we do not know. It is said to be "burnt" in the body, and to make its exit as carbonic acid and water; but no proof has yet been offered of this assertion. Some of it escapes in the breath, and in certain of the secretions; but how much escapes in this way, and what becomes of the rest, if any, is at present a mystery.

10. *Iron.* — We are passing from surprise to surprise as we in turn arrive at substances undoubtedly claiming rank among alimentary principles, which nevertheless, in the ordinary concep-

* MOLESCHOTT: *Lehre der Nahrungsmittel,* p. 162.

tions of men, are the very opposites of Food. After water, phosphates, starch, and alcohol, are we now to celebrate the nutritive qualities of iron? Even so. That metal circulates in our blood, forming indeed an *essential* element of the blood-discs—existing in all pigments—in the bile—in various other places — notably in the hair, where it is abundant in proportion to the darkness of the colour.

The quantity of iron in the blood is but small; varying in different individuals, and different states of the same individual; those who are of what is called the sanguine temperament have more than those of the lymphatic temperament; those who are well-fed have more than those who are ill-fed. It is in almost all our animal and vegetable food, so that we do not habitually need to seek it; but the physician often has to prescribe it, either in the form of "steel-wine," or in that of chalybeate waters.[*]

11. *Phosphorus* and *Sulphur* are also indispensable, but they are received with our food.

12. *Acids* are received with vegetable food; but they are also taken separately, especially the acetic acid, or vinegar, which, according to Prout, has either by accident or design been employed by mankind in all ages — that is to say, substances naturally containing it have been employed as aliments, or it has been formed artificially.

It is owing to their acids that fruits and vegetables are necessary to man, although not necessary to the carnivora. Dr. Budd justly points to the prolonged abstinence from succulent vegetables and fruits as the cause of the scurvy among sailors. Lemon-juice is now always given to sailors with their food; it protects them from scurvy, which no amount of vinegar is sufficient to effect.

We make cooling drinks with vegetable acids; and our salads and greens demand vinegar, as our cold meat demands pickles. Taken in moderation, there is no doubt that vinegar is beneficial, but in excess it impairs the digestive organs; and, as we remarked a little while ago, experiments on artificial digestion show that if the quantity of acid be diminished, digestion is

[*] "It is quite certain that if iron be excluded from food, organic life cannot be supported." — LIEBIG.

retarded; if increased beyond a certain point, digestion is arrested.

There is reason, therefore, in the vulgar notion, unhappily too fondly relied on, that vinegar helps to keep down an alarming adiposity, and that ladies who dread the disappearance of their graceful outline in curves of plumpness expanding into "fat," may arrest so dreadful a result by liberal potations of vinegar; but they can only so arrest it at the far more dreadful expense of their health. The amount of acid which will keep them thin, will destroy their digestive powers.

Portal gives a case which should be a warning: "A few years ago a young lady in easy circumstances enjoyed good health; she was very plump, had a good appetite, and a complexion blooming with roses and lilies. She began to look upon her plumpness with suspicion; for her mother was very fat, and she was afraid of becoming like her. Accordingly, she consulted a woman, who advised her to drink a glass of vinegar daily: the young lady followed her advice, and her plumpness diminished. She was delighted with the success of the experiment, and continued it for more than a month. She began to have a cough; but it was dry at its commencement, and was considered as a slight cold, which would go off. Meantime, from dry it became moist; a slow fever came on, and a difficulty of breathing; her body became lean, and wasted away; night-sweats, swelling of the feet and of the legs succeeded, and a diarrhœa terminated her life."

Therefore, young ladies, be boldly fat! never pine for graceful slimness and romantic pallor; but if Nature means you to be ruddy and rotund, accept it with a laughing grace, which will captivate more hearts than all the paleness of a Circulating Library. At any rate, understand this, that if vinegar will diminish the fat, it can only do so by affecting your health.

We have thus touched upon the chief Alimentary Principles, and will now review the Compound Aliments, or those articles of Food and Drink which constitute and vary our diet.

# CHAPTER II.

## (*Continued.*)

## FOOD AND DRINK.

### SECTION III. — ARTICLES OF FOOD.

Meats — The flavouring substance of meat, *osmazome* — The flesh of young animals — The age of animals in relation to the digestibility of their flesh — Effects of roasting, boiling, and baking — German and French meat — Digestibility of different meats — Sweetbread and tripe — Horse-flesh as food: experiments to establish the excellence of horse-beef — Quantities of horse-flesh consumed in various countries — The flesh of donkeys — Fish: digestibility of different kinds — Nutritive quality of fish — Are fish-eaters unusually prolific? — Eggs — Pastry: is it injurious? — Vegetables — Vegetarianism — Tea, coffee, and the narcotics: curious physiological paradox of their action — The quantity of food requisite for man — Individual varieties in the quantity needed — Error of applying arithmetic to vital problems — The gluttony of some races — Does a cold climate produce inordinate eating? — The rations of paupers and soldiers.

MAN is said, with but slight exaggeration, to be omnivorous. If he does not eat of all things, he eats so multifariously, that our limits would be insufficient to include even a superficial account of all the substances employed by him as Food. We must therefore be content to let attention fall on the principal groups.

1. *Meats.* — It is superfluous to dwell on the fact that the flesh of most herbivora, both wild and domestic, is both agreeable and nutritious; even the advocates of a purely vegetable diet do not dispute the flavour or the potency of flesh, whatever consequences they may attribute to the eating of it. It contains some of the chief alimentary principles: namely, albumen, fibrine, fat, gelatine, water, salts, and *osmazome*.

The last-named is a substance of reddish-brown colour, having the smell and flavour of soup (whence the name — ὀσμή, smell, and ζωμός, soup); it varies in various animals, increasing with their age. It is this osmazome, developed during the process of cooking, which gives their characteristic flavours to beef, mutton, goat-flesh, and birds, &c.

The flesh of young animals is tenderer than that of adults; and tenderness is one quality which favours digestibility. Nevertheless we shall err if, fixing our attention on this one quality, we assume that the flesh of young animals is always more digestible than that of adults; we shall find veal to be less so than beef, and chicken less so than beef. The reason given for the first of these exceptions is, that veal has less of the peculiar aroma developed in cooking; the reason given for the second is, that the texture of chicken is closer than that of beef, and, being closer, is less readily acted on by the gastric juice. Every one knows that veal is not very digestible, and is always shunned by the dyspeptic. On the other hand, in spite of chicken being less digestible than beef, it is more suitable for a delicate stomach, and will be assimilated when beef, or other meat, would not remain in the stomach,—an example which shows us that even the rule of nutritive value, being determined in a great measure by digestibility, is not absolute; and which further shows how cautious we should be in relying upon general rules in cases so complex.

The age of animals is very important. Thus the flesh of the kid is very agreeable; but as the kid approaches the adult period, there is so pronounced an odour developed from the hircic acid in its fat, that the flesh becomes uneatable. Whereas the ox and cow, fattened for two years after reaching full growth, have acquired the perfection of their aroma and flavour. The difference between lamb and mutton is very marked, especially in their fat, that of mutton containing more fatty acid, and being to many stomachs quite intolerable.

"All the savoury constituents of flesh are contained in the juice, and may be entirely removed by lixiviation (process of dissolving) with cold water. When the watery infusion of flesh thus obtained, which is commonly tinged red by some of the colouring matter of the blood, is gradually heated to boiling, the *albumen of flesh* separates, when the temperature has risen to 133⁰ Fahr., in nearly colourless cheesy flocculi; the colouring matter of the blood is not coagulated till the temperature rises to 158°.

"The proportion of the albumen of flesh separated as a coagulum by heat is very various, according to the age of the animal. The flesh of old animals often yields no more than 1 or 2 per cent; that of young animals as much as 14 per cent.

"The infusion or extract of flesh, after being freed by boiling from the albumen and colouring matter of the blood, has the aromatic taste, and all the properties of soup made by boiling the flesh. The residue of flesh, after exhaustion with cold water, is of the same quality in different animals; so that it is impossible in this state to distinguish beef from poultry, venison, pork, &c. On the other hand, the soup made of the flesh of different animals possesses, along with the common flavour in which all soups resemble one another, in each case a peculiar taste, which distinctly recalls the smell or taste of the roasted flesh of the animal; so that if we add to the boiled and exhausted flesh of roe-deer the concentrated juice of beef or poultry, the meat thus prepared cannot be distinguished by the flavour from roast-beef or fowl.

"The fibre of meat is, as we see from these facts, in its natural state steeped in and surrounded by a liquid containing albumen; and the tender quality of boiled or roasted meat depends on the amount of albumen deposited in its substance, and there coagulating, whereby the contraction, toughening, and hardening of the fibres are prevented. Meat is underdone, or bloody, when it has been heated throughout only to the temperature of coagulating albumen, or 133° Fahr.; it is quite done, or cooked, when it has been heated through its whole mass to between 158° and 165°."*

We may now understand the effects of cooking. When meat is *Roasted*, the outer layer of its albumen is coagulated, and thus presents a barrier to the exit of all the juice. To have a good and juicy roast, it is therefore necessary that the heat should be strongest at first. Let your cook, therefore, be careful not to set the joint down until the fire is vigorous and red. The heat may afterwards be much reduced. Besides this effect on

* Liebig: *Chemical Letters*, 1859, pp. 435-36.

the albumen, roasting converts the cellular tissue into gelatine ready for solution, and melts the fat out of the fat-cells.

In *Rapid Boiling* a somewhat similar result is effected, except that the albumen becomes less soluble. "If the flesh be introduced into the boiler," says Liebig, "when the water is in a state of brisk ebullition, and if the boiling be kept up for a few minutes, and the pot then placed in a warm place, so that the temperature of the water is kept at 158° to 165°, we have the united conditions for giving to the flesh the qualities which best fit it for being eaten."

In *Slow Boiling* a very different result is obtained. All the juices are extracted in the form of Soup, leaving a stringy mass of flesh behind. The thinner the piece of meat, the greater is its loss of savoury juices. To make the *best* soup we must chop the meat into fine pieces, and then, adding an equal weight of water, let the whole be slowly heated to the boiling point; it must be kept boiling for a few minutes, and then strained and pressed. We have then the strongest and most highly-flavoured soup that can be made from flesh; after which it may be diluted according to taste.

*Baking* exerts some unexplained influence on the meat, which renders it both less agreeable and less digestible. Those who have travelled in Germany and France must have repeatedly marvelled at the singular uniformity in the flavour, or want of flavour, of the various "roasts" served up at the *table-d'hôte*. The general explanation is, that the German and French meat is greatly inferior in quality to that of England and Holland, owing to inferiority of pasturage; and, doubtless, this is one cause, but it is not the chief cause. The meat is inferior, but the cooking is mainly at fault. The meat is scarcely ever *roasted*, because there is no coal, and firewood is expensive. The meat is therefore *baked;* and the consequence of this baking is, that no meat is eatable, or eaten, with its own gravy, but is always accompanied by some sauce more or less piquant. The Germans generally believe that in England we eat our beef and mutton almost raw; they shudder at our gravy, as if it were so much blood.

I have ascertained that it is really the cooking, and not the meat, which is in fault; for at the tables of great people, or re-

sident English, where *roast* meat is served, the flavour is excellent.    Moreover, the game, at a *table-d'hôte*, is almost as
tasteless as the poultry, partridges having little of their well-
known flavour:

"Longe dissimilem noto celantia succum;"*

and hare, that "well-flavoured beast," eulogised by Charles
Lamb, is rendered undistinguishable from beef, except perhaps in tenderness; while venison may be mistaken for kid.

In the inferior eating-houses of London the meat is also
baked, for the sake of economy, and is notoriously deficient in
that agreeable flavour which roast-meat possesses.    If it were
baked as thoroughly as it is in Germany, the meat in such
eating-houses would be as tasteless.

Dr. Beaumont has drawn up tables of the comparative digestibility of various substances, to which succeeding writers have
referred, without always perceiving that Dr. Beaumont's observations, being confined to what takes place in the stomach,
which is only *one* part of the digestive process, do not throw any
light upon what takes place in the intestines — by far the more
important part of the process** — and can only have a limited
value, because they can only apply to those substances which are
in any degree influenced by the gastric juice.    Bearing this in
mind, and accepting the following figures as indications only,
they will be found useful —

| | | | Hour. | Min. |
|---|---|---|---|---|
| Venison steak, broiled, | . | requires | 1 | 35 |
| Pig, sucking, roasted, | . | " | 2 | 30 |
| Lamb, fresh, broiled, | . | " | 2 | 30 |
| Beef, with salt only, boiled, | | " | 2 | 45 |
| Beef, fresh, lean, roasted, | . | " | 3 | 0 |
| Beef-steak, broiled, | . . | " | 3 | 0 |
| Pork, recently salted, raw, | . | " | 3 | 0 |
| Pork, recently salted, stewed, | | " | 3 | 0 |
| Mutton, fresh, broiled, | . . | " | 3 | 0 |
| Mutton, fresh, boiled, | . . | " | 3 | 0 |

* HORACE, *Sat.* ii. 8, makes this complaint of bad cookery in his day.
** See the next chapter, DIGESTION AND INDIGESTION.

| | | Hour. | Min. |
|---|---|---|---|
| Pork, recently salted, broiled, | requires | 3 | 15 |
| Pork steak, broiled, . . | „ | 3 | 15 |
| Mutton, fresh, roasted, . | „ | 3 | 15 |
| Beef, fresh, lean, dry, roasted, | „ | 3 | 30 |
| Beef, with mustard, &c., boiled, | „ | 3 | 30 |
| Beef, with mustard, &c., fried, | „ | 4 | 0 |
| Veal, fresh, broiled, . . | „ | 4 | 0 |
| Beef, old, hard, salted, boiled, | „ | 4 | 15 |
| Veal, fresh, fried, . . . | „ | 4 | 30 |
| Pork, fat and lean, roasted, . | „ | 5 | 15 |

As may be expected, the flesh of different parts has different qualities: the breast of birds, with its pectoral muscles, which move the wings, is tenderer than the legs; but the flesh of the legs, when the birds are young, is more juicy and savoury than that of the wings; and in the woodcock, old or young, the legs are always preferred, while in the partridge epicures select the wings.

The flesh of game is richer in osmazome than that of domestic birds; and when the bird has been kept till it is "high," it has — especially in the back — an aromatic bitter flavour very acceptable to epicures, but very nauseous to unsophisticated palates.

The flesh of all waterfowl, especially the goose, is penetrated with fat, which often becomes rancid and "fishy:" this renders the goose so notorious an offender, that he has to be "qualified" by a little brandy, euphuistically styled "Latin for goose." Dr. Beaumont found no difference between the digestibility (in the stomach) of roast goose and roast turkey, both requiring two hours and a half; but it should be observed that the fats are not digested at all in the stomach, and it is on the fats that the real digestive difference between goose and turkey depends. Turkey, roasted, requires two hours and a half for digestion; fowl, roasted, four hours, and ducks the same.

Besides the meat (muscle), the brains, livers, kidneys, and sweetbread of various animals are eaten. On account of the fat and oil contained in brain and liver, they are unsuitable for delicate stomachs, especially when fried. Kidneys are very tough, and difficult of digestion. Sweetbread forms a favourite food

with convalescents, when plainly dressed; its composition in
100 parts is as follows —

| | | | |
|---|---|---|---|
| Albumen, | . | . . . | 14.00 |
| Osmazome, | . | . | 1.65 |
| Gelatine, . | . | . | 6.00 |
| Animal fat, | . | . | 0.30 |
| Margaric acid,* . | . | . | 0.05 |
| Fibrine, . | . | . | 8.00 |
| Water, | . | . | 70.00 |
| | | | 100.00 |

' An excellent food, too much neglected, is Tripe, which is
simply the stomachs of ruminant animals. As it contains a large
proportion of albumen and fibrine, and requires not more than
one hour for its digestion in the stomach, we see the justification
of the practice popular in many families, of having Tripe for
supper. There is no nightmare in it.

2. *Horse-flesh.* — A Frenchman was one day blandly re-
monstrating against the supercilious scorn expressed by English-
men for the beef of France, which he, for his part, did not find
so inferior to that of England. "I have been two times in England," he remarked, "but I nevère find the bif so supérieur to
ours. I find it vary conveenient that they bring it you on leetle
pieces of stick, for one penny; but I do not find the bif supérieur." On hearing this, the Englishman, red with astonishment, exclaimed, "Good God, sir! you have been eating cat's
meat."

It is very true, he *had* been eating cat's meat; but had he
not at the same time been eating meat as succulent, savoury,
and wholesome as the marbled beef of which the Briton is so
proud?

Let the resonant shouts of laughter subside a little, and
while you are wiping the tears from your eyes, listen to the very
serious exposition we shall make of the agreeable and nutritive
qualities of horse-flesh. We are not going to press into the service of our argument the immense mass of evidence collected by

* Margaric acid is one of the fatty acids, and is produced from margarin
a pearly fat found in olive oil, goose grease and human fat.

M. Isidore Geoffroy St. Hilaire,* respecting the tribes and nations which habitually dine off horses; nor will we lay much
stress on the fact, that in the Jardin des Plantes the carnivora
are habitually fed on horse-flesh, which keeps them healthy in
spite of many unfavourable conditions. The sceptic might not
unreasonably ask whether our digestive power be *quite* as good
as that of the lion; and he would remark that the condor is
known to devour, with relish, food which Mr. Brown would
sturdily refuse. Unhappily no dietetic rules for men can be deduced from condors and lions. We must rely on the experience
of human stomachs.

Nor is this experience wanting. Without alluding to the
rumours which attribute to the Paris restaurateurs a liberal employment of horse-flesh among their *filets de bœuf*, M. St. Hilaire
collects an imposing mass of evidence to show that horses have
been eaten in abundance without suspicion, and without evil
consequences.

Huzard, the celebrated veterinary surgeon, records, that
during the Revolution the population of Paris was fed for six
months on horse-flesh. It is true, that when the beef was known
to be that of horses, some complaints were made; but in spite
of the strong prejudices, and the terrors such a discovery raised,
no single case of illness was attributable to this food.

Larrey, the great army-surgeon, declares, that on very
many occasions during the campaigns, he administered horse-
flesh to the soldiers; and what is more, he administered it to
the sick in the hospitals. Instead of finding it injurious, he
found that it powerfully contributed to their convalescence, and
drove away a scorbutic epidemic. Other testimony is cited, and
M. St. Hilaire feels himself abundantly authorised to declare that
horse-flesh is as wholesome and nutritious as ox-flesh.

Is horse-flesh as palatable as it is wholesome? Little will it
avail to recount how there are tribes of hippophagists, or how
soldiers during a campaign, and citizens during a siege, have
freely eaten of the *filet de cheval*: under such extremities an old

* *Lettres sur les Substances Alimentaires, et particulièrement sur la Viande
de Cheval.* 1856.

shoe has not been despised — nevertheless, *that* is not generally considered a toothsome morsel.

Feeling the necessity of having this point definitively settled, the advocates of horse-flesh have given banquets, both in Germany and France, at which the comparative merits of horses, cows, and oxen were to be appreciated. In 1835 the Prefect of Police chose a commission of eminent men to inquire into the quality of the flesh taken from horses which had died, or had been recently killed, in Paris and its environs. These commissioners all shared the general prejudice; yet in their report they avowed that "we cannot but admit this meat to be very good and very savoury; several members of the commission have eaten it, and could not detect any sensible difference between it and beef." In 1841, horse-flesh was openly adopted at Ochsenhausen (what irony in this name!) and Würtemberg, at both of which places it continues to be publicly sold, under the surveillance of the police; and five or six horses are weekly brought to market. In 1842, a banquet, at which a hundred and fifty persons assisted, inaugurated its public use at Königsbaden, near Stuttgart. In 1846 the police of Baden authorised its public sale; and Schaffhausen followed the example. In 1847, Weimar and Detmold witnessed public banquets of the hippophagists, which went off with *éclat;* in Karlsbad and its environs the new beef came into general use; and at Zittau two hundred horses are eaten annually. The innovation gained ground rapidly, and the public sale of horse-flesh is now general in Austria, Bohemia, Saxony, Hanover, Switzerland, and Belgium. In 1853, Berlin counted no less than five slaughter-houses, where three hundred and fifty horses were sold. In Vienna, during the same year, there was a riot to prevent one of these banquets; yet, in 1854, such progress had been made in public opinion that thirty-two thousand pounds' weight were sold in a fortnight, and now at least ten thousand of the inhabitants are hippophagists. A large quantity is also sold at the Lake of Constance, as I learned in 1858; and I *suspect* that I ate thereof on board the steamer.

These facts are very striking. When we consider, on the one hand, how strong is prejudice, and, on the other, how unreasoning the stomach, we must admit that horse-flesh could only gain acceptance in virtue of its positive excellence.  Nor will it suffice to meet these facts with a sarcasm on German beef, in comparison with which horse-flesh may be supposed to hold no dishonourable rank: we have the testimony of men accustomed to the *Café de Paris* and *Philippe's*, invited expressly to pronounce judgment, and proved, on trial, incapable of distinguishing horse-beef from ox-beef.

M. Renault, the director of the great veterinary school at Alfort, had a horse brought to the establishment with an incurable paralysis.  It was killed; and three days afterwards, on the 1st December 1855, eleven guests were invited to dine off it: they were physicians, journalists, veterinary surgeons, and *employés* of the Government.  Side by side were dishes prepared by the same cook, in precisely similar manner, consisting of similar parts of the meat from this horse, and from an ox of good quality.  The horse-soup was flanked by an ox-soup — the *bouilli* of horse by a *bouilli* of beef — the fillet of roast-beef by a fillet of roast-horse.  The guests *unanimously* pronounced in favour of the horse-soup; the *bouilli*, on the contrary, they thought inferior to that of the ox, though superior to ordinary beef, decidedly so to cow-beef.  The roast fillet, again, seemed to them very decidedly in favour of the horse.

Similar experiments have been subsequently repeated in Paris and the provinces, under varying conditions: the guests have sometimes been informed what they were going to eat; sometimes they have been totally unsuspecting; and sometimes they have been simply told that they were going to eat something quite novel.  Yet in every case the result has been the same.

It is on this evidence that M. St. Hilaire calls upon the French people to turn their serious attention to the immense mass of excellent animal food which lies within their reach, and which they annually suffer to waste, merely because of an absurd prejudice.  Difficult as it may be to overcome a prejudice, no army of ignorance can prevent the establishment of a truth which is at once easily demonstrable and immediately beneficial.  Prejudice may reject horse-flesh, as it long rejected tea and potatoes, the latter of which, Montaigne tells us, excited *l'estonnement et le dégoût*, but has nevertheless become European food.

If horses are eaten, why not donkeys? The Greeks ate donkeys, and we must suppose they had their reasons for it. Has any modern stomach been courageous enough to try?

Yes, the experiment has at least been made once. Dr. John Beddoe of Clifton sends me the following statement: — "Several years ago, I entertained six or eight medical students with a dinner, at which the *pièce de resistance* was nothing else than the hind-leg of a donkey which had been sacrificed to a physiological experiment. One or two of my guests were in the secret: to the others I represented the meat to be part of a fawn. They all partook of it, and 'even asked for more.' In flavour and appearance it most resembled mutton; but though young it was far from tender, and I did not care to repeat the experiment, to which I had been instigated partly by a passage in an Arabian tale, in which one of two gastronomic disputants, in reply to a commendation of a shoulder of lamb, is made to say, 'You know nothing: what say you to the neck of a young ass carefully roasted?'" Although Dr. Beddoe does not report very favourably of the tenderness, his guests found the meat sufficiently appetising, since they "asked for more." Besides, the animal may have been too fresh; another day or two might have given it the requisite tenderness. The point is worth investigating; for if the horse and donkey can be introduced among our meats, thousands who now rarely touch animal food may be supplied. So many horses are killed by accident, or killed because they are lame or vicious, that the supply would be enormous, without any necessity for killing horses expressly.

A new and noble kind of meat has recently been suggested by Prof. Owen, whose account of the flavour and capabilities of the Eland will doubtless induce noblemen to introduce that animal into their parks.

3. *Fish* is largely eaten by all classes, and is certainly nutritious. Great differences are noticeable in the different kinds. Many kinds have large quantities of oil — as the eel, salmon, herring, pilchard, and sprat; and these are therefore the least digestible. The oil is most abundant in the "thin" parts of salmon, which are consequently preferred by epicures. After spawning, the quality is very inferior. In the cod, whiting, had-

dock, plaice, flounder, and turbot, there is no oil except in their livers, so that these are easily digested, especially if they are not eaten with quantities of lobster or shrimp sauce, agreeable adjuncts very apt to exact large compensation from the delicate in the shape of acidity and flatulence.

Frying, of course, renders fish less digestible than boiling or broiling; and those whose digestions are delicate should avoid the skin of fried fish. They should also avoid dried, smoked, salted, and pickled fish; crabs, lobsters, prawns, and shrimps. The oyster is most digestible when raw, least so when stewed. Dr. Beaumont found the raw oyster took 2 hours 55 minutes to digest, the roasted oyster 3.15, and the stewed 3.30. What is called "scalloping" gives oysters a delicious flavour, but the heat coagulates the albumen and hardens the fibrine; besides, the effect of heat on the butter in which they are cooked renders it very unfit for the delicate stomach.

Respecting the nutritive quality of fish, opinions are divided. Let us hear old Leeuwenhoek. "It is the opinion of many medical persons," he says, "that various disorders in the human frame are caused by acid in the stomach, which coagulates the juices (!); and some condemn the use of acids, and also of fish, as articles of food. But to these opinions I cannot subscribe; for at a town in my neighbourhood, where the people get their living by fishing, and feed principally on fish, especially when they are on the sea, the men are very robust and healthy even to a great age; and with respect to myself, I have experienced that when my habit of body has been indisposed, I have been greatly refreshed by eating fish with sauce composed of a mixture of butter and vinegar, and I never found acid sauces disagree with me. It is also my opinion that a fish diet is more wholesome than flesh, particularly to those persons who do not use much exercise, because fish is more easily comminuted and digested in the stomach and bowels than flesh."*

But while fishermen are robust on a fish diet, it is notorious that those accustomed to meat find a certain debility follow the adoption of an exclusively fish diet — during Lent, for instance; and jockeys, when "wasting" themselves at Newmarket, take

* LEEUWENHOEK: *Select Works,* I. 154.

fish in lieu of meat. Lehmann cites the analyses of Schloss-
berger, which show "that the amount of nitrogen in muscular
fibre is throughout the animal kingdom essentially similar. The
flesh of fish contains the same amount as that of the higher animals; oysters, on the contrary, instead of containing more, as
common experience would lead us to conjecture, actually contain
less."[*] There is, however, as we have seen, a remarkable difference between being rich in nitrogen, and being good food. One
reason why fish is less nutritious than flesh, in spite of the simi-
larity in their composition, is said to be the absence of the osmazome which gives flavour to flesh.

One of the popular notions entertained even by some medical
men is, that eating fish increases fertility, and that the fish-
eating tribes are unusually prolific. We need not pause to refute
the physiological arguments on which this opinion is founded, as
the fact asserted, of fish-eating tribes being very prolific, is itself a fiction. Dr. Pereira remarks: —

"There is, I think, sufficient evidence to prove that the
ichthyophagous people are not more prolific than others. In
Greenland and among the Esquimaux, says Foster, where the
natives live chiefly upon fish, seals, and oily animal substances,
the women seldom bear children oftener than three or four times:
five or six births are reckoned a very extraordinary instance.
The Pessernis whom we saw had not above two or three children
belonging to each family, though their common food consisted of
mussels, fish, and seal-flesh. The New Zealanders absolutely
feed on fish, and yet no more than three or four children were
found in the most prolific families."[**]

4. *Eggs* are very nutritious, especially when poached or
lightly boiled; when boiled hard, or fried in butter, they are
difficult of digestion; and the same may be said of omelettes,
pancakes, and fritters.

But here, as indeed in all other cases, only general empirical
rules can be laid down — rules which individual experience must
rectify or confirm. There are persons who cannot eat the white
of egg; there are persons who cannot eat the yolk; and there are

[*] LEHMANN: *Physiol. Chemie*, III. 351.
[**] PEREIRA: *On Diet*, p. 288.

others who cannot eat egg in any shape whatever. To some persons of delicate digestion, eggs are found very suitable; while to others, whose digestion is generally good, they are hurtful. "In short," says Leeuwenhock, "we can much better judge for ourselves as to what agrees or disagrees with us, than pretend to advise other people what is good diet, or the contrary."* Experience, enlightened by vigilant good-sense, can alone determine such questions for each person. It is idle to assure a man who finds eggs disagree with him, that "they are really very wholesome;" and not less idle to warn him against eggs, or anything else, which his experience pronounces beneficial. The blissful being who knows not, except by rumour, what is the difference between digestible and indigestible, may smile at Science and its exhortations; the miserable being whose stomach painfully obtrudes itself upon his consciousness by importunities not to be evaded, and by clamours not to be outargued, may gather some guiding light from general rules, and thus by vigilance arrive at positive results for himself.

5. *Pastry.* — There are two kinds of pie-crust, called "puff" and "short" paste; of these, the latter is the most digestible, because the butter is thoroughly mingled with the dough, and is by this means in that state of minute subdivision which, when treating of Fats and Oils, we saw to be necessary for its proper digestion; morever, the starch is also thus more equally distributed.

In puff pastry this is not the case: the dough forms itself into thin and solid layers. "All pastry," according to Dr. Paris, "is an abomination. I verily believe that one-half of the cases of indigestion which occur after dinner-parties may be traced to this cause."

A hard sentence, this, on juveniles and pastry-lovers; but in mitigation, one may suggest that the offences of pastry lie less in its own sinful composition, than in the fact of its succeeding a chaos of meats, made-dishes, and mingled vintages. The gentleman who was found reeling forlorn and helpless against the railings, on his way home after dinner with a friend, hiccuped energetic denunciations against that "knuckle of ham" which had taken the steadiness from his legs and the singleness from

* LEEUWENHOEK; *Select Works,* I. 158.

visual objects; in like manner the tart, which is innocent when following a simple joint, may become as guilty as the knuckle of ham, at the rear of an elaborate dinner. We are all apt to over-eat ourselves, and then we throw the blame of our imprudence on some article of food not in itself more objectionable than the others.

6. *Vegetables.* — The immense variety of vegetable food cannot, of course, even be indicated in so rapid a survey as this. A volume might be written on the bread-plants alone. The tropical: rice, plantain, yam, sweet-potato, chayote, arrow-root, cassava, bread-fruit, sago, cocoa-nut, taro, and date; and the extra-tropical: wheat, rye, barley, oats, buckwheat, and potatoes; with maize, which is common to both regions — these alone support millions of human beings, and are justly named "the staff of life."

The tropical plants yield more than the others; wheat yields on an average only five or six fold in northern Europe, and eight or ten fold in southern Europe; but rice yields a hundred-fold. The plantain yields 133 times as much food as wheat on the same area. With a small garden round his hut the peasant can support his family. And how easy is subsistence in the Asiatic Archipelago, . where sago grows wild in the woods, and a man goes into the forest to cut his bread, as we to cut our firewood. He fells the tree, divides it into several pieces, scrapes the pith out, mixes it with water, strains it, and there is sago-meal ready for use.*

The bread-countries have been thus geographically indicated by Schouw: — "The *bread-line* extends furthest north in Scandinavia, for in Finmark we meet — only within the fiords, it is true — with barley and potatoes up to 70° N. latitude; from here it sinks both to the east and west. It is well known that neither Iceland nor Greenland possess bread-plants, although the south coast of the former lies in 63½°, and that of the latter in 60° N. latitude; and that in the Feröe Islands, although lying between 61¼° and 62½°, there exists but an inconsiderable cultivation of barley. On the east side of North America the bread-line sinks still further to the south, for Labrador and Newfoundland have no bread-plants, and the limit can scarcely be put here higher

* SCHOUW: *The Earth, Plants, and Man* (Trans.), p. 131.

than 50°, consequently much further south than in Denmark,
where the plains abound in corn. It extends a little further north
on the western coast of North America, which, as is well known,
possesses a warmer climate than on the east side. The few data
which we find here, render the determination of the north limit
rather uncertain; it can scarcely be placed higher than 57° or 58°
Turning from Scandinavia towards the east, we find a depression
of the bread-line even in European Russia, here coming by 67°
northward of Archangel. The curve is considerable in Asiatic
Russia; at Ob the north limit of bread comes to 60°, at Jenesi to
58°, at Lena 57½°, and in Kamtschatka, which has only a slight
cultivation of corn in the most southern part, it sinks to 51° —
thus to about the same latitude as on the east coast of North
America. The bread-line has thus two polar and two equatorial
curves, the former corresponding to the western, the latter to the
eastern sides of the continent."[*]

*Vegetarianism.* — On surveying the list of nations and tribes
whose food is principally, or entirely, vegetable, we are naturally
led to ask what confidence is due to that party in America and
England which proclaims Vegetarianism to be the proper creed
for civilised men, and vegetable food the healthiest and suit-
ablest in every way. Many years ago, I was myself a convert to
this doctrine, seduced by the example and enthusiasm of Shelley;
and, for the six months in which I rigidly adhered to its precepts,
could find no sensible difference, except that I was able to study
immediately after dinner. It soon became clear, however, that
the arguments on which the doctrine rests for support would not
withstand physiological scrutiny.

It is unnecessary to do more than allude to such fantastic arguments as that of Rousseau, who maintained vegetables to be
our proper food, because we have two breasts, like the vegetable
feeders; an argument as worthless as the counter-argument of
Helvetius, that flesh is our only proper food, because we have the
blind intestine short, like the flesh-feeders. The vegetarian
theory is at variance with the plain indications afforded by our
structure, and by the indications, no less plain, afforded by our
practice. The structure of our teeth and intestinal canal points

* SCHOUW; *The Earth, Plants, and Man* (Trans.), p. 131.

to a mixed diet of flesh and vegetable; and although the practice of millions may be to avoid flesh altogether, it is equally the practice of millions to eat it. In hot climates there seems little or no necessity for animal food; in cold climates it is imperatively demanded. In moderate climates, food is partly animal and partly vegetable. Against instinct, so manifested, it is in vain to argue; any theory of food which should run counter to it stands self-condemned.

Besides this massive evidence, we have abundant examples in individual cases to show how necessary animal food is for those who have to employ much muscular exertion. The French contractors and manufacturers who were obliged to engage English navvies and workmen, because French workmen had not the requisite strength, at last resolved to try the effect of a more liberal meat diet; and by giving the Frenchman as ample a ration of meat as that eaten by the Englishman, the difference was soon reduced to a mere nothing. It is worth noting that the popular idea of one Englishman being equal to three Frenchmen, was found by contractors to be tolerably accurate, one Englishman really doing the work of two and a half men; and M. Payen remarks that the consumption of mutton in England is three times as much as that in France, in proportion to the inhabitants.*

It is a fact of very great importance that the chemical constitution of the Blood is notably altered by an exclusively vegetable diet. Verdeil discovered that the blood of animals fed exclusively on flesh contained a quantity of phosphates, while the carbonates had disappeared; on the contrary, the same animals fed on vegetables had blood rich in carbonates, with but little of the phosphates. A dog was fed for a fortnight on flesh, and the ashes of its blood yielded as much as 12 per cent of phosphoric acid, combined with alkalies. The same dog fed on bread and potatoes showed only 9 per cent; and if it could have been fed on green vegetables, there would not have been more than 2 or 3 per cent — as in the blood of sheep and oxen.**

There are many conclusions to be drawn from this fact. One only need be hinted at here. Those who have any predisposition

* PAYEN: *Des Substances Alimentaires*, p. 8.
** VERDEIL in *Comptes Rendus de la Société de Biologie*, 1849, p. 71.

to the terrible disease called "the stone" should abstain as much as possible from animal diet, bread, and peas, since it is thence that the phosphoric acid in excess is derived, which will form the phosphate usually characteristic of the "stone." By a vegetable diet the blood is rendered alkaline; this will enable the uric acid to remain soluble; and thus, even if a stone be already formed, its progress will be arrested.

*Tea, Coffee, Chocolate, Wines,* and *Beers*, have been so amply and lucidly treated of by Johnston in his *Chemistry of Common Life*, that we need say nothing of them in this place, except to remark that they are all undeniably nourishing, although seemingly incapable of entering into the composition of any tissue, so that their physiological value is still a mystery.

There are few facts better established than that Tea and Coffee, no less than Wine and Beer, and Narcotics, *increase* the activity and power of the organism, while they *diminish* its waste. In Dr. Böcker's experiments on himself, it appeared that when for seven days, consecutively, he drank only water with *insufficient* food, he daily lost 12 ounces avoirdupois, more than when, with the *same* amount of food, he drank tea. Moreover, when he took a *sufficient* quantity of food he gained weight, if tea were added. He found tea very materially diminish the amount of urea and other excretions; and it also limited the amount lost in perspiration.

In Dr. Julius Lehmann's experiments on himself, with coffee, similar results were reached. They are thus stated by Dr. Chambers:[*]

1. That coffee produces on the organism two chief effects which it is very difficult to connect together — viz. the raising the activity of the circulating and nervous systems, and remarkably retarding the decomposition of the tissues.

2. That it is the reciprocal modifications of the empyreumatic oil and caffeine contained in the bean which call forth the stimulant effects of coffee.

3. That the lessening of the changes of decomposition which this beverage produces in the body is chiefly caused by the empyreumatic oil.

* CHAMBERS: *Digestion and its Derangements,* p. 249.

"What an important effect this is!" exclaimed Dr. Chambers. "The tea and coffee drinker may have less to eat and yet lose less weight — wear his body out less — than the water-drinker. At a comparatively small expense he may save some of the costly parts of his diet, those nitrogenised solids that entail so much thought, labour, and anxiety to obtain." The same is true of Alcohol, and all the Narcotics, as is irresistibly proved by Von Bibra in his comprehensive work.*

Let me call attention to a paradox which physiologists have seemingly overlooked, namely, that the physiological canon of "all activity being dependent on waste of tissue," seems here contradicted by a class of substances which notoriously increase the activity, and demonstrably decrease the waste. It is held that every evolution of force is produced by some chemical change; and every change tends towards final decomposition. In a vast variety of cases this is demonstrable. In the cases now under consideration nothing of the kind is apparent—the tissues are more active, and the waste is less. And what makes the paradox more striking is the fact that none of these substances enter, as such, into the composition of the tissues. They must be supposed, therefore, to act upon them; but how can they act upon them, evolving force, without producing decomposition?

I instituted some experiments with a view of determining, if possible, what the precise action was, and whether it was similar in each case. The fact that we ordinarily employ alcohol to *preserve* animal preparations — to protect them from that decomposition which would otherwise ensue if the substances were left to themselves — suggested the idea that when we drink alcohol, in wine, beer, or spirits, the action on our tissues may be of the same nature, only less energetic. If a *temporary* suspension of the inevitable process of decomposition were effected by alcoholic drinks — if the alcohol acted on the living as on the dead tissue, and arrested its molecular changes — we should then clearly understand how it is that alcoholic drinks diminish waste, how they are the "savings-bank of the tissues," and how they

* Von Bibra: *Die narkotischen Genussmittel und der Mensch.* Compare also Johnston: *Chemistry of Common Life:* "The Narcotics we indulge in."

lessen the quantity of food which is needful. But the mystery
would still remain how such an arrest of change could be coincident with an increase of power.

The point I endeavoured to establish was this: Are the tissues *preserved* by decoctions of Tea, Tobacco, and Coffee, in the
same way as by Alcohol? The experiments gave a decided ne-
gative; and I am now disposed to doubt whether the action of
Alcohol on the living tissues, when taken in the highly diluted
form of wine or spirits, has any notable resemblance to that
which concentrated Alcohol has on dead tissue. Consequently,
the mode of action of tea, coffee, and narcotics has yet to be explained; and when explained, there will still remain the paradox
of increased activity with diminished waste.

We have thus surveyed the great varieties of Food, and have
seen how far Science is from any accurate data respecting the
nutritive value of separate substances. It is doubtful whether
this last requisite will ever be attained, owing to the complexity
of the problem, and the shifting nature of the data.

The nutritive value of any substance is necessarily dependent
on the relation of that substance to the organism: but that relation cannot be constant, because the organism itself is frequently
changing. Moreover, a substance which under ordinary circumstances will be very nutritious, suddenly fails to nourish,
because some other substance is present, or some other substance is absent. Whenever the animal is a various feeder,
variety in food becomes indispensable. Majendie found that
rabbits could not subsist longer than a fortnight if fed on a single
article of their ordinary food, such as carrots, or cabbages, or
barley; and Ernest Burdach made the following experiment:
Taking three rabbits not quite full-grown, but all three from
the same litter, and as nearly alike as possible in size, strength,
colour, form, and sex, to the one he gave nothing but water
and potatoes, which were furnished in abundance; "it ate seven
ounces on the first day, six on the second, and gradually less
and less; its weight, which on the seventh day was 161 *gros*,
was reduced by the thirteenth day to 93 *gros*, when it died completely exhausted. The second was fed in the same way with
barley; it ate 20 *gros* the first day, 14 the third, and so on less

and less; in the fourth week it expired. The third rabbit was fed on alternate days with potatoes and barley, and its weight increased till the nineteenth day; and as its weight then remained stationary, in the third week both potatoes and barley were given together, upon which the weight continued to increase, and the animal retained its original vivacity."

VI. THE QUANTITY OF FOOD. — It has long been a question what quantity of Food is requisite for the proper sustainment and repair of the organism. Like most other questions of the kind, it can be answered only in a rough manner, precision being impossible. The differences of individual organisms, and the different conditions of these organisms, must always interfere with any attempt at accurate estimates. The same man must necessarily require more food when in activity than when in repose; in cold climates more than in hot climates; and although we may strike an average which shall be accurate enough as a matter of figures, of what use can an average be in Physiology? *The man to be fed is not an average.* A hundred men will consume an amount of food which may be accurately divided into a hundred parts; but these figures give us no real clue to the quantity needed by each individual; and rations founded on such estimates must necessarily be imperfect, one man receiving more, another less, than is required.

Individual experience can only be valid for the individual. Valentin, from experiments on himself, found that his daily consumption was rather more than six pounds of solid and liquid food; but Cornaro for fifty-eight years took no more than 12 ounces of solid food, and 14 ounces of light wine. Here are two individual experiences widely discrepant. It is clear to the physiologist that the very small amount of solid food taken by Cornaro was partly compensated by the nutritive value of the wine; and partly by the fact that his moderate activity caused a less demand than is usual among men; but even when due allowance is made for such elements, we are brought no nearer to a correct estimate, because we have not yet determined, and perhaps never shall determine, the nutritive value of the different articles of food; so that those elaborate arrays of *weights,*

which many chemists and physiologists are fond of producing as
evidence, are vitiated by the initial fallacy of supposing that
vital phenomena can be satisfactorily reducible to arithmetical
calculation.

We are tempted to pause here for a moment to notice one of
the most singular of these misleading applications of arithmetic
to Life. Both phrenologists and their antagonists constantly
invoke the weight of the brains of different men and animals, as
if they believed in an exact correspondence between so many
ounces of nervous matter, and so much cerebral activity. Nevertheless they, at the same time, maintain that size is *not* the
measure of power, unless "all other things are equal." Now
the truth is that "all other things" never *are* equal, in two different brains.* Nervous tissue is not like so much salt or chalk,
*definite* in composition, presenting everywhere precisely the
same quantities of water, phosphorus, sulphur, &c.; nor is it
everywhere precisely similar in *development;* the proportions and
directions of its fibres differing in different brains, and at different ages of the same brain. Yet it is on these two qualities,
of *composition* and *development*, that the functions of the brain
will greatly depend for their relative intensity; and these are not
ascertainable by measurement, or by weight. To weigh the brains
of two men, with a view of determining what the comparative intellectual power of the two men really was, is as chimerical as
to weigh two men in the scales, with a view of ascertaining what
amount of muscular energy, dexterity, and endurance each possesses. Indeed, the error never could have gained acceptance
for a moment, if a true conception of biological philosophy had
been prevalent, because such a conception would have repudiated
the attempt to explain vital or psychological phenomena by the
method effective only in Physics.

Quitting these estimates, and interrogating experience, we
find the most singular and inexplicable differences in the quantities of food which individuals require, and in the quantities
which they will consume if permitted.

As a general rule, more is eaten in cold climates than in hot
climates; but it is by no means clear to me that the reason of

* See *Biographical Hist. of Philosophy,* 1857, p. 637.

this is the one advanced by Liebig when he says, "Our clothing is merely an equivalent for a certain amount of food; the more warmly we are clad, the less urgent becomes the appetite for food, because the loss of heat by cooling, and consequently the amount of heat to be supplied by food, is diminished." The relation between cold and food is more complex than that; and when Liebig refers to the gluttony of the Samoyedes, he overlooks the gluttony of the Hottentots, which is quite as remarkable. "If," he says, "we were to go naked like certain savage tribes, or if in hunting and fishing we were exposed to the same degrees of cold as the Samoyedes, we should be able with ease to consume half of a calf, and perhaps a dozen of tallow candles into the bargain, daily, as warmly-clad travellers have related with astonishment of these people. We should then also be able to take the same quantity of brandy or train-oil without bad effects, because the carbon and hydrogen of these substances would only suffice to keep up the equilibrium between the external temperature and that of our bodies."

This sounds very plausible as long as we confine our attention to Samoyedes, but it is rendered questionable by the statement, recorded by Barrow in his *Travels in Southern Africa*, that the Hottentots are the greatest gluttons on the face of the earth. Ten Hottentots ate a middling-sized ox in three days; and three Bosjesmans had a sheep given them about five in the evening, which was entirely consumed before noon of the following day. "They continued to eat all night, without sleep and without intermission, till they finished the whole animal. After this their lank bellies were distended to such a degree that they looked less like human beings than before."

The inhabitants of the Alpine regions of Lapland and of Norway are not remarkable for their voracity, nor are the Icelanders: a sufficient proof that mere temperature is not the sole cause of *excessive* eating, since such excess is sometimes observable in hot climates, and not always observable in cold climates.

Although Liebig's statement cannot be accepted, being indeed only one of the conclusions deduced from his theory of respiratory food, there is ample evidence to show that, without

referring excessive gluttony to cold, we are justified in referring
an increase of appetite to cold; and the increase is perfectly intelligible: more exercise must be taken in cold weather to develop the necessary amount of animal heat, more tissue must
be wasted, and consequently more supply is needed for repair.
"He who is well fed," says Sir John Ross, "resists cold better
than the man who is stinted; while starvation from cold follows
but too soon a starvation in food." The same writer thinks, that
not only should voyagers to the polar regions take more food
than usual, but "it would be very desirable indeed if the men
could acquire the taste for Greenland food, since all experience
has shown that the large use of oil and fat meats is the true
secret of life in these countries, and that the natives cannot
subsist without it, becoming diseased, and dying, with a more
meagre diet."

The accounts which travellers give of the quantity of food
which can be consumed are extraordinary. Sir John Ross
estimates that an Esquimaux will eat perhaps twenty pounds of
flesh and oil daily. Compare this with Valentin's six pounds,
or with Cornaro's twelve ounces of solids and fourteen ounces of
wine!

Captain Parry tried, as a matter of curiosity, how much an
Esquimaux lad, who was scarcely full grown, would consume
if left to himself. The following articles were weighed before
being given. He was twenty hours getting through them, and
certainly did not consider the quantity extraordinary:

|                              |     | Lb. | Oz. |
|------------------------------|-----|-----|-----|
| Sea-horse flesh hard frozen, | .   | 4   | 4   |
| ,,      ,,    boiled,        | .   | 4   | 4   |
| Bread and bread-dust,        | .   | 1   | 12  |
|                              |     | 10  | 4   |

To this must be added one and a quarter pint of rich gravy-soup,
three wine-glasses of raw spirits, one tumbler of strong grog,
and one gallon one pint of water.

Captain Cochrane, in his *Journey through Russia and Sibe-
rian Tartary*, relates that the Admiral Saritchoff was informed
that one of the Yukuti ate in four-and-twenty hours the hind-

quarter of a large ox, twenty pounds of fat, and a proportionate
quantity of melted butter for his drink.  To test the truth of
this statement, the admiral gave him a thick porridge of rice
boiled down with three pounds of butter, weighing together
twenty-eight pounds; and although the glutton had already
breakfasted, he sat down to it with great eagerness, and consumed the whole without stirring from the spot.  Captain Cochrane also states that he has seen three Yakutis devour a rein-
deer at a meal; and a calf weighing about two hundred pounds
is not too much for a meal of five of these gluttons.*

These facts are curious, but of course they throw no light on
the question, how much food an individual requires to keep himself alive and active.  Nor, indeed, has any method yet been
devised which could elucidate that point.  We can never feel
confident that the quantity taken is not somewhat more, or
somewhat less, than would really be advantageous.  If a man
is active on six pounds daily, he might be perhaps stronger on
six and a half; and if six and a half should prove the precise
amount which kept his weight unaltered, it would only do so
under precisely similar conditions; and we know that on different days he will waste different quantities of tissue.

Some caterpillars daily eat double their weight in food; a
cow eats 46 lb. daily; and a mouse eats eight times as much, in
proportion to its own weight, as is eaten by a man.  But when
such facts are cited, we must bear in mind the enormous differences in the nature of the foods thus weighed, their relative
amounts of water and indigestible material.  The same caution
is requisite in speaking of man's diet.  It has been variously
computed.  Sanctorius estimated it at 8 lb., Rye at 5 lb. and
7 lb., Horne at 4 lb. 3 oz., and Valentin in his own person
at 6 lb.

Such estimates were too contradictory to afford any clue.
The chemists bethought them of securing the requisite precision
by taking the amount of carbonic acid expelled during the
twenty-four hours as the standard of the amount of carbon necessary, and the amount of urea expelled in the same period, as
the standard of nitrogen necessary.  Tables were then drawn

* PEREIRA: On Diet, pp. 16, 17.

up setting forth the separate items of food requisite to supply
this waste. But, apart from the profound distrust with which
such chemical reasonings should be regarded, there is this separate source of distrust, that each man necessarily wastes
different quantities of tissue under different conditions: if, therefore, our analysis of food correctly represented the amounts of
carbon and nitrogen assimilated (which it does not), we should
still have to construct a special table for each individual at each
season of the year, and under varying conditions.

The question is really one of importance, when we have to
apportion the rations of paupers, prisoners, soldiers, and sailors.
Here we are forced to strike an average, although we know that
on any average one man will necessarily have more, and another less, than is absolutely requisite; but the impossibility of
arranging matters otherwise, unless food be so abundant that
it may be left to the discretion of each to eat whatever amount
he pleases, forces the adoption of some standard which experience rectifies on the whole. Dr. Pereira has furnished several
dietaries adopted for masses of men, and from these the following is taken.

The scale of diet in the Royal Navy is thus given in the Re-
gulations: —

"There shall be allowed to every person the following quantities of provisions: —

| | | | | | |
|---|---|---|---|---|---|
| Bread, | . | . | . | . | 1 lb. |
| Beer, | . | . | . | . | 1 gallon. |
| Cocoa, | . | . | . | . | 1 oz. |
| Sugar, | . | . | . | . | 1½ oz. |
| Fresh meat, | . | . | . | 1 lb. |
| Vegetables, | . | . | . | ½ lb. |
| Tea, . | . | . | . | . | ¼ oz. |

"When fresh meat and vegetables are not issued, there shall
be allowed in lieu thereof —

Salt beef, ½ lb. } alter-  { Salt pork, ¾ lb.
Flour,      ⅜ lb. { nately } Pease, ¼ pint.

"And weekly, whether fresh or salt meat be issued —

| | | | | | |
|---|---|---|---|---|---|
| Oatmeal, | . | . | . | . | ½ pint. |
| Vinegar, | . | . | . | . | ¼ pint." |

The daily allowance to the common soldier in Great Britain
is 1 lb. of bread and ¾ lb. of meat, making together 196 oz. of
solid food weekly; for this he pays a fixed sum, namely, 6d.
daily, whatever may be the market price. He furnishes himself
with other provisions.

As to the quantity each man should eat when unrestricted,
it is to be determined by himself alone. We are notoriously apt
to eat too much, and consequently waste much food, even when
we do not injure ourselves. Our sensations are the surest guides,
yet they do not always tell us with sufficient distinctness when
we have had enough: one thing is very clear, that to force the
appetite — to continue eating after the stomach has once suggested "enough" — is sure to be injurious. Hospitable hosts,
no less than anxious parents, should refrain from pressing food
on a reluctant appetite; it is not kindness, although kindly
meant.

In closing here our survey, we must confess that it has exhibited few reliable scientific data. Indeed, to some readers it
may have seemed that our efforts have been mainly revolu-
tionary, shaking foundations which promised security, and
disturbing the equanimity of scientific speculation. It is a fact
that Physiology is at present in too incomplete a condition to
answer the chief questions raised respecting Food; and this fact
it was desirable to bring into the clear light of evidence; for on
all accounts it is infinitely better that we should understand our
ignorance, than that we should continue believing in hypotheses
which enlighten none of the obscurities gathering round the
question. It is in vain that we impatiently turn our eyes away;
the darkness never disappears merely because we cease to look
at it.

# CHAPTER III.

### DIGESTION AND INDIGESTION.

"LET good Digestion wait on appetite." Much of our happiness depends on health, and health cannot continue without digestion. Riches, and honours, and the applause of crowds, are but poor compensations for the loss of that perpetual spring of pleasure which arises from the harmonious activity of all the functions; and the most prosperous of men must envy children and animals their prosperity of digestion. The misery of mankind, springing from many causes, is intensified by Indigestion, which lessens the fortitude to endure calamities, and increases the tendency to indulge in painful forebodings. Sorrow, come whence it may, is more lightly borne, and is briefer in its visitations, when the health is vigorous; and it cannot be vigorous without good Digestion. To those whose troubled secretions predispose them to gloom and fretfulness, small evils become magnified into calamities, and evils anticipated have the force of realities.

The marvels of Nature are an inexhaustible source of reverence to the reverential mind, and among these not the least marvellous is the admirable complexity of the apparatus on which Digestion depends. No sooner do we become acquainted with this complexity than our surprise is, not that many of us, imprudent and reckless as we are, should suffer from derangements of that function; but that any of us should continue to perform it with success seven days together. The more we contemplate this mechanism, the more wondrous it appears. The more we study the process, the more intricate its problems seem. Formerly the process was thought to be very simple; increase of knowledge brought increase of doubt; and now, whoever looks closely into the results of modern investigation will be surprised to find how little the enormous labours in all directions have added to our positive knowledge. The conquests of science have consisted in explaining certain details of the process, and in analysing the whole function of Digestion into separate acts.

And here we may pause to consider in what *scientific explanation* peculiarly consists, namely, in the discovery of those intermediate facts, not obvious, which link together the obvious phenomena. Thus it is matter of vulgar observation that cattle eat grass, and that this grass returns, in the shape of manure, to effect the growth of fresh crops. The farmer, in knowing this, may be said to know as much as the philosopher; but the farmer only knows the facts which stand out, visible to all — the obvious arcs in the great orbit of life; whereas the philosopher, not content with these, seeks to detect the *hidden* facts — the intermediate links of cause and effect, which constitute the chain. In proportion to his success in discovering these intermediate links, and their order of succession, he approaches a *scientific explanation* of the vulgar *observation*. This scientific explanation has two great advantages: it ministers to the intellectual craving for knowledge, a craving which gives man his eminence; and it ministers to his practical aims, increasing his power over Nature by enabling him to foresee and to modify phenomena, and to adapt them to his uses. If he learns that

9*

silica* is an essential constituent of wheat, and that silica must
be in the ground before it can enter the wheat, he learns two
"intermediate facts" not at all obvious, which enable him to
adapt circumstances to his needs: if the earth be deficient in
silica, he will add a fresh supply.

It is the same with Digestion.  Every one knows that Food
of various kinds is taken into the mouth, chewed, and swallowed;
that it remains some time in the stomach, where it undergoes
certain changes; that it then passes into the intestines, and separates into two portions, one of which nourishes the body, while
the other is ejected as waste.  These are the vulgar facts.  But
we cannot rest content with these.  The intellect craves knowledge more precise, and practical wants require that the "intermediate facts" should be discovered.

THE FUNCTION OF DIGESTION. — The purpose of Digestion is
to make Blood.  To effect this there are many processes which,
although closely connected with Digestion, are not really implied in it: such are Chewing the food, and Absorption.  There
are many animals which do not chew; there are many which
have no absorbent vessels; yet all these digest.  The function
of Digestion is the function of the *alimentary canal*, which canal,
or tube, extends from the mouth downwards through the whole
trunk.  Digestion prepares the Food for its entrance into the
Blood.  In those animals which chew their food we perceive that
chewing aids in this preparation of the Food, and we shall therefore include it in our analysis of the process of Digestion, although, strictly speaking, it is not more digestive than cooking,
or carving.

In Digestion two kinds of processes concur: the *mechanical*,
such as trituration and maceration (or rubbing, and reducing to
a pulp); and the *chemical* decompositions and transformations.
My own investigations have led to the curious fact that in the
simpler animals, only mechanical processes are in operation: it
is not till we examine animals of a more complex organisation
that we meet with chemical processes in Digestion; these being

---

* *Silica* is the chief ingredient of flint, sandstone, and many earthy
minerals.

at first very feeble, and increasing in importance as the organisms become more complex.* In man, the chemical processes
predominate. We shall touch on both as they present themselves.

I. WHAT TAKES PLACE IN THE MOUTH. — Before Food can
enter the Blood it must be rendered *soluble*. It is very solid, for
the most part, when taken into the mouth, and must be torn
and ground by the teeth, the result of which is that the Food is
mashed and moistened till it can be swallowed with ease. We
first cook our beef; we then cut it into small pieces; and finally
we tear and mash it with our teeth, in which act the saliva aids.
These are mechanical preparations.

But now the question arises, whether the action of the Saliva
is purely mechanical, aiding only in the maceration of the Food,
or partly mechanical, and partly chemical, *i. e.* aiding also in
its transformation? This has been hotly debated, and has given
occasion to an immense amount of laborious investigation. I
will answer it at once, as I conceive the most trustworthy researches warrant, and afterwards examine briefly some of the
arguments and experiments which have been brought forward.

The action of the Saliva is mainly *mechanical*. It is also
*chemical*, but this in so slight a degree that it may be dispensed
with altogether if the food be otherwise prepared, and introduced directly into the stomach. Its chemical action is limited
to the amylaceous (starchy) substances, changing a small portion
of them into dextrine and sugar.

C. H. Schultz, whose experiments at one time created a great
sensation,** assigned the whole process of Digestion to the action
of the Saliva. He denied the existence of any such fluid as the
gastric juice; declaring that what was supposed to be gastric
juice was only saliva and the remains of food. It is unnecessary
nowadays to do more than mention this opinion, which is refuted

* As far as relates to the Sea-Anemones, these investigations are recorded
in *Sea-side Studies*, p. 207-217.
** SCHULTZ: *De Alimentorum Concoctione*, p. 31. The arguments are reproduced in his curious work, *Die Verjüngung des Menschlichen Lebens*, p. 77.

by abundant experiments, all proving that Saliva exerts no chemical action whatever on any except starchy substances.

Claude Bernard, on the other hand — one of the greatest experimental physiologists of our day — maintains that the ancients were correct in assigning only *mechanical* influence to the saliva in facilitating mastication, taste, and swallowing; the *chemical* influence being completely insignificant, if not altogether absent.* In his ingenious and interesting exposition of the phenomena which take place in the mouth, he maintains that the three separate liquids which issue from the three separate glands — the *parotid*, in the cheek, the *sublingual*, under the tongue, and the *submaxillary*, in the lower jaw (see p. 158, Fig. 7, *p*, *g''*, and *g*) — have distinct offices: —

1. The office of the parotid secretion is to assist chewing.
2. The office of the sublingual secretion is to assist swallowing.
3. The office of the submaxillary secretion is to assist taste.

A mixture of these three secretions with that from the mucous membrane of the mouth, constitutes Saliva; and it is this Saliva which alone exerts the slight chemical action that ever does take place; or, in other words, it is only the mucous secretion which can act chemically on starchy substances, the other three secretions separately, or mingled, being altogether without such chemical action. It is on this that Bernards founds his assertion that the Saliva has no part to play in the chemical processes of Digestion — an error in logic, I conceive; but let us see the results of experiment.

The first person who distinctly detected the chemical action of Salvia was Leuchs.** He found that in a few hours it converted a mass of cooked starch into sugar. This was subsequently confirmed by Schwann, in a celebrated paper,*** wherein he argued that inasmuch as the gastric juice was incompetent to effect any change whatever in starch, the sugar found in the stomach of animals who have had none given in their food, necessarily came from the action of the Saliva on starch.

     * BERNARD: *Leçons de Physiol. Expérimentale*, II. 168.
     ** BURDACH: *Traité de Physiologie*, IX. 268.
     *** MÜLLER's *Archiv*, 1836, quoted by BURDACH.

It should be remarked that these observations have not the cogency they were generally supposed to have, for nothing is better established than that many animal substances have the power of transforming starch into sugar; indeed, the *alterability* of cooked starch is so great, that almost any influence suffices to change it into *dextrine* (a substance having the same elementary composition, but different *properties*), and the dextrine into *glycose* (starch-sugar).

The researches of Mialhe[*] gave a new aspect to the question. He established the important fact that starch paste was changed into sugar *in less than a minute* in the mouth; as the sweet taste sufficiently indicated. It is this rapidity of action which distinguishes the Saliva from other organic substances (except the pancreatic juice), and which therefore confirms the position of Leuchs and Schwann. The same result is obtained out of the organism. Mix a little starch paste with Saliva, and it will very rapidly be converted into sugar. Mialhe conceived the idea that this action was due to a particular organic agent, similar to that known as the *diastase* of vegetables — an idea too plausible not to find ready acceptance; it is, however, now given up by the best authorities, and Bernard has shown that fibrine and gluten, in a state of decomposition, but *before* putrefaction has set in, acquire this very property of converting starch into sugar — whereupon he concludes that what is called vegetable diastase is really nothing but the spontaneous decomposition of the gluten.[**]

That a chemical action takes place in the mouth, during the ordinary process of eating, is very easily shown. Let the reader take a piece of ordinary bread, and he will perceive that when it is first introduced into the mouth no trace of sweetness is discernible for a few seconds; but as it rolls over the tongue, and the saliva mixes with it, a gradually increasing sweetness is discernible; in from 30 to 45 seconds a decided transformation into sugar has taken place. Moreover, he will find that those portions of the bread which have got fixed between his teeth, and have

* MIALHE: *Mémoire sur la Digestion et l'Assimilation des Substances amylacées et sucrées*, 1846.
** BERNARD: *Leçons*, II. 161.

thus been retained longer under the influence of the Saliva, are
noticeably sweeter than bread is wont to be.

The fact that Saliva does convert starchy substances into
sugar is thus placed beyond dispute. The researches of Donders,
Jacubowitch, Bidder and Schmidt,* moreover, show that if the
Saliva be *prevented* from entering the stomach, and starch paste
be introduced into the stomach through an opening, no sugar is
formed. Their conclusion is this: Although many organic substances convert starch into sugar, none do so with the rapidity
of the saliva and the pancreatic juice.

Starch itself is not assimilable. It must be changed into
dextrine and sugar before it can pass through animal membranes, and enter the Blood. Now, inasmuch as the starchy
substances form an important class of our aliments (see Food
and Drink), the chemical intervention of Saliva in the digestive
process is apparent.

We have thus arrived at a very different conclusion from that
of Schultz, who attributes to the Saliva the whole of the chemica!
transformations in Digestion; and from that of Bernard, who
denies that any chemical transformations are effected by it.
The truth is, that *no* albuminous substance is transformed by the
Saliva, and that *all* starchy substances are attacked by it.

Nevertheless we must not exaggerate this influence. It is
only a small portion of the starch which is normally acted on by
the saliva, either in the mouth or in the stomach; the greater
portion is transformed in the intestines by the action of the
pancreatic juice and intestinal juice. In consequence of this,
the action of the salivary glands may altogether be dispensed
with. When they are cut out, or when their secretion is prevented from flowing into the mouth, the animal seems to suffer no
material inconvenience.** And Bidder and Schmidt have made
the curious discovery that in young animals, during the period
of suckling, the salivary glands have no secretion whatever.***

* Donders: *Physiologie*, i. 199. Bidder and Schmidt: *Die Verdauungssäfte und der Stoffwechsel*, p. 15, seq. This latter work is the most elaborate
ever published on the digestive fluids, and will be largely laid under contribution in our pages.
** Budok: *Memoranda der speciellen Physiologie*, p. 83.
*** Bidder and Schmidt, p. 22.

Having vindicated the *chemical* character of this secretion, we must now remark that its *mechanical* character is the most important. The amount of *transformation* is insignificant; but the amount of *maceration* which the food receives in the mouth, by the combined action of the teeth and saliva, is very important, as a preliminary towards the indispensable *solution*, which all food must undergo.

"It is much easier to supply the place of chewing by mechanical preparation in animal food than in vegetable. We can grind things small, but we cannot make artificial saliva. Kitchen science may prepare the former for the stomach, but not the latter. Indeed, the cooking of starchy foods for weak stomachs often makes them more indigestible, by reducing them from a solid to a fluid form, and thus enabling them to be swallowed without that manipulation in the mouth which elicits a flow of its secretions. The best form in which starch can be taken is one in which the envelope of the granule has been ruptured by heat, and the whole mass made light so as to be capable, *by* mastication, of being broken up and fermented equally by fluids, but not capable of skipping over the salivary admixture, and being swallowed *without* mastication. Such are good stale bread, mealy, well-boiled potatoes, thoroughly cooked cabbages: such are *not* new rolls, waxy potatoes, &c., which mastication merely makes into small solid tough lumps; or gruel and sago, and other slops, which annoy the dyspeptic, though so often forced upon him by his female friends." *

There are animals that *bolt* their food. There are human beings who imitate these animals; but it is to be hoped that they have potent stomachs, since they thus throw upon that organ an amount of extra labour, which would better have been executed by the mouth. The food must be rubbed and macerated *somewhere.* If the mouth does not begin this process, the stomach must do it all.

II. STOMACHAL DIGESTION. — The food reaches the stomach in a state approaching that of pulp, and with a slight chemical change in its starchy elements. Formerly it was thought that

* CHAMBERS'S *Digestion and its Derangements*, p. 331.

the stomach did all. Digestion was thought to be the function of the stomach, and of it alone. But recent researches have profoundly modified this conception; they have circumscribed the action of the stomach to that of a still further preparatory process, the completion of which must be sought in the intestines.

Our knowledge of the stomachal process has been rendered more accurate and extensive, owing to a fortunate accident which befell the Canadian known all over Europe as Dr. Beaumont's patient. This man, Alexis St. Martin by name, had a large hole in his stomach caused by the discharge of a gun. He recovered perfect health, the wound healed, but the opening remained, and this opening was used by Dr. Beaumont for observation and experiment. He has recorded the results in a well-known work. * Since then, another case has fallen into scientific hands. Dr. Schröder and Dr. Grünewaldt, at different periods, experimented on an Esthonian woman, with what results we shall hereafter learn.** And quite recently Alexis St. Martin has again become the subject of experiment in the hands of Dr. Francis Smith of Philadelphia.*** The value of these cases cannot be over-estimated; and the results have been compared with observations on animals, since Blondlot conceived the happy idea of establishing an artificial fistula in dogs, through which gastric juice might be obtained when wanted, and substances introduced into the stomach, or removed from it directly.

1. *The mechanical action of the stomach.* — If we examine the stomach of a fasting animal we find its lining walls are pale and flabby, lying close together, and only separated from each other by a layer of mucus and saliva.

It was this appearance which suggested the idea that the sensation of HUNGER was due to the rubbing of the coats of the

* BEAUMONT: *Experiments and Observations on the Gastric Juice;* 1838.
** SCHRÜDER: *Succi gastrici Humani vis digestiva,* 1853. GRÜNEWALDT: *Disq. de succo gastrico Humano ope fistulæ stomachalis indagata,* 1853. I know these works only at second hand.
*** His memoir, originally published in the *Philadelphia Medical Examiner,* has been translated in the BROWN SÉQUARD'S *Journal de la Physiologie,* I. 144.

stomach; an idea which we saw in the first chapter to be altogether erroneous.

The arrival of the food changes this condition. The contractions of the œsophagus or gullet (see p. 158, Fig. 7, *a*), force the
food into the stomach (E), which distends its walls. This distension
goes on increasing and increasing as fast as fresh supplies arrive.
Gradually the distension becomes more and more difficult, and
this creates a sense of fulness, which warns us to desist from
eating. The blood-vessels of the stomach have now become
swollen; the secretions are pouring in actively; the whole condition of the stomach is changed, and its muscular activity is
roused.

This muscular activity is important, being to stomachal
digestion what the action of the teeth is in the preparation which
takes place in the mouth. The lining of the stomach is a mucous
membrane — a continuation, indeed, of that which lines the
mouth, but differing from it in the peculiar glands which characterise some regions of it. Under this mucous membrane lies a
muscular coat; this muscular coat gives, by the alternate contraction and relaxation of its fibres, a *rotatory* movement to the
food. According to Dr. Beaumont's graphic expression, the food
is *churned* in the stomach, carried round and round from right to
left around the large end, and from left to right along the large
bend, returning along the small bend.[*] In this churning movement the food is not only well "ground," but is more and more
mixed with the gastric juice. The process may be compared to
the rolling about of the food in the mouth by the tongue.

Blondlot maintains that this trituration and maceration constitute the whole of stomachal digestion: the food is rendered
liquid without being *chemically altered.* I have shown this to be
the case in the digestive process of the *Actiniæ;* but in all the
higher animals there is ample evidence of a positive chemical
change taking place. And this we shall now consider.

2. *The chemical action of the stomach.* — Before Réaumur

---

[*] This rotation has been denied by BXTS, who says the disposition of
muscular fibres in the stomach is against it. — CANSTATT, *Jahresbericht*, 1853,
p. 147. But it seems difficult to admit that Beaumont could have been mistaken when he says he saw the food thus rotate.

instituted his experiments, it was held that the stomach merely ground the food to a pulp, by the action of *trituration* or rubbing. He tested this opinion in a very ingenious way, considering that the backward state of chemistry could furnish him with none of the means now at our disposal. He filled hollow silver balls with

Fig. 4.

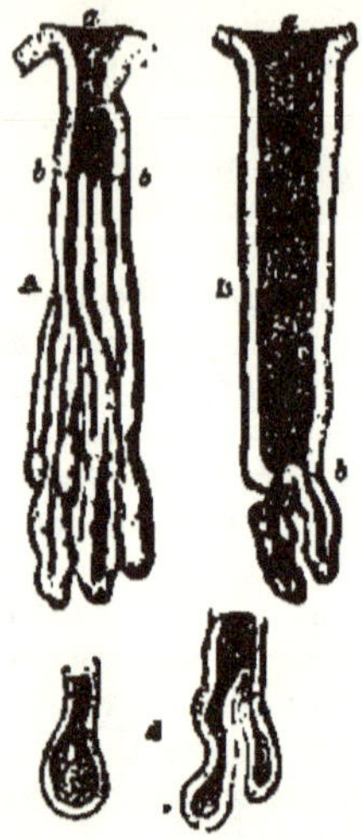

VERTICAL SECTION OF GASTRIC FOLLICLES, OR GLANDS, WHICH SE- CRETE GASTRIC JUICE. *From the stomach of a fasting dog, magnified.* A, a follicle from the middle of the stomach; B, one from the end near the intestine; *a a,* the openings through which the juice pours into the stomach; *b b b* mark the points where the structure becomes glandular; *d,* small py- loric tubes lined with epithelium to their ends. — After Todd and Dow- man.

meat, and perforating them in several places, caused a dog to swallow them. After they had remained some time in the stomach, he withdrew them by means of a thread. If, he argued, the digestive pro- cess were merely mechanical, the meat, protected by the silver covering, would not be altered; if, however, the process were chemical, the solvent fluid would have penetrated through the holes and acted on the meat; and so indeed it proved.— the meat was entirely *chymified;* that is, made into a pulp.

After this the gastric juice itself was obtained, and Réaumur and Spallanzani commenced that long series of experiments on *artificial* digestion which is not yet nearly concluded.

The stomach is lined by a mucous membrane. If we examine this membrane under the microscope, we find it crowded with minute finger-shaped tubes. These are the *gastric follicles*, or secreting glands, from which the gastric juice is poured into the cavity of the stomach, di- rectly the membrane is irritated by the presence of food (or indeed of any other substance).

Thirty-one pounds daily are said to be secreted from these glands in a healthy adult! Besides this gastric juice which flows on the entrance of food into the stomach, there is also present a secretion of mucus from the membrane, and the saliva, which is constantly being swallowed.

It would lead us too far, and into questions of too technical an interest, to examine the disputes which gather round the questions — What constitutes the gastric juice? and, What is its origin? For us it is enough to know that the gastric juice is an *acid* secretion, containing in all probability hydrochloric and lactic acids, containing also a peculiar organic substance named *pepsin.** The acids and the pepsin act chemically upon meats — that is, upon all albuminous and gelatinous substances — converting them into *peptones.* These peptones have all certain properties in common, no matter how various the substances from which they are derived; and it is owing to these properties, not possessed by the substances from which they are formed, that they are capable of being *absorbed* and *assimilated.*

Neither the acid, nor the pepsin, exerts more than a slight chemical influence on two great classes of Alimentary Principles, the Sugars and the Fats. Cane-sugar is changed into grape-sugar, owing, Dr. Harley believes, to the presence of a free acid: and fatty acids are sometimes developed from the fats. We may therefore set aside, for the moment, all starch, sugars, fats, and oils, which form so large a proportion of our food, and fix our attention exclusively on the albuminous substances. It is these which mainly undergo *chemical* change in the stomach. And we shall find that even these are not greatly changed; so that the popular idea of the stomach being the chief organ of Digestion will have to be considerably modified.

During the *churning* motion just described, the food is gradually mixed up with the fluids of the stomach. In consequence of this complete *saturation* it is reduced to a pulpy mass — the *Chyme;* and as it becomes more and more churned — more and more of semi-liquid consistence — it passes into the small intestines, there to undergo fresh changes. If we examine this pulpy

---

* The student may consult the great work of BIDDER and SCHMIDT, *Die Verdauungssäfte;* LEHMANN'S and MULDER'S Treatises on Organic Chemistry; DONDERS: *Physiologie;* CHAMBERS: *Digestion and its Derangements;* LONGET: *Physiologie:* BLONDLOT'S *Traité de la Digestion,* and his Memoirs in BROWN SÉQUARD'S *Journal;* and BERNARD'S *Leçons de Phys. Expérimentale,* II.

mass of Chyme just as it quits the stomach, we shall find that, however altered to the eye, its alterations have been for the most part physical, and but slightly chemical. That is to say, the *flesh* has become macerated, the *muscle-fibres* have become dissociated and broken into fragments, and the *cellular tissue* is dissolved; but many of these *muscle-fibres* retain their primitive structure; the *fat* is liquefied, but not often otherwise altered — not even emulsified; and the *gelatine* has become liquid peptone.

Fig. 5.

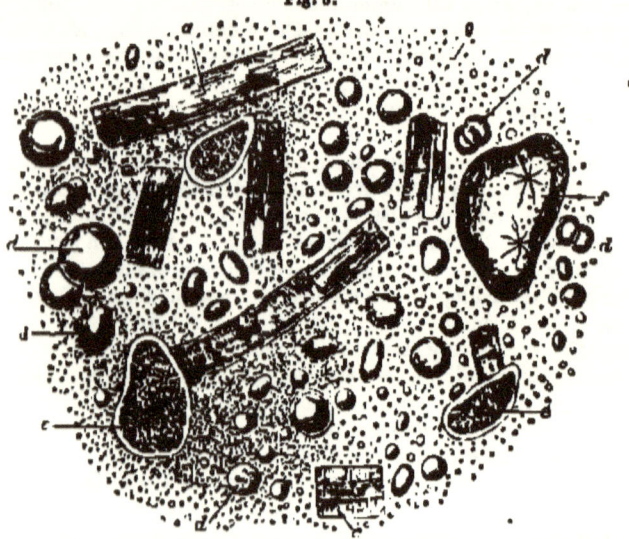

CHYME TAKEN FROM THE PYLORIC END OF A DOG'S STOMACH. *a*, muscular fibre from which the transverse markings have disappeared; *b*, muscular fibre in which these markings are partly visible; *c*, in which they are perfect; *d*, globules of fat; *e* and *f*, starch grains; *g*, granules. — After Claude Bernard.

This is what the microscope reveals, and this is assuredly not a *digested* mass.

Blondlot, indeed, declares that the Chymification we have been describing is the sole digestive process; and Chymification, according to him, is nothing but rendering the food *soluble*. Bernard takes a different view: Chymification he regards as only one part of the digestive process, and that exclusively confined to the albuminous and gelatinous substances, on which its action is precisely analogous to that of *boiling*.

If we attend closely to what goes on in the stomach, as reported by all the most trustworthy observers, we cannot, I think, come to any other conclusion than this: Chymification is mainly a physical process, but is also partly chemical; it liquefies and minutely divides one portion of the food, and it chemically transforms the other.

- Against the purely physical hypothesis there is one argument which seems to me overwhelming: Liquid albumen is very slightly absorbable, and not at all assimilable; but when acted on in the stomach, it becomes readily absorbable and assimilable. It seems, moreover, certain, that albumen is absorbed in small quantities from the stomach. The fact that the greater part of this substance passes undigested into the intestine, is no argument against the action of the stomach. The mouth begins, but does not complete, the conversion of starchy substances; the stomach begins, but does not complete, the conversion of albumen.

Albumen, on entering the stomach, in coagulated, and rendered insoluble in water. It must of course be again made soluble. This is effected by the gastric juice, which converts it into a *peptone*, not only soluble, but now incapable of coagulation.

If by heat you coagulate the albumen of the white of egg, and then dissolve it again, you can once more coagulate it by the application of heat. The change has been simply physical: the albumen was liquid, you made it solid; you can make it liquid again, and solid again; as you can turn water into ice, and ice into water. But you cannot do this with the peptone-albumen. *That* has undergone a chemical change, and has become a new body: it is soluble in water now, or in diluted alcohol (not in concentrated alcohol); and is incapable of coagulation, and of forming insoluble compounds *with salts*.

The gastric juice which does this, does so in virtue of its acid and its pepsin, acting together. Separately, these agents have no such power. In artificial digestion, if the acid be neutralised by an alkali—say the carbonate of soda—the action of the gastric juice is immediately suspended, to be resumed immediately on the addition of acid. Bidder and Schmidt have shown that the digestive power of the gastric juice is, up to a certain limit, in direct ratio to its amount of acid. Nevertheless it is not the acid alone which is operative. This is easily proved. Submit the gastric juice to a temperature of 212°Fahr., and it loses all its digestive power whatever; not because the acid has been destroyed, but because the pepsin has been destroyed. Pepsin is an organic substance which acts as a *ferment;* now, Chemistry teaches us that at 212° such organic substances coagulate, and when coagulated they cease to act as ferments.

Freezing the gastric juice has no such influence. Bidder and Schmidt found that when frozen it dissolved albumen as well as before — which, as they remark, must be a great comfort to the admirer of ices.

3. *Gastric Juice.* — Gastric juice is distinguished from among all other animals fluids by its *stability:* it resists decomposition longer than any other animal fluid. Nor does it lose its digestive virtue even when mouldy. One peculiarity must be insisted on, namely, its power of *arresting the putrefaction* of other organic substances. It is to this that we owe the impunity with which we eat "high" game and putrefying meat. Another curious fact is, that although the addition of organic acids increases the digestive power of this fluid, there is a limit at which this increase ceases, and beyond it, excess of acid suspends the whole digestive power. The power is also arrested by the presence of too large a quantity of organic substances, or peptones.

In this latter fact there is a lesson against over-eating. Digestion is impeded by too large a meal, first, in the arrest of the action of the gastric juice; and next, in overloading the stomach with more than it can properly move. There is another fact mentioned by Lehmann,[*] which is fertile in suggestion,

* LEHMANN: *Physiol. Chemie,* II. 47.

namely, that the addition of water, so far from weakening, *increases* the power of the gastric juice. In this fact we see the impropriety of that advice so often given by writers on Dietetics, to abstain from drinking at dinner, "because," as they assert, "liquid dilutes and weakens the gastric juice." Plausible as this assertion is, we see that it is directly contrary to fact. Our best guide in such cases is instinct; our sensations tell us when to drink, and when to leave off drinking; and we may rest assured that until Science can reconcile its dicta with the dicta of instinct, Science has still something to seek. As Goethe says in *Hermann und Dorothea:*

> "Ich tadlo nicht gern was immer dom Menschon
> Für unschädliche Triebe die gute Mutter Natur gab.
> Denn was Verstand and Vernunft nicht immer vermögen, vermag oft
> Solch ein glücklicher Haug, der unwiderstehlich uns leitet."[*]

Curiously enough, the digestion of albuminous substances is aided by the presence of *fat*. Whether this influence is simply one of contact (*catalysis*, as the chemists say), or whether the fat itself undergoes some slight chemical change, is undetermined; and at any rate, the quantity changed must be so small as to escape our estimate. The fact having been ascertained, we are led to speculate on its application. May not the custom of our eating bacon or ham with chicken, and not with ducks and geese, have something to do with it?

Saliva also lends its aid in the digestion of albuminous substances, although incapable of itself acting on them. Bidder and Schmidt, indeed, found that it hindered the digestion of coagulated albumen; but Donders found that cooked flesh was more rapidly digested when saliva was mingled with the gastric juice, than when the gastric juice alone was used; and even coagulated albumen was seen to be more rapidly digested when the gastric juice was made alkaline by the addition of saliva, in the case of the Esthonian peasant previously mentioned.[**]

---

[*] Of which the reader must accept the following prose version: — "I do not readily blame any harmless impulse which the kind Mother, Nature, has given to man. For often, the end which the understanding and reason are unable to attain, is arrived at by a happy instinct or inclination irresistibly leading us."

[**] DONDERS: *Physiologie*, I. 219.

The preceding paragraph suggests a serious doubt respecting the current theories on the chemistry of Digestion, and is apparently subversive of all those experiments which went to show that digestive power was intimately connected with the acid in the gastric juice. And I am the more disposed to call attention to this difficulty, because nothing is more certain than that a large quantity of alkaline saliva is normally present in the stomach, yet in spite thereof we know that digestion goes on; while it is equally certain that outside the organism, in artificial digestion, alkalies arrest the power of the gastric juice. Here are two contradictory facts: the alkaline saliva is found not to arrest Digestion in the stomach, and alkalies are found to arrest it out of the stomach. Can they be reconciled?"

In a former chapter (see p. 76) attention was called to the complication of all vital problems by the necessary interference of the organism itself. We have an illustration in Digestion. *In the organism*, although the alkali of the saliva may neutralise a certain amount of the acid of the gastric juice, it stimulates the gastric follicles to an *increased secretion*, so that, over and above the quantity neutralised, there is a *larger* quantity of gastric juice produced for the purposes of Digestion; and thus *in* the organism, saliva has practically a contrary result from that which it produces *out* of the organism.

Nor is this a mere hypothesis, without the warrant of analogy; for if carbonate of soda be administered with iron, the iron is more rapidly attacked by the gastric juice than when administered without the alkali; and this, says Bernard, is owing to the greater secretion of gastric juice which the carbonate of soda determines.

4. *Quantity of Gastric Juice.* — The quantity of gastric juice daily secreted has been very differently estimated, but the calculations of Bidder and Schmidt give the enormous amount of thirty-one pounds, or nearly one quarter of the whole weight of the body.[*] The quantity is of course variable. It depends on physical and mental conditions, and on the nature of the food

---

[*] At the Leeds Meeting of the British Association, Dr. Harley stated that he had never found any animal secrete more than one-tenth of its own weight in the twenty-four hours.

eaten; some substances exciting a more active secretion than others. The *quality* is also variable. Grünewaldt and Schröder found the gastric juice of the Esthonian peasant very different under different conditions. When Grünewaldt examined it, the woman was living well, at his expense, and in comfortable quarters; her gastric juice then contained 43 parts of solid matter in 100, and of these 43 no less than 36 were *pepsin*. When Schröder examined it, the woman had been living for some months on spare diet in her own hut, and her gastric juice then, instead of 43 parts in 100, contained only $5\frac{1}{4}$ parts of solid; and instead of 36 parts of pepsin, only 3 appeared!

In presence of differences so great as these, we must hesitate before drawing general conclusions from particular cases. We may also understand from it how food may be digestible at one time, which at another is indigestible.

To close these details respecting gastric juice, it may be mentioned that calculations have been made respecting the quantity of albumen which definite amounts are capable of dissolving. Lehmann estimates that 100 grammes* of juice dissolve 5 grammes of coagulated albumen, on the average. Schmidt estimates it at no more than 2 or 3 grammes. But even if we accept the largest of these quantities, we are forced to admit that the whole amount of the gastric juice secreted during the day would not suffice to dissolve more than *half* the albumen necessary for nutrition—another proof that stomachal Digestion is only one part, and that not the chief part, of the digestive process.

5. *Results of Inquiry.*— Let us now sum up in a few brief propositions the net results at which we have arrived respecting stomachal Digestion: —

1. In the stomach the food is churned, macerated, disintegrated, and much of it liquefied.

2. The Fats have been liberated from their cellular envelope, and have become Oils.

3. The Sugars have been little altered. The cane sugar has been changed into grape sugar, and probably a small proportion has been changed into lactic acid.

* A gramme is somewhat more than 15 grains.

4. The Vegetable matters have been more or less divided and made pulpy, but not chemically altered, except some of their starch, which has been altered by the saliva.

5. The Albuminous matters have been macerated, and some portion transformed into peptones. The whole has become a pulp.

Bernard, as we before stated, compares the action of gastric juice on fatty, saccharine, and albuminous matters, to that of boiling water. Boiling liquefies fat by dissolving the cellular envelope; gastric juice does no more, but it does so at a considerably lower temperature. Starch and sugar are not changed by boiling, except that they take up a proportion of water, which makes them what the chemists call *hydrates;* this also, he maintains, is the sole change effected in them by the gastric juice. Boiling *dissolves* the gelatinous parts of the bones and skin, leaving the earthy parts, and the muscular fibre, simply dissociated, but not altered; so does the gastric juice. Finally, Bernard calls attention to the fact that the *intestinal* fluid digests meat which has been boiled, but not raw meat — which shows that boiling may *replace* the action of gastric juice.

Were then the ancients correct in the supposition that stomachal Digestion is merely a process of cooking? To a great extent, yes. The process is in many respects analogous. It differs, however, in one important point, namely; the chemical transformation of the food into *peptones.*

6. *Action of Gastric Juice on the Stomach.* — Before quitting this subject we must glance at another ancient opinion, not yet universally discarded. When one of the Alchemists announced that he had discovered an *universal solvent*, Kunckell the chemist, with quiet wit, asked, "In what kind of vessel do you keep it?" The difficulty which Kunckell felt in conceiving a vessel that could resist the action of an *universal* solvent, was felt by the physiologists, who proclaimed that gastric juice was an universal solvent of animal substances which nevertheless did *not* dissolve the stomach. What protected the stomach? The mysterious entity, named "Vital Principle," which was the *deus ex machinâ*, and universal refuge in cases of difficulty, seemed to them the sole possible cause of this immunity enjoyed by the stomach. In

proof, they appealed to the fact that in the dead body the stomach is sometimes seen to be attacked by the gastric juice. Not content with attributing this immunity of the stomach to the Vital Principle, which "suspended the action of chemical laws," they urged this fact of immunity in the living stomach as a proof of the existence of that very Vital Principle which effected it. Logicians call this arguing in a circle; but let us see if we cannot explain the facts without having recourse to any Vital Principle suspending and superseding chemical laws. *

In the first place, as a matter of fact, the Vital Principle, granting its existence, has *no* power whatever of arresting the action of gastric juice. The proof is easy. Place a little juice under the skin of a *living* animal, and you will find in a short time that the cellular tissue is dissolved, and the parts in contact with the fluid chymified. Bernard kept the hinder extremities of a living frog in contact with gastric juice, and found they were digested by it, in spite of that Vital Principle which, according to its advocates, can suspend all chemical laws.

We thus see that it is not the mere fact of the animal being alive which prevents the gastric juice from acting on its stomach, Life having no mysterious power of "suspending" such actions; but that, whether dead or alive, the gastric juice will dissolve animal tissues. Why then is the stomach protected during life? For precisely the same reason that many poisons which rapidly destroy life when entering the blood, as in wounds, are perfectly harmless when entering the stomach. The savage slays his game with poisoned arrows, and eats the poisoned flesh with impunity. This is an interesting, but by no means mysterious, fact. The poison is harmless in the stomach because it cannot be absorbed from the stomach; and unless it be absorbed, and enter the blood, it cannot operate as a poison. There is no question of a Vital Principle here; it is simply a question of Absorption. Let but the epithelial lining** of the stomach be destroyed in any

* In our final chapter, on LIFE AND DEATH, we shall examine this ancient hypothesis of a Vital Principle, and expound the modern substitute for it.

** The *epithelium*, or delicate layer of cells which lines the wall of the stomach, is another form of that layer of cells called *epidermis*, or scarf skin (see fig. 2, p. 24) which is the outermost and protecting membrane of the body.

spot, and the poison will there enter in spite of a Vital Principle. The case is analogous with the gastric juice; the pepsin cannot be absorbed, because the epithelial lining of the stomach opposes that absorption. This epithelium, however, is very rapidly and easily destroyed; and in the dead stomach the *destruction*, not being compensated by as rapid a *renewal*, leaves the tissue unprotected against the action of the gastric juice. *

Life therefore endows the stomach with immunity, not because Life suspends the ordinary actions of matter, but because it here *renews* the protecting epithelium as fast as it is destroyed; and thus the phenomenon is explained by clear physiological principles, without invoking the interference of a Vital Principle, the very essence of which is inconceivable, and its modes of action wholly supposititious.

III. INTESTINAL DIGESTION. — The food has become *Chyme;* we have now to trace its transformation into *Chyle.* It has been, so to speak, cooked; we have now to see it digested.

The pulpy mass of Chyme enters from the stomach into the intestinal canal, and there undergoes its final changes during its passage through an organ the enormous size of which (*thirty feet,* and upwards, in length) is alone sufficient to indicate its importance; and this indication is further borne out by the fact that large and important glands, such as the Liver and the Pancreas, pour their secretion into it. This thirty-feet canal is by anatomists distinguished as if it were two organs, though in reality it is one continuous tube. They speak of it as the Small Intestines — comprising the *Duodenum*, the *Jejunum*, and the *Ileum;* and the Large Intestines — comprising the *Cæcum*, the *Colon*, and the *Rectum* (see p. 158, fig. 7).

Here it is that *Vegetables* are made to yield whatever digestible material they contain; *fats* are reduced to an emulsion

* BERNARD: *Leçons*, ii. 406, *seq.* BASSLINGER gives a very absurd explanation — namely, that nervous influence produces a state of tension in the molecules of the tissue which prevents their being acted on. — MEISSNER, *Bericht über Physiol.*, 1857, p. 201. Since this was in type, I have learned that Dr. Harley has shown by experiment that the layer of mucus covering the walls of the stomach is the chief protector against the absorption of gastric juice. This does not disturb the argument in the text.

which permits their being absorbed; *starch* is completely converted into *glycose* (starch-sugar); and the undigested *flesh* is converted into peptones.

In the Stomach the *mechanical* processes are predominant; in the Intestine, these are subordinate to the *chemical* processes due to the influence of three fluids, the Bile, the Pancreatic juice, and the Intestinal juice. These we must now separately examine.

1. *The Bile.* — Into the first of the Small Intestines (*Duodenum*) the Liver pours its secretion of Bile at a slight distance from the stomach (see p. 158, fig. 7, B·). No less than three or four pounds of this fluid are daily poured in. The quantity is of course variable, like that of every other secretion, being dependent on individual peculiarity, and on the nature of the food eaten. Fats, and fatty foods, *diminish* the quantity in a notable degree, according to Bidder and Schmidt, who found that cats fed solely on fat secreted no more than 0.327 of a gramme per hour, whereas their secretion on ordinary diet was 0.807 grm.

Although far from denying the conclusion of these able experimenters, I cannot help pointing out a source of fallacy in this experiment, which seems to have escaped criticism. We know that the quantity of Bile secreted is always larger on a full diet than on a spare diet, larger on flesh-diet than on mixed diet; when therefore cats were fed on fat alone, they were fed on a diet which was equivalent to almost none at all, since all animals starve on fat alone. That this objection is valid may be seen in the fact that the quantity secreted by these fat-fed cats is actually the quantity which is secreted by the fasting animal. Had Bidder and Schmidt fed the cats on pure albumen, I believe they would very soon have found the secretion of Bile was no greater than that from fat diet; and for the same reason: pure albumen soon becomes equivalent to almost no food at all. The only positive conclusion I can draw from their experiment is one sufficiently curious — namely, that in spite of Bile being the most hydrocarbonaceous substance in the body, and of fat being a hydrocarbonaceous food, there seems *no* definite relation between the formation of the one and the presence of the other.

There is an important practical question directly connected with this influence of fat on the secretion of Bile. Fats are said to make people bilious.  On the other hand, some medical men advise bilious people to eat bacon for breakfast.  Now we must distinctly understand that even some medical men talk of "biliousness," when in truth the evil is simply Indigestion; and as fat, if decomposed in the stomach, produces Indigestion, fat may in *this* sense be said to make people bilious.  There is, however, a frequent "attack of biliousness" from which some unhappy people suffer, and this arises from a deficiency in the secretion of Bile.  The sluggish Liver leaves its work undone, like the over-fed servants of a great house.  The best of all stimulants is continued exercise in the open air.  But if it could be proved that fat has a tendency to diminish the secretion of Bile, we should therein see the perfect explanation of the common belief that "fats make people bilious."

In the preceding section it was noted that water increased, instead of diminishing, the digestive power of the gastric juice.  Its value in digestion is further shown in the fact that it increases the quantity of Bile — not only its amount of liquid, but also its amount of solid matter.  A dog, after eating 185 grammes of beef without water, secreted 2.289 grm. of Bile, containing 0.135 solid matter.  He was subsequently allowed to take the same weight of water — 185 grm. — without beef, and he secreted 5.165 grm. of Bile, containing 0.143 solid matter.  On another occasion, after only 25 grm. of beef and 158 grm. of water, he secreted 4.000 of Bile.  Very surprising facts, which show the immense importance of water in nutrition.

Flesh increases the secretion considerably beyond that produced by vegetable diet.

2. *The part played by the Bile.* — It would be easy to fill a small volume with the controversies which have long been raging respecting the part played by this secretion in the animal economy; but the reader will not expect anything of the kind here, and may be content with two facts which, if not absolutely beyond dispute, are at any rate fixed on so broad an inductive basis as to command confidence:  These are, First, that the Bile is formed *in* the Liver, and *by* the Liver; it does not pre-exist in the blood, although of course its elements are there:  Secondly, that it is at once a *secretion* and an *excretion:* the Liver separates

from the blood substances which it *forms anew* into a fluid, this fluid taking its part in the digestive process, afterwards to be *reabsorbed* into the blood; and the Liver also separates from the blood, or forms anew, substances which, though constituting not more than one-eighth of the whole Bile (probably much less), are ejected from the organism as injurious.*

In the stomach *Bile at once arrests Digestion*. If from any cause it has risen into the stomach, as unhappily it sometimes does, we are seized with nausea and vomiting. The evidence for this is so plain that we cannot wonder if many writers have founded on it their disbelief in the digestive influence of the Bile, which they regard as a pure excretion. They overlook one important consideration, however, and forget that, when in the stomach, Bile is out of its right place. The intestine is its right place, and *there* its influence is digestive, although it there also counteracts the action of the gastric juice.

This leads us to a very curious example of the complication and seeming contradiction of organic processes. Bile undoubtedly arrests the influence of the Gastric Juice, inside as well as outside the body. Place a piece of meat in a glass vessel with some gastric juice; the meat will soon manifest a commencement of digestion, the fibres will be dissociated, and the cellular tissue dissolved. If now a little bile be added, the digestive process is suddenly arrested: the gastric juice preserves its acidity, but loses its digestive influence. If, in a second vessel, meat be left in contact with gastric juice only, we find at the end of a few hours that a complete chymification has been effected; whereas the meat to which bile was added remains unaltered, and will continue so for a very long period.

What is the nature of this action? Bernard maintains that it is nothing else than this: the ferment *pepsin*, which is operative in gastric juice, is *precipitated*, as the chemists say (separated and thrown down), and the albuminous substances are once more rendered *insoluble*,** and cease to undergo chemical change.

The reader will remember that the albuminous substances were rendered *soluble* in the stomach by the gastric juice. On

* Comp. BIDDER and SCHMIDT, p. 217.
** BERNARD; *Leçons de Physiol. Expérimentale*, II.

reaching the intestine, and there coming in contact with the Bile, they are once more rendered *insoluble:* a yellow precipitate is formed, which sticks to the coats of the intestine; and thus, while the starchy, fatty, sugary substances continue their progress unchanged, the albuminous substances are arrested, and all that was so laboriously achieved in the stomach seems undone again. If there were nothing to counteract this influence of the bile, the digestion of meat would be impossible; fortunately the delay is temporary, and by the action of the pancreatic and intestinal juices, the albumen is once more rendered soluble.

We may now perhaps explain some points which have seemed very puzzling and contradictory. Experiments have been made which prove that when the gall duct, through which the bile pours into the intestine, is opened, and the bile by removal is prevented from entering the intestine, the animal loses weight, and dies in a fortnight or three weeks. This result is intelligible when we reflect that normally the bile is mostly *reabsorbed*, only one-eighth of it passing away as an excretion; so that the loss of all the bile must be an immense drain on the system.

But other experiments seemed flatly to contradict this result. The bile was removed, yet the animal lived on, apparently uninjured. Blondlot had a pointer who lived for five years with an artificial opening, or "fistula" in its gall duct; she annually suckled her pups, and went out shooting with her master, as if nothing were the matter. On the strength of this it has been argued that bile is an excretion, and totally useless in Digestion.

The contradiction has been explained thus: when the bile is removed, a much larger quantity of food becomes necessary, indeed as much again must be eaten, to preserve the standard weight. The extra supply of food compensates for the drain occasioned by the loss of the bile.

But we have still to prove that the bile has a digestive action. And that *some* material difference is produced by the bile is clear from the highly fetid odour of the excreta, and the unusual development of gas, when the bile is prevented from pouring into the intestine. Flatulent dyspepsia is the result of a languid secretion from the liver.

We have already seen that the action of bile arrests the

digestion of albuminous substances; on sugar and starch its action is inappreciable; on fat its action is peculiar. There is no dispute that the bile greatly assists in the absorption of fat; but *how* it does so is disputed.* Wistinghausen's experiments show that whereas oil can only be made to penetrate an animal membrane when submitted to a high pressure, it penetrates without any pressure at all, if the membrane be moistened with bile. Now all absorption in the organism takes place through membranes, and not through orifices: the absorbent vessels have no open mouths to suck up fluids; the fluids pass into them through their delicate walls.**

3. *The part played by the Pancreatic Juice.* — Under its form of "sweetbread" every one is familiar with the Pancreas. It lies along the under-side of the stomach, and pours its secretion into the intestine through a duct (sometimes two ducts) which enters a little way below the bile-duct (see p. 158, Fig. 7, W).

If Bernard's views of its function are correct, it is the most important organ in the whole course of the alimentary canal, for it possesses the property of forming *fats* into an emulsion, of transforming *starch* into sugar, and of acting on *albuminous substances* — both those precipitated by the bile, and those also which the gastric juice has not yet dissolved. But, he says, it possesses this power over albuminous substances only *after* they have been acted on by the bile. If we take food directly from the stomach, and submit it to the action of the Pancreatic Juice, *no* such effect ensues; whereas if the food taken from the stomach be first mixed with a little bile, and then submitted to the Pancreatic Juice, the digestive effect is obtained. Thus the successive actions of Gastric Juice — Bile — and Pancreatic Juice, form a necessary series.***

There has been great dispute respecting the functions thus

* Mr. Marcet has recently advanced cogent reasons for supposing that the bile assists in the absorption of the fatty acids, and that these are produced in the stomach from the fats of the food. — *Medical Times*, 28th Aug. 1858. I know only the analysis of this paper given by BROWN SÉQUARD: *Journal de la Phys.*, 1. 806.

** See the explanation of *Endosmosis* in the chapter on FOOD AND DRINK, p. 72.

*** BERNARD: *Leçons*, II. 441.

attributed to the Pancreas, and although Bernard replies to his
antagonists with great skill and ingenuity, the researches of
Colin and Bérard* place beyond a doubt that fat is absorbed
even when the Pancreas has been extirpated; and, moreover,
the fact of animals digesting when their bile is removed, proves
that the Pancreatic Juice *does* act on the food even without the
previous action of the bile. We must, therefore, somewhat
qualify Bernard's statement, and say that the action of the Pancreatic Juice alone is much less energetic than when following
that of the bile; and that although the Pancreas may greatly assist the absorption of fat, it is not indispensable to it.

The united influence of the bile and Pancreatic Juice transforms such portions of the starch as have escaped the action of
the saliva into *dextrine* and *glycose* (see p. 135), into which the
starch must pass before it can be observed; it renders the fats
easy of absorption; and it dissolves albuminous substances.

4. *The Intestinal Juice.* — Although the processes just named
are capable of digesting all alimentary substances, the process of
Digestion is not really completed by them, but is continued and
finished during the passage of the food along the whole length of
the intestine, by means of the Intestinal Juice, a fluid secreted
from the glands which are imbedded in the lining coat of
the intestine. Fig. 6, on the next page, represents three of these
glands, named after Brunner, Lieberkühn, and Peyer, their
discoverers.

The action of this Intestinal Juice has been demonstrated by
Bidder and Schmidt in the following ingenious experiment. A
coil of a dog's intestine was drawn through an opening, and a
thread tied round it, so as to cut off the influx of the gastric
fluids; into this intestine, small muslin bags were introduced,
containing coagulated albumen and meat; the coil was then replaced. After periods of from six to fourteen hours, the dogs
were killed. The bags were found in different regions of the intestine, some having scarcely moved, some having been carried
down as far as the cæcum (Fig. 7, *q*, p. 158); but in every case
the albumen and meat were more or less changed, and had lost

* See MEISSNER: *Bericht*, 1857, p. 205.

weight, some having lost 18, and others 85 per cent of their solids.

Fig. 6.

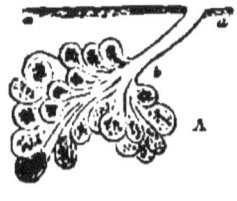

GLANDS IN THE INTESTINE WHICH SECRETE THE INTESTINAL JUICE.

A. *Brunner's gland* — *a a* the mucous membrane of the intestine; *b* the grape-like gland, each lobe of which pours its secretion through a common duct.

B. *Lieberkühn's glands*, being finger-like depressions of the mucous membrane, very like the glands in the stomach.

C. *Peyer's glands* — the one to the right is empty, its contents having been discharged: these are figured above. Peyer's glands project on the surface of the intestine, instead of being depressions from it.

In the Sea-Hare (*Aplysia*) I have more than once traced this action of the intestine. The food quits the stomach in a very imperfect state of digestion, and may be traced gradually along the whole length of the intestine, digestion not being finally completed till the *colon* is reached. Indeed, *a priori*, one might have drawn such a conclusion. The function of Digestion is performed by the whole alimentary canal, and if particular parts of this canal have a special office, in virtue of some special development, the whole organ is necessary for the whole result.

p Parotid gland;
g submaxillary
gland; g' sublin-
gual gland; œ
œsophagus or gul-
lot; cc carotid ar-
teries; pp lungs,
that on the left
being opened to
show the bron-
chial tubes, ar-
teries, and veins;
VC' superior vena
cava; k aorta; h
right auricle of
the heart; h' left
auricle; f right
ventricle; o left
ventricle; p' pul-
monary artery; tt
thoracic duct; F
liver; B gall blad-
der, entering the
intestine by the
duct B'; E sto-
mach; R spleen;
S Pecquet's reser-
voir; j lympha-
tics; æ mesenteric
ganglia; VP trunk
of portal vein; Vp
Vp branches of
portal vein; W
pancreas; VC in-
ferior vena cava;
d duodenum; Vl
lacteals; i small
intestine; q cœ-
cum; r colon, or
large intestine.—
After Bernard.

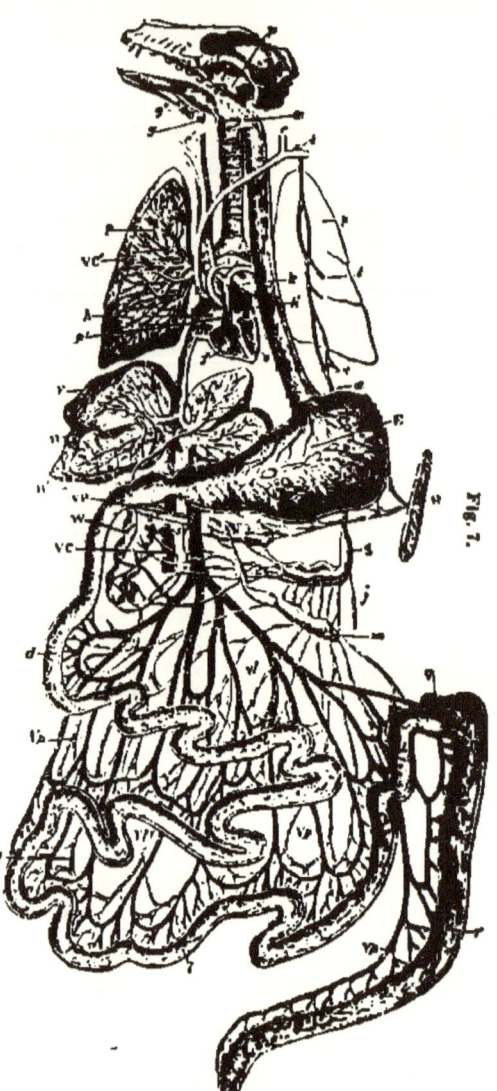

Fig. 7.

THE DIGESTIVE TRACT.

IV. The Nature of the Chyle. — We have thus completed our history of tho digestive process. The food has become Chyme, the Chyme has become Chyle, and the Chyle will be absorbed, and become Blood.

The preceding diagram, copied from Bernard, may assist the amateur in following the course of the digestive tract.

In the mouth the food is acted on by the saliva issuing from the *parotid* (p), the *submaxillary* (g), and the *sublingual* glands (g''). It passes along the *œsophagus* (œ), and reaches the *stomach* (E), whence it passes into the *duodenum* (d), and the whole length of the *small intestine* (i), to the *cœcum* (q), and *colon* (r).

During its course, such portions of the food as have become soluble are absorbed — 1, by the *Portal Veins* (Vp), which carry them to the *Liver* (F), and, 2, by the *lacteals* (Vl), minute absorbent vessels which carry them to the *reservoir of Pecquet* (S), from whence they are transmitted by the *thoracic duct* (tt) to the *subclavian vein*, where they join the blood. The other parts of this diagram will be explained hereafter. Meanwhile, if the reader considers for a moment the immense preponderance of the absorbent portal veins over the absorbent lacteals, he will see that the popular notion of the Chyle, which is found in the lacteals, being the quintessence of the food, is altogether erroneous. If we call Chyle that which is found in the intestine before absorption, we may, be justified in the assertion that the object of digestion is to make Chyle. But if we suppose that the fluid circulating in the chyliferous vessels (lacteals) is all the Chyle, we shall greatly err. *This* Chyle is really little more than ordinary lymph and fat. The chief part of the digested food, chief in quality as in quantity, *never* enters the lacteal vessels, but is carried by the portal veins to the liver. Comparative anatomy, teaching as it does that birds have *no* lacteals, that reptiles have none, and that fishes have none, plainly teaches that the function of these vessels must be special, and Claude Bernard maintains that it is limited to the absorption of fat.

V. Causes of Indigestion. — In unfolding the various stages of the digestive process, we have at the same time unfolded

several of the causes which may disturb that process, and
afflict human beings with a slight or terrible attack of Indigestion.

It is certain that if the food be not well masticated and
saturated with saliva, we must have the powerful gastric juice of
a dog, or a lion, to compensate this deficiency; otherwise a
larger proportion of the unchanged food will be transmitted to
the intestines than they can well manage, or will lie like a load
oppressing the stomach. The starch will descend in lumps, and
although much of it will be dissolved by intestinal digestion,
some will pass away undigested.

If the secretion of Gastric Juice be languid, or if that fluid be
not sufficiently acid, chymification will be laborious and painful.
If the bile rise in the stomach, digestion will cease; if the secretion of bile be too scanty, the food will lie like a burden, and produce diarrhœa or sickness; and so on to the end of the chapter.
Let there be only a little less acid, or a little more alkali, each
of which depends on complex conditions, and Digestion, which
to the young and healthy is as easy as it is delightful, becomes
the source of misery.

Ill-selected food is one source of these evils; but it has been
touched on in a previous chapter, and need not detain us now.
Want of fresh air and exercise is another source. The action of
the liver is particularly affected by exercise; and all who suffer
from biliousness should pay their fees to the livery stable and
waterman, horse-exercise and rowing being incomparably the
best of prescriptions. A walking excursion, especially in mountain districts, and with resolute avoidance of walking too much,
will be of great service to the dyspeptic. It is important to bear
in mind, moreover, that although sedentary habits are very injurious to the Digestion, they are less so than bad ventilation;
those who sit long, and sit in bad air, are sure to suffer. We shall
touch on this point in the chapter on RESPIRATION AND SUFFOCA-
TION.

The influence of the Nervous-System is perhaps even more
prominently manifested than that of any other cause of Indigestion. It is comparatively rare to meet with Indigestion among
artisans, in spite of their ill-cooked food, their exposure to all

weathers, and other hardships; and it is as rare to meet with
good Digestion among the artisans of the brain, no matter how
careful they may be in food and general habits. Protracted
thought, concentrated effort in the directions of Philosophy,
Science, or Art, almost always exact a terrible price. Nervo-tis-
sue is inordinately expensive. But it is worthy of remark, that
mere intellectual activity, when unaccompanied by agitating
emotion, never seems to affect the Digestion, unless the effort be
of an unusual intensity. Our passions are destroying flames.
Anger, Ambition, Envy, Despair, Sorrow, and even sudden Joy,
immediately disturb the digestion. A letter bringing bad news,
the sight of anything which painfully affects us, a burst of temper, or an anxious care, will sometimes render the strongest of
us incapable of digesting a meal. If the food be swallowed, it
will not be digested, or digested only at a vast expense. And
herein may be learned a lesson against a very common mistake
committed by very sensible people. When a friend is over-
whelmed with grief, we try to force him gently to take the food
he obstinately refuses. "Do try and eat a mouthful: it is necessary for your strength; you will fall ill." Perhaps our entreaties
succeed; he takes a little food "as a support." Error! the food
will weaken, not strengthen him. In such cases Instinct may
safely be relied on. When a man is hungry, he will eat. When
he will not eat, he should be left in peace until hunger prompts.
If in compliance with the entreaties of friends he takes a meal,
it will do him harm rather than good. There are, indeed, people
who think that to eat in times of sorrow, is a proof of want of
feeling, and that their appetite is a sign of disrespect; as if appetite were subject to the will. Such people must be reasoned
with, and told that it is as foolish to refuse food when the appetite
demands it, as to eat it when the system rebels against it.

There is another direction in which the Nervous System influences Digestion, although it can only be briefly alluded to
here. When we come to treat of nervous phenomena, we shall
more particularly examine the nature of Reflex Action; at present it is enough to say, that certain parts of the organic mechanism are so intimately allied in action, that they are said to *sympathise* with each other. All parts of the alimentary canal sym-

pathise. Whenever the saliva is profusely secreted, the gastric
juice "sympathises," and is also secreted; and any irritation of
the mucous membrane of the stomach increases the flow of saliva.
This is a fact to be borne in mind, the more so as few persons
seem thoroughly aware of it, although it serves as a simple indication of an irritated state of the stomach, which they might well
note. In my own person I have frequent experience of it; and
the presence of an unusual flow of saliva is always a warning to
me that the mucous membrane of my stomach is affected. Dr.
Gairdner mentions the remarkable case of a man who secreted
from six to eight ounces of saliva during a meal of broth which
was injected into his stomach; and the reverse has been observed — an excitation of the nerves of taste producing a flow
of gastric juice and bile.*

The deduction from these facts is simple and important. All
who are troubled with a deficiency of gastric juice should be
careful to let their food be as full of *flavour* as possible. Tasteless
food, by leaving the nerves of taste comparatively quiet, leaves
the secretion of gastric juice proportionately feeble. Food
which has a relish can be more easily digested. Every one
knows that we can eat a variety of dishes with less labour in digestion, than a smaller quantity of one kind of food, simply because the variety of "relish" makes the digestive process more
active.

It is, I conceive, from the same law of sympathetic action that
smoking, after a meal, assists digestion. There has been much
discussion respecting the injuriousness of smoking, ever since
Tobacco was first discovered; but as Physiology was — and still
is in most circles — little understood, a very considerable amount
of nonsense has been, and continues to be, uttered on this question. It is a positive fact that the gastric secretion can at any
time be produced by simply stimulating the salivary glands with
tobacco; and, as before stated, whatever stimulates the secretion
of saliva promotes that of the gastric juice. Smoking does this.
A cigar *after* dinner is therefore to that extent beneficial. Not
so *before* a meal.

* GAIRDNER: *Edin. Med. and Surg. Journal*, xvi. 355; BROWN SÉQUARD:
"Lectures" in *Lancet*, Nov. 1858, p. 467.

But the action of tobacco is not confined to this — it has other influences, some beneficial, some injurious; the amount of injury depends on the nature of the organism; and therein each person must judge for himself. There is only one caution which it is right to place before the reader. When tobacco is said to be not injurious, but beneficial, it must always be understood to mean tobacco in small quantities. Excess in tobacco is very injurious; so also is excess in alcohol; so also would be excess in mutton-chops. All excess is dangerous. All stimulants should be used sparingly. Yet the man who never thinks of exceeding his half a pint of wine, or pint of beer, daily, makes no scruple of smoking a dozen cigars. From my own experience, rendered vigilant as I am by a delicate digestion, and an easily disturbed organism, I can conscientiously say that two cigars daily, always taken after, and never before, the chief meals, have proved themselves to be decidedly beneficial in many directions; but I should no more think of increasing that quantity, than of increasing my daily quantity of coffee or beer. Other organisms could of course endure greater quantities. Each must determine the proper limit for himself, and having determined it, *abide* by it.

Among the many slight causes of impaired digestion is to be reckoned the very general disregard to eating between meals. The powerful digestion of a growing boy makes light of all such irregularities; but to see adults, and often those by no means in robust health, eating muffins, buttered toast, or bread-and-butter, a couple of hours after a heavy dinner, is a distressing spectacle to the physiologist. It takes *at least four hours to digest a dinner;* during that period the stomach should be allowed repose. A little tea, or any other liquid, is beneficial rather than otherwise; but solid food is a mere encumbrance: there is no gastric juice ready to digest it; and if any reader, having at all a delicate digestion, will attend to his sensations after eating muffin, or toast, at tea, unless his dinner has had time to digest, he will need no sentences of explanation to convince him of the serious error prevalent in English families of making tea a light meal, quickly succeeding a substantial dinner.

11*

Regularity in the hours of eating is far from necessary; but regularity of *intervals* is of primary importance. It matters little at what hour you lunch or dine, provided you allow the proper intervals to elapse between breakfast and luncheon, and between luncheon and dinner. What are those intervals? This is a question each must settle for himself. Much depends on the amount eaten at each meal, much also on the rapidity with which each person digests. Less than four hours should never be allowed after a heavy meal of meat. Five hours is about the average for men in active work. But those who dine late — at six or seven — never need food again until breakfast next day, unless they have been at the theatre; or dancing; or exerting themselves in Parliament; in which cases a light supper is requisite.

———

We have thus traced Food through its metamorphoses into Chyle. As Chyle, it is absorbed by the lacteals and veins to join the Blood. It is this complex fluid which we have now to examine.

———

# CHAPTER IV.

## THE STRUCTURE AND USES OF OUR BLOOD.

Blood the river of life — Erroneous notions about medicines "purifying" the blood — How it circulates — Capillary vessels — The substances it carries: iron and soap — The blood-discs: their discovery by Malpighi and Leeuwenhoek — Hewson's researches — Size of the discs in various animals — The nucleus — The colourless corpuscles: analogy between them and the Amœbæ — What is an Amœba? — The parasite which lives in our blood — Development of blood-cells — Is the blood alive? — Coagulation and its cause — Chemical composition of the blood — Variations of, in different people — Differences between arterial and venous blood — The gases they contain — Cause of the change of colour — The marvel of the circulation — Quantity of our blood — Blood-letting — Transfusion: history of the attempts; when it may be successfully employed — Blood does not form the organs — Vivifying elements of blood: arterial nourishes, and venous excites the tissues — Oxygen as a condition of nutrition — How does the blood nourish? — Each organ determining the nutrition of the rest — Relation between circulation and assimilation.

BLOOD is a mighty river of life! It is the mysterious centre of chemical and vital actions as wonderful as they are indispensable, soliciting our attention no less by the many problems offered to speculative ingenuity, than by the important practical conclusions to which our ideas respecting the Blood necessarily lead. By some the Blood is regarded as the source of all diseases, and to "purify the Blood" is the object of their treatment. Many quacks seize on this notion, and in sublime ignorance of the nature of the Blood they profess to purify, and of the means by which their drugs could possibly purify it, make fortunes out of the credulity of the public. I would warn my readers at the outset against this notion of "purifying" their Blood. Not that the Blood is always healthy and pure, free from hurtful substances, and rich in needful substances; but Nature herself takes this purification in hand, whenever it is possible — or, to speak less ambiguously, the organic processes upon which our existence depends for its continuance are themselves the means by which the Blood is kept at its proper standard, hurtful substances removed, and needful substances carried to it. The Blood is not like a river into which anything, and in any amount, may be introduced from without. It gets rid of, or destroys, all substances which do not form part and parcel of its own structure; or, failing in that, it ceases to act as living blood. And of those substances which form part and parcel of its structure, it will only take up, or retain, certain definite quantities — the surplus is rapidly got rid of. Let a man drink gallons of water, and his blood will not be more watery than before. Let him take quantities of salt, and his blood will not be more saline. In the incessant changes which take place within the circulating system, the Blood itself constantly tends towards uniformity of composition.

Nor is this all. On the supposition that we could "purify the blood" of a diseased patient, nothing would be gained by it, as respects his cure; for the malady under which he labours does not lie in the blood, but in the tissues; and when they are in a diseased condition, it is of no use to present them with purer blood; because, although they take from the blood all the materials for their nutrition, they can only take such as their condition allows. But we shall explain this more fully hereafter.

This river of Life is impetuously rushing through every part of the body, by means of an elaborate network of canals. In the course of the year, these canals carry not less than three thousand pounds' weight of *nutritive* material *to* the various tissues, and three thousand pounds' weight of *wasted* material *from* the tissues.

At every moment of our lives there is something like ten pounds of Blood rushing along in one uninterrupted throbbing stream, from the heart through the great arteries, which branch and branch like the boughs of a tree, the vessels becoming smaller and smaller as they subdivide, till they are invisible to the naked eye, and are then called *capillaries* (hair-like vessels), although they are no more to be compared in size with hairs, than hairs are to be compared with cables. These capillaries form a network much finer than the finest lace — so fine, indeed, that if we pierce the surface, at almost any part, with the point of a needle, we open one of these vessels and let out its contents. But as even this will not convey an idea of the fineness of the capillary network, we will give a figure of the vessels on the surface of a rabbit's liver, magnified eleven times.

This, which we have copied from Virchow, shows us how densely crowded the vessels are; they seem to form nearly the whole bulk of the liver.

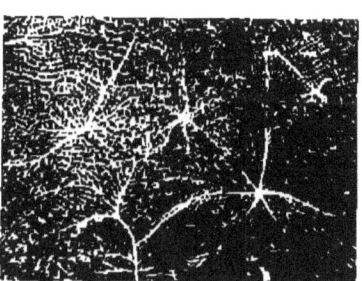

CAPILLARY BLOOD-VESSELS OF THE LIVER.

Through the *walls* of these capillaries, the Blood suffers some of its nutritive material to ooze, receiving in exchange the worn-out material of the tissues. The Blood has now ceased to be arterial, and has become venous. The stream continues its course through the veins, which, commencing in the capillaries, reverse the arrangement we noticed in the arteries, and become less and less numerous, their twigs becoming branches, and their branches trunks, till they reach the heart.

In this ceaselessly-circulating stream forty or more different substances are hurried along: it carries gases, it carries salts, it carries metals — nay, it carries what may be called soaps. The iron, which it washes onwards, can be separated; and Prof. Bérard used to exhibit a lump of it in his lecture-room — so that one ingenious Frenchman was led to suggest that coins should be struck from the metal extracted from the blood of great men! Lest this statement should mislead the reader, I will add that the quantity of iron in the blood is extremely small; but as the quantity of blood is large, and is perpetually being renewed, it affords the chemist the means of extracting a lump of iron from it.

Let us now examine the principal constituents of this organic structure — first its solid, and then its liquid parts.

1. *The Blood-discs.* — Although to the naked eye the blood appears a simple fluid, having a colour more or less scarlet, the microscope assures us that it is a fluid which carries certain solid bodies of definite shape and size — so definite, indeed, that a mere stain, no matter where, will, to the experienced eye, betray whether it be the blood of a mammal, a bird, a reptile, or a fish.

Prick your finger with a needle, place the drop on the glass-slide under your microscope, cover it with a thin glass, and

Fig. 9.

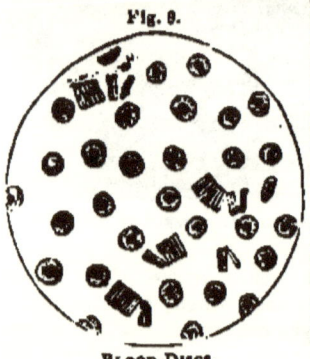

BLOOD-DISCS.

look. You will be surprised, perhaps, to observe that the blood which had so deep a tint of scarlet in the mass, is of a pale reddish yellow, now that it is spread out on the slide; whereupon you conclude that the depth of tint arose from the dense aggregation of those reddish-yellow *discs*, which you observe scattered about, some of them sticking together, and presenting the appearance of piles of half-sovereigns.

It is these "floating solids" of the blood upon which your attention must now be fixed. They are variously named *Blood-corpuscles*, *Blood-globules*, *Blood-cells*, and *Blood-discs*. It is a pity that one term is not finally adopted; and blood-discs seems on the whole the best, as being descriptive, without involving any hypothesis. Meanwhile, since physiologists use all these terms, the reader must be prepared to meet with all.

The first person who saw these blood-discs was undoubtedly Swammerdamm, in 1658; but as his observations were not published till a century afterwards, and as in Science priority can only rightfully be awarded to him who first publishes, the title of discoverer is given to Malpighi, who saw and described them in the blood of a hedgehog in 1661. He saw them, but did not understand them. They appeared to him to be only globules of fat.

The commencement of accurate knowledge dates from Leeuwenhoek, who, in 1673, detected them in human blood. "These particles," he says, "are so minute, that one hundred of them placed side by side would not equal the diameter of a common grain of sand; consequently, a grain of sand is above a million times the size of one such globule." *

We have now the exact measurement of these discs, which was not possible in his day. Extending his observations, Leeuwenhoek found that in birds and fishes, as well as in quadrupeds, the *colour* of the blood was due to these discs. He seems to have been puzzled by the fact, that in fishes the discs are not round, but oval; and he at first attributed this to the compression exercised by the vessels. It is instructive to hear him confess that he could not persuade himself "that the natural shape of the particles of blood in fishes was an oval; for inasmuch as a spherical seemed to me the more perfect form." **
He was too good an observer, however, to permit such metaphysical conceptions long to mask the truth, and, accordingly, he described and figured the blood-discs in the fish as oval. ***

It is to Hewson that science is indebted for the most accurate and exhaustive investigation of the blood which has been made from 1770 down to our own time; and it has been even asserted by one whose word is an authority, † that Hewson's works contain the germ of all the discoveries made in our own day.

There is something at once painful and instructive in the fact, that, after the publication of researches so precise and important as those of Leeuwenhoek and Hewson, the whole subject should have been suffered for many years to lapse into ignorant neglect; and instead of any progress being made, we find the

* LEEUWENHOEK: *Select Works*, L. 69.
** LEEUWENHOEK, *Select Works*, ll. 233.
*** In the larva of the *Ephemeron* the blood-discs are as nearly as possible oal-shaped.
† MILNE EDWARDS: *Leçons sur la Phys. et l'Anat. Comp.*, i. 44. The works of HEWSON have been edited, and in a very valuable manner, by Mr. GULLIVER, for the "Sydenham Society."

most eminent physiologists at the beginning of the present century (Richerand and Majendie, for example) denying positively
that the blood-discs existed, or that the microscope could tell us
anything about them.* Nevertheless, there is not an amateur
of the present day who is not familiar with them. Science has
carefully registered the exact measurements and forms of these
discs, in upwards of five hundred different species of animals.

Contempt of microscopic research seriously retarded the
progress of Physiology; it has its parallel in a similar contempt
inspired by the great Linnæus respecting the application of the
microscope to Botany; and as the physiologists of this century
have had to rediscover what was known to Leeuwenhoek and
Hewson, so also have the botanists had to rediscover what was
familiar to Malpighi.

2. *Influence of the Form of the Discs.* — There must assuredly be some relation between the *form and size* of these discs
and their *function;* but what that relation is, no one has yet
made out. In general, the larger discs are found in the less
advanced organisms; that is to say, they are larger in the
embryo than in the adult, larger in birds than in mammals,
larger in reptiles and fishes than in birds. But they are largest
of all in the Triton and Proteus, which being reptiles are exceptions to this rule. Nor can the rule be taken absolutely, even
within those limits we have named, since although reptiles are
less advanced in organisation than mammals, and have larger
discs, it is not the least advanced among the mammals that have
the largest discs; — for instance, the ruminants are less advanced than the quadrumana, yet among mammals the ruminants have the smallest discs; and in man they are as large
as in rodents. **

3. *Structure of the Discs.* — The structure of these bodies is
necessarily difficult of study. Leeuwenhoek, and others, observed that in the discs of the fish and reptile there is always

---

* MILNE EDWARDS notices a similar denial made by M. GIACOMINI at the
Pisa Congress of scientific men in 1839 — a denial which pretended to be
based on original investigations.

** In man their diameter varies between ₃₂₀₀ and ₃₇₀₀ of an inch; and
their average thickness is ₇₃₀₀ of an inch. VIERORDT estimates that in
about ₁₁₈ of a cubic inch there are as many as 5,055,000 of these discs.

a central spot, which appears dark, or clear, according as it is viewed by transmitted, or reflected, light. This appearance was interpreted as indicating a hole in the discs, which made them resemble quoits. But Hewson settled the point by proving the central spot to be a solid *nucleus*, which he saw escaping from its envelope, and floating free in the liquid — an observation subsequently confirmed.

It is worthy of remark that this nucleus is seen with difficulty when the blood is newly drawn from a vessel, although it speedily becomes distinct, especially if a little water be added. This has led Valentin, Wagner, Henle, Donders, and Moleschott to the conclusion that the nucleus is *not* present in living discs, but arises from *internal coagulation* on exposure of the discs to the air: a conclusion rejected by Mayer and Kölliker, the former averring that he has *seen* the nucleus while the blood-discs were still circulating in the capillaries of a young frog's foot. I have not been able to see this in the large discs of the Triton, and know not if Mayer's observation has been confirmed by any other microscopist.

The most perfect opportunity I ever enjoyed of seeing the nucleus, under the circumstances mentioned by Mayer, was with Professor von Siebold, when examining the gills of the embryo of *Salamandra atra*. This salamander brings forth its young alive; but it lives high up in the mountains, out of the reach of water, and its young would perish were they to come into the world like the young of other salamanders; namely, as tadpoles. Instead, therefore, of going through its metamorphoses in the water, the young *Salamandra atra* goes through them in its mother's body, and is born with perfect lungs, and without gills. Professor von Siebold removed two or three of these young ones before they had completed their metamorphoses, while therefore they were still in the tadpole state; and the elegant appearance under the microscope of their long delicate gills, like gelatinous fern-leaves, was exquisite. The excessive transparency of these gills rendered our observation of the circulation peculiarly favourable; but although I gave special attention to it, I could not detect the nucleus.

But there are other grounds on which I should be disposed to

accept the fact of the nucleus being normally present, and not
simply the result of coagulation: the chief of these is, that in
the embryo of every mammal we discover nuclei in the discs,
whereas in the adult animal no nuclei are discoverable, even
after long exposure to the air; and the philosophic zoologist well
knows in how many minute particulars the *embryonic* state of the
higher animals represents the *permanent* state of the lower.   In
the discs of all adult mammalia the nucleus is absent; what has
sometimes been mistaken for it is simply a central depression
of the disc, which gives it the form of a bi-concave lens.  Nevertheless, although the nucleus is absent in the adult, it is present
in the embryo.

Robin says that *almost* all the discs have a nucleus when
first the blood appears, but even then some are without it.  "By
the time the embryo has attained a length of thirty *millimètres*,
at least one-half of the discs are without a nucleus, and the
number goes on increasing, although even as late as the fourth
month a few rare examples may be found."  From that period,
he says, they are no longer visible in the *human* subject;[*] but I
have seen on two occasions what may have been the nucleus in
a few discs of a newborn kitten, and *one* in a drop of blood of
an adult mole.[**]

4.  *The Colourless Corpuscles.* — There are other bodies in
the blood beside these, and they are known as the *colourless corpuscles,* which consist of two, if not three, different kinds.   The
true colourless corpuscle (and it will be convenient to confine the
term disc, or cell, to the *red* corpuscle) is much larger than the
disc, and seems to be a round vesicle containing a number of ex-

---

* C. ROBIN: *Sur quelques points de l'Anat. et de la Phys. des globules
rouges,* in BROWN-SÉQUARD's *Journal de la Physiologie,* I. 288.

** Mr. WHARTON JONES, one of our best investigators, says that the blood
of the elephant and the horse contains a few of these nucleated discs.  NASSE
has seen them in the blood of pregnant women, and Mr. BUSK found one in
that of a man.  KÖLLIKER disputes the accuracy of these observations, and
thinks that in each case the nucleus was produced by some alteration of the
contents; and VIRCHOW makes it very probable how the optical illusion could
be produced. — *Cellularpathologie,* 1858, pp. 10 and 126.  At any rate, the
presence of nucleated discs is the indication of physiological inferiority, and
we may perhaps find them in certain cases of disease.

cessively minute particles imbedded in a gelatinous substance. This corpuscle has the property of *spontaneous expansion and contraction*, which forcibly reminds the observer of the contractions and expansions of that singular microscopic animalcule, the *Amœba*, probably the very simplest of all organic beings.

Some of my readers are probably not acquainted with even the name, much less the nature, of this microscopic animal, which is nevertheless so interesting to naturalists that a goodly array of authorities may be cited when it is mentioned. A few words of explanation will suffice here.

The Amœba is a single cell: it has no "organs" whatever, but crawls along the surface by extemporising an arm or a leg out of its elastic body; this arm or leg is speedily drawn in again, and fresh arms are thrown out; thus, as you watch it, you perceive it assuming an endless succession of forms, justifying the name of Proteus originally bestowed on it.

So like the Amœba is the colourless blood-corpuscle, that many observers have not hesitated to adopt the opinion that these corpuscles are actually animalcules, and that our blood is a select vivarium; an opinion which is not very tenable, and is far from necessary for the purposes of explanation. We may admit, and the point is of philosophic interest, that the blood-corpuscles are *analogous* to the Amœbœ, without admitting them to be parasites.

Considering the wondrous uniformity in the organic creation, considering how Life seems everywhere to manifest itself under forms which through endless varieties preserve an uniformity not less marvellous — so few and simple seem to be the laws of organic combination — there is nothing at all improbable in the idea that as the Amœba is a starting-point of the animal series, an analogous form may also be developed in the blood. In many of the lower animals the blood abounds in these Amœba-like cells. *
Moreover, the very substance of the fresh-water Polype *sometimes*

* They have been seen in molluscs, crustacea, and insects. I have seen them in the beautiful transparent *Corethra* larva.

breaks up into several distinct masses, which can in no respect be distinguished from Amœbæ.*

Although it is wrong to consider these Amœba-like corpuscles to be parasites, I may mention, in passing, that the blood *has* its peculiar parasite, and a very singular animal it is. Bilharz describes it, under the name of *Distoma hæmatobium*, as a double animal, the sexes being perfectly separate, the male lodging the female in a sort of tube extending along its stomach. With two heads and two tails, it seems only to have one body. This specimen of "two single parasites rolled into one," is only found in the blood of man, and is as limited in its choice of a home as the parasite which finds a home in the brain of the sheep (producing there the "staggers," well known to farmers), or the parasite which gives pigs the "measles."**

The colourless corpuscles are not numerous in healthy human blood, and play but a secondary part, unless we assume, with many physiologists, that they are the early stage of the red-discs. Professor Draper speaks unhesitatingly to this effect. He says there are three periods in the history of our blood-cells. Those of the first period originate simultaneously with, or even previously to, the heart — these are the embryonal cells which are colourless and nucleated. These becoming liquid internally, are developed into the cells of the second period, which are red, nucleated, and oval, like the normal cells of reptiles. The cells of the third period replace these, "the transition being clearly connected with the production of lymph and chyle corpuscles." This change takes place at the close of the second month of fœtal life; and from henceforwards no change is observable; the cells continue to be red, bi-concave, non-nucleated, and circular. "The cell of the first period is therefore spherical, white, and nucleated; that of the second, red, disc-shaped, and nucleated; that of the third, red, disc-shaped, bi-concave, and non-nucleated. The primordial cell advances to develop-

---

* Sometimes, but often not; so that the phenomenon probably depends on the state of the animal. Eckek describes a "contractile substance" in the Hydra, which he likens to the Amœba, but his figures do not at all resemble the contractile masses which I saw, and which indeed were so like Amœbæ as to make me believe at first that the Polype had swallowed them.

** BILHARZ in SIEBOLD u. KÖLLIKER's *Zeitschrift*, 1849, p. 207.

ment in different orders of living beings. The blood of the in-
vertebrated animals contains coarse granule-cells, which pass
forward to the condition of fine granule-cells, and reach the
utmost perfection they are there to attain in the colourless
nucleated cell of the first period of man. In oviparous vertebrated animals, the development is carried a step further, the
red nucleated cell arising, and in them it stops at this, the
second period. In mammals the third stage is reached in the
red non-nucleated disc, which is therefore the most perfect
form."*

The resemblance here indicated between the *transitory* forms
of the blood in the higher animals, and the *permanent* forms of
the blood in the lower animals, points at a hidden law of organic
combination which will perhaps one day be detected, and which
will effect for Biology as much as the law of definite proportions
has effected for Chemistry. No one can have studied the development of animals, without being profoundly impressed with
the conviction that there is something deeper than coincidence
in the recurrence of those forms, however transitory, which
characterise the permanent condition of some animals simpler
in organisation.

The colourless corpuscles are found by Moleschott to be far
more numerous in children than in adults. The difference between the blood of youth, manhood, and old age, is but trifling;
yet there is a continual decrease with age. Women, when in
their ordinary condition, have fewer corpuscles than men; but
during pregnancy, and other periods, the quantity increases,
without, however, reaching that in the blood of children. Albuminous food increases the quantity.**

5. *Is the Blood alive?* — After making ourselves acquainted
with these blood-cells and their history, which even the amateur
may do with pleasure and profit, we shall have to meet the question — *Is the blood alive?* — a question often debated, and not
without its interest to the speculative mind. Harvey*** held the

* DRAPER: *Human Physiology*, p. 115.
** *Wiener Med. Wochenschrift*, 1854. No. 8.
*** HARVEY: *Anatomical Exercitations concerning the Generation of Living
Creatures*, 1653. Exe. 51, p. 276.

blood to be the "primigenial and principal part, because that
in and from it the fountain of motion and pulsation is derived;
also because the animal heat or vital spirit is first radicated and
implanted, and the soule takes up her mansion in it." We see
here the influence of the ancient philosophy. Harvey further
declares, "Life consists in the blood (as we read in Holy Scrip-
ture), because in it the Life and Soule do first dawn and last
set. ... The blood is the genital part, the fountain of Life, *pri-
mum vivens, ultimum moriens*."

Harvey's views were taken up, with modifications, and argued
earnestly by Hunter, in his celebrated work *On the Blood*. The
constant objection urged against Hunter by his contemporaries
and successors, was their inability to conceive a *living liquid;*
but Milne Edwards meets this by saying that it is not the *liquid*
which is alive, but the *cells* floating in that liquid, and these he
regards as organisms.

The reader must feel that the discussion of such a question
cannot be brought to an issue, unless preceded by an accurate
definition of the terms employed. What is meant by the blood
being alive? If it be meant that an organic structure, having a
specific composition, and passing through a definite cycle of
changes — such as Birth, Growth, Development, and Death,
can truly be said to *live*, then blood, which manifests these
eminent phenomena of life, must be pronounced to be alive.

This, however, no one would think of denying. But if it be
meant that blood has an *independent* vitality, unlike the vitality
of any other tissue, a vitality which can be manifested apart
from the organism, the opinion seems wholly untenable. Blood
is vital, and has vital properties; but so has every tissue of the
body, and in no sense can we attribute to it independent life.

6. *The liquid Plasma of the Blood.* — Having touched upon the
floating solids, we must now direct attention to the liquid in
which they float. This is called the plasma, or liquor of the
blood — *liquor sanguinis*.

Although this plasma is perfectly liquid when in the vessels,
yet no sooner does it pour from them, than there separates from
it a sort of jelly, leaving behind a yellow fluid. This jelly-like
mass is *Fibrine;* the yellow fluid is the *serum*. As the Fibrine

separates, and becomes solid, it entraps some of the red-discs in its meshes, and the two are then named the *clot*. The process of becoming solid is called *coagulation*.

The following figure, copied from Virchow, represents the aspect of this coagula-
ted Fibrine, magnified 280 times. At *c* the discs may be observed entrapped in the mesh-es. The Fibrine itself takes the form of fine and broad fibres, as seen at *a* and *b*.

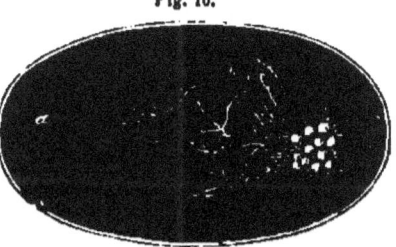

Fig. 10.

FIBRINE.

The fact of coagula-tion has always been known; indeed, it could not have escaped observation, being the almost constant result of exposure of blood to the air. The blood of all vertebrate, and many invertebrate animals, has this pro-perty; but having observed in several of the Mollusca that no coagulation takes place, I propose, when my researches are finished, to draw up a list of all the animals which are thus ex-cepted from the general law, hoping that these data will furnish some interesting result.

Although the fact was known to the ancients, it was only in the 17th century that this coagulation was discovered to be de-pendent on the solidification of a peculiar substance. Malpighi* washed the clot free from its discs, and found that the remaining substance was a mass of white fibres. Borelli, at the same epoch, declared this substance to be liquid in the blood, and that it coagulated spontaneously when the blood was drawn from the veins. Ruysch discovered that by whipping the blood, as it poured out, the whipping twigs were covered with a mass of white elastic filaments, exactly similar to that which was got in washing the clot free of its discs.

This substance was named Fibrine by Fourcroy, and it was universally believed to be identical with the substance of muscu-lar fibre. The idea was too plausible not to be at once accepted.

* MALPIGHI: *Opera Omnia*, 1866, p. 123; cited by MILNE EDWARDS.

The formation of muscle-fibres from fibrine seemed the easiest thing in the world; although really, when the idea comes to be closely examined, it is as wide a departure from all that we know of the formation of muscle, as the notion of eating brains to get more brains, or drinking milk to make milk. We now know that blood-fibrine is *not* the same substance as muscle-fibrine (which is called *musculine*, or *syntonin*), and we know that muscles are not formed by this spontaneous coagulation.

What fibrine is, whence it comes, and what purpose it subserves, are questions upon which science is at present so far from settled that I shall say nothing here about them.*

There is one point, however, which must be noticed. It has been universally held that the coagulation was simply the solidification of the liquid Fibrine. Nor can there be any doubt but that the chief part is played by the Fibrine. Nevertheless, some observations of Claude Bernard tend to show that the blood entirely deprived of its fibrine can and will coagulate. He whipped out all the fibrine from some blood, and found that, even when it was impossible to get any more, the blood subsequently coagulated. He found, moreover, that the blood of the veins from the kidneys contains no fibrine, yet it coagulates. And he reminds us that pancreatic juice sometimes shows a kind of coagulation which cannot be attributed to the fibrine.**

While it thus seems as if blood could coagulate without fibrine, it is known that blood will sometimes not coagulate even when its fibrine may be assumed to be present. Thus Dr. Richardson, to whose valuable researches this question is greatly indebted, informs us that he had described the blood as quite fluid after death in only four cases: all these were cases in which death ensued from slow arrest of the respiration. Drs. Peters, Goldsmith, and Moses, three American physicians, have published a report on the appearance of the blood in 20 cases of death resulting from the excessive use of ardent spirits. In every

* The student will do well to consult SIMON: *lectures on Pathology*, p. 49 et seq. BROWN-SÉQUARD's *Journal*, I. p. 290. BRÜCKE: *Ueber die Ursache der Gerinnung des Blutes* in the *Archiv für path. Anat.* xii. 81. VIRCHOW: *Cellular-pathologie*, 149. BERNARD: *Liquides de l'Organisme*, I. 455, 466-8; and the works already cited of LEHMANN, MULDER, and MILNE EDWARDS.

** BERNARD: *Liquides de l'Organisme*, I. 418, 456.

case the blood was fluid and dark, was of a cherry-juice appearance, and showed no tendency to coagulate. In deaths from narcotic poisons, from delirium tremens, typhoid fever, and yellow fever, the blood is generally described as thin and uncoagulable. Dr. John Davy found the blood fluid and uncoagulable on exposure in cases of drowning, hanging, suffocation from the fumes of burning charcoal, and effusion of blood into the pulmonary air-cells."*

I said that we might assume the fibrine of the blood to be present in these cases, although it is certainly allowable to assume that it may not; but in the following curious example there can be no doubt whatever that the fibrine is present. Dr. Richardson has observed, that not only is the blood drawn by a leech entirely uncoagulable, but that the bite of the leech seems to affect even the blood remaining in the bitten vessels; since that blood continues to flow much longer from the wound, than from a wound made by the lancet; and this, he thinks, can only be because the wound is not stopped up by the coagulation.

7. *Cause of the Coagulation.* — Why does the blood coagulate out of the vessels, and not in them? The question has frequently been put, and answered in very contradictory terms. In the form in which it is often put, it seems not less idle than to ask why roses have thorns, why the cohesion of iron is greater than that of clay, or why stupid querists are not entertaining companions? Fibrine coagulates because it is the property of fibrine to coagulate, and would always do so spontaneously, were there not some obstacle present. We may study the conditions which assist, and the conditions which arrest this tendency, but it is hopeless to inquire into the cause of the tendency.

It is said that the blood would remain fluid were there no fibrine present; but this fibrine has a spontaneous tendency to coagulate, which can only be prevented by the presence of some solvent. What is that solvent? The researches of Dr. Richardson satisfactorily establish some points which go very far towards a demonstration of the true cause, namely, the presence of ammonia in the blood. He shows, in the first place, that ammonia *does* preserve the fluidity of the blood, if it be present in

* RICHARDSON: *The Cause of the Coagulation of the Blood,* 1858, p. 34.

quantities amounting to 1 in 8000 parts of blood containing 2.2 per thousand of fibrine. He shows, in the second place, that the blood does normally contain this volatile alkali, which is rapidly given off during coagulation. And he shows, moreover, that the causes which *retard* coagulation are causes which *obstruct* the giving out of ammonia, whereas the causes which *favour* the giving out of ammonia *hasten* the process of coagulation. Finally, he shows that if the vapour arising from blood be caught in a vessel, and then passed through another mass of blood, the coagulation of this second mass is suspended. The numerous and ingenious experiments by which Dr. Richardson has established these important propositions must be sought in his work, which gained the Astley Cooper prize.

There still remain some difficulties, however, which are not cleared up by this hypothesis: I refer especially to the cases in which the blood does not coagulate in spite of exposure to the air, and to several of those mentioned by Brücke in the memoir previously cited.

Brücke's hypothesis is, that contact with the living blood-vessels is the necessary condition which arrests the spontaneous tendency to coagulation. The blood of a carp, he says, will remain uncoagulated for twenty-five hours in contact with the walls of the blood-vessel; but if a glass tube be inserted, so as to preserve the blood from contact with the walls, all the blood inside the tube coagulates just as it would in the open air. This does not explain why the blood is incoagulable after death from suffocation, typhus fever, &c. In fact, we have as yet no demonstration of the cause sought, and must await the result of further researches.

8. *Chemical Composition of the Blood.* — Before concluding our description of the blood, we must glance at its chemical composition; for if the microscope reveals it to be far from a simple fluid, chemical analysis further assures us that it contains water, salts, sugars, fats, and albuminates. In spite, however, of numberless analyses made with the greatest care, our present knowledge is only approximative — a rough estimate, and that is all; the excessive difficulty of making an unexceptionable analysis being acknowledged by all who have attempted it. We

know tolerably well what the *elementary* composition is — that is to say, how many atoms of carbon, hydrogen, &c. are included in every 1000 parts; but what the *immediate* composition is — that is to say, in what forms these atoms exist in the blood — we do not know so well. The elementary composition of ox blood, when all its water is removed, is as follows: —

| | | |
|---|---|---:|
| Carbon, | . . . . . . | 519.50 |
| Hydrogen, | . . . . . | 71.70 |
| Nitrogen, | . . . . . | 150.70 |
| Oxygen, | . . . . . | 213.90 |
| Ashes, | . . . . . . | 44.20 |
| | | 1,000.00 |

The following may be taken as the nearest approach to a table of the substances which form the *immediate* composition of every 1000 parts of human blood: —

| | | | |
|---|---|---|---:|
| Water, | | . . . . . . . | 784.00 |
| Albumen, | | . . . . . . | 70.00 |
| Fibrine, | | . . . . . . | 2.20 |
| Cells, | Globulin, | . . . . . | 123.50 |
| | Hæmatin, | . . . . | 7.50 |
| Fats, | Cholesterine, | . . . . | 0.08 |
| | Cerebrine, | . . . . | 0.40 |
| | Seroline, | . . . . . | 0.02 |
| | Oleic and margaric acid, . .⎫ Volatile and odorous fatty acid, ⎬ . Fat containing phosphorus, ⎭ | | 0.80 |
| Salts, | Chloride of sodium. . . . . | | 3.60 |
| | Chloride of potassium, . . | | 0.36 |
| | Tribasic phosphate of soda, . . | | 0.20 |
| | Carbonate of soda, . . . . | | 0.84 |
| | Sulphate of soda, . . . . | | 0.28 |
| | Phosphates of lime and magnesia, . | | 0.25 |
| | Oxide and phosphate of iron, · . | | 0.50 |
| Extract, salivary matter, urea, colouring matter of bile, accidental substances, | | | 5.47 |
| | | | 1,000.00 |

In this table sugar is omitted, yet we know that sugar, in varying quantities, always exists in the blood quitting the liver, where it is formed from albuminous matters, and is also generally found in blood at other parts of the organism; but, because this sugar rapidly undergoes transformation into other substances, its amount cannot be estimated.

All analyses of the Blood hitherto have been only rough estimates. In fact, the fluid itself is constantly changing. The following table, drawn up by Lehmann,[*] gives the results of analyses of the solid red-discs, and the fluid or *liquor sanguinis*, separately examined: —

### 1000 *parts Red Discs are composed of* —

| | |
|---|---|
| Water, . . . . . . . | 688.00 |
| Solid remains, . . . . . | 312.00 |
| Specific weight, . . . . | 1.0885 |
| Hæmatin, . . . . . . | 16.75 |
| Globulin and cell membrane, . . . | 282.22 |
| Fat, . . . . . . . | 2.31 |
| Extractive matters, . . . . | 2.60 |
| Mineral substances, excluding iron,[**] . . | 8.12 |
| Chlorine, . . . . . . | 1.686 |
| Sulphuric acid, . . . . . | 0.066 |
| Phosphoric acid, . . . . . | 1.134 |
| Potassium, . . . . . | 3.328 |
| Sodium, . . . . . . | 1.052 |
| Oxygen, . . . . . . | 0.667 |
| Phosphate of lime, . . . . | 0.114 |
| Phosphate of magnesia, . . . . | 0.073 |

### 1000 *parts Liquor Sanguinis are composed of* —

| | |
|---|---|
| Water, . . . . . . | 902.90 |
| Solid remains, . . . . . | 97.10 |
| Specific weight, . . . . | 1.028 |
| Fibrine, . . . . . . | 4.05 |

[*] LEHMANN, II. 131.
[**] The iron is reckoned with the hæmatin.

| | |
|---|---|
| Albumen, . . | 78.84 |
| Fat, . . . | 1.72 |
| Extractive matters, | 3.94 |
| Mineral substances, | 8.55 |

| | |
|---|---|
| Chlorine, . . . . | . 3.644 |
| Sulphuric acid, . . . | . 0.115 |
| Phosphoric acid, . . . | . 0.191 |
| Potassium, . . . . | . 0.323 |
| Sodium, . . . . | . 3.341 |
| Oxygen, . . . . | . 0.403 |
| Phosphate of lime, . . | . 0.311 |
| Phosphate of magnesia, . | . 0.222 |

But, granting that Chemistry had succeeded in making a perfect analysis, we should still have to bear in mind that all the constituents vary in different individuals, and in different states of the same individual. The blood of no two men is precisely similar; the blood of the same man is not precisely similar in disease to what it was in health, or at different epochs of life.

The iron which circulates in the veins of the embryo, is more abundant than the iron in the veins of the mother; and this quantity declines after birth, to augment again at puberty.

The fats vary, in different individuals, from 1.4 to 3.3 in 1000.

The blood-cells vary with the varying health.

The albumen fluctuates from 60 to 70 parts in 1000, the proportion being greater during digestion.

The fibrine, usually amounting to about 3 in a 1000, may rise as high as 7½, or fall as low as 1.

9. *Arterial and Venous Blood.* — Such are the chief points ascertained respecting the blood in general. We must now call attention to the different *kinds* of blood in the different parts of the circulation; for although we speak of "the blood" as if it were always one and the same thing, it is, in truth, a system of various fluids, a confluence of streams, each more or less differing from the other.

The first grand division is familiar to all men — namely,

that of venous and arterial blood; the former being dark
purple — "black blood," as it is called — the latter bright
scarlet.

To many it will seem that this is but a distinction of colour —
a distinction so easily effaced, that no sooner does the dark blood
come in contact with the atmosphere than it brightens into
scarlet. The distinction of colour is, however, the sign of an
important difference. Between the two fluids a profound difference exists; and yet the venous blood has only to pass through
the lungs in an atmosphere not overcharged with carbonic acid,
and at once it becomes transformed into a life-giving fluid.
Wherefore? Analysis of the two detects but trifling variations
in their solids, the most notable being the larger amount of red-
discs and the smaller amount of fibrine in venous blood. But in
their gases an important difference is detected. In both there
are nitrogen, oxygen, carbonic acid, and ammonia, either free,
or combined so feebly that they are easily disengaged. The quantity of nitrogen is much the same in both; that of ammonia
probably does not vary, but the oxygen and carbonic acid vary
considerably. Indeed, there is a notion current in popular
works that venous blood contains carbonic acid, and arterial
blood oxygen — *that* being the difference between the two fluids.
But the physiologist knows that both fluids contain large
amounts of both gases, the difference being only in the relative
amounts contained in each. The experiments of Magnus were
for a long while held to be conclusive of the opinion that arterial
blood contained absolutely *more* carbonic acid than venous
blood, although in relation to the amount of oxygen the amount
was less; that, in short, it contained more of both gases, but the
larger proportion of oxygen gave it its distinction. Recent investigations have considerably shaken this conclusion, but they
leave unaltered one result — namely, that arterial blood contains a large amount of carbonic acid, and a still larger amount
of oxygen.[*]

Where does the oxygen come from? The atmosphere.
Where does the carbonic acid come from? We do not know.

---

[*] On the quantity of gases in the two bloods, see BERNARD, i. 367.

The most generally accepted hypothesis is, that the carbonic acid comes from the oxidation of tissue. On this point, however, the evidence seems to me extremely defective, but as I dare not venture here on the discussion, I will content myself with stating the received opinion, referring the student to Bernard's latest work for some grounds of doubt.[*] This is the hypothesis: The blood which flows *to* the tissues is scarlet, but in the capillaries it parts with some of its oxygen; and as it flows *from* the tissues it is dark, and will become scarlet again on its passage through the lungs. When we know that arterial blood contains carbonic acid as well as oxygen, the idea suggests itself, that on parting with some of this oxygen it might assume the dark colour, owing simply to the carbonic acid retained; but this idea is set aside by the fact that unless an *exchange* take place, no oxygen will be liberated. The carbonic acid is said to be the product of the vital activity of the tissues, and as such is taken up by the blood in exchange for its oxygen; for if the nerves which supply a limb be cut, and vital activity be thus arrested, the current of blood will not be darkened; precisely as it will not be brightened in its passage through the lungs, if there be a surplus of carbonic acid in the air. The experiments of Bruch[**] are very instructive on this point. He found that blood saturated with oxygen became darker in *vacuo*, while blood saturated with carbonic acid did not change colour.

What causes the change of colour when venous blood is submitted to oxygen? Formerly it was held to be due to the iron in the discs; but the iron may be removed without this removal affecting the phenomenon; so that the opinion now held is that the change of colour is due solely to the difference in the *form* of the discs, which become *brighter* as they become more *concave*, and *darker* as they become more *convex*. Oxygen renders them concave, carbonic acid renders them convex.

Arterial blood is everywhere the same: it is one stream perpetually flowing off into smaller streams, but always the same fluid in its minutest rills as in its larger currents.

* BERNARD: *Liquides de l'Organisme*, I. 336-346; and compare ROBIN et VERDEIL: *Traité de Chimie Anatomique*, II. 86 *et seq.*
** SIEBOLD U. KÖLLIKER: *Zeitschrift für Wissenschaftliche Zoologie*, iv. 873.

Not so venous blood. *That* is a confluence of many currents, each one bringing with it something from the soil in which it arises; the streams issuing out of the muscles bring substances unlike those issuing out of the nervous centres; the blood which hurries out of the intestine contains substances unlike those which hurry out of the liver.

Not only is venous blood different in different parts of the body, but it has even differences of colour: it is not always black, it is sometimes scarlet, without, however, ceasing to be venous. The discovery of this curious fact is due to Claude Bernard,[*] who found that, in the renal veins, during the *activity* of the kidney, the blood is always scarlet, and black during the *repose* of that organ. He has extended his observation to the sub-maxillary and parotid glands; and the conclusion he draws is this: while the venous blood from the active muscles is always black, the blood from the secreting glands, when active, is always scarlet; and *vice versâ*, the venous blood is scarlet in the muscles when they are perfectly quiet, and black in the glands when they are quiet. This leads Bernard to establish a distinction between the functional and mechanical activity of the glands: when the chemical process of forming the secretion is going on, he considers the gland to be in a state of functional activity, and then its venous blood is black; when the mechanical process of pouring out that secretion is going on, he considers the gland to be in a state of mechanical activity, and then the blood is scarlet. Although his interesting experiments open a new field of speculation, they are far from having satisfactorily established the cause of this change of colour.

Disregarding these minor variations, we may still keep to the broad distinction of scarlet and black, as characteristic of arterial and venous blood. But these variations help us to conceive how, while arterial blood is everywhere the same, venous blood is everywhere fluctuating in its composition, according to the organs from which it comes.

Wondrously does the complex machine work its many pur-

---

[*] *Mémoire lu à l'Académie des Sciences*, 25th January 1858. See his *Leçons sur les Liquides de l'Organisme*, 1859; and BROWN-SÉQUARD's *Journal*, 1858.

poses: the roaring loom of Life is never for a moment still, weaving and weaving,

"Geburt und Grab,
Ein ewiges Meer,
Ein wechselnd Weben,
Ein glühend Leben."[*]

· It is difficult for us to realise to ourselves the fact of this incessant torrent of confluent streams coursing through every part of our bodies, carrying fresh fuel to feed the mighty flame of life, and removing all the ashes which the flame has left. Sudden agitation, setting the heart into more impetuous movement, may make us aware that it is throbbing ceaselessly; or we may feel it beating when the hand is accidentally resting on it during the calm hours of repose; but even then, when the fact of the heart's beating obtrudes itself on consciousness, we do not mentally pursue the current as it quits the heart to distribute itself to the remotest part of the body, and thence to return once more — we do not follow its devious paths, and think of all the mysterious actions which attend its course. If for a moment we could with the bodily eye see into the frame of man, as with the microscope we see into the transparent frames of some simpler animals, what a spectacle would be unveiled! Through one complex system of vessels we should see a leaping torrent of blood, carried into the depths and over the surfaces of all the organs, with amazing rapidity, and carried from the depths and surfaces through another system of vessels, back again to the heart: yet in spite of the countless channels and the crowded complexity of the tissues, nowhere should we detect any confusion, nowhere any failure. Such a spectacle as this is unveiled to the mental eye alone, and we cannot contemplate it, even in thought, without a thrill.

10. *The Quantity of Blood.* — It is a natural question, and often asked, but difficult to answer, What *quantity* of blood circulates every minute in our bodies?

Anything like an accurate answer to this question is rendered impossible by the fact overlooked by most physiologists, or

* "Birth and the grave, an eternal ocean, a changing motion, a glowing life." — *Faust.*

unknown to them, that the blood necessarily *varies* in quantity
every hour.  I was surprised to find striking differences in the
amount of blood which flowed from two decapitated Tritons of,
as nearly as possible, the same size; but on proceeding to open
them, I found the one animal was in a state of active digestion,
whereas the other had not eaten for a long while.  Since this
note was made, Claude Bernard has published his experiments on rabbits and dogs, upon which he founds the startling
opinion that the blood of the same animal may, during digestion,
amount to double the quantity during fasting;* for he finds that
from a rabbit, during digestion, he can remove 30 grammes of
blood without killing it; whereas the same rabbit, fasting, is
killed by the removal of 15 grammes.  The knowledge of this
fact will be very important to surgeons about to perform any
operation which entails considerable loss of blood; and it points
also to the eminent advantage there would be in giving soldiers
a hearty meal before battle.

We thus perceive that no estimate can pretend to be very
accurate; nor need we notice those which earlier writers have
given: only those of Lehmann, Weber, and Bischoff now command general attention.  Lehmann says that his friend Weber
aided him in determining the quantity of blood in two decapitated criminals.  The quantity which escaped was thus
estimated: Water was injected into the vessels of the trunk and
head, until the fluid, escaping from the veins, had only a pale
red or yellow colour.  The quantity of blood remaining in the
body was then calculated by instituting a comparison between
the solid residue of this pale red aqueous fluid and that of the
blood which first escaped.  The living body of one of the
criminals weighed 60.140 grammes,** after decapitation 54.600
grammes, consequently 5.540 grammes of blood had escaped;
28.560 grammes of this blood yielded 5.36 of solid residue; 60.5
grammes of sanguineous water, collected after the injection,
yielded 3.724 of solid substances.  There were collected 6050
grammes of the sanguineous water that returned from the veins,

* BERNARD: *Liquides*, I. 419.
** A *Gramme* is somewhat more than 15 *grains.*

and these contained 37.24 of solid residue, which corresponds to
1.980 grammes of blood.  The estimate, therefore, turns out as
follows: 5.540 grammes escaped after decapitation, and 1.980
remained in the body, thus making 7.520 grammes; in other
words, the weight of the whole blood was to that of the body
nearly in the ratio of 1 to 8.

It is obvious from the account of the experiment that only an
approximation could be arrived at.  And Bischoff's more recent
investigations on the body of a criminal, carefully weighed before and after decapitation, lead to the conclusion that the blood
amounted to 9½ lb., or *exactly one-fourteenth of the whole body.*
This nearly corresponds with his former investigations, which
gave the weight as one-thirteenth of the whole body.

If we say ten pounds for an adult healthy man, we shall probably be as near the mark as possible.  The quantity, however,
necessarily varies in different persons, as well as in different
conditions, and seems from some calculations to be greater in
women than in men.  In the Seal its quantity is enormous, sur-
passing that of all other animals, man included.

11. *Blood-letting.* — In former days, blood-letting was one of
the "heroic arms" of medical practice; and it is sometimes almost appalling to read of the exploits of practitioners.  Haller
mentions the case of a hysterical woman who was bled one
thousand and twenty times in the space of nineteen years; and
a girl at Pisa is said to have been bled once a-day, or once every
other day, during several years.  A third case he mentions of a
young man who lost seventy-five pounds of blood in ten days; so
that if we reckon ten pounds as the utmost which the body contains at any given period, it is clear that this young man's loss
must have been repaired almost immediately.  In truth, the
blood is incessantly being abstracted and replaced during the
ordinary processes of life.  Were it not continually renewed, it
would soon vanish altogether, like water disappearing in sand.
The hungry tissues momently snatch at its materials, as it hur-

* See his Memoir in SIEBOLD u. KÖLLIKER: *Zeitschrift,* ix. 72.  HEIDEN-
HAIN: *Dingn. criticæ et experimentales de sanguinis quantitate,* also arrives at
a somewhat similar result.

ries through them, and the active absorbents momently pour fresh materials into it.

12. *Transfusion.* — In contemplating the loss of blood from wounds or hemorrhage, and in noting how the vital powers ebb as the blood flows out, we are naturally led to ask whether the peril may not be avoided by pouring in fresh blood.

The idea of *transfusion* is indeed very ancient. But the ancients, in spite of their facile credulity as to the effect of any physiological experiments, were in no condition to make the experiment. They were too unacquainted with physiology, and with the art of experiment, to know how to set about transfusion. Not until the middle of the seventeenth century had a preparation been made for such a trial. The experiments of Boyle, Graaf, and Fracassati, on the injection of various substances into the veins of animals, were crowned by those of Lower, who, in 1665, injected blood into the veins of a dog.

Two years later a bolder attempt was made on man. A French mathematician, Denis, assisted by a surgeon, having repeated with success the experiments of Lower, resolved to extend the new idea. It was difficult to get a human patient on whom the plan could be tried; but one evening a madman arrived in Paris, quite naked, and he was daringly seized by Denis as the fitting subject for the new experiment. Eight ounces of calf's blood were transfused into his veins. That night he slept well. The experiment was repeated on the succeeding day; he slept quietly, and awoke sane!

Great was the sensation produced by this success. Lower and King were emboldened to repeat it in London. They found a healthy man willing to have some blood drawn from him, and replaced by that of a sheep. He felt the warm stream pouring in, and declared it was so pleasant that they might repeat the experiment.

The tidings flew over Europe. In Italy and Germany the plan was repeated, and it now seemed as if transfusion would become one more of the "heroic arms" of medicine. These hopes were soon dashed. The patient on whom Denis had operated again went mad, was again treated with transfusion, and died during the operation. The son of the Swedish minister,

who had been benefited by one transfusion, perished after a
second. A third death was assigned to a similar cause; and in
April 1668 the Parliament of Paris made it criminal to attempt
transfusion, except with the consent of the Faculty of Paris.
Thus the whole thing fell into discredit, to be revived again in
our own day, and to be placed at last on a scientific basis.

It occurred to Majendie that the ill success of the experiments
arose from the supposition that the blood of all quadrupeds was
the same, and that it was indifferent whether a man received
the blood of another man, or of a sheep or calf. This supposition
he thought altogether erroneous. His opinion was, that only
the blood of animals of the same species can be transfused in
large quantity without fatal results. The blood of a horse is
poison in the veins of a dog; the blood of a sheep is poison in the
veins of a cat; but the blood of a horse will revive the fainting
ass. From this it followed, he thought, that when transfusion
is practised on human beings, human blood must be employed;
and so employed, the practice is in some urgent cases not only
safe, but forms the sole remedy. But the recent investigations
of Brown-Séquard have proved that transfusion is successful
with the blood of different species. Blundell has the glory of
having revived and vindicated the practice of transfusion,* and
he has seen his idea amply confirmed. Bérard cites fifteen
distinct cases of hemorrhage in which transfusion has saved
life.**

So startling and so important is this success of Transfusion,
that it is very necessary we should distinctly understand in what
cases it may with advantage be employed. And these cases are
very simple, since it is only when there has been a dangerous
loss of blood that any benefit can accrue from transfusion. In
all cases of disease it is useless, or worse. The ancients, indeed, thought that by infusing new blood into an old and failing
organism, new life would be infused; and wild dreams of a sort

---

* BLUNDELL: "Experiments on the Transfusion of Blood," *Medico-
Chirur. Trans.* 1818, p. 56.
** BÉRARD: *Cours de Physiologie,* III. 220. It is from this work, and the
*Leçons* of MILNE EDWARDS and BÉRARD, that all the details on this subject
in the text have been taken.

of temporal immortality were entertained.  Completely as these notions are banished, the initial error of supposing that the blood *forms the organs* — and that if blood be *purified* the organs will be restored to health and vigour — this error is still general, even among men of science.  It rests on a misconception of the laws of Nutrition.*  Because the organs are nourished by materials drawn from the blood, and because, unless blood be duly supplied, the organs will decay, it has been supposed that the point of departure of Nutrition was in the blood itself, and that the blood formed the organs.  It is not so.  The organs are, many of them at least, in existence before blood appears;** and even afterwards the process of Nutrition always consists in the assimilation of certain materials from the blood by the organs; not in the organisation of this blood itself.  In vain will you carry generous food to a sick stomach — it cannot digest the food; in vain will you carry young blood to old organs — they cannot draw their youth from it.  The blood is always young, for it is always being renewed.  The organs get daily older, and different.  Between the blood of an infant, and the blood of a patriarch, no appreciable difference can be found; but how great is the difference between their organs!  That which is true of old age, is likewise true of disease.  The tissue which is in an unhealthy condition cannot be made healthy by bringing to it a "purer" blood (were such obtainable); it can only be brought back to its healthy condition by the cessation of those causes which keep up the morbid action, and these are not in the blood.***

13.  *Which are the Vivifying Elements?* — Seeing that blood has a power of reanimating the failing body, it is natural we should

* These laws will be expounded in our final Chapter on LIFE and DEATH.
** The young fish *Clypeus* has been observed by Filippi to quit the egg and swim vivaciously before there is any trace of circulation — before, indeed, the blood-discs are formed. — *Annales des Sciences*, 1847, vii, 67.  If the student desires an easy mode of studying this point, let him carefully watch the development of tadpoles; and he will see, in their transparent tails, how the vessels gradually appear, and how the blood-discs, which at first are in all respects the same as the cells of the general substance, gradually lose their large fat-globules, and assume more and more the character of blood-discs.
*** On this extremely important subject the student should weigh carefully the whole of VIRCHOW'S *Cellularpathologie*.

inquire to which element of the blood this is due — to the cells, or the plasma? We know that it is only necessary to withdraw blood from a part, or prevent its access by a ligature round the arteries, and the part gradually loses all its vital ·properties; but even after the rigour of the muscles announces death, we have only to readmit the blood by removing the ligature, and the vitality will be restored.

Unless the circulation be maintained In the nerves, their power almost instantaneously disappears; which proves that in the nerves the chemical changes must be very rapid. Swammerdamm, and others since, have shown this by the experiment of tying the aorta; immediately the circulation is interrupted, the power of voluntary movement disappears. This is only true, however, of warm-blooded animals. Frogs may have the aorta tied, and still possess the power of hopping about for some hours. They will even do this for an hour, when the heart and all the viscera are taken away, according to Stilling.* Schiff thinks that they do this in virtue of the remnant of stored-up force retained in their nerves, and the remnant of blood still retained in the parts.** The difference between frogs and warm-blooded animals in this respect, seems to me solely referable to the difference in the normal rapidity of their nutritive changes. The warm-blooded animal "lives fast," and unless fresh blood be constantly present to supply the waste, the vital changes rapidly cease. The frog can live for months without food, which shows that its nutritive changes are comparatively slow. It will therefore require a much longer time before the interruption of the circulation in a frog will interrupt all manifestation of vitality, than in the case of a warm-blooded animal.

Every one knows how loss of blood causes man to faint; and how checking the action of his heart instantly produces unconsciousness. Our nervous centres demand incessant supply.

Blood, as we said at starting, is the river of life, and where it ceases to flow, all organic action soon vanishes. But blood is composed of two things — the plasma and the cells, or discs.

* STILLING: *Untersuchungen über die Functionen des Rückenmarks*, 1842, p. 38.
** SCHIFF: *Lehrbuch der Physiologie*, 1858, p. 103.

And we return to the question: Which of these is the vivifying element? It has been ascertained that the plasma of the blood, deprived of its cells and fibrine, has no reanimating power when injected, being in fact not more effective than so much warm water. It has also been ascertained that blood, deprived of its fibrine only, produces the same effect as pure blood; whereby it appears that as neither the plasma nor the fibrine possesses the vivifying power, that power must belong to the cells. This is a great step gained, but the restless spirit of inquiry cannot content itself with such a gain, and it asks, What gives to the blood-cells this specific power? Let us see the answer that can be made to such a question.

We know that the cells (discs and corpuscles) carry the oxygen, either in slight combinations, or free, as in vesicles. We know this, because we find that the blood-plasma is unable to absorb much more than one per cent of its volume of oxygen, whereas the blood containing cells absorbs from ten to thirteen times that amount. The change of colour exhibited by the discs as they take up or give out oxygen, and the fact that, if they are placed in a vessel containing air, they absorb oxygen from that air, whereas the plasma does nothing of the kind, are proofs of the cells being the transporters of oxygen.

But this is not all. The experiments of M. Brown-Séquard seem to establish the important fact that it is to the oxygen carried by these cells that we must attribute their *nutritive* agency, and to the carbonic acid carried by them that we must attribute their *stimulating* agency.*

Blood has two offices: it furnishes the tissues with their food, and it stimulates them into activity. Unless the tissues be endowed with certain vital properties, they cannot be stimulated into activity; and when stimulated, this activity brings about a destruction, which must be repaired. If stimulus be applied without equivalent nutrition, the force is soon exhausted. This double office the blood performs, according to M. Brown-Séquard, chiefly through the oxygen, as the *agent of nutrition*, and of carbonic acid, as the *agent of excitation*.

* BROWN-SÉQUARD: *Journal de la Physiologie*, 1858, I. 91.

Without accepting his conclusions in all their absoluteness, we may accept thus much of them, for we see him operating on dead animals, or dead parts of animals, by means of *venous* blood charged with oxygen, and producing therewith precisely the same effects as with *arterial* blood; and we see him showing that arterial blood, charged with carbonic acid, acts precisely as venous blood. The conclusion, therefore, is obvious, that the vivifying difference between the two fluids is simply owing to the difference in their amounts of oxygen.

He takes the blood from a dog's vein, and the blood from its artery, whips both till the fibrine be extracted, and till both have become equally scarlet from the absorption of oxygen. He then injects one of these fluids into the right thigh artery of a dead rabbit, in which the rigidity of death has set in for ten minutes, and the other fluid into the left thigh artery. The result is precisely similar in both limbs, namely, in about five minutes both recover their muscular irritability, which they both retain for twenty minutes. Repeating this experiment with blood drawn from vein and artery, but charged with carbonic acid instead of oxygen, he finds a similar result as to the *exciting* power.

Having thus made clear to himself that, as respects nutrition and excitation, there is no other difference between arterial and venous blood than is assignable to their differences in the amount of oxygen and carbonic acid contained in each; that venous blood, charged with oxygen, acts precisely as arterial blood; and that arterial blood, charged with carbonic acid, acts precisely as venous blood, M. Brown-Séquard proceeds with his demonstration, that unless the blood be highly oxygenated it has *no* power of nourishing the tissues; and unless it be highly carbonised, it has *no* power of stimulating them.

We cannot here afford sufficient space to give any account of the experiments by which these conclusions are reached, and must refer the curious reader to the memoir itself.[*] But as the idea of the stimulating power of the blood residing chiefly in the carbonic acid, will be novel and startling to most physiological readers, it may be useful to mention one of the experiments. A rabbit was suffocated; and, as usual in such cases, the intestine

* *Journal de la Physiologie*, I. 95.

exhibited very powerful disorderly movements. Into a coil of this agitated intestine he injected some *venous* blood highly *oxygenated.* Immediately the movement ceased. He then injected *arterial* blood highly *carbonised*, and the movements were at once resumed. Again he injected oxygenated blood, and again the movements ceased, to appear on the second injection of carbonised blood. "It is possible," he says, "to produce two conditions of the organism essentially different, one of which consists in the presence of a greater amount of oxygen than usual, both in the venous and in the arterial blood, the other of which consists in the presence of an excess of carbonic acid in both fluids. In the first of these conditions, life ceases in spite of the extreme energy of the vital properties, simply because the stimulating power of the blood is insufficient. In the other of these conditions, the stimulating power, being excessive, causes an activity which is soon spent, because it cannot be reproduced."

Even should we accept to the full the ingenious hypothesis just propounded, we must guard against an exaggeration of its application. Oxygen may be the one chief *condition* for that exchange between the blood and the tissues which constitutes Nutrition, and without a due supply of oxygen Nutrition may be brought to a stand-still; but we shall greatly err if we suppose that oxidation is itself the process of Nutrition, or that the cells are the sole agents. The albumen, the fats, and the salts which the tissues draw from the blood, are not drawn from the cells, but from the plasma. It is, therefore, quite possible, indeed M. Séquard's experiments render it eminently probable, that the blood-cells, by their oxygen, furnish the indispensable *condition* of Nutrition, the material being furnished by the blood-plasma. It is also probable that the cells, by their carbonic acid, furnish the condition of muscular excitement; so that arterial blood, when containing more than its usual amount of carbonic acid, causes an excess of the stimulating over the repairing processes. This may account for the greater cerebral excitement succeeded by languor, consequent on exposure to the vitiated atmosphere of a theatre, a ball-room, or a lecture-room.

14. *Relation of Blood to Nutrition.* — Such is the wondrous fluid we name Blood, and such its properties, as far as Science

hitherto has learned them. Before quitting our survey, it will be desirable to say a few words respecting the relation which blood bears to Nutrition, since that relation is not generally understood.

Every one knows that all the tissues are nourished by the blood. But in what way is this effected? Blood, in itself, is perfectly incapable of nourishing the tissues — so incapable that, if it be poured on them from the rupture of a vessel, it hinders nutrition, and acts like a foreign substance. Accordingly, we see it rigorously excluded from them, shut up in a system of closed vessels; but as it rushes along these vessels, *certain of its elements ooze through the delicate walls* of the vessels, and furnish *a plasma from which the tissues are elaborated.* In exchange, certain products of waste are taken up by the blood, and carried to the organs of excretion.

An image may render the process memorable. The body is like a city intersected by a vast network of canals, such as Venice or Amsterdam; these canals are laden with barges which carry to each house the meat, vegetables, and groceries needed for daily use; and while the food is thus presented at each door, the canal receives all the sewage of the houses. One house will take one kind of meat, and another house another kind, while a third will let the meat pass, and take only vegetables. But as the original stock of food was limited, it is obvious that the demands of each house necessarily affect the supplies of the others. This is what occurs in Nutrition: the muscles demand one set of principles, the nerves a second, the bones a third, and each will draw from the blood those which it needs, allowing the others for which it has no need to pass on.

This leads us to notice a luminous conception, attributed by Mr. Paget to Treviranus, but really due to Caspar Friedrich Wolff, whose doctrine of epigenesis reposes on it;[*] namely, that "each single part of the body, in respect of its nutrition, stands to the whole body in the relation of an excreting organ." Mr. Paget has illustrated this idea with his accustomed felicity.[**] Every part of the body taking from the blood those substances

[*] WOLFF: *Theorie von der Generation.* 1764.
[**] PAGET: *Lectures on Surgical Pathology,* L. 34 et seq.

which it needs, acts as an excretory organ, inasmuch as it removes that which, if retained, would be injurious to the nutrition of the rest of the body. Thus the polypes excrete large quantities of calcareous and silicious earths: in the polypes, which have no stony skeleton, these earths are absolutely and utterly excreted; but in those which have a skeleton, they are, though retained within the body, yet as truly excreted from the nutritive fluid and the other parts as if they had been thrown out and washed away. In the same manner, our bones excrete the phosphates from our blood. The hair in its constant growth not only serves its purposes as hair, but also as a source of removal from the blood of the various constituents which form hair. "And this excretion office appears in some instances to be the only one by which the hair serves the purpose of the individuals; as, for example, in the fœtus. Thus in the fœtus of the seals, that take the water as soon as they are born, and, I believe, in those of many other mammals, though removed from all those conditions against which hair protects, yet a perfect coat of hair is formed within the uterus, and before, or very shortly after birth, this is shed, and is replaced by another coat of wholly different colour, the growth of which began within the uterus. Surely in these cases it is only as an excretion, or chiefly as such, that this first growth of hair serves to the advantage of the individual."

Mr. Paget also applies this principle to the explanation of the rudimental hair which exists all over our bodies, and to that of many other rudimental organs, which subserve no function whatever. He also, without apparently being aware of Wolff's ideas on this point, applies it to the explanation of the embryonic phases. "For if it be influential when all the organs are fully formed," he says, "and are only growing or maintaining themselves, much more will it be so when the several organs are successively forming. At this time, as each nascent organ takes from the nutritive material its appropriate constituents, it will co-operate with the gradual self-development of the blood, to induce in it that condition which is essential, or most favourable, to the formation of the organs next in order to be developed."

This principle further enables us to understand how the existence of certain materials in the blood may determine the formation of structures in which these materials are to be incorporated, and it enables us to understand the "constitutional disturbance," or general state of ill health, which arises from some local disturbance, such as a cold in the head; for, "if each part in its normal nutrition is an excreting organ to the rest, then cessation or perversion of nutrition in one, must, through definite changes in the blood, affect the nutrition of the rest.

How evidently the special condition of the organism determines the growth or decrease of certain organs, may best be seen in the sudden development of the beard and the voice at the period of puberty. Birds in the pairing season acquire their most brilliant plumage, and express the tumult of their emotions in perpetual song. Stags at the same epoch develop their antlers, and make the forest ring with their hoarse barking. Mr. Paget justly says — "Where two or more organs are thus manifestly connected in nutrition, and not connected in the exercise of any external office, their connection is because each of them is partly formed of materials left in the blood on the formation of the other."*

Does not this throw a new light upon the blood? and do you not therein catch a glimpse of many processes before entirely obscure? It assures us that the blood is not "flowing flesh" — *la chair coulante* — as Bordeu called it, to the great delight of his successors; nor is it even liquid food. It is an organic structure, incessantly passing through changes, which changes are the *conditions* of all development and activity. Food and Drink become subjected to a complicated series of digestive processes. The liquid product of Digestion is carried into the blood-stream, undergoing various changes in its route. It is now blood; but other changes supervene before this blood is fitted for the nourishment of the tissues; and then certain elements pass from it, through the walls of the capillaries, to be finally assimilated by the tissues. In the simpler animals, the liquid product of digestion is itself the immediate agent of Nutrition, and does not pass through the intermediate stage of blood. It escapes from the digestive canal into the general substance of the body, which it permeates and nourishes much in the way that the

* PAGET, p. 32.

blood-plasma nourishes the substance of the more complex animals. But in the simplest animals there is not even this approach to blood. There is no liquid product of digestion, for there is no digestion at all, the water in which these animals live carrying organic matter in solution; *this* permeates the substance, and is assimilated: thus does the water play the part of blood, carrying the food, and carrying away the waste.

Let the speculative mind traverse the marvellous scale of created beings upwards, from the simplest to the most complex, and it will observe that Assimilation first takes place by means of the direct relation of the organism to the surrounding medium; next arrives the interposition of agencies which *prepare* the food for the higher effects it has to produce; and instead of relying on organic substances in solution, the organism is seen extracting nutriment from other organisms; finally is seen the operation of still more complicated agencies, which impress on the digested food still higher characters, converting it into blood. This blood is retained in a system of vessels everywhere closed. Yet, in spite of the absence of orifices or pores, it is distributed impartially to the most distant parts of the organism, and it is distributed according to the momentary requirements of each part, so that when an organ is called upon to put forth increased energy, there is always an increase of food sent to supply that energy. If the stomach has been quiet for hours while the brain has been active, the regulating power of the circulation has adapted the supply of blood to each organ; and no sooner will the stomach be called upon to exert itself, than an abundant supply of blood will instantly be directed to it. This simple and beautiful fact in the animal economy should warn men against the vicious habit of studying at, or shortly after, meals, or of tasking the brain when the stomach is also tasked.

# CHAPTER V.

## CIRCULATION OF THE BLOOD: ITS HISTORY, COURSE, AND CAUSES.

Was Harvey the discoverer of the circulation? — Course taken by the blood — History of seventeen centuries — Three errors removed by Galen, Vesalius, and Colombo — What then remained for Harvey? — Discovery of the valves — Exaggeration of their importance: veins without valves — Discovery of the fact of the circulation — Reception of the discovery by contemporaries — Deficiencies in Harvey's doctrine — Discovery of the capillary vessels: their structure and uses — Discovery of the lymphatics — Harvey's opposition to it — Statement of Harvey's real claims — The cause of the circulation — Influence of the heart; not the sole cause — Rapidity of circulation — Circulation in absence of the heart — Motions of the heart; cause thereof; nerves and ganglia of the heart — The heart continuing to beat after death — Action of the Arteries — Circulation in the capillaries — Draper's hypothesis — Spallanzani's observations — Circulation and Respiration.

Did Harvey discover the circulation of the blood? To many, the question will sound like an impertinence. To those who have critically examined the historical evidence, the question wears another aspect, and their answer will run somewhat thus: Harvey did, and he did *not*, make the discovery; he made a very great discovery, which has given an imperishable glory to his name, but it was not precisely that which is popularly attributed to him. In endeavouring to mark clearly out that which he discovered, and that which he did not discover, no attempt will be made here to diminish the fame England is justly proud of, by ransacking the archives of science to detect stray passages of meaningless vagueness, wherein older authors may have indicated something like the truths which Harvey established on the firm basis of experiment and reasoning. Erudite prejudice has done its worst in this direction, and its worst has only set Harvey's merits in a clearer light.

Harvey discovered the *fact* of the circulation; but he did not discover the *course* of the circulation, nor the *causes* of the circulation. He knew that the blood was carried from the heart through the arteries to the tissues, and from the tissues, through the veins and lungs, back again to the place whence it started. But he knew not *how* the blood passed from arteries to veins; he knew not *why* the blood thus moved. In our day Science is in possession of the exact *course* of the circulation, but the exact *causes* are still under question. We know that the circulating system consists of *heart, arteries, veins, capillaries,* and *lymphatics.* Harvey knew not the capillaries and lymphatics; so that his knowledge of the course taken by the blood was necessarily incomplete.

To put the reader in possession of what is now known on this subject, and to enable an estimate to be formed of what Harvey discovered, we will first take a rapid view of the circulation.

The following diagram will convey a general conception of the course of the circulation: —

Fig. 11.

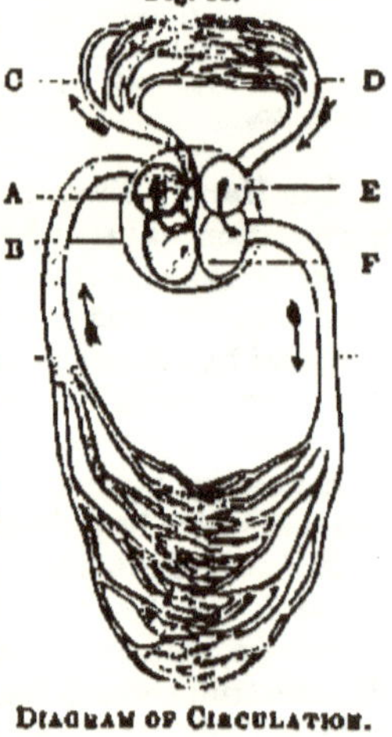

The reader will understand that this figure is a *diagram*, not a *picture*: it represents, in an ideal manner, the relation of the various parts of the circulating system to each other, and shows how a circle is formed by the blood starting from the *right auricle*, A, of the heart, and passing thence into the *right ventricle*, B; from this again it is driven by a strong contraction of the *pulmonary artery*, C, into the lungs; from the lungs it is carried by the *pulmonary veins*, D, back to the *left auricle*, E, of the heart, and from that to the *left ventricle*, F, whence it is poured into the arteries, and passes from these through the *capillaries* (described in our last chapter, p. 166, and represented by DIAGRAM OF CIRCULATION.

dotted lines in fig. 11) into the veins, and thus is once more carried back to the heart.

Such is the diagram, or *theoretic* view, of the circulation. But lest the reader should be misled by this, which is intended to simplify the conception, I will now give a representation of a part of the actual disposition of the circulating apparatus, which he can complete by the aid of the theoretic diagram.

The heart is composed of four cavities, two *auricles* or antechambers, and two *ventricles* or chambers. Into the right auricle (*ó*) the blood enters by means of the two great trunk-veins, the

Fig. 12.²

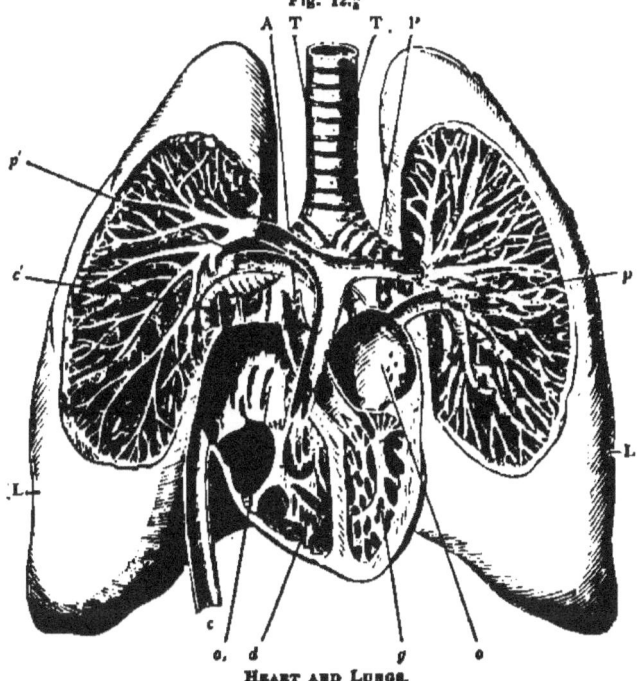

HEART AND LUNGS.

superior and inferior *venæ cavæ* (*c'* and *c*). After passing thence into the right ventricle (*d*) it is driven by the *pulmonary artery* (P)

into the lungs. This vessel is called an artery although it contains venous blood; for vessels do not receive their names from
the nature of the blood they carry, but from the nature of their
office : those which carry blood to the heart are called veins,
those which carry it from the heart are called arteries.

In the lungs (L L) the blood comes in contact with the oxygen
of the atmospheric air, admitted to the air-cells of the lungs
through the windpipe, or *trachea* (T) which branches off, and
ramifies through the lungs as *bronchial tubes*. The action of the
oxygen changes the blood from venous into arterial.

The blood now returns from the lungs by the *pulmonary veins*
(p p') and enters the left auricle (o), whence it passes into the left
ventricle (g). It is then driven into the arteries, through the
great arterial trunk, the *aorta* (A), and is by them distributed to
the various tissues.

The arterial blood having served its purpose, and having
yielded some of its materials to the tissues through which it
flowed, has now to return once more to the heart, to be reinvigorated by passing through the lungs. In the diagram we saw
this return effected by means of the veins. But there is another
system of vessels, different from veins and capillaries, of which
no notice is taken in the diagram. This is the Lymphatic system.

The Lymphatics, like the roots of plants absorbing nutriment
from the earth, absorb lymph from the various organs in which
they are distributed, as we shall learn more particularly hereafter. These lymphatics pour their contents into the venous
current, which thus becomes a confluence of streams, all flowing
towards the heart.

This is the circuit taken by the blood, from the right auricle
of the heart back again to that starting-point.

I⁰. Story of the Discovery. — The story of this discovery is
one of the most interesting and instructive in the whole range of
science, and it has recently been re-written by M. Flourens in a
very agreeable style.* He declares that before him no one had
accurately narrated it. In some sense this is true; but there

* Flourens: *Histoire de la Découverte de la Circulation du Sang*, 1854.

are important omissions in his own account; and while availing myself of his labours, I shall endeavour to complete them. It is a story whose episodes extend over not less than seventeen centuries; and the two centuries that have elapsed since the discovery, have not sufficed entirely to complete it. Seventeen centuries is a vast span of time for the elaboration of the discovery of a fact which, now we know it, seems so obvious that the marvel is why it was ever unknown; and the moral of the story lies precisely there, teaching, as it does, the remarkable servility of the mind in the presence of established opinions, and the difficulty which is felt, even by eminent men, in seeing plain facts, when their eyes are hoodwinked by preconceived notions. To those who are unfamiliar with the practical investigation of science, it seems singular that errors, so baseless that they vanish immediately they are challenged, should continue to find believers: and to men who have never trained themselves in the difficult and delicate art of Observation, it seems singular that facts, extremely simple when observed, should continue to be overlooked. But the truth is, observers are at all times rare, because *new* observation requires singular independence of mind; and, unhappily, those who never made an observation themselves, are always ready to dispute the accuracy of new observations made by others.

1. *Three errors which masked the truth.* — In the case now before us there were three capital errors, which for seventeen centuries masked the fact of circulation; and the reader will probably learn with surprise what those errors were.

——The first error was, the belief that the arteries did not contain blood.

— The second error was, the belief that the two chambers of the heart communicated with each other by means of holes in the partition dividing them.

——The third error was the belief that the veins carried the blood to the various parts of the body.

How was it possible that errors so flagrant as these could have maintained their ground a single day after men began seriously to examine the subject? It was obvious that air entered the body, and entered it by the trachea, or windpipe. The conclusion was natural, in the early days of science, that the air, thus entering by the trachea and bronchial vessels, should continue its course through other vessels. When the arteries of a dead body were examined, they were found empty, and consequently the arteries were chosen as the veritable air-channels: hence their name (air-containers," from ἀηρ and τηρεω).

What, then, becomes of the air inspired? Galen said it did not enter the parts of the body, but was thrown out again after performing its office, that office being to cool the blood. If you open an artery, said Galen, blood will issue, but not air: whence the conclusion seems inevitable, that the arteries do not contain air, and do contain blood. Modern science has proved that atmospheric air is not contained in the arteries, but only its oxygen with a slight amount of nitrogen, and a certain amount of carbonic acid gas. And as the composition of the atmosphere was not suspected in the days of Galen, the presence of blood, and the absence of air, were facts so firmly established by him, that, in spite of all antagonists, they finally assumed the place of incontestable truths.

Here, then, we see one error removed. The others still remained. Galen, and all his successors, maintained that the two chambers of the heart communicated directly by means of holes in their partition; an opinion perfectly intelligible when we learn that it rested on a theoretical assumption. Theory wanted the fact, and men saw the fact they wanted. Theory distinguished between venous blood, and spirituous or arterial blood: The venous blood nourishing all the coarser organs, such as the liver; the spirituous blood nourishing all the delicate organs, such as the lungs.

In our day we should demand some proof, before accepting such a theory; but the ancients had a very vague idea of the necessity of proof; and were equally vague respecting the nature of proof; so long as an opinion was logical and plausible, it was held to be irresistible.

The spirituous element was supposed to be formed in the left ventricle of the heart; but inasmuch as even venous blood requires some of this spirit for the purposes of nutrition, it was necessary that the two bloods should mingle; and, to meet this necessity, holes were assumed in the partition dividing the two ventricles. So deeply impressed were anatomists with reverence for what Galen had said, and what theory required, that they one and all *saw* the holes — which do not exist. Berenger de Carpi had, indeed, an uneasy doubt on the subject, which he naïvely expressed in the admission that the holes were only to be seen with great difficulty — *cum maximâ difficultate videntur;* but, by straining the eyes sufficiently, he doubtless saw what Galen required him to see — as thousands daily see what they believe they ought to see. The first man who had sufficient strength of mind to use his eyes, and say what he saw, was Vesalius,[*] the father of modern anatomy: for whom Titian did *not* draw the figures which illustrate his work. [**]

Thus was the second error overthrown in 1543. This third error — namely, that of the veins carrying the blood *to* the tissues — was somewhat more complex. If the venous and arterial bloods do not mingle in the heart, where do they mingle? *We* know it is in the lungs that the one passes into the other; but it was an immense discovery to make; and there is something piquant in the fact that it was first divined by a restless and daring theologian, whom Calvin burned, with affectionate zeal, for speculations of another kind.

Michael Servetus was the first to announce the existence of the circulation in the lungs; and he announced this in the *Christianismi Restitutio*, a work which was burned by the theologians. Two copies of this work exist: one, still reddened and partly consumed by the flames, is in the Royal Library of Paris; and copious extracts from it are printed by M. Flourens in his "History." Servetus there describes the passage of the blood from the heart to the lungs, "where it is agitated, prepared, changes its colour, and is poured from the pulmonary artery to the pulmonary vein." [***]

* VESALIUS: *Opera Omnia*, edit. 1725, I. 519. The first edition of the Anatomy was published in 1543.
** The real artist was Calaar, a pupil of Titian's, called by Vasari, Giovanni Fiammingo. I do not know how the tradition arose which attributes the figures to Titian — (CUVIER, *Hist. des Sc. Nat.*, II. 21). Vesalius himself names *Johannes Calcarensis* in his preface, and makes no mention of Titian.
*** "Fit autem communicatio hæc, non per parietem cordis medium, ut

This idea was as novel as it was true; but the critical reader will probably not agree with M. Flourens in regarding this as a *discovery*, in the strict sense of the term; for although Servetus had some notion of the anatomical evidence furnished by the large size of the pulmonary artery, which enables it to carry a far greater quantity of blood than could be needed for the nutrition of the lungs, yet we have only to read the passages in which he describes this pulmonary circulation to perceive that he had no accurate idea of it: he speaks confidently of the nerves being continuations of the arteries, and describes with great precision how the air passes from the nose into the chambers of the brain; and how the devil takes the same route to lay siege to the soul. All we can say is, that Servetus made one lucky guess among his numerous guesses by no means of the lucky kind. I think it right to insist on this point, because, owing to the rarity of the book in which the guess was promulgated, very few persons have been able to form a correct idea of what Servetus really meant. Thus Cuvier, among others, emphatically asserts that "the physiological phenomenon of the pulmonary circulation is explained in a very clear manner,"[*] and that Servetus says, "in a positive manner, that the whole mass of the blood passes through the lungs." The copious extracts given by M. Flourens now enable every one to see what Servetus really did assert. He announced the fact of the pulmonary circulation, and may receive from History the whole credit of such priority; he also guessed rightly that in the lungs, and not in the liver, the blood received its elaboration, passing from venous into arterial.

But whatever merit may be assigned to Servetus, no influence can be attributed to his discovery, since both he and his treatise were roasted by Calvin; and no one heard of the pulmonary circulation. Six years afterwards, Realdo Colombo re-discovered the pulmonary circulation;[**] and that the discovery was ready to be made on all sides, is seen in the fact of its being also made

vulgo creditur. Sed magno artificio a dextro cordis ventriculo longo per pulmones ductu, agitatur sanguis subtilis: a pulmonibus præparator, flavus efficitur, et a vena arteriosa in arteriam venosam, transfunditur."

[*] CUVIER: *Hist. des Sciences Nat.*, II. 15.
[**] COLOMBO: *De re Anatomica*, edit. 1572, p. 325.

by Cæsalpinus, the great botanist, who does not seem to have been aware of what Colombo had written, since he makes no mention of him, and, as M. Flourens observes, *le grand mérite est toujours probe.* Cæsalpinus, moreover, was the first to pronounce the phrase "circulation of the blood."[*]

2. *Discovery of the general Circulation.* — Here the reader may ask, What further remained for Harvey to discover? and it may surprise him to hear the answer: Everything! Such is pretty nearly the fact. The pulmonary circulation takes place only through a small arc of the great circle traversed by the blood. Besides this arc, there is the other greater arc, through which the *systemic*, or general circulation, takes its course; and of this no one, except Cæsalpinus, had even a suspicion. Every one supposed that the veins carried the blood *to* the tissues, and nourished them; no one suspected that this function was reserved for the arteries, and that the veins carried the blood only to the heart. It was thought that the arteries had their origin in the heart, and the veins in the liver; from the liver the veins carried the blood to every part.

A single fact, familiar to every surgeon, and to every barber who ever opened a vein, ought to have revealed the error; since every time a ligature was applied, the operator must have seen that the vein swelled *below* the ligature, and not *above* it; from which the deduction seems obvious that the blood in the vein flowed *to* the heart, and not *from* it.

But here, as in so many other cases, familiar facts were not *observed;* they were seen, but not interpreted. Cæsalpinus was the first who observed it; but he has only the merit of having suspected the cause to be the current setting towards the heart.[**] His suspicion was not a demonstration; and we are surprised to find De Blainville saying, "that the circulation was known to Cæsalpinus, although he had not demonstrated it." In Science, the difference between a guess and a demonstration is as great as that between the fame which an unwritten poem may achieve,

---

[*] CÆSALPINUS: *Quæst. Peripatet.*, edit. 1583, lib. v. p. 125. Flourens gives the passage, as well as that from Colombo.

[**] "Quia tument vonæ citrà vinculum, non citrà. Debuisset autem opposito modo contlo..., si motus sanguinis et spiritus a visceribus fit in totum corpus." — *Quæstionum Medicarum.* lib. II. p. 234.

and the fame which a great poem *has* achieved. If guesses
counted as achievements, the temple of fame would be thronged
with the statues of heroes.

De Blainville says that the reason why Haller and others
have denied the claim of Cæsalpinus, it because they did not
read what he had said in his work *On Plants.*[*] Now, if we turn
to the passage in question, we shall see how far the writer
really was from the truth, and yet how near his guess went
to the truth. "In animals, we see the food carried by the
veins to the heart, as to a centre of innate heat; and there,
having acquired its final perfection, it is distributed over the
whole body through the arteries, by the agency of the spirit,
which is engendered in the heart by this same food."[**]

Easy as it is for us to *read into* this passage almost all that we
understand by the circulation, a close historical criticism detects
in it nothing but a guess; and as Bérard remarks, we ought not
to confound two such vague statements as these, themselves requiring demonstration, and by Cæsalpinus himself subsequently
contradicted, with the clear ideas, and imposing proofs, on
which Harvey established his discovery.[***]

The convincing evidence of Harvey's originality is, that not
only was the guess advanced by Cæsalpinus without any influence on the theories of that day, in spite of his deserved
authority; but that when Harvey promulgated his theory, he
found, all over Europe, the greatest difficulty in getting it accepted. Bérard maintains, that so far from any one before Harvey
having had a clear idea of the true theory, no one had even
accurately conceived the true theory of *pulmonary* circulation;
for although Servetus, Colombo, and Cæsalpinus knew that the
blood passed through the lungs, they fancied only so much
passed as was necessary for the reception of the "vital spirits,"

---

[*] De Blainville: *Hist. de Sciences de l'Organization*, II. 227 — a statement repeated by Isidore Geoffroy St. Hilaire: *Histoire Générale des
Règnes Organiques*, I. 44.
[**] Cæsalpinus: *De Plantis*, I., c. 2, p. 3. — "In animalibus videmus
alimentum per venas duci ad cor tanquam ad officinam caloris insiti, et adeptâ
inibi ultimâ perfectione, per arterias in universum corpus distribui agente
spiritu, qui ex eodem alimento in corde gignitur."
[***] Bérard: *Cours de Physiol.*, III. 581. Compare Milne Edwards: *Leçons
sur la Phys. et l'Anat. comparée*, III. 20.

— a quantity which their predecessors fancied took its course through the holes in the partition of the heart. But they had no conception of the entire mass of blood traversing the lungs; and even had they known so much, they would have been wholly at a loss to say whence it came, and whither it went. It was necessary to understand the whole circulation before any part of it could accurately be understood.

3. *Discovery of the Valves.* — The discovery that the veins had valves, opening and closing like doors, brought the discovery of the circulation within compass. It was made in 1574 by Fabrice d'Acquapendente, under whom Harvey studied at Padua. In the following figure the valves *b b b* are represented in the course of the venous trunk, and at the entrance *b* of the venous branches. These valves, preventing any flow from the heart, but admitting the flow to the heart, might have suggested to their discoverer the true interpretation of their use. But five-and-forty years elapsed before any one arose, who had the sagacity to perceive the real

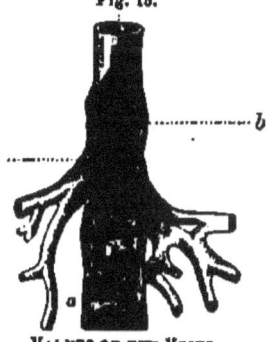

Fig. 13.

VALVES OF THE VEINS.

value of this anatomical structure in respect to the blood-currents; and during these five-and-forty years, everything that had been discovered or surmised respecting the circulation, was familiar to every anatomist of the great Paduan school in which Harvey studied: nevertheless, when Harvey promulgated his theory, it was vehemently opposed.

In 1619 Harvey first publicly taught what he had discovered; and in 1628 he published, for the benefit of Europe, his celebrated treatise, *Exercitatio Anatomica de Motu Cordis et Sanguinis*, which may justly be called the basis of modern physiology. That the theory was new, and would be opposed as a heresy, no one more clearly divined than he did.[*] The great-

* "Adeo iis nova erunt et inaudita, ut non solum ex invidia quorundam metuam malum mihi, sed vereor ne habeam inimicos omnes homines, tantum

ness of the discovery, and the force of genius required to make
it, can only be appreciated by those who, familiar with the
state of opinion in those days, read the evidence and arguments
by which Harvey established his doctrine. It is true that he
appeared at a particular epoch, when the confluence of various
discoveries rendered his discovery possible; but that a man of
genius was necessary to interpret and co-ordinate those discoveries, is evident in the fact, that no one except Harvey
had, for nearly half a century, seen the significance of the facts.

Here, however, a caution must be interposed. The importance of the valves has been greatly exaggerated, and their real
bearing on Harvey's discovery misconceived. They are thought
to have rendered the discovery facile, because, inasmuch as they
prevent the blood from flowing backwards, while permitting it
to flow outwards, the idea of the circulation, it is said, must
necessarily have emerged from the contemplation of these
valves.

Against this supposition there is one decisive fact: no one
*did* deduce the conclusion which is said to have been so necessary.

Moreover, in many cases, circulation takes place entirely
without their aid. There are *no* valves in the veins of the Inver-
tebrata,* *none* in the veins of fishes and reptiles, and *very few* in
birds; yet the circulation is as complete in these animals as in
man.

Nay, even in man the *chief* veins are destitute of valves, although writers on Natural Theology, and even better-informed
physiologists, are in the habit of speaking of them as if they were
universal and indispensable: it may, therefore, be useful to mention, that there are no valves whatever in the great venous
trunks, the venæ cavæ, and portal veins — none in the hepatic,
renal, and uterine veins — none in the brachio-cephalic, spinal,
and iliac veins; and they are rarely present in the azygos and
intercostal veins.

consuetudo aut semel inhibita doctrina, altisque defixa radicibus, quasi altera
natura apud omnes valet, et antiquitatis veneranda opinio cogit." — *Exercit.*
p. 88.

    * In the aorta of the *Eolis* there is a semilunar valve.

4. *Harvey's Originality.* — M. Flourens says, that when Harvey appeared everything had been suspected or indicated, but nothing established. This seems to me even less than the truth, for I cannot ascertain that any one had the slightest conception of the real process.

Acquapendente could make nothing of the valves he had detected. He thought their office was simply to prevent a too great accumulation of blood in the lower parts of the body, and a diminution from the upper parts.

Colombo thought with his contemporaries, that the veins had their origin in the liver, and carried blood to the tissues.

Cæsalpinus, in spite of his recognition of pulmonary circulation, thought the blood also passed from the right chamber of the heart to the left.

But Harvey not only conceived a clear idea of the process, he described it minutely and accurately. He noticed the successive contractions which forced the blood into the ventricle when the

Fig. 14.

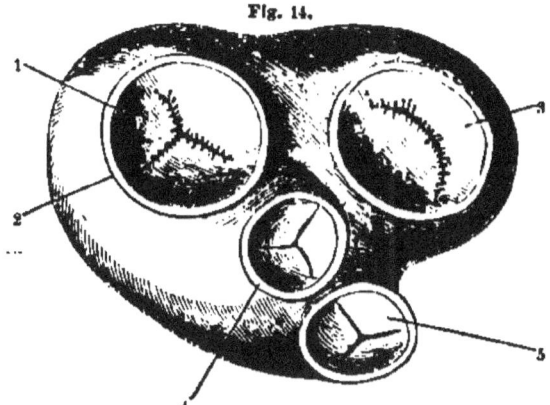

VALVES OF THE HEART AND ARTERIES.

Upper surface of the heart, the auricles having been removed.
1. Valve between right auricle and ventricle; 2. Fibrous ring; 3. Valve between left auricle and ventricle; 4. Valve of the aorta; 5. Valve of pulmonary artery.

auricle contracted, and forced it from the ventricle into the lungs when the ventricle contracted; a process repeated on the left side with the blood which had come in contact with air in the lungs. And at each passage of the blood from one cavity to another, there were the valves, or "little doors" (*ostiola*), opening to let the current pass, and closing to prevent its reflux.

These valves are represented in the above figure, which shows the upper surface of the heart, when the *auricles* are removed: —

Harvey described the course of the blood along the arteries, which he attributed to the pulsations of the heart; and in this, instead of in Galen's "pulsific virtue," he recognised the cause of the blood's movement.

5. *Reception of the new Doctrine.* — By Harvey the overthrow of ancient authority was completed. Men dared no longer swear by Galen — they swore by Harvey, who had discovered the greatest fact in the animal economy — a fact totally unknown and unsuspected by Galen, or any other ancient. The new era had commenced.

It was not in the nature of things for the old system quietly to accept the new; accordingly, the opposition was loud and vehement. Like many other parts of this history, and like most oppositions to new doctrines, it has been immensely exaggerated by historians, and by writers who have chosen it as a theme for rhetoric. It is true that the Faculty rejected the new doctrine; but it is no less true that eminent men accepted it with enthusiasm. If Guy Patin was caustic in opposition, Molière laughed at Guy Patin's prejudice; and Boileau ridiculed the Faculty. Some anatomists accepted the doctrine, and the great Descartes warmly espoused it.[*] Swammerdamm and Malpighi, two of the

---

[*] The carelessness with which history is often written, is exhibited in the criticism of M. ISIDORE ST. HILAIRE: *Hist. des Règnes Organiques*, I. 49; on the passage in CUVIER, *Hist. des Sciences Nat.*, II. 53, where Harvey is said to have had the rare happiness of seeing his discovery accepted by Descartes. M. St. Hilaire remarks that this is an error, because Harvey died in 1657, and Descartes did not publish his *Traité de l'Homme* until 1662. This remark is doubly unfortunate, Descartes having expressed his adherence to the doctrine in his very first work, the *Discours de la Méthode*; and Harvey having, in his Second Reply to Riolan, expressed his gratification at this flattering approval of Descartes.

great names of the century, speak of Harvey with reverence; and soon no one spoke of him in any other tone.

6. *Gaps in the Doctrine of Harvey.* — It is impossible to read Harvey's work without the highest admiration for the scientific genius it displays, and the conviction that here the circulation was not only demonstrated, but for the first time conceived. The experiments and arguments by which he establishes the fact are still worthy of study, as models of investigation.

But there were necessary gaps in his doctrine. The *course* of the circulation was not known to him, could not indeed have been discovered by any instruments at his disposal. He supposed the blood passed from arteries to veins by two paths, either through anastomosis (that is to say, the arteries opening directly into veins), or through the porosities of the parts — *aut porositates carnis et partium solidarum pervias sanguini.* He thought it necessary that so much of the blood as was required by the tissues for their nutrition, should *remain behind* in the tissues, and the rest be carried onwards to the heart. The error is considerable; and its bearing on the theory of the circulation will be appreciated by any one who reflects on the fact that venous and arterial blood being so obviously distinguished, it is necessary that the passage of the one into the other should be demonstrated — not surmised — before the theory of the circulation could be accepted as complete; for any one might reasonably assume that the blood in the veins is altogether another fluid from that in the arteries, and not merely another state of that fluid.

This, indeed, *was* assumed by the adversaries of Harvey, and has found supporters even in our own day. Burdach cites two German physiologists — Willbrand and Runge — whom he thinks worthy of refutation, and who maintained that arterial blood was transformed in a mass into the tissues, and that venous blood was the re-transformed tissues. Unless the passage of the blood into the veins be clearly traced, there can be no reason against supposing that the veins simply absorb from the tissues, in the same way as the lymphatics and lacteals absorb their fluid. To prove that the blood makes a circuit, that circuit must be traced; and Harvey plainly declares that, with all his diligence, he could not succeed in tracing any connection between arteries and veins; in only three places did he find them presenting anything like an anastomosis; in every other place he imagined porosities.

7. *Discovery of the Capillaries.* — Nor, with the means at his disposal, *could* Harvey have traced the complete course of the blood. The Microscope was needed; and the first to employ the microscope in such researches was Malpighi, who, four years after Harvey's death, in 1661, detected those Capillaries which form the channel of communication between arteries and veins. (See fig. 11, p. 202.) He says that, at first, he thought the blood poured out from the minute arteries in streams, without his detecting any vessels for these streams; but afterwards he detected the distinct walls of these vessels; and he describes the modes of examining them in the lung of the frog. Their network arrangement on the pulmonary cells is well described by him.[*] Nevertheless, in 1668, Leeuwenhoek describes them as if previously they had been quite unknown. "I used every means I could devise," he says, "to see the complete circulation of the blood — namely, that one of the smallest of those vessels which we call veins, arose from another which is called an artery, and afterwards conveyed its contents to a larger vein; but I found this to be impossible, for when I followed the course of the artery until it became so small as only to admit of one or two globules to pass through it at a time, I then lost sight of it." This was in the wing of a bat; but subsequently he was more fortunate with the tail of a tadpole: "a sight presented itself more delightful than any that my eyes had ever beheld; for here I discovered more than fifty circulations of the blood in different places. I saw that not only the blood in many places was conveyed through exceedingly minute vessels, from the middle of the tail towards the edges, but that each of these vessels had a curve or turning, and carried the blood back towards the middle of the tail, in order to be conveyed to the heart. Hereby it appeared plainly to me that the blood-vessels I now saw in this animal, and which bear the names of arteries and veins, *are, in fact, one and the same —*

---

[*] MALPIGHI: *Epist. II. de Pulmonibus*, in *Opera Omnia*, II. 327 of the 4to edition. From the *Opera Posthuma*, p. 9, it appears that the date of this discovery was 1661. I am indebted to Professor SHARPEY for this reference.

that is to say, that they are properly termed arteries so long as they convey the blood to the farthest extremities of its vessels, and veins when they bring it back towards the heart."[*]

Thus, then, was the demonstration of the *course* of the blood completed; and we must confess that it is with surprise we find all historians overlooking the great gap in the doctrine which had been left by Harvey, a gap only filled up by Malpighi and Leeuwenhoek in their discovery that these capillaries formed the true passage of arterial into venous blood.

It is necessary to bear in mind that the capillaries are a distinct set of vessels, differing from the arteries and veins which they connect, in their anatomical structure, and in their arrangement as a network (Fig. 8, p. 167). Bichat was the first who systematically conceived them as a distinct system; but their structure was not known until investigated by Henle, in 1841, and by subsequent histologists. The existence of these vessels is not only important to the theory of the circulation, but is even more important to the theory of nutrition; since it assures us that not only does the blood truly circulate, but circulates in a system of *closed* vessels, so that only by oozing through the walls of those vessels can it reach the tissues, and nourish them. Indeed, those who imagined that the blood was poured on to the tissues, were not aware that blood under such circumstances would act like a foreign substance: instead of nourishing, it would destroy.

If the reader feels any difficulty in understanding how the blood can ooze through the walls of the vessels in sufficient quantities for the purposes of nutrition, he is referred to the explanation previously given of Endosmosis (see p. 72). Having there learned with what facility the passage takes place when the membrane separates two fluids of unequal density, he will be prepared to understand how it may take place even in the Slug, which has a continuous layer of *chalk* imbedded in the walls of its blood-vessels — a fact which considerably surprised me when I first observed it. In other animals the walls of the blood-vessels are more delicate.

8. *Discovery of the Lymphatics.* — Harvey did not live to hear

[*] LEEUWENHOEK: *Select Works*, i. 09.

of the Capillaries; but there is another system of vessels, of
which indeed he heard, although he failed to appreciate their
significance. We allude to the Lymphatics, or Absorbents.
They are minute vessels, abounding in all the viscera, rare in
the muscles, and not yet detected in the nervous centres; when
they rise from the alimentary canal, they are called *Lacteals*, or
chyliferous vessels, and as such were, until quite recently, supposed to be the chief channels for the conveyance of the chyle to
the blood. But in the chapter on DIGESTION we learned that this
chyle is not the quintessence of the digested food, and that the
lacteals only differ from all other lymphatics in carrying a larger
proportion of fat, which gives their fluid its milky aspect during
digestion. Lymph is blood without its cells. Chyle is lymph
with the addition of fat, and perhaps also the addition of some
other products of digestion. Lymph contains albumen, fibrine,*
fat, salts, and extractive matters, like the blood: and, like the
blood, it coagulates at certain temperatures. The chief differences between lymph and blood are the absence of the cells,
and the presence of a greater proportion of water. By absorbing
its water, lymph leaves the plasma bathing the tissues in a more
concentrated state. Lymph is one of the streams which set towards the heart, and join the venous current.

The discovery of the Lymphatics is due to Aselli, Pecquet,
Rudbeck, and Bartholin. Anatomists taught that there were
three kinds of vessels in the body: the veins, which carried
blood; the arteries, which carried spirituous blood; and the
nerves, which carried "animal spirits." To the surprise of
all, the news came that an Italian anatomist, Aselli, had
discovered a fourth kind, which carried the chyle. This 'discovery was announced in 1622 — three years after Harvey first
announced *his* discovery, but six years before his book was
published.

Aselli was dissecting a dog, and, to his surprise, on opening
the abdomen he saw a network of delicate white vessels. What
could they be? Did they contain the chyle? He pricked one,

* VIRCHOW considers the fibrine of the Lymph to be different from that of
the Blood. It is certainly less easily coagulated. We may, perhaps, assume
it to be an early form of blood-fibrine.

and, in a transport of delight, exclaimed *Eureka!* as he saw a
milky fluid flowing out. But on opening another dog, he was
greatly discouraged, for there was not a vessel of the kind to be
seen. Had he been deceived? Was his joy premature? In this
perplexity it occurred to him that the first dog had been fed a
little while before it was opened; whereas the second dog was
fasting. With the insight of genius, Aselli detected here the
clue which might lead him to the truth. He fed another dog;
four hours afterwards he opened it, and had the intense satisfaction of once more seeing the milky vessels.

But although Aselli made Europe aware of a new system of
vessels, which he named Lacteals, he failed to trace their issue.
He thought they conducted the chyle to the liver.

In 1648, a French anatomist, Pecquet, distrusting the conclusions of that "mute and frigid science," as he calls the dissection of dead bodies, determined to seek the truth in the
living organism, and began a series of vivisections. He was
rewarded by the discovery of the course taken by the chyle in the
lacteals, as it passes into the Reservoir, still named after him,
and along the Thoracic Duct, to be poured into the subclavian vein, and thence, mingled with the blood, into the
heart.

In 1650, Rudbeck, a young Swede, discovered the lymphatics
in the liver, and their connection with the reservoir of the
chyle.'

In 1652, Bartholin, another Frenchman, completed this discovery by finding the lymphatics in the viscera and limbs, and
by tracing them into a common trunk.

These discoveries, following in such quick succession,
greatly disturbed the equanimity of the Faculty, whose members
swore by Galen, and could not tolerate the idea of the ancients
being supposed to have overlooked anything. "Un chacun in-
vente à présent! — Everybody must needs be a discoverer nowadays," was the indignant sarcasm of Riolan, the most renowned
teacher of that day — the only adversary whom Harvey con-
descended to answer, and of whom he stood in such awe, that,
even when answering his attacks, he declares the book which
contains those attacks "will live for ever, and when marble shall

have mouldered, will proclaim to posterity the glory which belongs to your name."*

Harvey knew indeed of the existence of the lacteals, and says that he had observed them before Aselli published his book. But he denied that they contained the chyle, and he is twitted by Riolan for his disbelief. In consequence of this, a tradition has come down, that Harvey showed the same spirit of opposition towards the novelties of others, as was shown by others towards the novelties he advocated; but this is a mistake. If the reader will turn to Harvey's letter to Dr. Morison of Paris, he will see a very circumstantial and temperate exposition of the objections which Harvey felt against the notion of the lacteals conveying the chyle: many of these objections are of great force, and still remain unshaken. His chief error is in supposing that the fluid in the lacteals is milk. But he insists very properly that it should be demonstrated that this fluid is really chyle brought from the intestines, and that it supplies nourishment to the whole body; "for unless we are agreed upon this point, all discussion is vain." Subsequent investigations have cleared up what was obscure, and have shown that the lacteals convey lymph mingled with fat, and that the lymphatics convey whatever they can absorb from the tissues, in which they are imbedded like the roots of a tree in the earth. The lacteal and lymphatic streams are confluent with the great venous streams, and thus form parts of the circulation.

It may now be convenient to state in a few brief sentences the results of all these discoveries, and the course taken by the circulation. For this purpose, let us cast a glance at the disposition of the organs represented in figure 15, on page 221.

The Food having become chyle in the intestines, is from them carried to the heart by these two courses:

1°. The system of *portal veins* (*Vp*) which conduct the chief mass to the liver; from the liver, the chyle, now become Blood, passes along by the inferior vena cava to the right auricle of the heart (*h*).

2°. The system of *Lacteals* (*Vl*), which conduct the fluid

---

* *Exercit. de Circul. ad Riolanum*, 1649; last paragraph.

Fig. 15.

THE DIGESTIVE TRACT.

*p* Parotid gland;
*g* submaxillary
gland; *g''* sublin-
gual gland; *œ*
œsophagus or gul-
let; *cc* carotid ar-
teries; *pp* lungs,
that on the left
being opened to
show the bron-
chial tubes, ar-
teries, and veins;
VC superior vena
cava; *k* aorta; *h*
right auricle of
the heart; *A'* left
auricle; *f* right
ventricle; *o* left
ventricle; *p'* pul-
monary artery; *tt*
thoracic duct; F
liver; B gall blad-
der, entering the
intestine by the
duct B'; E sto-
mach; R spleen;
S Pecquet's reser-
voir; *j* lympha-
tics; *x* mesenteric
ganglia; VP trunk
of portal vein; *Vp
Vp* branches of
portal vein; W
pancreas; VC in-
ferior vena cava;
*d* duodenum; *Vi*
lacteals; *i* small
intestine; *g* cœ-
cum; *r* colon, or
large intestine. —
After Bernard.

through the mass of mesenteric ganglia, *m* (not to be confounded
with nervous ganglia), to the Reservoir of Pecquet (*S*) along the
thoracic duct (*t, t*), whence it is poured into the subclavian vein,
and there mingling with the venous blood, it is afterwards carried to the heart and through the lungs to be arterialised.

Thus the Food reaches the heart as Blood. From the heart
it takes the course already described.

The arteries carry the blood to all parts of the body by a
system of subdividing branches, the twigs of which are Capillaries. Through the walls of these capillaries some of the
elements of the blood pass to nourish the tissues.

The Capillaries are continuations of the arteries, and the
veins are continuations of the capillaries (or more correctly
speaking, the capillaries are intermediate vessels uniting these
two). Into the veins that portion of the blood enters which has
lost its arterial character in the passage through the capillaries.
Into the veins also the Lymphatics pour their fluid, which is
partly the unused plasma of the blood absorbed from the tissues,
and partly the products of waste in the tissues. When the
Lymphatics arise from the intestines they are called *Lacteals*, or
chyliferous vessels, and carry some portions of the digested food,
as well as lymph. This compound of altered blood, unused
plasma, wasted tissue, and food, forms venous blood, and is
carried by the innumerable veins, ramifying all over the body,
to two great venous trunks, the *venæ cavæ*, inferior and superior
(*Vc* and *Vc'*), which pour the whole mass into the right auricle of
the heart.

9. *Harvey's Claims.* — From the preceding exposition of the
march of discoveries, it is clear that Harvey did not discover all
that *we* mean by the circulation of the blood; but he discovered
the great fact, that the blood does circulate, propelled from the
heart along the arteries, and back to the heart and lungs through
the veins.

Having thus shown that he did not discover the whole *course*
of the circulation, we have now to show that he did not discover
its whole *cause*. Before doing so, it will be interesting to remark,
that in one important respect he was behind Servetus, for he
thought that the blood returned to the heart, as to a fountain,

there to receive the additions necessary to its perfection — *tan-quam ad fontem sive ad lares corporis, perfectionis recuperandæ causa reverti.* Servetus correctly stated that it was in the lungs, and not in the heart, that this perfection was attained. Instead of perceiving that arterial blood acquired its bright colour by its exposure to the air, Harvey maintained that this colour was owing to the lighter part being "strained" from the heavier in its passage through minute openings. "In blood-letting, when the blood forcibly escapes to a distance in a full stream, it is thicker and darker; but when flowing from a small orifice drop by drop, it is brighter because it is then strained, and the thinner portion alone escapes." We know that the difference is owing to a more perfect exposure of the whole mass to the air when it issues slowly in drops, and *that* is why the blood is then of a brighter hue. Harvey, having no suspicion of this atmospheric influence, is driven to ingenious devices to explain the change of colour. "In the lungs," he says, "it is more florid than in the arteries, because it is strained through the pulmonary tissue." His notion of the office of the lungs was, that they served to *cool* the blood, "and prevent it from boiling up."

II⁰. CAUSE OF THE CIRCULATION. — What is it which causes the blood to circulate? "The heart," answers an unhesitating reader. That the heart pumps blood incessantly into the arteries, and that this pumping must drive the stream onwards with great force, there is no doubt; but although the most powerful agent in the circulation, the heart is not the sole agent; and the more we study this difficult question, the more our doubts gather round the explanation.

1. *Circulation in the absence of a Heart.* — Let a few of the difficulties be stated. There have been cases of men and animals born without a heart; these "acardiac monsters" did not live, indeed could not live; but they had grown and developed in the womb, and consequently their blood must have circulated. In most of these cases there has been a twin embryo, which was perfect; and the circulation in both was formerly attributed to the heart of the one; but it has been fully established that this is not the case. Further, Dr. Carpenter reminds us that "it has

Fig. 16.

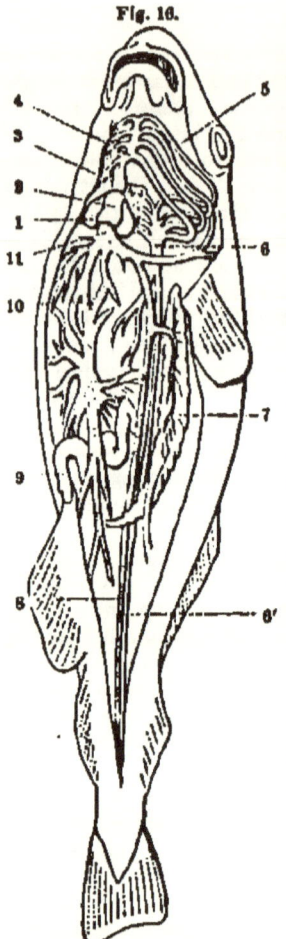

occasionally been noticed that a degeneration in the structure of the heart has taken place, during life, to such an extent that scarcely any muscular tissue could at last be detected in it, but without any such interruption to the circulation as must have been anticipated if this organ furnishes the sole impelling force."[*]  On the other hand, an influence acting on the capillaries will give a complete check to the action of the heart although that organ is itself perfectly healthy and vigorous.

Professor Draper conceives that circulation in the liver is peculiar, since a complete circuit is there performed by the blood, yet no heart, or pulsating organ, is found in that circle; the small vessels which belong to the intestine converge into a large trunk, and this portal vein on entering the liver ramifies over it in the manner of an artery — that is to say, it branches and branches into the minutest subdivisions, and terminates in capillaries; these once more converge into venous trunks, and carry the altered blood from the liver.  Here is a complete circle, analogous to that larger circle which traverses the whole body.  But this circulation is dependent on the primary

CIRCULATION IN THE FISH.
1. Auricle; 2. Ventricle; 3. Arterial bulb; 4. Artery of the gills; 5. Vessels of the gills 6 6'. Aorta or dorsal artery; 7. Kidney; 8. Vena cava; 9. Intestine; 10. Portal veins 11. Large venous sinus.

[*] Human Physiology, p. 349.

impulsion given by the heart; and Prof. Draper would have to show that without the heart the circuit would still be performed, before he could claim the liver as an illustration of his views. He also refers to the circulation in the fish.

The fish has a heart, but that heart only drives the blood into the gills; it does not suffice for the rest of the body — it is a pulmonary, not a systemic heart. This will be understood by reference to the preceding figure, which represents the circulation in a fish.

The blood, propelled from the auricle into the ventricle, is aërated in the capillaries of the gills, and descends through them into the aorta, *not* into the heart; and from the aorta it passes to the rest of the body, from whence it returns through veins to the heart.

Thus we perceive that in the fish, although the blood performs a complete circuit, it only once enters the heart; whereas in the mammal it twice enters the heart, going to and returning from the lungs. The following *theoretic* diagram (copied from Milne-Edwards like the preceding) may assist the reader in forming a distinct conception of the fish circulation.

This diagram should be compared with that at p. 202, in order to detect the important differences between the circulation in the fish and the mammal.

It is possible to meet these difficulties, but the objections to the Harveyan doctrine do not end here. The heart may be removed in cold-blooded animals, and the capillary circulation will continue for some time, in spite of that

Fig. 17.

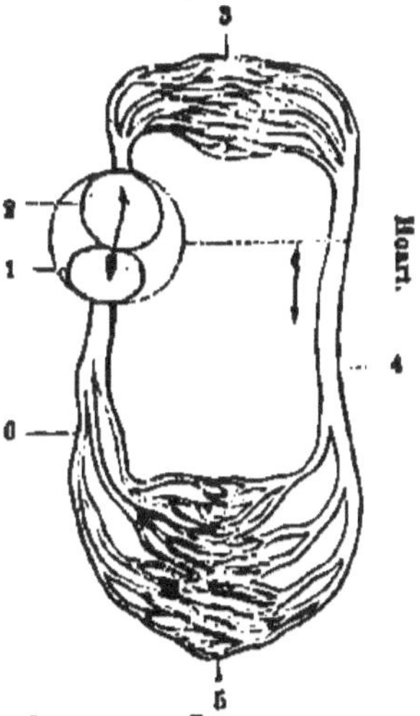

DIAGRAM OF CIRCULATION IN THE FISH.

1. Auricle; 2. Ventricle; 3. Vessels of the gills passing into arteries; 4. Arterial system passing at 6 and 6 into the venous.

removal. This has been observed more than once; and although I had myself observed it some time ago, yet, in preparing these pages for publication, I again investigated the point; and for this purpose removed the heart of a Triton, with as much care as possible, and found the circulation going on in the tail for some minutes afterwards; nor did it entirely cease on separating the tail from the body.*

While the fact was thus indubitable, I had many doubts as to the cause. But the fact is enough for our present purpose; and that it is also true of warm-blooded animals may be inferred, since after death various processes of secretion, and some even of *growth* (as of hair, beard, &c.), are known to take place; and this seems to imply capillary circulation. "After most kinds of death," says Dr. Carpenter, "the arterial system is found, subsequently to the lapse of a few hours, almost or completely emptied of blood; this is partly, no doubt, the effect of the tonic contraction of the tubes themselves; but the emptying is commonly more complete than could thus be accounted for, and must therefore be partly due to the continuance of the capillary circulation. It has been observed by Dr. Bennet Dowler, that in the bodies of individuals who have died from yellow fever, the external veins frequently become so distended with blood, *within a few minutes* after the cessation of the heart's action, that when they are opened the blood flows in a good stream, being sometimes projected to the distance of a foot or more. It is not conceivable that the slowly-acting tonicity of the arteries could have produced such a result as this; which can scarcely therefore be

---

* A curious fact connected with this investigation may here find a place. Having some doubts as to the cause of the continued circulation, I proceeded to repeat the experiment with another Triton; but no sooner was the thorax opened than I was seized with a sudden giddiness and faintness, which caused me instantly to throw open the window, and breathe energetically for some minutes; and, of course, to give over the experiment. I should have fainted away, had not the remembrance of a passage in Mr. BUCKLAND'S *Curiosities of Natural History* warned me of the danger. He describes a similar effect as having arisen during his dissection of a Triton recently dead. Another note-worthy circumstance is, that the effect is by no means constant. I have dissected scores of Tritons, but this was the only occasion on which any effect was perceptible.

attributed to anything else than the sustenance of the capillary circulation by forces generated within itself."

2. *Rapidity of the Circulation.* — Those who have never watched with attention the circulation in the capillaries, may perhaps imagine that the mere force of the heart which propels the blood into the gills, will suffice to propel it also through the general circuit. They will see the heart of the fish beating vigorously, and will imagine these pulsations suffice. But this will no longer seem so plausible, if we place the tail of a tadpole, or the foot of a frog, under the microscope, and delight ourselves with the wondrous spectacle. We shall immediately perceive that the blood flows with far greater rapidity in the arteries than in the capillaries; we shall note that, although the heart continues its vigorous pulsations, and the blood in the arteries advances in regular leaps, the currents in the capillaries are very irregular, sometimes momently arrested, and even reversed. Instead of the *leaping rush*, we perceive an *unsteady flow*, which is never at any time equal in rapidity to the flow in the arteries.

This slackening of the capillary current is held to be an important point in the present discussion. Although precise estimates are excessively difficult in such cases, we need accept the estimates yet made as only approaching the truth, and the argument is equally fortified by them, for the difference in the rate is enormous: in the main arteries the blood rushes at the rate of a *foot* per *second;* in the capillaries only an *inch* per *minute.*[*]

What does that indicate? It indicates that, when the heart has driven the blood along the arteries at a rapid rate, there is a considerable *retardation* occurring in the capillaries, which must call for some new force to *restore* the rate.[**]

[*] This is Valentin and Weber's estimate. Draper makes the rate in the capillaries an inch in three minutes, which would imply that the arterial current was 2160 times more rapid than the capillary current.

[**] The force of this argument is destroyed by the remark of a friend of mine, that the slackening of the capillary current may be explained on the principle of Hydraulics, that "if in any part of a closed current the sectional area of the current is increased, the velocity is diminished." Where a river

Not further to multiply examples, we may take our stand on
these, and pronounce the Harveyan doctrine to be incomplete,
since it fails altogether to account for many important phenomena.   Whatever influence the action of the heart may exert, it
is not the sole cause of the circulation, but only *one* of the causes.
But before attempting to assign the other causes, let us see the
part actually assignable to the heart.

3. *The Motions of the Heart.* — The motions of the heart consist in the alternate contractions and relaxations of its muscular
walls.   The process is this: The two antechambers (*auricles*)
suddenly contract; immediately afterwards, *but while the auricles are still contracted*, the two chambers (*ventricles*) also
contract, having been powerfully expanded by the rush of blood
from the auricles.   This contraction is named the *systole* of the
heart.   It continues for a moment, and is followed by a relaxation of the two auricles, which is immediately succeeded by the
relaxation of the two ventricles.   This relaxation is named the
*diastole.**

During each beat, two sounds may be heard; one dull, which
may be imitated by pronouncing the word *lubb;* the other,
quickly succeeding it, has a sharper sound, like *dup.*   The
former sound is supposed to be due to the contraction of the
muscular fibres of the ventricles, and the thump of the heart
against the chest; aided, no doubt, by the rush of blood and
the closing of the valves.   The latter sound is caused by the
shutting of the semilunar valves of the aorta and pulmonary
artery.

4. *The Pulse.* — The number of pulsations varies greatly,
not only between different sexes and different individuals, but

widens, its velocity slackens, and is recovered again where it narrows.  The
total sectional area of the capillaries being much greater than that of the
arteries supplying them, there is no need of any other cause to explain the
retardation and recovery of the velocity.  This objection destroys the force of
the argument derived from the retardation in the capillaries, but it does not
touch the other arguments.

* Although Harvey describes the process correctly, Haller, and, until
quite recently, all succeeding writers, described the contraction of the auricles
as coincident with the relaxation of the ventricles.  The movement is really
wave-like, and the contraction passes on from one cavity to another before the
relaxation supervenes.

at different ages and conditions of the same person. The following table shows the average at several epochs: —

| | Beats per Minute. |
|---|---|
| In the fœtus in utero, | 150 to 150 |
| Newly-born infant, (wt~~~~) | 130 ,, 140 |
| During the 1st year, | 115 ,, 130 |
| During the 2d year, | 100 ,, 115 |
| During the 3d year, | 95 ,, 105 |
| From the 7th to 14th year, | 80 ,, 90 |
| From the 14th to 21st year, | 75 ,, 85 |
| From 21st to 60th year, | 70 ,, 75 |
| Old age, | 75 ,, 80 |

These figures open a wide field for speculation, especially when coupled with the differences noticed between the sexes, the female having greatly the superiority over the male in respect of frequency, her pulse beating from ten to fourteen times a minute beyond that of man. It must be remembered, however, that a quick pulse and a strong pulse are very different things. The rate of the pulse varies at different periods of the day, gradually diminishing from morning to night, and notably declining during sleep. It is quickened during exercise and digestion. It is slower when we lie down than when we sit, slower when we sit than when we stand.*

5. *Cause of the Pulse.* — What is it causes the beating of the heart? Haller and his school attributed it to the irritability of the muscular walls, which are stimulated by the presence of the blood. There is this fact in favour of such an hypothesis, namely, that *after* the heart has ceased to beat, and its irritability is extinct, a little arterial blood injected into it will cause it instantly to resume its pulsations. This, however, is met by another fact, that the heart continues to beat long after it is empty of all blood.

Nor is the common statement correct, that the heart *retains* its irritability longer than any other muscle; I have found the tail and lower extremities of a Triton preserving their irritability,

* A valuable collection of details respecting the frequency of the pulse will be found in MILNE-EDWARDS: *Leçons*, iv. 50 *et seq.*; and BERNARD: *Liquides de l'Organisme*, i. 221.

and, indeed, almost all their vital properties, several hours after
the heart had ceased to beat: and Budge found the amputated
leg of a Frog retain its irritability as long as the heart.[*]

Not, therefore, by the possession of any greater irritability
is the heart distinguished from other organs, but by the possession of a power of spontaneous contraction, such as they do not
manifest. Other muscles will contract if some stimulus be applied, but they remain quiet so long as they are undisturbed.
The heart does not remain quiet. Remove it from the body, and
you will see its rhythmic pulsations continuing almost as if it
were within a living breast. Cut it lengthwise into two halves,
and each half will continue beating.[**] Cut it across, through
both auricles and ventricles, and both sections will beat as
before.

This is one of the spectacles that assail the mind of the anatomist with somewhat of a tremulous awe. The beating of the
heart, which from his childhood he has learned to associate in
some mysterious manner with life and emotion, he here sees occurring under circumstances removed from all possible sugges-
tions of emotion or life. What mean those throbbings? They
are not the equable movements of Life; they are not the agita-
tions of terror; they are not the impulses of instinct. Dead and
destroyed is the wondrous mechanism of which this heart but
lately formed the mainspring; and yet, beside the inert body
lies this beating organ, as if in the expiring agonies of struggle.

Why is this? For many years no explanation could be
given. We now know that in the substance of the heart
there is a complete little nervous system, consisting of ganglia
and nerves.[***] This system is not made up of the nerve-
filaments which come from the *pneumogastric* nerve. It is a
system belonging to the heart. Ganglia are to be found at
the base of the auricles and ventricles. The *auricular septum* of the frog's heart is the best place in which to study
these ganglia, because its transparence permits microscopic

---

* DONDERS: *Physiologie des Menschen*, I. 49.
** Harvey was acquainted with this fact.
*** In Chapter VIII. the reader will learn what is meant by ganglia; for the
present it is enough to say they are the nerve-*centres*.

investigation, without any preparation, which might alter the
natural disposition of the parts.* In mammals the ganglia may
be found on the surface of the auricles; and according to
Remak, who may be considered the discoverer of this ganglionic
system,** they are also on the surface of the ventricles. Todd
and Bowman,*** however, declare they could not find them in
the ventricle of the calf. I was equally unable to find them in
that of a pig, a mole, a mouse, a cat, and a kitten; and Eck-
hard† saw fibres, but no ganglia, in the septum of the tortoise.
It is probable, therefore, that there are considerable variations
in the distribution of these ganglia; but the fact of their existence is enough for us.

From these ganglia nerves are distributed through the muscular substance. That it is to this nervous apparatus we are to
ascribe the spontaneous activity of the heart is easily proved;
for if any part be severed from all connection with the ganglia,
the pulsations cease at once in that part; but if any part be
severed which still retains a ganglion, the pulsations will continue. The movements during life or death are thus seen to be
due to the ganglia.

But why these ganglia retain their power after the circulation has been destroyed, and why a similar power is not observable in other ganglia, still remains a problem. It seems
certain that the power is only retained during the continuance
of those molecular changes which we vaguely name vital; for if

* Few, I think, who examine a ganglion thus, can resist the conclusion
that the fibres pass beside and round the cells, but are *not* all in direct connection with them. I never saw any but "apolar cells" in these ganglia; and
three very eminent anatomists have assured me that they also have failed to
detect a single cell in direct connection with a fibre. If these negatives do not
affect the positive statement of those who say they have seen such cells in connection with fibres, at least they establish the fact that this connection is by no
means *necessary*. For my own part, attentive study of the nervous tissue in
every class of the animal kingdom, has convinced me that the theoretical conception of cells being necessarily in direct connection with fibres is untenable.
** REMAK in *Müller's Archiv*, 1844. — Compare also LEE: *On the Ganglia
and Nerves of the Heart*, Philos. Trans., 1849.
*** TODD and BOWMAN: *Physiological Anatomy*, II. 342 (where the two previous references are given).
† ECKHARD: *Beiträge zur Anat. u. Physiol.*, p. 151.

the heart be subjected to the influence of foreign gases, or be dipped in oil, its pulsations suddenly cease: on the contrary, if arterial blood be injected long after the cessation of all movement (provided decomposition has not commenced), the contractions are resumed. * It has been observed to beat in an exhausted air-pump; which excludes the idea of the atmosphere being the stimulus that sets it going.

. The heart pulsates in the embryo long before it contains blood, and long before any nerves have been developed in it — when, indeed, it is nothing but a mass of cells. Nor have we any evidence of the existence of nerves in those pulsatile sacs which constitute the hearts of the simpler animals: not only is there no evidence of such a structure, but all the evidence is decidedly against our supposing that these pulsatile sacs derive their contractions from nervous influence.

Here the reader probably thinks he sees a flagrant contradiction in our statements. We first do our utmost to show that the heart contracts only under nervous agency, and we then quietly assert that the embryonic heart, no less than the heart of various animals, is under no such agency whatever, yet it pulsates with a vigour not to be gainsaid.

But the contradiction is only apparent. The student of Physiology must expect to meet with such at every stage of inquiry. Extending his investigations into the vast field of animal life, he will gradually learn that Contractility is one of the vital properties of tissue, which may be excited by *various* stimuli. We happen to know with tolerable certainty, that, in the heart of the complex animal, the stimulus acts through the agency of a nervous system; in the embryonic heart of that animal, or in the permanent heart of simpler animals, we do not know the agency by which the stimulus is conveyed, nor do we know what the stimulus is.

Before quitting this beating heart, we may remark, that while on the one hand the pulsations are not in themselves

---

* Harvey says that one day, after the heart of a pigeon had ceased to beat, he placed his finger on it wetted with saliva, and in a short time, under the influence of this "fermentation," as he calls it, the heart recovered its vigour, and both auricles and ventricles pulsated.

evidence of life, on the other hand their cessation is no evidence of death, but only one among the many signs of death.

When death follows on a long or painful illness, the irritability of the heart vanishes almost with the vanishing breath; but if the decease be sudden, the heart will continue beating for some time afterwards. Harless observed it beating in the body of a decapitated murderer one hour after the execution. Margo found the right auricle beating two hours and a half after the execution, although not a trace of irritability could be detected in the other parts of the heart. Dietrich, Gerlach, and Herz, found that both ventricles contracted, if one were irritated, forty minutes after death.* Remak observed the rhythmic contractions in the hearts of birds and mammals two days after death; and Em. Rousseau mentions that a woman's heart had these rhythmic movements seven-and-twenty hours after she had been guillotined.

It is not always, indeed, that the pulsations cease even when the death has been gradual. Vesalius had a terrible experience of it. That great anatomist, who had nobly braved so much odium because he would not, as his predecessors had done, content himself with the dissection of animals, but suffered his scalpel to traverse the complexities of the human frame, one day opened the body of a young nobleman, whose medical attendant he had been, to ascertain, if possible, the cause of his death. Imagine the horror which ran through all present at the sight of the heart still equably beating! Vesalius was accused of having dissected a live man; nor was the accusation unreasonable in those days. He had to appear before the Inquisition, and narrowly he escaped with his life. A pilgrimage to the Holy Land was his punishment; but he never outlived the scandal created by this unfortunate occurrence.

6. *Action of the Arteries.* — Having made ourselves acquainted with the action of the heart, let us now inquire into its influence on the circulation. Every time the blood is pumped into the arteries a pressure is exerted, the force of which is estimated at *thirteen pounds.* This pressure, being on a column of liquid, it will, by the known laws of hydrostatics, not only

* Doedens: *Physiologie,* 1. 49.

drive that liquid onwards, but will also cause a great *lateral*
pressure, and thus distend the arterial tubes. These tubes are
eminently elastic, owing to the elastic tissue of their outer walls.
They are also eminently contractile, owing to the muscular
tissue of their inner walls. The elasticity is a physical property, and continues after death. The contractility is a vital
property, and vanishes with the disappearance of the molecular
changes of Nutrition.

Although the arteries are elastic and contractile throughout
their whole length, they are so in varying degrees: the elasticity
decreases, and the contractility increases, as the vessels become
smaller in calibre. What follows? Why, that when fresh blood
is impetuously poured into them from the heart, it dilates them;
and no sooner is the pressure taken off by the reopening of the
ventricles, than muscular contraction once more restores the
arteries to their former size, and in so doing forces the column
of blood onwards.

The heart's influence is thus decomposed into two portions:
one, which is of momentary duration, lasting no longer than the
contraction of the heart; another, which is occupied in expanding the artery. This second action is not lost, because the
contraction of the artery gives it back to the blood. At each injection of blood there is a pulsation. The distension does not
occur at the same instant in all the arteries; those nearest the
heart yield first, and those more distant a little later. There is,
consequently, a *wave of distension* passing along the whole length
of the vessel, and another *wave of motion* in the blood itself.
The interval of wave-motion from the heart to the wrist is only
one-seventh of a second.

7. *Action of the Capillaries.* — The sudden push and continuous pressure which the column of blood thus receives, suffice to carry it with great velocity to the network of capillaries,
which, be it observed, are elastic, but *not* contractile. In them
a very noticeable change occurs. Instead of the *rushing, leaping
movement*, which characterises the flow in the arteries, we observe an *equable current* of much less velocity: it no longer jets
like a spring, it wanders like a canal. The absence of contractility
in the capillaries prevents their assisting in driving the blood

onwards; and when we reflect that the *capillary area* traversed by the blood is *five hundred times greater than the arterial area*, and further reflect that, after traversing the capillaries, the blood has to pass through the veins to the heart, we shall understand why it has been held that some new force originates in the capillary area capable of effecting such a movement.*

What is that new force which comes into play when the force of the heart is nearly spent? A perfectly satisfactory answer to this question cannot, perhaps, be given in the present state of science; but we will give the hypothesis recently revived by Professor Draper.** He grounds it on a well-known physical law, namely, that if two fluids communicate in a capillary tube, which have *different* degrees of affinity for the walls of that tube, the fluid having the highest affinity for the tube will drive the other fluid before it. The two fluids in the blood-vessels are arterial and venous, and the greater affinity of arterial blood for the tissues causes it to drive the venous blood onwards.

Professor Draper commences by applying this principle to the circulation of the sap in the cells of plants.

"The motions of the sap in plants are clearly dependent on this principle. Leaving out of consideration the minor movements which take place for special purposes, or at specific epochs in the development, it may be truly said that the *nutritive changes occurring in the leaf are the primary cause of the motion*; for as the ascending sap presents itself on the sky-face of the leaf, it receives carbon under the influence of the sunlight from the air, and becomes converted into a gummy glutinous liquid. And just as in the pores of a bladder, or in those of any pervious mineral, pure water will drive out gum water, and occupy the pore, so will the ascending sap expel the gummy solution from the capillary tubes or intercellular spaces of the leaf. As fast as this takes place the active liquid becomes inactive, by itself changing into a gummy solution, and the movement is perpetuated. And this ensues not only in the leaf, but in every

---

* Unless we adopt the suggestion offered in the note to p. 227.
** DRAPER: *Human Physiology*, 1856, p. 142 *et seq.* The idea was casually thrown out by MÜLLER, and elaborately argued by ALISON: *Outlines of Phys.*, 3d ed. p. 62 *et seq.* It is restated by DRAPER with great ingenuity.

part of the plant; *the liquid to be changed presses upon that which has changed, and forces it onwards.*"

The motion of the blood depends on the same principle. The arterial blood, charged with oxygen, passes to all parts of the body in search of organic particles, for which it has affinity. No sooner is this affinity satisfied, than the blood becomes venous, and is pressed onwards by the eager column behind. "In my view of this subject, it is therefore the arterialisation of the blood in the lungs which is the cause of the circulation. I consider the circulation as the consequence of respiration; and though, in one sense, the minor causes are numerous, each portion of nervous material, each muscular fibre, every secreting cell, working its own way — these subordinate actions are all referable to one primordial act, and that is, the exposure of the blood to the air." Professor Draper then refers to the fact that whatever interferes with respiration, interferes with circulation. If an unbreathable gas is thrown into the cells of the lungs, the passage of the blood is instantly arrested, and suffocation occurs. If the access of air be prevented, as in drowning, in vain will the heart throb convulsively — the blood is not driven forward.

Professor Draper's hypothesis, then, is briefly this: the arterial blood has an affinity for the tissues, which causes it to press forwards in the capillaries; and no sooner is that affinity satisfied, than the blood becomes venous, and is pressed forward by the advancing column. In the lungs, venous blood presses forward to satisfy its affinity for the oxygen which is in the air. Having satisfied this, and become arterial, it is pressed on by the advancing column.

If the reader will station himself at the door of a theatre, and watch the column of eager playgoers struggling to get to the money-takers, he will see an image of the forces of the circulation. Each visitor is anxious to put down his half-crown in exchange for a ticket. No sooner has he satisfied that "affinity," than he finds himself pressed forward by the man behind him, still in a state of unsatisfied affinity; and so the rush continues. An image is not an explanation, but it may render an hypothesis more intelligible; and having attempted

to make Professor Draper's hypothesis intelligible, we will add,
by way of criticism, that it has one serious defect. It rests on
the notion of chemical affinity, yet chemical affinity acts only at
*insensible* distances, and here the distances are *sensible*. That
liquids should circulate in a tube, when one of them has a
greater affinity than the other for the walls of that tube, is not
evidence that the liquids will circulate in a tube in virtue of an
affinity supposed to exist between one of them and the tissues
*outside* the tube, because these tissues, being at sensible distances, cannot exert their affinity. If instead of "affinity" we
substitute "leakage" — if we remember that the action of en-
dosmose is necessarily set up between the blood and the tissue-
plasma, the hypothesis may be more acceptable.

- Spallanzani, in his celebrated *Mémoires sur la Respiration*,
relates that, when snails were confined in vessels, and had absorbed all the oxygen from the contained air, the movement
of their lungs ceased, and with it ceased all movement of the
heart — the circulation was arrested. He had only to remove
the top of their shells, which could be effected without injury,
and the phenomenon was easily watched. By keeping a snail
thus confined, at a temperature gradually diminishing, the gradual diminution of the respiration and circulation became very
evident. When the temperature fell to zero, the heart ceased
to beat altogether, and the blood was stagnant in the veins. In
this state of suspended animation the animal was kept for several hours; but on raising the temperature, the lungs began
once more to inflate, the heart to beat, the blood to circulate;
and, as in the palace of the Sleeping Beauty, all was vivid
activity where a minute before all was the image of death.

> "The hedge broke in, the banner blew,
> The butler drank, the steward scrawl'd,
> The fire shot up, the martin flew,
> The parrot scream'd, the peacock squall'd,
> The maid and page renew'd their strife,
> The palace bang'd, and buzz'd, and clackt,
> And all the long-pent stream of life
> Dash'd downward in a cataract." *

* TENNYSON.

The same effect of torpor was produced by the absence of oxygen and the absence of heat. Spallanzani placed a snail in a vessel containing mephitic gas. In eleven minutes the heart was still, and remained so during five hours. On reintroducing atmospheric air the lungs once more began to move, and life returned. To prove that it was the oxygen of the air, and nothing else, which caused this reanimation, Spallanzani repeated the experiment, substituting nitrogen gas for atmospheric air, as the replacer of the mephitic gas; but no movement was visible. Thus it appeared that the animal ceased to breathe because it had ceased to absorb oxygen. It ceased to absorb oxygen under two conditions — when there was none present in the air, and when the temperature was too low — the absorption of oxygen being always in a direct ratio to the temperature; and under both conditions the cessation of the absorption of oxygen was followed by the arrest of the circulation.

Viewing the Circulation in connection with Respiration, we see many arguments favourable to Professor Draper's hypothesis; but that there are some difficulties not easily reconcilable with that hypothesis, cannot be denied. For the present, however, it is enough to have mooted the question, and to have touched on some of the difficulties in the way of our accepting the heart as the sole agent in propelling the blood. "The relation between the interspaces of the capillaries, and the blood thus introduced to them, continues the current. The oxidising arterial blood has a high affinity for those portions that have become wasted; it effects their disintegration, and then its affinity is lost. The various tissues require repair; they have an affinity for one or other of the constituents of the blood; they take the material they need, and their affinity is satisfied; or secreting cells originate a drain upon the blood, and the moment they have removed from it the substance to be secreted, they have no longer any relation with it. So processes of oxidation, of nutrition and secretion, all conspire to draw the current onwards from the arteries, and push it towards the veins."*

We have now brought to a close our survey of the course and

* DRAPER, p. 145.

cause of the Circulation, and assigned to each labourer in this difficult field of research his share in the work. As an episode in the History of Science, the discovery of the circulation will always command the interest of readers; and if the foregoing sketch has had the good fortune to secure the attention of any medical readers, we hope it may have the further effect of inducing them to go carefully through the immortal works of WILLIAM HARVEY.*

Several times in the course of our exposition we have been forced to allude to the passage of the blood through the lungs, and the changes there impressed on it. Indeed, without such changes blood could serve no purpose in the organism. Respiration is the mainspring of animal existence. In the next chapter we shall attentively examine it.

* HARVEY'S works have been ably translated by Dr. R. WILLIS, and published in one volume by the Sydenham Society.

# CHAPTER VI.

## RESPIRATION AND SUFFOCATION.

Two suicides — Suffocation of seventy-two persons on board the "London-derry" — History of our knowledge of respiration — The air we breathe — Distinction between respiration as an Animal Function and as a Property of Tissue — Oxygen the life-giver — Varnished eggs will not develop; tail of a tadpole developing after separation from the body — The breathing-mechanism in various animals — The process of breathing — Tight-lacing — Alterations of the air in respiration — Necessity of ventilation — German taverns — How the organism accustoms itself to bad air — Effect of bad air in depressing the vital functions — Respiration a vital, not a physical, problem — Suffocation: various forms of — Carbonic acid not a poison — Oxide of carbon a poison: its effects on the blood — Deaths by suffocation: escape of gas: drowning — Respiration not a process of oxidation — The balance of nature — Trees not beneficial in streets — Varieties of animal respiration — Respiration during sleep — Effect of temperature on respiration — Why do we breathe?

A few years ago a young Frenchman, named Déal, finding his hopes of making a figure in the world were daily becoming more chimerical, resolved to die; and that he might not quit the world without producing some "sensation," he left this written account of his dying moments: — "I have thought it useful, in the interest of science," he wrote, "to make known the effects of charcoal upon man. I place a lamp, a candle, and a watch on my table, and commence the ceremony. It is a quarter past 10; I have just lighted the stove; the charcoal burns feebly.

"Twenty minutes past 10: the pulse is calm, and beats at its usual rate.

"Thirty minutes past 10: a thick vapour gradually fills the room; the candle is nearly extinguished; I begin to feel a violent headache; my eyes fill with tears; I feel a general sense of discomfort; the pulse is agitated.

"Forty minutes past 10: my candle has gone out; the lamp still burns; the veins at my temples throb as if they would burst; I feel very sleepy; I suffer horribly in the stomach; my pulse is at 80".

"Fifty minutes past 10: I am almost stifled; strange ideas assail me... I can scarcely breathe... I shall not go far... There are symptoms of madness...

"Sixty minutes past 10: I can scarcely write... My sight is troubled... My lamp is going out... I did not think it would be such agony to die... 10..." Here followed some quite illegible characters. Life had ebbed. On the following morning he was found on the floor, a corpse.

A few hours later, she whom he loved, and who loves him, hears of this rash act, which annihilates even hope. In her despair she flings herself into the dark and sullen Seine. The next morning a corpse is exposed at the dreadful Morgue. The casual spectator gazes on it with undefinable awe, as he thinks of the stillness of that wondrous organism, which but a few hours before was so buoyant with life. Where is all that mystery now? The body is there, the form is there, the wondrous structure is there, but where is its activity? Gone are the graceful movements of those limbs, and the tender sweetness of those eyes; gone the rosy glow of youth; gone the music of the voice, and the gaiety of the heart. The mystery of Life has given place to the mystery of Death.

What has thus suddenly arrested the wondrous mechanism, and, in the place of two palpitating, vigorous beings, left two silent corpses? The cause seems so trifling that we can only marvel at its importance, when revealed in the effect; it was the same in both cases, in spite of the difference of the means: that which killed the one, killed the other; the fumes from the charcoal pan, and the rushing waters of the Seine, interrupted the exchange of a small quantity of gases, and by preventing the blood from getting rid of its carbonic acid, in exchange for an equivalent of oxygen, the fervid wheels of life were suddenly arrested.

To get rid of its carbonic acid for an equivalent of oxygen — that is to say, to make a slight exchange of gases—seems a very trifling process; and only the impressive lessons of tragic experience can persuade men that this process is extremely important. Every child knows that we must have air to breathe; every one knows how unpleasant it is not to have *fresh* air to breathe; but the mass of mankind have no conception that air which is *not* fresh, is as bad as poison.

A very painful illustration of this ignorance is afforded by the calamity which occurred on board the "Londonderry," a steamer plying between Liverpool and Sligo. On Friday, 2d December 1848, she left for Liverpool, with two hundred passengers on board, mostly emigrants. Stormy weather came on, and the captain ordered every one to go below. The cabin for the steerage passengers was only 18 feet long, 11 feet wide, and 7 feet high. Into this small space the passengers were crowded; they would only have suffered inconvenience, if the hatches had been left open; but the captain ordered these to be closed, and — for some reason not explained — he ordered a tarpaulin to be thrown over the entrance to the cabin, and fastened down. The wretched passengers were now condemned to breathe over and over again the same air. This soon became intolerable. Then occurred a horrible scene of frenzy and violence, amid the groans of the expiring and the curses of the more robust: this was stopped only by one of the men contriving to force his way on deck, and to alarm the mate, who was called to a fearful spectacle: seventy-two were already dead, and many were dying; their bodies were convulsed, the blood starting from their eyes, nostrils, and ears.

The cause of this tragedy was owing to the ignorance of the captain and his mate. They had never learned the vital importance of fresh air. They had never been taught, that air which has once been breathed, cannot be breathed over again without injury; never been taught the fact, that air which has once passed to and fro in the lungs is vitiated, and that vitiated air is as bad as poison.

It is the same cause, acting with milder force, which makes the faces pale of those who issue from a crowded church, and gives a languor to those who have sat for some hours in a theatre, concert-room, or any other ill-ventilated apartment, in which human beings have been exhaling carbonic acid from their lungs. A breath of fresh air quickly restores them, and after breathing this fresh air, during a walk home, they scarcely feel any evil results of the late partial suffocation. Had the young man's door

been burst open, and fresh air admitted to his room, or had the
girl been rescued from the river, and made to breathe within a
few minutes after her plunge, or had the hatches been broken
open in time, all these victims would have been finally restored,
as our concert-goers are restored; and the concert-goers, if kept
much longer in that ill-ventilated room, would have perished, as
the others perished.

Amongst the earliest experience of mankind must have been
the necessity of fresh air for the continuance of life; but the
complete explanation of the fact, in all its details, is a scientific
problem, the solution of which only began to be possible when
Priestley discovered the gases of which the air is composed, and
the relation these bear to the organism; nor is the problem even
now entirely solved, in spite of the labours of so many illustrious
men. We have learned much, and learned it accurately; but
the difficulties which still baffle us are many and considerable.
. The ancients really knew nothing of this subject; nor did the
men of the sixteenth and seventeenth centuries lay any solid
foundation-stone. That was laid by Priestley, when he discovered
the oxygen contained in atmospheric air to possess the property
of converting venous into arterial blood. Lavoisier carried out
this discovery, and founded the chemical theory of Respiration.
Goodwyn (1788) applied the new views to Asphyxia (Suffocation),
showing, by a series of experiments, that when air was excluded,
venous blood remained unchanged; and when it remained unchanged, death inevitably followed. Bichat concluded from a
number of striking experiments, that an intimate relation
existed between Respiration, Circulation, and Nervous Action;
he showed how the access of venous blood to the brain stopped
its action, and subsequently stopped the action of the heart.[*]
Legallois extended these observations to the spinal chord.
But by far the most brilliant investigations on the subject
of Respiration are those of Spallanzani, whose *Mémoires* still
deserve a careful study, both as models of scientific research,

* Claudo Bernard has recently shown that venous blood is *not* poisonous,
although incapable of sustaining life; and that Bichat's experiments consequently must be otherwise interpreted. — BERNARD, *'Liquides de l'Organisme,*
. 507-18.

16*

and as storehouses of valuable facts. He was succeeded by W. F. Edwards, whose *Influence des Agens Physiques sur la Vie* (which may be found on the old book-stalls for a couple of shillings) still remains one of the best books the science can boast of. During the present century, hundreds of physiologists have devoted labour to the elucidation of the various difficulties which darken this subject, and a vast accession of valuable facts has been the result. The chief points which have been cleared up we may now endeavour to exhibit.*

1°. *The Air we breathe.* — In Respiration there are two objects to be considered, namely, the Air which is breathed, and the Breathing-mechanism. This air, which no man can *see*, is nevertheless a very material substance. We stuff cushions with it; and the chemists analyse it into well-known substances. It forms an atmospheric ocean forty-five miles in depth, surrounding our planet, and whirling with it, as it whirls around the sun. It is an ocean subject to incessant fluctuations, or tides, as we may call them. Like the other ocean it carries a variety of substances in its restless currents, but preserves a constant composition of its own, not affected by these substances. It is chiefly composed of two gases — Oxygen, which forms about one-fifth, and Nitrogen, which forms nearly the remaining four-fifths; that is to say, there are twenty-one parts of Oxygen to seventy-nine parts of Nitrogen. But besides these, there is always a *Fraction* of carbonic acid gas even in the purest atmospheric air: at ordinary elevations there are about two parts of carbonic acid in 5000 parts of air; so that we may reckon this gas as forming the $\frac{1}{2500}$ of the atmosphere. There are also traces of ammonia, but they are very slight.

The air of inhabited rooms, or of caves and dungeons, although constantly *tending* towards the standard of composition,

* In the following works will be found most of the facts cited or alluded to in our exposition: — SPALLANZANI: *Mémoires sur la Respiration;* EDWARDS: *De l'Influence des Agens physiques sur la Vie;* CLAUDE BERNARD: *Leçons sur les Effets des Substances toxiques;* MILNE EDWARDS: *Leçons sur la Phys. et l'Anat. Comp.;* LEHMANN: *Physiologische Chemie;* Dr. JOHN REID's article *Respiration* in the *Cyclopædia of Anat. and Phys.;* and the Treatises on Physiology of BÉRARD, MÜLLER, VALENTIN, LONGET, FUNKE, and DRAPER, already cited.

is, of course, subject to great variations. The respiration of animals and plants, and the decay of organic matters, incessantly alter the composition of the air in these places, and unless these alterations be quickly counteracted by free access of fresh air, the result is an atmosphere *injurious* or *unbreathable*. The air is vitiated by its proportion of oxygen being lessened, and its carbonic acid increased. It may be vitiated by other causes, such as the presence of injurious gases and effluvia, but the chief cause is the one just named.

When we breathe, and burn candles, or lamps, in a room, the breathing and the burning have a similar bad effect on the air, robbing it of oxygen, and loading it with carbonic acid; there is neither breathing, nor burning of candles without these effects. When Dalton analysed the air of a room in which, during two hours, fifty candles had been burning, and five hundred persons breathing, he found that instead of the proportion of carbonic acid being only two gallons in five thousand of air (which would have been the proportion in the air of the street), it was not less than one gallon in every hundred! This air would soon have become unbreathable. Leblanc analysed the atmosphere of three hospitals in Paris, and found that it contained five, ten, and twelve times as much carbonic acid as the air of the streets.

2°. *The Breathing-mechanism.* — Before describing the organs by which we breathe, it will be necessary first to define what is meant by breathing. It will perhaps strike some readers as an idle question, to ask What is Respiration? And yet until a distinct answer to that question is given, there can be no philosophical comprehension of the present subject; and as the purpose of these pages is to furnish philosophical students with material for reflection, no less than to furnish explanations of vital processes, we must endeavour to answer this question.

Reduced to its simplest terms, Respiration appears to be nothing more than the interchange of carbonic acid and oxygen, which takes place between the blood and the atmosphere. Our analysis comes down to this; and yet we shall be led into error if we accept this as the true answer to our question: for this is the *physical fact* implied in the process, it is not the *vital function* itself. This physical fact is not only manifested by the breathing apparatus, but by every tissue in the body, even when it is separated from the body. Take a fragment of muscle, rid it of its blood, and leave it exposed to the atmosphere; it will absorb oxygen, and give out carbonic acid. But no one would say that the muscle breathed; because breathing is an animal function, not a mere interchange of gases: a function dependent upon this interchange, but dependent *also* on the organic apparatus which performs it. We are thus led to distinguish between Respiration as the *Function of an apparatus of organs*, and that interchange of gases which is merely a Property of the tissues.

In the higher animals we see this Function performed by two different organs — gills and lungs. In both organs we find that a large quantity of blood is exposed to the air by means of a net-work of vessels spread over the surface. The blood arrives there black, and passes away scarlet. It has exchanged some of its carbonic acid for some of the oxygen of the air; it has become changed from venous into arterial blood. This *oxygenation of the blood* is therefore the special office of Respiration; and although all animals exhale carbonic acid and absorb oxygen — although every tissue does so — yet we must rigorously limit the idea of Respiration, as an animal Function, to that which takes place in the gills or lungs. True it is, that the simpler animals effect such exhalation and absorption by their *general surface*, and not by any *special modification of it* — such as gills or lungs; true it is, that even fish and reptiles, furnished with gills, also respire by their skin; and that, when the lungs of a frog are removed, the necessary oxygenation of the blood may be effected through the skin, if the temperature be low; nay, it is also true, that even man himself, in a slight degree, *respires by the skin;* so that the student tracing upwards the gradual complication of the organic apparatus, and finding, *first,* the whole of the general surface effecting the aëration needed; *secondly,* a part of the surface formed into a gill, in which aëration is far more active; and, *finally,* finding this gill replaced by a lung, may be tempted to say, "If the aëration of the blood is the office of Respiration, and if this is effected in some animals by the skin alone, in others by the skin and the gills, and in others principally by the lungs, but still in a slight degree also by the skin, how can you pretend to establish a distinction, other than a simple distinction of degree; how can you expect me to lay much stress on a verbal difference such as that between Function, and general Property of tissue?"

In reply to this plausible objection, we must observe that in science verbal distinctions are often extremely important; they keep attention alive to real, though subtle, distinctions. It is difficult to keep to such distinctions, for, as Bacon says, "words are generally framed and applied according to the conception of the vulgar, and draw lines of separation according to such differences as the vulgar can follow: and when a more acute intellect, or a more diligent observation, tries to introduce a better distinction, words rebel." In strict physiological language, no animal without blood ought to be said to *breathe;* for Respiration in such animals is not effected by a special apparatus of breathing organs; and in physiology *the idea of Function is inseparably connected with that of Organ,* as the Act is with its Agent. Professor Bérard says that, penetrated with the idea of a special organ being necessary for Respiration, he experienced a singular disappointment in reading the experiments of Spallanzani, which proved that every tissue of the body absorbed oxygen, and gave out carbonic acid; and he "only recovered his contentment on perceiving that the essence of Respiration consisted in this interchange of gases, so that, wherever a nutritive fluid was in contact with the atmosphere, Respiration must take place." Here the professor seems to us to have made an oversight, confounding the general with the particular, as completely as if a savage visiting England, and observing the transport of men and goods by railways, and "penetrated with the idea of a special method of transit being necessary," were afterwards to observe that vans, carts, and wheelbarrows also conveyed goods, from which he would conclude that the essence of transport being the removal of goods from one place to another, every means of transport must be a railway. The interchange of gases, like the transport of goods, may be effected by various means, but we only call the one Respiration, when it is effected by gills or lungs; and the other Railway transit, when it is effected by Railways. Professor Bérard was right in conceiving that a special organ was necessary for Respiration; and his error arose from confounding the *action of the organ* with the *result of that action*. Respiration effects the interchange of gases, and the aëration of the blood, by means of a peculiar organic apparatus, without which the due aëration would not take place in the higher animals. In the simpler animals this apparatus is not needed, because the nutritive fluid, being easily accessible, requires no apparatus to bring it into contact with the air; but no sooner does the organism become so complex that a direct aëration of the nutritive fluid ceases to be possible, than an apparatus is constructed, the function of which is to effect this aëration. In the gills and lungs we see such an apparatus.

Unless distinctions like these are established, Respiration ceases altogether to be a vital process; and every interchange of carbonic acid and oxygen, no matter where effected, will have an equal claim to be designated as a respiratory act. Therefore, as it is of the first importance in all physiological inquiries to keep constantly in view the part played by the organism in modifying physical laws, the philosophic reader will see at once that any verbal distinction which aids us in this must be of advantage.

If now we ask, What is Respiration? the answer will be this: *The function of the lungs or gills, by means of which the blood absorbs oxygen, and parts with carbonic acid and some other noxious elements.* Oxygen is the great inciter of vital changes; its presence is the indispensable condition of life. It is at once fuel and flame: it feeds, and it destroys: constantly withdrawn from the blood by the ceaseless activities of vital change, it is as constantly drawn into the blood by the process of Respiration. If the blood rushing through our lungs does not meet there with a supply of oxygen, the torrent carries to the tissues venous in lieu of arterial blood, and the consequence is an arrest of all the vital changes. If in passing through the lungs the blood only meets with a small supply of oxygen, an imperfectly arterialised fluid is carried to the tissues, and a partial arrest takes place, which is seen in the diminished vigour of the organism: all the functions are depressed; and if this depression continue, death arrives.

That oxygen does play this life-giving part, is familiar to all readers; but I will here cite two illustrations for the sake of their intrinsic interest. The chick inside its shell develops only when the air can penetrate the pores of that shell. If a varnish be rubbed over the surface of the shell, development is arrested; and although it appears that even varnish does not utterly prevent the penetration of gases, yet it so considerably diminishes it that the chick cannot develop. It is noticeable, moreover, that the precise point at which the development ceases, is that of the establishment of the first circulating system, when the vascular area begins to form. If one of these varnished eggs be freed from its varnish, and once more placed under the hen, it will develop.[*] Here we observe the absence of oxygen causing a complete arrest of vital changes. In the following case we shall see the reverse, namely, vital changes going on under free access of oxygen, with no other stimulus that can be detected. The case is so remarkable that I have thought it right to verify it by repeating the experiments several times.

Spallanzani, and after him numerous physiologists, found, that if the tail of a tadpole were cut off, it grew again rapidly. M. Vulpian thought of inquiring what became of the tail thus cut off? and he found that not only did it live many days, but it exhibited activity and development: it wriggled when touched, or when exposed to the air, and it developed new parts, as well as new forms.[**] I cannot say that I was fortunate enough to observe all the curious facts recorded by M. Vulpian; but respecting the main fact, namely, that the cells daily pass from their rudimentary state into that of actual muscle fibres, vessels, and pigment cells — in a word, that a regular process of development takes place — I can confirm his statement. These tails separated from the organism are without food, and the means of procuring food; yet the free access of oxygen is sufficient for a time to keep up the process of vital change.

To absorb oxygen is an animal necessity. The Blood, which is the great agent of Nutrition, must constantly be supplied with oxygen from the air.

It matters not whether the animal lives in air or in water — the real respiratory medium is always the air — for water, deprived of its air, or of its due proportion of oxygen, is as fatal

---

[*] See DARESTE: *Comptes Rendus de la Société de Biologie*, 1857, p. 101-120.

[**] See BROWN SÉQUARD's *Journal de la Physiologie*, I. 803.

to aquatic as to terrestrial animals. It matters not by what organ or surface the respiratory exchange takes place, it is always a twofold act of exhalation of carbonic acid on the one hand, and of absorption of oxygen on the other.

The variety of respiratory organs is great. In the Molluscs we find some kinds having no "organs" at all; some kinds having gills, others having lungs, and one kind (*Oncidium*) having both gills and lungs. In the Crustacea we find rudimentary gills. In spiders there are both gills and lungs. Fish have only gills. Frogs, toads, tritons, and salamanders begin life with gills, which disappear and give place to lungs. Reptiles, birds, and mammals, have lungs of different degrees of complexity.

Animals are said to breathe by their skin when the air, either in the water or as atmospheric air, comes in contact with the moist skin in which the blood is circulating.

Fig. 18.

*Gill-Respiration* is effected in a similar way: the water, rushing over the delicate surface, parts with oxygen, and takes up carbonic acid.

In *Lung-Respiration* the air is no longer outside, but inside the organ: it is drawn in from the atmosphere; the exchange is effected *in* the organ, and the altered air is then driven out, to be replaced by fresh air.

To understand the mechanism of Pulmonary Respiration, let us commence with an examination of the Water Newt (*Triton*), which presents us with the simplest form of the lung, and will therefore best enable us to understand the more complex forms. On opening the chest of this Newt, recently caught from a neighbouring pond, we observe two elongated air-sacs of thin membrane: these are the lungs.

Let us remove one of these sacs, and place it under the microscope. This is what we see: A delicate membrane, down one side of which we observe the pulmonary artery *a*, and running

LUNG OF TRITON (after Wagner).

up the other side, the pulmonary vein $b$; between these trunks, we observe smaller branches and innumerable capillaries, the meshes of which are indicated by the white spots.

After the air has entered the windpipe it passes into this sac, and there comes in contact with the delicate blood-vessels, through the walls of which the oxygen passes freely into the blood, and the carbonic acid passes out of the blood. How will the air, which is now in the sac, and which is vitiated by the presence of carbonic acid, and the loss of oxygen, be got rid of, to make way for fresh air? Simply by a contraction of the animal's abdominal mus-

Fig. 19.

cles. If you watch a live Triton in a glass-jar of water, you will see this contraction, and the bubble of gas, which is expelled.

Let us now take a live Triton, and examine its lungs under a magnifying power of 150 diameters; we can only see a very small bit at a time, but that bit will show us the circulation in the capillary net-work — a wondrous spectacle, indeed.

The lung of a man is little more than a repetition on a large scale of this very scheme: a myriad of small air-sacs are crowded together in the cavity of his chest. The Trachea, or windpipe, divides and subdivides into a number of *bronchial tubes*, which, when

CIRCULATION IN LUNGS OF TRITON
(after Wagner).

inflamed, as in violent colds, are the seat of the disease so familiar to all — *bronchitis.* A glance at Fig. 20, copied from Dr. Dalton, will enable the reader to understand the relation of these tubes to the lungs.

The tubes are seen to end in little islets of lung-substance: these are the "pulmonary lobules." If we now apply the microscope, each lobule is seen to be a cluster of air-cells (Fig. 21), of which, it is calculated that the human lungs contain six hundred millions. This, which is copied from Kölliker, is partly a real and

Fig. 20.

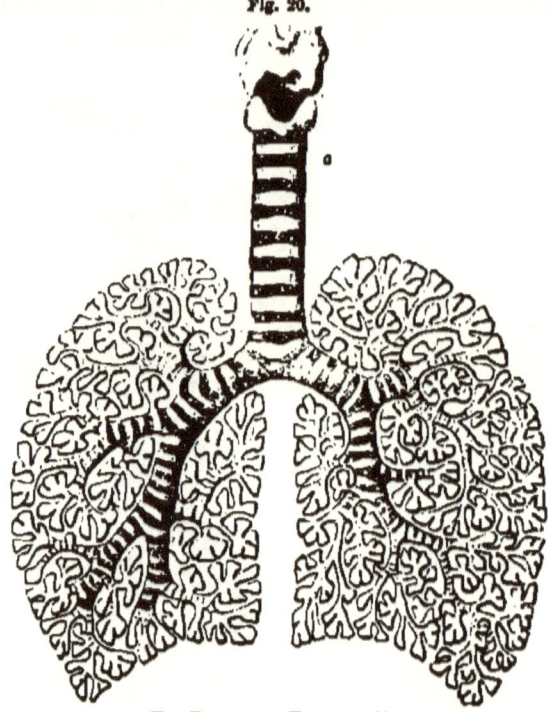

THE BRONCHIAL TUBES OF MAN
a, Windpipe branching off into minute tubes.

partly a diagrammatic representation. It enables us to understand how the air passes through the bronchial tube into the air-cells, between which, and outside of which, run the capillaries. These vessels are densely crowded; as may be seen in Fig. 22, also from Kölliker, magnified sixty times.

3⁰. *The Process of Breathing.* — Having thus ascertained the chief points respecting the air breathed and the breathing organ, we must now glance at the process. When we breathe, we draw in the air by our nostrils, which penetrates the trachea or wind-pipe, from thence passing into the bronchial tubes and tubelets, and from thence into the air-cells. Here it yields part of its oxygen to the blood, receiving carbonic acid in exchange. It was drawn in by a dilatation of the chest, and is driven out again by a con-traction of the chest. Science has accurately measured the amount of air thus inspired and expired — namely, about 20 or 25 cubic inches each time. But we never *empty* our lungs by an expiration;

Fig. 21.

A SINGLE BRONCHIAL TUBE WITH AIR-CELLS.

there is always a much larger quantity of air remaining in the air-cells; this quantity varying, of course, with the force of the effort. Herbst found that, while 25 cubic inches was the quantity expelled in ordinary quiet breathing, the quantity would rise to 90, and even 240 cubic inches, by very energetic efforts. It is therefore calculated that an adult man, with a well-developed chest, will retain about 170 cubic inches of air in his lungs, after each expiration, during ordinary breathing; and as 25 inches will be added at the next inspiration, there will be alternately 175 and 200 cubic inches of air acting on the blood which rushes over the vast area of the lungs. The phrase "vast area" is no exaggeration; for small as the bulk of those organs

Fig. 23.

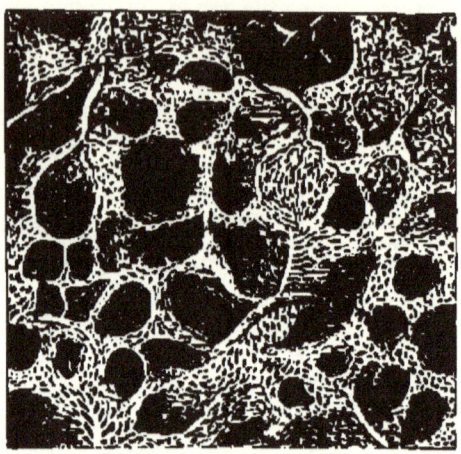

CAPILLARIES OF HUMAN LUNGS.

truly is, the amount of *surface* on which blood is exposed to the air in them, has been calculated by Lindenau at not less than 2642 square feet. Is it not wonderful to reflect that, in the course of a single year, 100,000 cubic feet of air have been drawn in and expelled, by something like 9,000,000 of separate and complicated actions of breathing, to aërate more than 3500 tons of blood?

4°. *Tight-lacing.* — The injurious effect of tight-lacing has often been pointed out, and in England, at least, women have pretty generally learned to see the danger, if not always the hideousness, of those wasp-waists once so highly prized. A single fact elicited in the experiments of Herbst will probably have more weight than pages of eloquent exhortation. It is this: the same man who, when naked, was capable of inspiring 190 cubic inches at a breath, could only inspire 130 when dressed: now, if we compare the tightness of women's stays with the tightness of a man's dress, we shall easily form a conception of the serious obstacle to efficient breathing which stays must present; and the injurious effect of this insufficient breathing consists, as we shall see hereafter, in its inducing a *depression of all the vital functions.*

5⁰. *Alteration of the Air in Respiration.* — In Respiration we draw in and give out a *similar quantity* of air; but this air is by no means of *similar quality.* It has been altered — vitiated. The ancients had no other notion of Respiration than that it served to cool the blood, as the air cools the heated brow. This is not its office. It serves to supply the indispensable conditions of vital changes, by removing carbonic acid from the blood, and supplying its place with oxygen. The air which is expired differs from that which was inspired: it has lost much of its oxygen, and has gained from 3 to 6 per cent of carbonic acid, a large amount of vapour, traces of ammonia, hydrogen, and volatile organic substances. The latter being very putrefiable, gives a fetid taint to the moisture condensed from the air on the window-panes, and to the moisture which soaks into all porous substances in the room. It was pure breathable air when it entered, and is now so vitiated that after a few repetitions of the process it becomes unbreathable. It is made unbreathable by the carbonic acid.

It is not difficult to demonstrate the production of carbonic acid in Respiration. Fig. 23 is an apparatus which beautifully demonstrates it.

A bird is placed in the bell-glass A, which is reversed over mercury. A vessel of water, B, serves to establish a current of air as the water flows out, and this current of air entering by the tubes 1 2, which contain pumice-stone moistened with a solution of potass, abandons there its carbonic acid; and the proof that it does so, is seen in the fact that it passes through Liebig's apparatus c (in which there is lime-water) *without* producing that milky appearance which would result if any carbonic acid were present, because this carbonic acid would unite with the lime, and form the carbonate of lime, or *chalk.* From c, therefore, the air enters the bell-glass entirely without carbonic acid. It is here breathed by the bird. The air which the bird expires passes from the bell-glass into the apparatus D, and there it meets with lime-

Fig. 23.

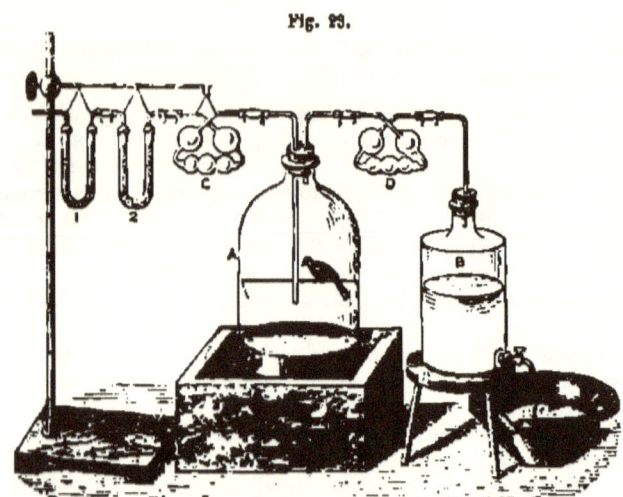

water, which it [renders milky by precipitating chalk; and thus proves that carbonic acid has been given out by the bird.

If any one thinks that the carbonic acid may have had some other origin, he can convince himself by simply breathing through a glass-tube into a glass of lime-water: its instantaneous milkiness will assure him that there was carbonic acid in his breath. The quantity of this gas which is momently thrown into the atmosphere by each individual, varies according to sex, age, physical and mental condition, and according to the season of the year, and time of day. We are constantly exhaling carbonic acid, but not in constant quantities. Men exhale much more than women; during the ages of from 16 to 40 the quantity exhaled by men nearly doubles that exhaled by women of the same ages. In men it is observed that the amount gradually increases from the age of 8 to that of 30, making a sudden start at the period of puberty. From the age of 30 it decreases gradually, till at extreme old age the amount is no greater than it was at 10. In women, a noticeable phenomenon is observed; the amount increases from infancy to puberty, just as in men; but at that epoch the increase suddenly ceases, and remains stationary till the change of life, when the amount increases. Besides such variations dependent on age and sex, there are others dependent on the muscular activity and physical condition of the individual. The amount of carbonic acid exhaled during digestion is greater than that exhaled during fast, and greater in sunlight than in darkness. Wines, spirits, tea, coffee, and narcotics lessen the amount; not, however, because they interfere with the process of Respiration, but because they cause less carbonic acid to be produced by the organism.

The exchange of these gases, considered simply as an exchange, is a physical fact resting on well-known physical laws. There have been, and there still are, disputes as to whether the gases are *free* in the blood, as in water, or are in a state of slight chemical combination; but the facility with which the exchange is made seems to be as great as if they were free. If blood be shaken in a vessel containing air, it will absorb from that air more than a tenth of its volume of oxygen. It is then *saturated;* and if now poured into a vessel containing carbonic acid, and there shaken, it will abandon almost all its oxygen, and absorb carbonic acid. This is a simple illustration of the interchange effected in the lungs and in the tissues; for, as previously indicated, the delicate walls of the blood-vessels oppose no obstacle to this interchange. It is only necessary that the blood should be brought in contact with an atmosphere, or a fluid, of a composition specifically different from its own. If we substitute hydrogen for oxygen, the animal confined in a vessel containing this gas will be found to exhale carbonic acid with the same facility as when atmospheric air is breathed. No animal can continue long to breathe hydrogen, simply because that gas does not furnish the conditions of vitality; but while the animal breathes in hydrogen, the exhalation of carbonic acid is as perfect as at any other time; thus showing that the exhalation depends on the difference in the nature of the gases in the atmosphere, and in the blood.

6°. *Necessity of Ventilation..* — When we breathe over and over again the same air, we gradually vitiate it by the constant exhalation of carbonic acid, which gradually brings the air up to the point where the difference between it and the blood — as regards the proportions of carbonic acid — disappears. The blood ceases to be arterialised, and the vital functions are arrested. In vain does the air still contain a quantity of life-giving oxygen; the blood cannot take it up, because it cannot get rid of the carbonic acid, and it cannot get rid of its carbonic acid because the conditions of the exchange are absent. To place an animal in air overcharged with carbonic acid, is equivalent to a gradual prevention of his breathing at all. Suffocation results from vitiation of the air in precisely the same manner as from interception of the air. Although burking and gagging are crimes which appal the public, that public seems almost indifferent to the milder form of the same murder when it is called "want of ventilation." In spite of the historical infamy of the Black Hole at Calcutta, our prisons, hospitals, theatres, churches, and other public buildings, were left disgracefully neglected, until, thanks to the energetic labours of our sanitary reformers, public attention was aroused. That thousands have been the victims of public ignorance on this important matter, may be shown by a single example. The deaths of new-born infants between the ages of 1 and 15 days, which in the Dublin Lying-in Hospital amounted in the course of four years to 2944 out of 7650 births, were suddenly reduced to only 279 deaths during the same period, after a new system of ventilation had been adopted. Thus more than 2500 deaths, or 1 in every 3 births, must be attributed to the bad ventilation.

In England the public is daily becoming more enlightened on the subject of ventilation, although a dangerous indifference, springing from want of elementary knowledge, is still prevalent, and taxes the patience of reformers; but in the country where these lines are written, it is painful to observe that even highly cultivated men seem almost insensible to the importance of fresh air. The Germans sit for hours in low crowded rooms, so dense with tobacco-smoke that on entering you cannot recognise your friends; and so vitiated is the atmosphere by the compound of breath, bad tobacco, exhalations of organic putrefiable matters, and an iron stove, that at first it seems impossible for you to breathe in it. Even in their private rooms they breathe a hot, musty, dry air, which makes an Englishman gasp for an open window. It is true that after a while you get accustomed to the air. You also get accustomed to that of the smoke-filled tavern. On entering, you felt it would be impossible to stay in it ten minutes; but in less than ten minutes it has become quite tolerable, and in half an hour scarcely appreciable. If you quit the room for a few minutes, and return once more after having breathed fresh air, again you perceive the poisonous condition of the atmosphere, but again you will get accustomed to it, and seem to breathe freely in it.

Was this atmosphere really not injurious? or have your sensations, like sentinels asleep, ceased to warn you of the danger? To answer this, we will first bring forward some experiments instituted by Claude Bernard on the influence of vitiated air (Fig. 24). A sparrow left in a bell-glass to breathe over and over again

Fig. 24.

A, Bell-glass; M. Mercury; C, Trough.

the same air, will live in it for upwards of three hours; but at the close of the second hour—when there is consequently still air of sufficient purity to permit *this* sparrow's breathing it for more

17*

than an hour longer — if a fresh and vigorous sparrow be introduced, it will expire almost immediately. The air which would
suffice for the respiration of one sparrow suffocates another. Nay
more, if the sparrow be taken from the glass at the close of the
third hour, when very feeble, it may be restored to activity; and
no sooner has it recovered sufficient vigour to fly about again,
than, if once more introduced into the atmosphere from which
it was taken, it will perish immediately. Another experiment
points to a similar result. A sparrow is confined in a bell-glass,
and at the end of about an hour and a half it is still active,
although obviously suffering: a second sparrow is introduced;
in about ten minutes the new-comer is dead, while the original
occupant flies about the lecture-room as soon as liberated.

One cannot try experiments on human beings as on animals,
but accident and disease frequently furnish us with experiments
made to our hand. What has been just related of the birds, is
confirmed by an accident which befell two young Frenchwomen.
They were in a room heated by a coke-stove. One of them was
suffocated, and fell senseless on the ground. The other, who
was in bed, suffering from typhoid fever, resisted the poisonous
influence of the atmosphere, so as to be able to scream till assistance came. They were both rescued, but the healthy girl, who
had succumbed to the noxious air, was found to have a paralysis
of the left arm, which lasted for more than six months. Here, as
in the case of the sparrows, we find the paradoxical result to be,
that the poisonous action of a vitiated air is better resisted by
the feeble, sickly organism, than by the vigorous, healthy organism.

This paradox admits of a physiological explanation. In the
vitiated air of a German *Kneipe*, as in that of the houses of the
poor, we find those who have had time to adjust themselves to it,
breathing without apparent inconvenience, although each new-
comer feels the air to be vitiated; and because they "get accustomed to it;" people very naturally suppose that no injurious
effect can follow. Here lies the dangerous fallacy. They get
accustomed to it, indeed, and only because they do so are they
contented to remain in it; but at what price? by what means?
By a gradual *depression of all the functions* of nutrition and secre-

tion. In this depressed condition less oxygen is absorbed, and therefore less is needed in the atmosphere. A vitiated air will suffice for the respiration of a depressed organism, as it would amply suffice for the respiration of a cold-blooded animal. When we enter a vitiated atmosphere, our breathing becomes laborious; the consequence of this is a depression of all the organic functions, and *then* the breathing is easy again, because we no longer require so much oxygen, and we no longer produce so much carbonic acid. Were it not for this adjustment of the organism to the medium, by a gradual depression of the functions, continued existence in a vitiated atmosphere would be impossible; we see the vigorous bird perish instantaneously in air which would sustain the enfeebled bird for upwards of an hour.

Thus does Physiology explain the paradox; but at the same time it points out the fallacy of supposing that bad air can be harmless because we "get accustomed" to it. It is a fortunate circumstance for those who have to breathe bad air, that the organism is quickly depressed to such a point as to render the air breathable, yet no one will deny that depressions of this kind are necessarily injurious, especially when frequently experienced. There is indeed a wonderful elasticity in the organism, enabling it to adapt itself to changing conditions; but a frequent depression of functional activity must be injurious, and fatal if prolonged.

It is interesting to observe the effect of a *gradual* adjustment of the organism, as contrasted with one less gradual. The longer the time allowed, the easier is this adjustment. Thus a bird will live three hours in a certain quantity of air; in the same quantity, two birds of the same species, age, and size, will *not* live one hour and a half, as might be supposed, but only one hour and a quarter. Conversely, the bird which will live only one hour in a pint of air, will live three hours in two pints.

7°. *Respiration a vital Problem.* — Enlightened by these remarkable results, we shall now be able to regard Respiration as a physiological function rather than as a simple physical process. On more than one occasion we have had to protest against the tendency to explain vital phenomena by physical and chemical laws only, without regard to the order of conceptions specially

belonging to vital phenomena; and we must repeat that protest
in the present case. That Respiration is ultimately dependent
on physical laws, no one thinks of disputing; and in the arduous
endeavour to detect the operation of those laws, it is natural that
men should neglect the still more difficult study of vital laws.
But we think it can be shown that however far analysis may trace
the operation of the laws of gaseous interchange and diffusion,
and the condensing action of moist membranes, these will only
conduct us to the threshold; they will never open for us the
temple. These physical laws reveal only one part of the mystery.
Respiration is not a simple physical fact.  It is the function of a
living organism, and as such receives a specific character from
that organism.  No sooner do we cease to regard the exclusively
physical aspect of this function — no sooner do we fix our attention on the organism and *its* influence, than the theory raised on
the simple laws of gaseous interchange suddenly totters and
falls.

It seems easy to explain why warm-blooded animals cease to
breathe in an atmosphere charged with a certain per-centage of
carbonic acid, although there may still remain sufficient oxygen
to permit a candle to burn in it, and even to permit continued respiration if the carbonic acid be removed.  The presence of a
certain amount of carbonic acid in the air *prevents* the exhalation
of carbonic acid from the blood. , As we read the explanation,
nothing can seem clearer, and we admire the skill with which the
laws of the absorption of gases are brought to bear on the question.  But as we pursue our researches, various difficulties arise;
and as we extend the inquiry from the respiration of warm-
blooded to that of cold-blooded animals, we learn that the fact
is not at all true of the simpler organisms.  Let us for a moment
consider one striking contradiction: the air which has once
passed through the lungs of a man, and which, in losing four or
five per cent of its oxygen, has become charged with three or four
per cent of carbonic acid, will yield but very little of its remaining oxygen when again passed through the lungs; and if this air
be breathed over and over again, until the sense of suffocation
forces a cessation, the air will still be found to contain ten per
cent of oxygen — that is to say, nearly half its original quantity.

In air thus vitiated the respiratory process is impossible, but *only impossible for warm-blooded animals in health:* frogs, reptiles, fish, and molluscs, instead of perishing when the air has lost about half its oxygen, continue to breathe, and to absorb oxygen, almost as long as there is any left. Spallanzani, Humboldt, and Matteucci, have placed this beyond a doubt by their experiments; and when we consider how long these experiments have been before the world, it is a matter of surprise that the contradiction they give to all the purely physical theories of Respiration has not been insisted on. If the process depends *simply* on the proportion of gases in the atmosphere, how is it that one animal can continue to breathe in an atmosphere unbreathable by another? If it be *simply* the interchange of oxygen and carbonic acid, and this interchange be frustrated whenever eleven per cent of oxygen has disappeared, the law must be *absolute:* it must be as applicable to reptiles and molluscs as to birds or mammals. Instead of this, we find that reptiles can continue to breathe long after such a limit has been passed; they continue to absorb oxygen as long as even only three per cent remains, in spite of the continually increasing proportion of carbonic acid. How is it that the physical laws of absorption frustrated the Respiration of one class of animals, and were powerless with another class? Why is it that, when a bird and a frog are confined in the same vessel, the frog will continue to absorb oxygen from the vitiated air in which the bird has long perished? Clearly the cause of this difference lies in the difference of the organisms; and we must no longer seek in the mere quantities of gases an explanation of interrupted respiration; we must no longer say that "breathing becomes impossible when the air is charged with a certain amount of carbonic acid, *because* that amount prevents the gaseous interchange;" but we must say that such an amount prevents the gaseous interchange, because it interferes with the organic action of the pulmonary apparatus. The distinction becomes palpable when we have an organism which is not affected by this amount of carbonic acid, and is even more palpable when we see a warm-blooded animal capable of breathing for a long period the air which, under a different condition, it would find unbreathable. We have seen how a bird, with its functions depressed, can continue to breathe for an hour in an atmosphere which immediately suffocated another bird of the same species; whereby it became clear that the lungs of one warm-blooded animal could absorb oxygen from an atmosphere in which there was such a proportion of carbonic acid, that sufficient oxygen could not be absorbed by a vigorous animal of the same species.

The intervention of organic conditions, modifying the simple physical laws of gaseous exchange, is sufficiently evident from what has just been said; but we have as yet no clear insight into the nature of this intervention; we do not know why blood, charged with carbonic acid, cannot in the one case exchange that gas for the oxygen, of which ten per cent still remains, since in another case the same blood *can* effect the exchange when there is even less than ten per cent of oxygen.

Atmospheric air contains only twenty-one per cent of oxygen. But if fifty per cent of oxygen be mixed with fifty of carbonic acid, a warm-blooded animal is suffocated in it, in spite of there being more than double the amount of oxygen present in the ordinary atmosphere. Bernard, who made the experiment, thinks that the carbonic acid in this mixture prevented the oxygen from entering the blood, not only because of its greater solubility, which gives it a tendency to displace the oxygen, but also because of the obstacle it presents to the exhalation of carbonic acid. On the other hand, the extensive and careful experiments of Regnault and Reiset show that Respiration will take place quite well in an atmosphere which contains as much as twenty-three per cent of carbonic acid, if at the same time it contains as much as forty per cent of oxygen. How are we to reconcile such facts as those just cited? In the one case we see that fifty per cent of oxygen is insufficient, if the amount of carbonic acid be also fifty per cent; in another case we see that forty per cent of oxygen suffices, if the carbonic acid do not exceed twenty-three per cent; and we could explain both by saying, that unless the amount of oxygen nearly doubles that of carbonic acid, respiration is impossible, were it not for the irresistible objection that reptiles breathe in an atmosphere which has become charged

with carbonic acid, and has gradually lost all but three per cent
of its oxygen.

We have raised difficulties which we cannot pretend to remove.  It is enough to have called attention to the physiological
problem involved, as a justification of our scepticism in presence
of the purely physical explanations.  Respiration is not a simple
interchange of gases, but an organic function, which chiefly consists in exhaling carbonic acid and absorbing oxygen: whatever ·
interferes with the exhalation or the absorption, checks Respiration, no matter what may be the condition of the atmosphere.  As
a final proof of the correctness of this conception, we will add
that oxide of carbon, by preventing the exhalation of carbonic
acid from the blood, prevents all Respiration, whatever amount
of oxygen may be in the air.  Moreover, experimenters are now
agreed that there is no accurate correspondence between the
amounts of oxygen absorbed and carbonic acid exhaled, as there
ought to be were the process one of simple exchange.

II. SUFFOCATION. — With this explanation of the process of
Respiration, let us now approach the terrible phenomenon of
Suffocation, or Asphyxia, which is the consequence of a continued interruption of the breathing process.  This interruption
may be owing either to the air being prevented from entering the
lungs — as in drowning, hanging, gagging, &c. — or by the air
which enters being too poor in oxygen, or too rich in carbonic
acid, or in oxide of carbon.  To tighten a cord round a man's
neck, to hold his head under water, or to burn charcoal in his ill-
ventilated room, are three modes of producing the same result.
Every one can understand that if you forcibly prevent an animal
from breathing, you must cause its death, because breathing is
necessary to life; but every one does not understand that air
which has been vitiated by the breathing of animals, or the burning of candles and gas, is kept out of the blood as certainly as if
a pillow were pressed upon the face.

One very general, indeed almost universal, misconception r
this subject is, that carbonic acid is poisonous in the blood; ᴵ
the truth seems to be that the carbonic acid is noxious only v
it prevents the access of oxygen.  There is always carboni·

in the blood, both venous and arterial. Its accumulation in the blood is only fatal when there is such an accumulation *in the at-mosphere* as will prevent its exhalation; its mere presence in the blood seems to be quite harmless, even in large quantities, provided always that it be not retained there to the exclusion of oxygen. Carbonic acid, when absorbed into the blood, which is alkaline, cannot there exert its irritant action as an acid, because it will either be transformed into a carbonate or be dissolved. Bernard has injected large quantities into the veins and arteries, and under the skin of rabbits, and found no noxious effect ensue. The more carbonic acid there is in the blood, the more will be exhaled, provided always that the *air* be not already so charged with it as to prevent this exhalation.

This is a sufficient answer to the Tectotal argument, that Alcohol *must* be poisonous, because it is said to cause an accumulation of carbonic acid in the blood. This is not true, as a matter of fact; and if true, it would in no way affect the breathing process; the extra quantity of carbonic acid would be got rid of as easily as the usual quantity.

But *oxide of carbon* is a poisonous gas. Every reader will remember the *blue* flame which rises from lighted coals or wood; that is oxide of carbon; and being notoriously poisonous, it has by some writers been selected as the real agent in those numerous deaths occurring from voluntary and involuntary exposure to the fumes of charcoal in closed chambers. Carbonic acid was said to be innocent, and oxide of carbon had to bear the whole infamy. There is no doubt, however, that although carbonic acid is not a poison, it will produce asphyxia, and deaths from charcoal-fumes may occur either from this asphyxia, or from poisoning by oxide of carbon, or from a conjunction of the two. Oxide of carbon is truly called a poison, because its action is deleterious even in slight doses, no matter what may be the state of the atmosphere; but carbonic acid is only deleterious when the quantity in the atmosphere is such that the absorption of oxygen is frustrated.

Carbonic acid passes to and fro; leaving the blood otherwise unaltered; but oxide of carbon really kills the blood. If we take a little venous blood and expose it to oxide of carbon, it becomes instantly scarlet. In appearance the change has been nothing more than would have occurred had oxygen, instead of the oxide, been employed. But in fact, the change has been very considerable.

Fig. 25.

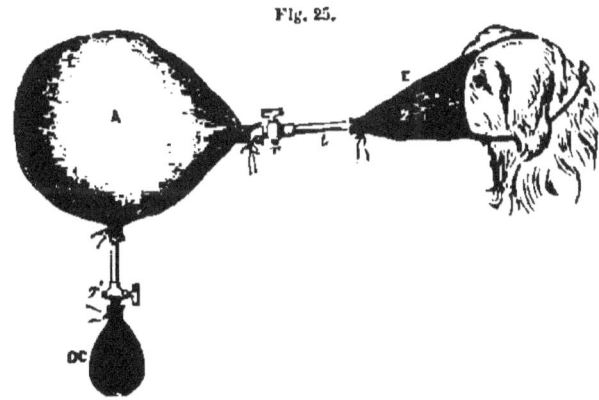

In Fig. 25 we see how Bernard causes a dog to breathe the oxide of carbon. At first the gas, which is in the bladder, is kept from the dog, and the blood flowing from an opened vein is seen to be black. But on turning the cock, and causing the oxide to mingle with the air breathed, the blood is rapidly seen to be scarlet; and unless the operation is suspended immediately, the dog will die suffocated. This scarlet blood will not become black again on exposure to carbonic acid, as would be the case if oxygen had given the scarlet colour. On the contrary, the scarlet colour is retained for weeks.

Prussic acid produces a similar effect. Poisoning by prussic acid, or by oxide of carbon, may be detected by this scarlet colour of the venous blood.

The effect of oxide of carbon is to render the blood-discs incapable of that process of exhalation, on which, as we have seen, the activity of the organism depends. The blood, to all appearance, preserves its vitality, for neither the form nor the colour of its discs is altered; but the blood is really dead, because its restless changes are arrested. Ever wonderful is the fact constantly obtruding itself upon us, that Life is inseparably linked with Change, and that every arrest is Death. Only through incessant destruction and reconstruction can vital phenomena emerge, an ebb and flow of being. The moment we preserve organic matter from destruction, we have rendered it incapable of the restless strivings of Life. A spirit like that of Faust seems ranging through all matter; and if ever it should say to the passing moment, "Stay! thou art fair," its career will be at an end.

*Deaths from Suffocation.* — We have seen that a current of fresh air prevents carbonic acid from being noxious, unless the quantity be very considerable; and it is on this account that coal, coke, candles, gas, &c. can be burned in our apartments without injury. But it is important to know that a current of fresh air will not always prevent death from suffocation. It is important to know that there is no absolute safety in the fact of the room being ventilated; the mere presence of carbonic acid will not cause suffocation in such a room, but unhappily the carbonic acid is frequently accompanied by oxide of carbon, and it is to *this* we must attribute those accidents which have occurred in manufactories, when the workmen, seated at tables under which coke was burning, have fallen back suffocated. Dr. Marye cites a case of asphyxia which occurred in a room, one of the window-panes of which was broken, so that a current of air must have circulated in it. In 1835, a shopkeeper of Paris was found suffocated in his bed, although the room in which he slept was over the shop, communicating with it by an open staircase, and the shop had its windows, opening on the street, imperfectly closed. In spite of this free access of air, the noxious vapours from a stove in which coke and coal were burning, suffocated him.

Gas is a great spoiler of the air; but it has the merit of giving timely warning of the danger, by the horrible smell which accompanies its escape. This smell is perceptible when there is only one part in a thousand parts of air; becomes very offensive when the proportion is $\frac{1}{750}$ or $\frac{1}{540}$, and is almost insupportable as the proportion increases. If the gas has escaped from a crack in the pipes, and been allowed to mingle with the air in which a free circulation by ventilation is impossible, so that the proportion of gas amounts to $\frac{1}{14}$, it explodes on the introduction of a candle. This was the cause of that terrible accident some twenty years ago in Albany Street, when a whole house was blown up, as if a powder-mill had been ignited. Gas, when burning, is also very injurious, and seems to have a particularly bad effect upon the nervous system, as all persons know who have attended to their sensations. It produces excitement, headache, lassitude, and often sickness. While ventilation is in all cases indispensable, it becomes more and more urgent in proportion to the amount of gas or coke which is burning in the room; and when we reflect on the compound of evils which meet together in a theatre, concert-room, or lecture-room — the air robbed of its oxygen by the burning and the breathing, and loaded with carbonic acid, animal effluvia, and heat, there can be little surprise if a violent headache, or unusual languor, is the result of staying three hours in such an atmosphere.

Death from drowning is also a form of suffocation. On sinking into the water, a man first struggles to the surface, and gasps for breath; but with the air there enters some water, and this makes him cough; in coughing to expel the water, he expels a great part of the air which he had drawn in. In a few seconds his strength fails; he can no longer rise to the surface, the urgent demand for fresh air forces him to open his mouth, and this only allows more water to enter, and asphyxia results. But this is not always the course of the phenomena. Sometimes the man receives such a shock that he is instantaneously deprived of the use of his faculties — he faints in the water, and dies without a struggle. Sir Benjamin Brodie tells a story of a man who was recovered from drowning, and who described it as being a very calm and blissful mode of death. The last thing he was conscious of was, that he quietly counted the pebbles on the bottom.

III. Theories of Respiration. — It is hoped that the fore-going pages have furnished the reader with many important hints for practical guidance, and have duly impressed him with the serious necessity of attending to ventilation in bed-rooms, sitting-rooms, and manufactories; but there are also speculative points which might profitably detain us, after we have fully satisfied ourselves on the practical points. A few of these may now be touched on.

And, first, of that popular theory which declares Respiration to be a process of Oxidation. It probably caused the reader a pleasant feeling of surprise when he first heard that the burning of a candle, the rusting of iron, and the process of breathing, were only three forms of the same process — three names for three different forms of combustion or oxidation. There is, in-deed, a fascination in such generalisations. One almost regrets to find them not correct. I am sorry to say this one is not correct. The burning of a candle and the rusting of iron are, indeed, two forms of one process of combustion. They are oxidations; but respiration can no longer be considered, in any sense, as a process of oxidation. The combustion-theory is a mistake from first to last. Respiration, as a process, is two-fold — the exhalation of carbonic acid, and the absorption of oxygen.

The interesting experiments of Priestley will enable us to set forth the differences between Respiration and Combustion. He placed mice in a bell-glass, where in due time they were suffo-cated by the air which they had vitiated; other mice were in-troduced, and they expired immediately. In another bell-glass a candle went out, after having in its combustion absorbed a part of the oxygen; another burning candle was introduced, and it was at once extinguished by this vitiated air. In both of these vessels some mint was now placed, where it flourished, and so completely revivified the air, by absorbing its carbonic acid and giving out oxygen, that mice could again breathe in the one, and a candle burn in the other. In these experiments we *seem* to have a demonstration of the identity of Combustion and Re-spiration — and this, indeed, was the conclusion drawn; but

that the conclusion is erroneous, appears from the experiments
of Claude Bernard, who takes a bell-glass containing an atmosphere of 15 per cent of oxygen, and 2 per cent of carbonic
acid — the rest of the oxygen having disappeared to form water
with the hydrogen of the candle which has just gone out. In
this atmosphere, in which a candle will not burn, a linnet will
breathe at ease for some time. Bernard then reverses the experiment, and makes an atmosphere in which a candle will burn, but
in which an animal instantaneously perishes — an atmosphere
composed half of oxygen and half of carbonic acid, in which a
candle will burn *better* than in the air, because of the greater
amount of oxygen; but in which the animal perishes, because,
in spite of the amount of oxygen, that oxygen cannot be absorbed. The bird, when about to expire in vitiated air, will be
recalled to life if the carbonic acid be removed by the introduction of potash — showing that it is owing to the presence of
this carbonic acid that Respiration is impeded; but we cannot
thus restore the expiring flame of the candle by removing the
carbonic acid. Place lighted candles in two bell-glasses, and
as soon as the combustion grows feeble, introduce into one glass
some potash to remove the carbonic acid, you will, nevertheless,
find that the candles in both glasses will go out at the same instant. The experiment is very simple, and its significance is
plain. By it we see the difference between Combustion, which
is only oxidation, and Respiration, which is not *oxidation* but
*exchange*. In the combustion of the candle the oxidation is
everything, and no process of exchange takes place. In the
breathing of an animal the exchange is everything, and no oxidation takes place. The candle expires because there is not
enough oxygen in the air; the animal expires because there is
too much carbonic acid in the air.

Further, to prove that Respiration is an exchange of gases
in the lungs, and not a process of oxidation, we need only refer
to the experiments of Spallanzani and W. Edwards — experiments so celebrated, that one is amazed to find one's-self
citing them in this discussion, which they ought long ago to
have closed.

A frog was placed in a bell-glass containing pure hydrogen gas, reversed over mercury: Fig. 26. Before placing it there, all the air had been pressed out of its lungs. For eight hours and a half it continued to breathe this hydrogen, and continued to give out carbonic acid. The same experiment will succeed also with warm-blooded animals, if tried on those newly born; but after they have breathed for some hours they are unable to stand the test. These experiments prove that carbonic acid pre-exists in the blood, and is not formed during respiration by the oxygen as it enters; and prove, likewise, that the respiratory process is a double one of *exhalation and absorption*, which can take place as well with hydrogen as with oxygen: and we are thus forced to exclude the idea of oxidation altogether. Although respiration can take place without oxygen, life will not long continue without it; for, as before stated, oxygen is the power which burns organic matter into life.

Fig. 26.

There is another form of the combustion-theory, held by those who give up the idea of carbonic acid being formed in the lungs. It is this: "The oxygen of the air burns the carbon of the tissues into carbonic acid, and the hydrogen into water." Widely as this hypothesis has been accepted, there is not one bit of direct evidence that carbonic acid and water are ever formed in this way in the organism; it is purely inferential, and there are many reasons against our accepting it even hypothetically. But even on the supposition that such direct oxidations were the source of the carbonic acid and water, we should still have to declare that Respiration was not a process of Combustion. If oxidation of tissue is one *result* of Respiration, it is not the *process*.

Why is death inevitable when the access of fresh oxygen is excluded? The fact we know — of the reason we are ignorant. There still remains a large quantity of oxygen in the blood of the expiring animal; nor will death be sensibly retarded if fresh oxygen is injected into the veins and arteries. How is this? The process of respiration brings oxygen to the blood; yet, if the oxygen be brought there through a more direct channel while respiration is impeded, the animal will die as quickly as if left to itself. Bernard tied a dog's head in a bag, which would in a certain time produce suffocation, and he found that period by no means retarded when he injected oxygen into the arteries.

2⁰. *The Balance of Nature.* — Quitting for a moment this labyrinth of difficulty and doubt, which alternately fascinates and disheartens us when we strive to gain some explanation of the myriad processes of Life, let us stand apart and contemplate the marvel of respiratory interchange, no longer as an animal function, but rather as a planetary phenomenon; let us endeavour to picture to ourselves the silent creative activity everywhere dependent on this interchange. The forests, the prairies, the meadows, the cornfields, and gardens — the mighty expanse of plant-life covering mountain and valley — these subsist on the carbonic acid which is exhaled from the lungs and bodies of animals. Plants take up this carbonic acid from the atmosphere, mould the carbon into their own substance, and set free the oxygen, once more returning it to the atmosphere. Animals reverse the process, taking up the oxygen, and giving out carbonic acid for the nourishment of plants. This beautiful rhythmus of organic life has been so often described that it has almost become a commonplace, without, however, losing its charm for the contemplative mind.

The dependence of plant on animal, and of animal on plant, united in one mystery, and ever acting each for the advantage of the other, is not an idea to lose its charm by becoming familiar; but it sometimes leads to misconceptions. What, for instance, seems more natural than that the influence of trees planted in our cities should be very beneficial? If trees can thus withdraw the noxious carbonic acid from the vitiated air of cities, would it not be desirable — nay, ought it not peremptorily to be demanded — that as many trees should be planted in our streets as we can find room for? Such conclusions are soon reached by swift logicians. But Nature is apt to elude the grasp of swift logicians, and she repeatedly declines to fall into the most symmetrical of their formulas. Not that Nature is capricious or illogical; but logicians are apt to draw inferences before they have collected sufficient data. Nature, in the present case, point-blank declares that the influence of vegetation on the atmosphere is totally *inappreciable*, unless the atmosphere be in a closed chamber or vessel, and *then* the influence is striking. Human wit has discovered no test delicate enough to appreciate the influence of plants on the free atmosphere in which we live. The depth and compass of this air-ocean are too vast, and the amount of oxygen absorbed by animals too trivial in comparison, for any effect to be appreciable; moreover, the mixture of the gases in the air, and their mutual diffusion, is so rapid, that no difference has yet been detected in the proportions of oxygen and carbonic acid in the air of crowded towns or wooded valleys. The air of cities will hold more noxious exhalations suspended in it, but its gaseous composition will be the same as that of the country. To give an idea of the insignificant part played by animals as vitiators of the great air-ocean, we may mention the calculation made by the distinguished chemist Dumas, that all the oxygen consumed by all the animals on the surface of the globe during one hundred years would not amount to more than the $\frac{1}{1000}$ of the quantity in our atmosphere; and even supposing all vegetation to be annihilated, consequently no oxygen to be returned to the air by the incessant reduction of the carbonic acid, there would still need a period of ten thousand years before the diminution of the oxygen could become appreciable by any instruments we have hitherto invented.

3⁰. *Varieties in Animals.* — The fact that Respiration is an animal function, dependent upon a peculiar organic apparatus, leads us at once to suspect that it will exhibit great varieties — not only in various animals, but in the same animal under different conditions.

We learn, for example, without surprise, that animals of

large bulk consume more air than the smaller animals; horses and oxen more than men; men more than dogs and cats. But, to use an Eastern figure, it raises the eyebrow of astonishment when we learn that the proportion of carbonic acid exhaled by a man and a horse bears no sort of correspondence to the differences in their relative bulk — the proportion being 187 to 16. We are, in like manner, puzzled to find that a full-grown cat only exhales 1¼ of carbonic acid, where a rabbit produces more than 2. How is this to be explained? Is there not a streak of light trembling on this question when we bring forward the fact previously mentioned, that the vegetable feeders uniformly exhale more carbonic acid than the animal feeders, and that carnivorous animals exhale more than their usual quantity if they are fed on vegetables? Some light may fall from this source, but it does not suffice to clear up the obscurity.

Another interesting problem also arises here: — Although the larger the animal, the greater the *absolute* amount of carbonic acid it produces,* yet the smaller the animal the greater is the *relative* amount it produces. Thus, supposing the production of carbonic acid be estimated according to each pound-weight of the animal, we shall find that the smaller the animal the greater will be its proportion. But it is not size and weight alone which determine the differences in the amount of air consumed; far greater differences will arise from the varieties of organisation. We may accept it as an axiom in physiology, that the activity of Respiration is inseparably connected with vital activity — not simply muscular activity, as some writers maintain, but all processes whatever, involving chemical change within the body. The most striking confirmation of this axiom is perhaps to be seen in the phenomena of hybernation or winter-sleep. No sooner are the vital functions reduced to this extremely feeble condition, in which we may almost say life is suspended, than these hybernating animals are so incapable of

* This applies, of course, only to animals of the same kind. "Vous seres étonné," says Spallanzani, "quand je vous dirai qu'une larve du poids de quelques grains s'approprie presqu' autant d'oxygène dans le mômo tems, qu'un amphibie mille fois plus volumineux qu'elle." — *Mémoires sur la Resp.*, p. 69. This is because the insect lives so much more rapidly than the reptile.

18*

ordinary respiration that they may be placed in an atmosphere of pure carbonic acid, and remain there unhurt for four hours; whereas if they were placed in such an atmosphere when their breathing was going on, they would instantly perish.

One would imagine, on hearing this, that our ordinary Sleep would also bring with it a diminution of the quantity of air consumed. And in as far as sleep may be considered a diminution of the vital activity, such a conclusion must be correct. But in how far is sleep a diminution? That is a question not hitherto asked, consequently as yet without an answer. In sleep there is very obvious diminution of some forms of vital activity, but we are by no means sure that the organic changes are so much less rapid on the whole. We are led to this doubt by the experiments of Moleschott and Böcker, which establish that the chief cause of the difference noticed between the amount of carbonic acid produced during the day and night is the influence of *sunlight;* and that a man lying quietly awake will produce *less* instead of more than a man asleep, if the conditions of light and temperature are the same. Sleep, *as* sleep, seems not therefore a diminution of the vital activity; although the sleep which we take at night after the fatigues of the day must of course be considered as accompanied by a diminution. It is quite certain that, partly from fatigue and partly from the absence of sunlight, less carbonic acid is formed at night than during the day. Boussingault found that the same turtle-doves during day and night showed a difference of 94 and 59 on one occasion, and of 75 and 53 on another. Lehmann confirmed the observations.

If it is true that all vital activity increases the amount of carbonic acid exhaled, and if every diminution is accompanied by a corresponding diminution of the amount, we may readily believe that intellectual fatigue, and the lassitude which succeeds mental or emotional excitement, will be accompanied by a corresponding depression of the respiratory function. Nay, even the concentration of the mind on any subject will produce this. Every one knows the state of "breathless attention." Whenever the mind is preoccupied by a powerful impression of some duration, the breathing becomes so feeble that from time to time we are forced to compensate this diminished activity by a deep inspiration. This is the rationale of *sighing*, an action commonly attributed only to grief, but which is the accompaniment of all mental preoccupation. The philosopher, brooding over his problem, will be heard sighing from time to time, almost as deeply as the maiden brooding over her forlorn condition. All men sigh over their work, when their work deeply engages them; but they do not remark it because the work, and not their feelings, engages their attention, whereas during grief it is their feelings which occupy them.

It is an interesting fact, and one which throws light on the intimate connection between respiration and vital activity, that a very considerable increase in the production of carbonic acid swiftly follows after eating, consequently an enormous reduction in the amount is found to accompany starvation. The fact was established by Spallanzani, and has been repeatedly confirmed. Boussingault found that pigeons, when fasting, did not produce half the amount which they produced when well fed. Spallanzani suggests that the food during digestion gives off carbonic acid, and this passing into the blood, is exhaled in respiration — a suggestion which receives additional force from the fact that vegetable food uniformly produces more carbonic acid in respiration than animal food. But this will scarcely account for the whole of the increase, and we are led to seek for the other cause in the greater activity of the nutritive processes: the fasting animal has a depressed vitality.

Temperature has considerable influence on respiration. The fact has been ascertained by experiment, but it might have been deductively established; for the influence of temperature on the vital activities is well known, and whatever influences them must affect respiration. It is only by the aid of such an axiom that we can find our way amid the apparent contradictions of this subject. The remarkable difference noticed between the capabilities of warm and cold blooded animals in breathing vitiated air, is not less than the difference in the effect of temperature on those two classes. We remember our astonishment on learning from Spallanzani that increase in the temperature brings with it an uniform increase in the amount of oxygen absorbed by molluscs and reptiles; it was a statement in direct contradiction to the well-established fact in human physiology, that more oxygen was absorbed in cold than in hot weather. Our difficulty was lightened, however, when we learned that Spallanzani's statement is only true of cold-blooded animals, and true of them only within certain limits: too great a heat ceases to increase the amount, and gradually diminishes it, as with warm-blooded animals. What are these limits, and why this cessation of increase? The limits are these: take a frog and place it in an atmosphere a little above the freezing-point; as the temperature rises from 36° to 45° Fahrenheit, the amount of oxygen absorbed uniformly increases; it remains nearly stationary from 45° to 57°; at 58° it begins to decrease, and this decrease continues till 104° is reached, and then the frog perishes. The reason is very simple: a certain amount of heat stimulates all the vital functions of the frog, and consequently increases its need for oxygen; when the heat becomes too great it ceases to be a stimulant, and depresses the functional activity, till at length a point is reached when the organism can no longer exist.

On warm-blooded animals the effect of temperature is apparently different, but really the same. Every increase of heat is found to *diminish* their respiration, every increase of cold to *augment* it. Thus it is ascertained that the smaller mammals, at a temperature of 86° to 104° Fahr., consume only half the quantity they consumed at freezing-point. Various experiments on man have elicited the general fact, that under the influence of a moderately cold atmosphere the respiration is increased by one-sixth more than in a moderately warm atmosphere. Precisely as too intense a degree of heat diminishes the respiration of the frog, by enfeebling its vital activity, does too intense a degree of cold diminish the respiration of a warm-blooded animal by enfeebling its vital activity. There are certain limits of temperature within which every increase of heat raises the respiration of the frog, because the increase raises its vital activity; and there are certain limits within which every decrease of heat raises the respiration of the man, because the decrease raises his vital activity; but if these limits be overstepped, the stimulant is changed into a debilitant.

We see this very curiously illustrated by the hybernating

animals, such as the dormouse, marmot, bat, hedgehog. They occupy, in this respect, an intermediate position between the cold-blooded and warm-blooded animals; for although they are really warm-blooded animals, the effect of temperature on them is closely allied to that produced on the cold-blooded. With every fall of external temperature their respiration diminishes. Unlike the rest of warm-blooded animals, their organism seems to have little power of resisting the changes of external temperature; they cannot produce heat with sufficient rapidity to counterbalance the loss they sustain from the surface of their bodies when the air is cold. Instead of acting on them as a stimulus, which would accelerate the respiratory process, cold acts on them with a depressing influence, which gradually reduces their respiration almost to zero. But no sooner have they passed into this winter-sleep, and their organic activity has become very feeble, than we can at pleasure reawaken it to any degree by raising the surrounding temperature; and as the vital activity once more begins to manifest itself, the respiration (which is only one form of vital activity) likewise becomes manifest.

*Why* do we breathe? The foregoing pages have given some answer to the question, *How* do we breathe? but have not hinted at the *why;* yet after reading about the respiratory process, a natural curiosity prompts the inquiry as to its cause. Unhappily nothing but extremely vague answers can be given. We know that the chest expands and contracts with beautiful rhythm, and, mostly, as an involuntary, automatic process. We know that our attention is not required, that no effort is needed, and indeed that no effort of ours can prevent the regular alternation of inspiration and expiration. We can by an effort accelerate or retard these motions, but we cannot prevent them. The process, then, clearly depends on a stimulus given to the involuntary part of the nervous system: it is called into action by nervous stimulus, and physiologists have vainly endeavoured to discover the nervous apparatus which is involved, and the rationale of its action. The pressure of carbonic acid in the air-cells, or of venous blood in the capillaries, may act as a stimulus to the pneumogastric nerve; but what is the rationale of making a new-born child draw breath, by whipping its back and continuation? Generally, the stimulus of the cold air on the child's face suffices to make it draw breath, which it expires again in a well-known cry, to mothers' ears most musical; but this stimulus is often insufficient, and the doctor or nurse initiates the little stranger into that experience of "external local applications" which, in later years, will also be freely used as a stimulus to virtue or learning. The fact we know; but why such "local applications" excite the respiratory activity, we do not know, for we do not know the nervous apparatus which regulates the actions of respiration. It is probable that the researches of physiologists will, ere long, clear up this point, as they have cleared up so many others; meanwhile we must content ourselves with vague answers to our question, Why do we breathe?

———

# CHAPTER VII.

## WHY WE ARE WARM, AND HOW WE KEEP SO.

Animals have a temperature of their own — This not owing to a "Vital Principle" — Description of the various instruments employed in measuring animal heat — Mistake of supposing that there are cold-blooded and warm-blooded animals — Man preserves his temperature in all climates and all seasons — His power of enduring great heat — The cooling apparatus of his organism — Perspiration carries off superfluous heat — Difference between cooling hot and being hot — Influence of age, sex, and food on our temperature — Young animals cannot well resist cold — The notion of "hardening" infants erroneous — Is food warmth? — Influence of the seasons — Effect of a cold wind — Why is the east wind felt to be cold? — Where is cold dangerous? — Can cold water be drunk with safety when we are hot? — The theory of animal heat — Respiration is not the cause of animal heat — Heat in dead bodies — Relation between respiration and animal heat in various classes of animals — Hybernating animals — Frogs and tritons in winter and summer.

A BIRD-CAGE hangs above a small aquarium: in the cage there is a bird; in the glass tank, seaweeds, zoophytes, molluscs, and fish. The atmosphere of the apartment varies with those variations of temperature which accompany the earth's daily rotation and annual movement. The summer sunlight streams in through the windows; the icy north wind rushes through the crevices; the shadows of night, and the evaporations of morning, bring with them perpetual risings and fallings of the temperature of that room; and with these risings and fallings there are corresponding fluctuations in the temperature of the glass and water of the tank, the brass and woodwork of the cage. This is according to the law by which an equilibrium of temperature is always established among inorganic bodies. The warmer atmosphere rapidly warms the glass and water — the cooler atmosphere rapidly cools them; it is true that the water will always be somewhat colder than the atmosphere, because it loses heat in evaporation, but nevertheless, as the external temperature rises and falls, that of the water also rises and falls.

While these changes, so familiar and so easy of explanation, have been taking place, the bird has been neither colder nor warmer; throughout the fluctuations of external temperature it has preserved almost uniformly the very high degree of warmth which, as a bird, belongs to it. Neither the beams of an August sun, nor the nipping east wind of December, have raised or lowered its normal heat at any time more than one or two degrees. You may perhaps imagine that it has been kept warm through the winter by its envelope of feathers, but this is true only to a very slight extent; strip it of its feathers, and you will still find its heat greatly above that of the air; whereas, if a heated sub-stance be enveloped in feathers, and left exposed to the air, it will soon become as cold as the air. Driven from this explana-tion, you will ask, How is it that the bird is enabled to preserve a steady temperature of a high degree amid unsteady influences from without? The answer is obviously to be sought in the organism and its processes, not in any external influence; and a certain Philosophy, somewhat rash and ready, fond of phrases and impatient of proof, will assure you that the bird, as an organised body, is absolved from the law of equilibrium which rules all inorganic bodies, because the bird is endowed with a "vital principle which suspends the action of physical laws."

This explanation, which to many has seemed satisfactory, labours under two disadvantages — first, that it invokes the operation of a "vital principle," of which we can form no definite conception; and secondly, that the assumed suspension of phy-sical laws is a pure figment. The organism, living or dead, radiates heat with equal facility; but when living, it produces heat to compensate the loss; and when dead, it no longer pro-duces heat, so that it speedily becomes as cold as the external air. The processes of Life do not "suspend" the operation of physical laws, although, by the introduction of more complex conditions, they bring about results which, superficially con-sidered, look like a suspension of those laws. A close analysis always detects the physical laws. No one thinks of attributing to a spirit-lamp, when lighted under a vessel of water, the power

of suspending the equilibrium of temperature, because it keeps
the water boiling, in spite of the constant loss of heat by evaporation.  Without the lamp, the boiling water would speedily
cool below the temperature of the air; *with* the lamp, it may be
kept indefinitely at the boiling-point, if fresh water be from time
to time added to replace what has evaporated.  There is no
"lamp-principle" suspending physical laws.  Nor is there any
such mysterious agent in Animal Heat.  Just as the temperature
of the water is kept constant by the continual reproduction of
heat equalling the amount lost, so is the temperature of the bird
kept constant by a continual reproduction of heat within; and
although the vital processes by which that reproduction is
effected are very far from exhibiting the simplicity of the spirit-
lamp, and are indeed still involved in great obscurity, yet we
know that physical laws are in no sense suspended thereby, and
that the living animal has the tendency to establish an equilibrium between its temperature and that of the objects surrounding it.

We have only to extend our investigations and examine the
temperature of the other organised bodies—seaweeds, zoophytes,
molluscs, and fish—during these changes which *seem* not to
have affected the bird, to find that this mysterious "vital principle" suddenly fails altogether.  It here abdicates its autocratic
power.  It suspends no laws; on the contrary, it permits equilibrium to be established unopposed.  The seaweeds are, within a
very slight fraction, as cold as the water, and get warmer as the
water warms.  The zoophytes have no appreciable superiority of
temperature.  The fish are only two or three degrees warmer.
Either we must give up the explanation which the vital principle
seemed to afford, or we must deny that the cold-blooded animals,    .
as they are called, have any vital principle at all.  In vain will a
refuge be sought in the greater cooling agency of water over that
of air; for although something must be allowed for this, we cannot by it account for the enormous disproportion between the
temperature of the fish and the bird; and for these reasons: The
Bonito, equally subject to this cooling agency of water, preserves .
a constant temperature of $20^{\circ}$ above the sea; and the temperature of the Narwhal is nearly that of man — namely, $96^{\circ}$ Fahren-

heit. Moreover, while some marine animals are thus independent of the temperature of water, serpents, lizards, and frogs are dependent on the temperature of the air.

Before entering further into this subject, it will be well to glance at the instruments by which physiologists measure the delicate differences in amount of heat which different animals and plants produce. Of the various thermometers we need say

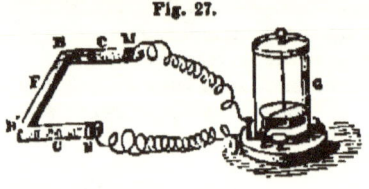

Fig. 27.

nothing. But there are thermo-electrical instruments which need explanation. Fig. 27 represents a thermo-electric couple. Its construction rests on the fact that two metals soldered together develop electric currents when their solders are maintained at different temperatures. Two bars of copper (c, c) are soldered to a bar of iron (f), and their two extremities (m, n) are in contact with the wires of the galvanometer (o); so long as the solders (b, b') remain at the same temperature no electric current passes; and the magnetic needle of the galvanometer remains motionless. But the instant one of these solders is heated, the needle moves. It is on this principle that Becquerel invented his *thermo-electric needles with median solder* (Fig. 28). Each

Fig. 28.

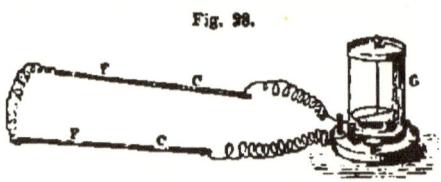

needle is composed of a copper and an iron half of equal length and thickness, soldered end to end. At one extremity each iron half (f) is united to the other by an iron wire, long enough to permit of their being kept at some distance apart; at the other extremity each copper half (c) is fixed to the wires of the galvanometer.

With such an instrument we are enabled to penetrate, without disturbance, into the interior of the animal tissues, and accomplish what no thermometer could attempt. We can test by it the temperature of a muscle, or of the blood in an artery, without troubling the circulation. For instance, let us desire to know the temperature of the muscles of the arm, at rest and in contraction. Fig. 29 will show the method of procedure. One

Fig. 29.

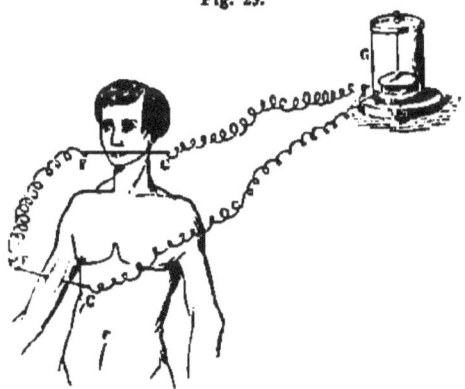

needle is passed through the muscles; the other is placed in the mouth. The patient breathes only by the nostrils during the experiment; and all the time a small thermometer is placed under his tongue, to prove that the temperature of the mouth does not vary. The direction of the needle indicates in which part there is an excess of heat; and this is afterwards calculated.

Another application of the same principle is that of Dutrochet's *needles with latero-terminal solder* (Fig. 30). An

Fig. 30.

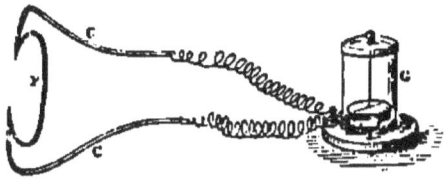

iron needle (r), bent at both ends, is soldered by these bent ends to two copper needles (c, c). With this instrument he compared the temperature of a living and a dead insect, as represented in Fig. 31.

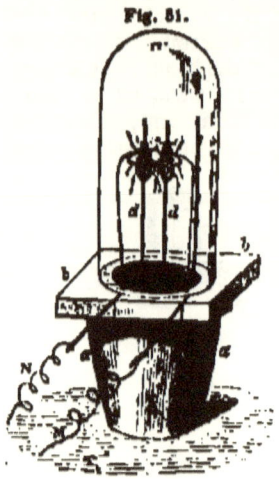

Fig. 31.

Each insect was fixed on a stick, d d, planted in the earth of a flower-pot a. The needles were then thrust into corresponding parts of the living and dead insect, and being in communication with the galvanometer by the wires M N, the deviation of the galvanometer gave the measure of the temperature possessed by the living insect. The same instrument serves to measure the heat of plants, Fig. 32. An asparagus, c, is freshly cut and placed in water to keep it alive; another asparagus, b, is killed, and the two are then tested as the living and dead insects were tested.

Fig. 32.

There are other methods unnecessary to mention here. The result which has been arrived at is that every living organism has within it a source of self-supplying heat. The amount of heat thus supplied will depend on the amount and nature of the chemical changes which take place within the organism. Even in the microscopic animalcules such a supply exists. We might assume this a priori, but we can establish it experimentally: if water be gradually frozen under the microscope, it will be seen that the last drops which solidify are those which surround the animalcules, and have been kept liquid by their heat.

Organic beings are thus distinguishable from the inorganic in possessing, as a necessary consequence of their vital activity, a self-supplying source of heat; and organic beings are distinguishable *among each other* by the rapidity with which this heat is *supplied,* and the facility with which it is *radiated;* and not, as the current classification implies, into animals with warm blood, animals with cold blood, and plants with no heat at all. There are no animals with cold blood, and all plants produce heat. But plants, except during their periods of germination and flowering, when they are sensibly warmer than the air, produce heat so slowly, and part with it so easily, that their temperature always follows that of the medium in which they live; and the so-called "cold-blooded animals" produce heat so slowly that they are never more than two or three degrees above the medium, and sometimes even *below* it, owing to the rapidity of evaporation from their surfaces. Insects — bees, for instance — produce heat with a rapidity equal to that of birds; but they part with it so rapidly that their temperature is little above that of the air. When bees are collected together in the hive, the heat they radiate is found to be very great.

Many writers object to the old distinction of warm and cold-blooded animals as unphysiological, and suggest that the distinction should be, that the warm-blooded are independent of, and the cold-blooded dependent on, the external temperature: the one class preserving its normal heat under all variations of the external medium, and the other class growing warmer and colder as the external medium rises and falls. But against this distinction we would urge three arguments. First, — Both classes of animals are dependent on the external temperature, and both are independent of it; they are *dependent,* because it accelerates or retards their vital activities by which their own heat is evolved; they are *independent,* because whatever may be the amount of external heat or cold, their own temperature, being really evolved in their vital processes, is always restrained within certain limits, and is almost always *somewhat* above that of the external medium,* until a limit is reached, and then, if the external temperature continue to increase, they perish, or their heat falls below that of the medium.

Secondly, — The young of many warm-blooded animals are as much dependent on external temperature as frogs and fish; and even the adult animals of the hybernating class are in this category: no sooner does the external temperature fall, than their heat sinks, and this depression continues till they are only three degrees warmer than the air.

Thirdly, — While the foregoing arguments have shown that the distinction is not tenable in the presence of facts, we would further remark that, granting the distinction to be valid, the cause would still have to be sought, and we should ask, why one class of animals was independent and another dependent on the external temperature? In fixing attention on the physiological differences of *rapid supply* and *rapid radiation*, as the real ground of distinction, we avoid the objections just brought forward; at the same time, inquiry into the cause of animal heat is disengaged from many a perplexing digression.

The marvellous balance between supply and loss exhibited by the human organism, and indeed by that of most warm-blooded animals, may be best seen in the following facts. Our temperature is 98°, and this is the standard, no matter what may be the external heat. In the tropics, the thermometer during several hours of the day is 110°. In British India it is sometimes as high as 130°. In the arctic zones it has been observed by our voyagers as low as 90°, *and even* 102°, *below freezing-point.* Nevertheless, amid such extensive variations of the external temperature, that of the human organism has but slightly varied, and a thermometer placed under the tongue of an arctic voyager will show the same degree of heat as one under the tongue of a soldier before the walls of Delhi. Throughout the scale of 200° which represents the variations of climate borne by our voyagers and soldiers, the average temperature of the

---

* I once found the temperature of a "cold-blooded" lizard to be 56° in the mouth, when the air was at 54°. A list of observations on the temperature of the cold-blooded animals will be found in GAVARRET: *De la Chaleur produite par les êtres vivants*, p. 123.

human organism remains steady at 98⁰. We say *average*, because the same man is not always at the same degree; his temperature varies at different seasons, different hours, and under different conditions; and of course different men vary among themselves. Dr. Livingstone remarks, "If my experiments are correct, the blood of an European is higher than that of an African. The bulb of the thermometer held under my tongue stood at 100⁰; under that of the natives, at 98⁰."* This was most likely nothing more than an individual difference; but the point is worth investigating.

It is the opinion of M. Gavarret, who has earned the right to speak with authority on this subject, that even in our moderate climates the temperature of the adult man will oscillate as much as a degree, *i. e.*, between 36⁰.50 and 37⁰.50 centigrade.**

Although the organism can endure a heat greater than its own, yet this would soon be fatal if continued. For a short period the excess of temperature can be resisted; and it is astonishing what a power of resistance we possess. Chabert, the once celebrated "Fire-King," who used to exhibit in public, amazed his audience by entering an oven, the heat of which was from 400⁰ to 600⁰; and although we have no details as to his own temperature when subject to that heat, we may be sure that it could not have risen many degrees above 98⁰, otherwise he would have perished; for the experiments of Berger and Delaroche*** prove that, when the temperature of animals is raised 11⁰ or 13⁰ above the normal standard, they perish. Workers in iron-foundries and gasworks are constantly obliged to remain for some time in air which is as high as 250⁰, yet their own temperature remains tolerably uniform. A dog confined in a heated chamber at 220⁰-236⁰, in which he remained half an hour, was found to have gained only 7⁰; and while the external temperature stood as high as 236⁰, his own stood only at 108⁰.

It thus appears that warm-blooded animals, besides their central source of heat, which keeps up their temperature in spite

* LIVINGSTONE'S *Travels in South Africa*, p. 509.

** GAVARRET: *De la Chaleur produite par les êtres vivants*, 1855, p. 100. This work is a perfect encyclopædia of information on the subject of Animal Heat. It is from it we have borrowed the figures given above.

*** Quoted by W. EDWARDS, *De l'Influence des Agens Physiques sur la Vie*.

of external cold, have also a cooling apparatus by which their standard of heat is preserved in spite of excessive heat outside. What is this process, which prevents the equilibrium of heat, and can keep the animal temperature more than one hundred and fifty degrees *below* that of the atmosphere? We can easily understand why a kettle of water can be kept at boiling-point in

Fig. 33.

a cold atmosphere, so long as a flame is underneath it; but how can that water be kept *cold* when the temperature of the air is many degrees above boiling-point? A man whose temperature is 98° in an atmosphere of 60°, suddenly steps into an atmosphere of 200°, and yet his own warmth is scarcely elevated. The ordinary explanation of this surprising fact is, that the evaporation and exhalation of vapour and water from the surface are so accelerated by the excessive heat, that they suffice to keep the man's temperature from rising. Let us look more closely into this.

All over the surface of our bodies there are scattered millions of minute orifices which open into the delicate convoluted tubes lying underneath the skin, and are called by anatomists *sudoriparous glands* (Fig. 33). Each of these tubes, when straightened, measures about a quarter of an inch; and as, according to Erasmus Wilson, whose figures we follow, there are 3528 of these tubes on every square inch of the palm of the hand, there must be no less than 882 inches of tubing on such a square inch. In some parts of the body the number of tubes is even greater; in most parts it is less. Erasmus Wilson estimates that there are 2800 on every square inch, on the average; and as the total number of such inches is 2500, we arrive at the astounding result

SWEAT-GLAND.
a is the cuticle or scarfskin (epidermis), the deeper layers, dark in colour, being the *rete mucosum*; b are the papillæ; c the cutis or true skin (dermis); d the sweat-gland, in a cavity of oily globules.

that, spread over the surface of the body, there are not less than *twenty-eight miles of tubing*, by means of which liquid may be secreted, and given off as vapour in *insensible* perspiration, or as water in *sensible* perspiration. In the ordinary circumstances of daily life, the amount of fluid which is thus given off from the skin (and lungs) during the twenty-four hours, varies from 1¾ lb. to 5 lb.; under extraordinary circumstances the amount will of course rise enormously. Dr. Southwood Smith found that the workmen in the gasworks employed in making up the fires, and other occupations which subjected them to great heat, lost on an average 3 *lb.* 6 *oz.* in forty-five minutes; and when working for seventy minutes in an unusually hot place, their loss was 5 *lb.* 2 *oz.*, and 4 *lb.* 14 *oz.*

Whatever stimulates the circulation of the blood at the surface, will necessarily increase the action of the sweat-glands. A warm atmosphere or a warm bath immediately causes the surface-circulation to be increased. Muscular exertion does the same. That the ordinary amount of evaporation and exhalation will be greatly raised on our entrance into an atmosphere of 200° is very certain; but the question is, whether this amount is sufficient of itself to account for the enormous difference between the temperature of the animal and that of the atmosphere? We must remember that not only is man's temperature more than 100° lower than iron or wood in such an atmosphere, but it is this amount lower *in spite of the incessant production of heat* taking place in his own organism, by the chemical changes on which vitality depends—a production of heat which will suffice to preserve his temperature at the same height, if, on quitting this atmosphere of 200°, he plunges into a snow-bath. For a short period a man can enter a furnace the floor of which is red-hot, the air being 350°, yet his own heat will remain two hundred and fifty degrees *below* this; and we cannot suppose that, in this brief period, he has lost enough heat by evaporation to prevent his own temperature rising. What, then, is the cause? We must confess inability to answer this question. For some time we fancied an explanation might be gained from the low-conducting power of the animal envelope, which would prevent the external temperature from gaining access to the internal organs. Wrap

19*

a jug of ice in flannel, and the ice will not melt, even in a very warm room, until a considerable time has elapsed. It is on this principle that, in China, they *bake ices*. An ice is enveloped in a crust of delicate pastry, and introduced into the oven. The paste is quickly baked, and the ice is still unmelted, having been protected from the heat by its envelope; and thus the epicure has the delight of biting through a burning crust, and then immediately cooling his palate with the grateful contents. But although the envelope of the warm-blooded animal is unquestionably a bad conductor, and would therefore suffice to account for the animal's not getting warmer during a brief exposure to high temperature, this explanation fails when confronted with experiments which show that, during a longer exposure, the temperature has been still at its old limit. The following experiment by Berger and Delaroche is very instructive:—They introduced into a furnace at 126⁰-143⁰ a porous vase, containing two wet sponges and a frog. The temperature of the sponges and the vase had been previously raised to 101⁰-105⁰; that of the frog was 70⁰. At the close of the first fifteen minutes, the vase, the sponges, and the frog had almost an uniform temperature, *which did not exceed that of warm-blooded animals;* and this was maintained pretty constant during two hours. It is remarkable that, to reach this standard, the vase and the sponges *fell* in temperature about a degree and a half, whereas the frog rose as much as twenty-nine degrees in fifteen minutes. But frog, sponges, and vase maintained themselves from twenty to forty-five degrees *below* the external temperature — namely, at the temperature of warm-blooded animals. From this it would seem as if the temperature of warm-blooded animals was the limit which could be reached by organic bodies coincident with a free evaporation of water from their surfaces. The vase and the sponges were introduced into a furnace very considerably higher than themselves in temperature; and this excess of heat caused an evaporation of their water, which lowered their temperature to that point where the rapidly-rising temperature of the evaporating frog would stop. Now, although the evaporation from the surface of the frog would have had a cooling influence from the first minute of the experiment, yet we see that this cooling

influence was not great enough to withstand the rapid rise of
the animal's temperature, until the point was reached at which
the fall of the vase and sponges had ceased; and this point is
the very limit which we find uniformly in the warm-blooded
animals, no matter what the external temperature may be.

The temperature of man is constant: neither the fluctuations
of the seasons, nor the differences of latitude, bring any variation in his standard. No fact in science is better established;
but we must guard against a misconception, and add, that when
this temperature is spoken of as constant, it is not the heat of
individual parts, nor of individual men at every hour of the day
or under all circumstances, it is the *average* temperature of the
internal organs. The limits of oscillation are narrow indeed,
but within those limits the oscillation is incessant. I found that,
when a thermometer is used which marks fractions of a degree
so small as one-tenth, if placed in the mouth of a man or dog, it
will exhibit an incessant oscillation; and it is well known that
very obvious variations occur at different periods of the day, and
under different circumstances. Dr. John Davy found that, when
at rest in a temperature of $37^0$, his own temperature fell as low
as $96^0.7$; in a room at $92^0$, he found the heat of a workman had
risen to $100^0$. Gierse observed that, before dinner, his temperature under the tongue was $98^0.78$, and after dinner, $99^0.5$.

*Unsophisticated Reader.* — "We want no scientific authority
for the belief that variations take place, since the daily complaints of our fellow-citizens, shivering or perspiring, render the
fact too obvious for thermometers to be needed."

*Physiological Lecturer.* — "Excuse me, sir; but you do want
scientific authority. Without the thermometer, you cannot say
whether you are warmer or colder than you were."

*U. R.* — "What! do you tell me I don't know when I feel
colder?"

*P. L.* — "I only tell you that you don't know when you *are*
colder. What you may *feel* is another question altogether.
Thermometers do not measure feelings."

*U. R.* — "This is too much! You will tell me next that I ought
to trust your thermometer, and distrust my sensations. Before
venturing to light a fire in my room, I must place a thermometer

under my tongue to see if I am really as cold as I feel; and next July, when I am sweltering in the sun, you will perhaps assure me that I am wrong to complain of the heat, since I am only at 98⁰ — not a degree hotter than I was in December!"

*P. L.* — "O Unsophisticated Reader! if we are to talk science, let us be accurate. If we are to talk the language of the market and the dining-room, we shall never come to a clear understanding. Were you ever attacked by an intermittent fever?"

*U. R.* — "Yes; and remember distinctly the vehement shivering-fit which commenced it. Perhaps you will tell me I was not colder then, nor warmer when that fit disappeared and I seemed on fire, eh?"

*P. L.* — "Your ironical question warns me of your incredulity when I shall answer: No, you were *not* colder when you shivered under the heap of blankets which they in vain threw over you. You were some degrees warmer. The application of that thermometer, which you seem to treat lightly, would have shown that, whatever your sensations may have said, the actual heat of your skin had *risen six or seven degrees;* and when that sensation of cold was succeeded by a sensation of burning heat, the thermometer, which knows nothing of sensations, but measures heat only, would have shown that you were really not hotter than during the cold fit."

*U. R.* — "That is very staggering. But fevers are exceptional things, so let us come to ordinary life. Do you mean to say that, when I feel cold in winter, I am really not colder than when I come in from the walk which — according to my sensations — has warmed me?"

*P. L.* — "As an Unsophisticated Reader, liable to chilblains, your feet are doubtless colder and warmer under these two conditions; and the thermometer placed between your toes before you walk will show a temperature of 66⁰ perhaps, while that of the air is 60⁰; and after the walk, the same test will show your feet to have risen as high as 96⁰.5. But if I regard you as a scientific *datum*, and think only of your Animal Heat as an average, I am forced to assure you that your temperature, variable in feet and hands, has remained constant in the blood and internal organs. A thermometer under your tongue would show 98° before and after your walk. Exercise had increased the circulation in your limbs, and consequently increased the warmth of those parts; but the source of your heat is the Blood, and that has not warmed or cooled with exercise. Dr. John Davy found, after a walk in the open air at 40°, that the temperature of his feet rose to 96°.5; of his hands, to 97°; while his tongue remained at 98°. Another day, after a walk in the air at 50°, his feet were 99°, his hands 98°, and tongue 98°. Here the feet were even warmer than the tongue. I can now answer your question without equivoque. When you feel colder, it is because the circulation in your extremities, or at the surface, is less active than usual, and either exercise or external warmth is necessary to restore that circulation; but the temperature of your blood, and, consequently, of those internal parts more abundantly and constantly supplied with blood — in a word, your Animal Heat — remains unaltered."

Our Lecturer, had he been questioned, would have stated that, in spite of this remarkable constancy in animal heat, there are oscillations even in that of the internal organs. The temperature varies according to Age, Sex, Food, and other circumstances. We cannot, it is true, speak with any confidence as to the exact share which any one of these circumstances has in the variations observed; the case is so complex, and implies the concurrence of so many separate influences, that considerable discrepancies will be found in the results attained by different investigators. Thus the majority of writers agree that in Infancy the temperature is higher than in maturity. A thermometer under the armpit of a new-born infant will stand nearly at 100°; and although it falls rapidly to 95°, yet in the course of the next four-and-twenty hours it will rise again to 99°.5. Between the ages of four months and six years, the average is 98°.9, and between the ages of six and fourteen it is 99°.16. On reading these figures the physiologist is tempted to see in them the simple expression of the fact that, during infancy and childhood, the growth is much more rapid than it afterwards is; and this rapidity of growth implies a greater production of heat, because a more rapid chemical action. Nevertheless, the extensive observations of M. Charles Martins * and W. F. Edwards ** disturb the simplicity of this explanation, and cast some doubt on it. M. Martins, comparing the temperature of fifty-six ducks and ninety-seven geese, finds that in infancy it is somewhat *less* than in maturity. This fact is in direct contradiction to the physiological explanation; but it may possibly have some connection with the very important fact established by W. Edwards, namely, that young animals are distinguished from the adult less in the *degree* of heat which they attain than in their want of power to resist cold by *rapid production* of heat. This, as we attempted to show just now, is the distinguishing characteristic of what are called the warm-blooded and cold-blooded animals; and we shall now see that it is a characteristic of Age. Edwards removed a new-born puppy from its mother, and left it exposed to the air at 50°-60°. It rapidly grew cold, until at the expiration of three hours it was only two or three degrees above the temperature of the air. A similar result was observed with new-born rabbits, in a shorter space of time. With the new-born guinea-pig nothing of the kind was observed. It had a temperature equal to that of its mother; and this it preserved whether left with the mother or removed from her. Dogs, cats, rabbits, and other warm-blooded animals, therefore, seem in their earlier periods of existence to resemble the cold-blooded animals, and to be dependent on external warmth; but this is not true of all the warm-blooded classes. Edwards divides those classes into two groups, one of which comes into the world cold-blooded, the other warm-blooded. If we examine these groups closely, to discover some external sign by which they may severally be known, we find that one group comes into the world with its eyes closed, and the other with its eyes open. The reader, probably, thinks this sign of very small value, until we beg him further to remark that the puppy, whose temperature was so dependent on external warmth during the early part of its existence, becomes less and less so as he grows older, till at the end of a fortnight he is almost as capable as his parents of

* *Mémoire sur la Température des Oiseaux du Nord*, in BROWN-SÉQUARD: *Journal de la Physiologie*, 1. 22.
** W. EDWARDS: *De l'Influence des Agens Physiques*, p. 132.

resisting external cold — and at this epoch his eyes are open. Thus the cold-blooded period is precisely coincident with the blind period.

Is, then, Animal Heat dependent upon vision? — is it in any degree regulated by vision? The phenomena are, indeed, intimately connected, but their connection is not that of cause and effect: it is that of two effects determined by one cause. Animal Heat is evolved by the vital changes which take place in the organism; and only when that organism has attained a certain degree of development has it the power of evolving sufficient heat to resist external cold: now, the development of the eyes is an indication of the degree of development reached by the organism, and no sooner is the animal sufficiently developed to use its eyes, than it is also sufficiently developed to preserve its normal temperature. The young puppy cannot see, and is forced to remain near its mother to be warmed by her; but tho young guinea-pig sees perfectly well, and runs about seeking food for itself. It is the same with birds. Young sparrows, taken from the nest where they were kept warm by their mother and by each other, rapidly lost about $30^0$, although the external air was moderate ($63^0$), so that their own temperature fell to three degrees above that of the air. A similar result was obtained with the air at $72^0$. As these birds are born without feathers, their loss of heat might be supposed to be owing to the absence of the warm covering which protected their parents. It is not so, however. Edwards completely stripped an adult sparrow of its feathers, and exposed it to air at $65^0$, in company with a young sparrow taken from the nest; the young one had the advantage of down, and in some parts of feathers to protect it, nevertheless its temperature quickly fell to two or three degrees above that of the air, while that of the adult scarcely varied, and remained $36^0$ above that of the air. Although the young sparrows, and those birds which are born imperfectly developed, require the heat of the nest and of their mother, the young chick preserves its temperature as well as the grown hen; but the chick quits the egg in a state of development which permits it to run about and feed itself.

Have these facts any application to man? Are we born cold-blooded, like blind puppies? Not exactly; yet the same laws are in operation in our organisms as in the organisms of the puppy and the sparrow. Edwards relates that one of his patients gave birth to a seven-months child, with such ease that the child came before assistance could be got. He arrived two or three hours afterwards, and found the child vigorous, well swaddled in clothes before a good fire; yet its temperature, even under these circumstances, was only 90°, or five degrees below that of the average of a child born at the proper period. Every precaution was taken to keep the infant warm; had not such precautions been taken, it would have perished as a puppy would have perished.

Maternal instinct has in all ages and in all climates taught women to keep their infants warm. Philosophers have at various times tried, by logic and rhetoric, to thwart this instinct. Philosophy has been eloquent on the virtue of making infants "hardy," and has declared that cold baths and slight clothing must be as "strengthening" to the infant as to the adult. Listen to none of these philosophers, ye mothers! They are to be suspected when they are talking physiology, for under such circumstances they are the worst of guides, deceiving themselves and you by that fatal facility which intellectual power gives them of making ignorance look like knowledge, and of so speciously arraying absurdity that it looks like plain common-sense. It is bad, very bad, to listen to grandmothers, mothers-in-law, and nurses: their heads are mostly mere lumber-rooms of crotchets and absurdities; but it is better sometimes to listen to them than to philosophers who inspire more respect, and cannot irreverently be treated as "old women." Maternal instinct must not be perverted by such unphysiological teaching as that of "hardening" infants. It is true that strong infants can endure this process, but it is certain that in all cases it is more or less injurious; for the universal law is, that the younger the animal, the feebler its power of *resisting* cold, in spite of its possessing a higher temperature than the adult.

An interesting fact is elicited by Edwards from his researches, namely, that although the younger the animal the less its ability to resist cold, this peril is to a great extent evaded by the com-

parative impunity with which the young animals can be subjected to a fall in their temperature. The adult better resists
external cold; but if the resistance be overcome, there is greater
difficulty in re-establishing the normal heat. In proportion as
the faculty of developing heat increases, the faculty of developing it after a considerable fall decreases. One sees the beneficial
operation of this law in nature. The most careful bird is forced
to quit her young from time to time in search of food, and during
her absence they necessarily become colder; if she is absent
long, or if the nest be not very warm, they will undergo a loss of
heat which would be perilous to an adult. But no sooner does
she return to warm them, than they regain their temperature
with facility.

Old people are commonly said to have a lower temperature
than those of middle age; but Dr. Davy's observations do not
confirm this; he found no such difference, nor are we aware of
any evidence by which the notion can be established. It is true
that cold is not so well resisted in old age. Herein old age and
infancy agree.

The influence of *Sex* has not been much investigated; yet,
considering the differences in the blood and respiration of the
sexes, we might expect to find some striking results elicited from
a careful comparison of temperatures. The only extensive investigations with which we are acquainted are those of M.
Martins, previously cited: from one hundred and ten observations on ducks and drakes, he finds the temperature of the
females to be somewhat higher than that of the males; but their
temperature is also more *variable*, differing between individuals
more than is the case with the males. Between women and
men there seems to be no appreciable difference, which is the
more striking from the known differences in their blood and respiration.

"Food is warmth," says the physiologist; and in one sense
this is strictly true, namely, that Food, by rendering a continuance of the vital processes possible, must bring with it the
heat to be evolved in those processes. But it is *not* true in the
sense in which the aphorism is frequently employed, namely,
that Food is the fuel which is burned for animal heat (like coke

in a furnace), and that particular kinds, the so-called Respiratory Foods, are those we ought to employ as fuel. The warmth you feel after eating a hearty dinner is not really an increase of your temperature, but a *diffusion* of it to the extremities and the surface. Place a thermometer under your tongue before dinner and after it, and you will find that, in spite of your sensations, the thermometer points to the same degree at each period. Yet, as this admits of another interpretation, we shall adduce the less equivocal observations of M. Martins. The ducks belonging to a miller near Montpellier were fed well on grains every morning before being turned out to enjoy themselves in the river, and every evening on their return they were fed again; close by, there lived a poor waiter on the lock, who also kept ducks, but could not afford to feed them on grains, like his richer neighbour, so that they were reduced to forage for themselves. Here accident had arranged the conditions of a good scientific experiment. Living in the same air, the same temperature, and in the same lock of the river, these two flocks differed only in respect of the grain on which one was daily fed. The influence of food would, therefore, here be manifest. What did observation detect? A superiority of temperature amounting nearly to a degree centigrade (about 1½° Fahr.) in favour of the well-fed ducks. M. Martins adds that he has since then often been able to affirm whether a bird has been well or ill fed, by simply ascertaining its temperature.

On a superficial consideration, this would seem to be convincing evidence that those physiologists are correct who assert " food to be warmth," in the crude sense of food being fuel; but closer attention will show that the evidence supports our view of food. Indeed, M. Martins has furnished us with irresistible evidence; " for," as he remarks, "we shall greatly deceive ourselves if we imagine that a better quality of food will suffice to raise the temperature in *a short period*. Two drakes, after five days of abstinence, were found to have a temperature of 41°.83 centigrade (about 107° Fahr.); I then fed them entirely on bran and herbs, and twenty-five days afterwards their temperature was 42°.14 (not quite 108° Fahr.) Two other drakes, with a temperature of 41°.40, were fed abundantly on maize and hay;

at the end of twenty-five days of such diet their temperature was
41º.76" — that is to say, actually *less* than those which had been
ill fed! This may seem to be in contradiction with M. Martins'
previous observation on the well-fed and ill-fed ducks; but the
contradiction is only superficial: the reader will notice that,
although the temperature of these well-fed drakes was actually
less than that of the ill-fed, it was also less when the experiment
began; and if we compare the rise in the temperature which took
place in both, we shall find that in the ill-fed it was only 0º.30,
and in the well-fed 0º.36. This difference, slight as it may seem,
is in favour of the well-fed; and when such slight elevations are
continued month after month, they may, and will, attain a
superiority amounting to one degree. Although, therefore, this
experiment confirms the previous observation of the influence of
generous food in elevating the degree of animal heat, it strikingly
discredits the notion that the food is burned as fuel in the organism.

"Food is warmth," because food furnishes the pabulum of the
tissues, and warmth is evolved in the chemical changes which go
forward in the formation and destruction of the tissues. But
food is not fuel only, as some physiologists would have us believe.
If anything is burnt, it is the tissues, not the food; our warmth
comes from the organic processes which make and unmake the
tissues. The proof of this is seen, not only in the foregoing
experiments, but even more convincingly in the experiments on
starvation which Chossat and Martins have performed. We shall
not here repeat those of Chossat, because they are well known,
and the results are accessible in almost every text-book; but
those of Martins will be new to our readers, and may therefore
briefly be indicated. He took four drakes, and submitted them
to several successive periods of abstinence, separated by periods
in which they were abundantly fed. They were left in a tub of
water in which to bathe, and their habits were unaltered; nothing
but the solid food was withheld during the days of the experiment; and in order to avoid the diurnal variations of temperature
from complicating the problem, the thermometer was always
applied at the same hour of each day. The birds commenced the

period of fasting with a temperature of 42⁰.20 (108⁰ Fahrenheit), at the close of a period of ample nourishment.

| | | | | |
|---|---|---|---|---|
| After 24 hours' abstinence | the temperature | | | *sank* to 41⁰.84. |
| „  48 | „ | „ | „ | *rose* to 41⁰.89. |
| „  72 | „ | „ | „ | *rose* to 41⁰.91. |
| „  96 | „ | „ | „ | *rose* to 41⁰.94. |
| „  120 | „ | „ | „ | *sank* to 41⁰.62. |

Here we see that twenty-four hours' fast have produced a striking reduction of temperature; and those writers who attribute warmth to the combustion of food may fancy they see evidence for their opinion in such a fact; but, as the fast is prolonged, the temperature does not continue falling; it rises: so that, after ninety-six hours of complete abstinence, the temperature has risen nearly to what it was when the animal was crammed with food. We have only to add, that this is in perfect accordance with the observations of Chossat on pigeons. It is true that, after the fifth day, the temperature suddenly sinks; but the mere increase, as the abstinence is prolonged during the first four days, is sufficient to show that animal heat is not evolved by the combustion of food.

Having examined the influence of Age, Sex, and Food, we may now cast a glance at the influence of the Seasons. Although man preserves his standard of 98⁰ in the tropics and in the arctic zone, he does so in virtue of the power his organism possesses of adjusting itself to changing circumstances. We adjust ourselves to the changing seasons. In winter we are as warm as in summer, because in winter we produce more heat, and lose less by evaporation and exhalation. A cold day in summer is incomparably more unpleasant and injurious than a day of equal temperature in autumn; and the coldest day in summer would be mild to us in winter. The reason is, that in summer the cold day finds us unprepared. The organism during summer has been adjusting itself to the production of less and less heat, and if a cold day now occur, we have less power of resistance; we are somewhat in the condition of the infant animal, which has not yet acquired its full power of heat-making. It is on this principle that we may explain the death of animals exposed during summer to a degree of cold which in winter would scarcely lower their temperature.

We are not all blessed with the same capacity for rapidly developing heat; we are not all blessed with the same activity of the circulation. Yet each is apt to make himself the standard. B. shivers, and complains of the cold; thinks he must have the fire lighted, though it be June. C. is amazed that any one can possibly be cold on such a day; C. is quite warm. Perhaps, after reading these pages, B. will learn to understand that it is quite possible for C. to be comfortable in this temperature; and C. will learn to sympathise with the less fortunate B.'s, who shiver when he is warm. The differences may arise from two causes: the heat-producing capacity may be less, or the circulation feebler. The stimulus of the external cold increases the activity of the organic processes in one man, and depresses it in another. That this is the real cause, will appear on examining the influence of cold on the various classes of warm-blooded animals. One class — the hybernaters — is so incapable of resisting cold by an adequate increase of its own temperature, that it falls into a torpor; other classes are forced to seek external warmth in nests and holes, as we seek it in warm clothing and heated rooms; others, again, need nothing but their own temperature. In spite of the active respiration of a mouse, it needs a warm nest, and, unless in active exercise, will perish if exposed to a temperature which we should consider moderate: we, again, should perish in a temperature which the cat or dog could endure without uneasiness.

Among men there are some who resemble the mouse, and others who resemble the cat. The slightest fall of temperature causes the first to put on warmer clothing, or to light the fire; at which their robuster friends are liberal in sarcastic allusions, spoken or thought, and are somewhat impatient of this "coddling." These sarcastic friends are the cats.

It is important to bear in mind, however, that this inadequate production of heat does not always translate itself by the expression of "chilliness;" the effect of cold is often totally unlike that of a chilly sensation: it produces a vague uneasiness, a feeling of depression, resulting from the lowering of the organic

activity; and many periodic forms of disease are probably connected therewith. Without positively "feeling cold," the person
so affected need only enter a well-warmed apartment, to be at
once aware of a reinvigorated condition.

There is a misconception respecting cold which may here be
rectified. Capt. Parry tells us that with the thermometer at 55°
below zero — that is to say, 87° below freezing-point, — if no
wind be stirring the hands may remain uncovered for a quarter of
an hour without inconvenience; whereas with a fresh breeze,
even when the thermometer is at zero, few persons can keep the
hands exposed without pain. The fact is familiar to all, that
wind makes the bitterness of a winter day; and that even in
summer an east wind is bitter and sometimes painful. But why
is it so? Why are our sensations at variance with the thermometer? Why do we *feel* the cold to be greater on a windy day?
The reason is that we *are* colder; we *feel* the cold to be greater
because our loss of heat is more rapid. The air is a bad conductor, and unless it be blowing upon us, thus continually bringing fresh air in contact with our warm bodies, we produce heat
fast enough to replace what is carried off; but when the air
carries off heat faster than we can produce it, — when the evaporation from our skin is more rapid than the replacement, then
we have a continuous sensation of cold, because then our skin
really is cold. A dry wind, like the east wind, is cold because it
promotes a rapid evaporation; a moist wind, like the west wind,
is warm because its moisture retards evaporation.

Dr. Watson, in his Lectures, gives a very useful caution
against the readiness with which we may confound the effects of
long exposure to cold with those of intoxication. "There is too
much reason to believe that poor wretches, who have been picked
up by the constables in the streets at night during periods of
hard frost, have been supposed to be drunk, when in truth they
were only stupefied by cold."*

When is cold dangerous? It is always dangerous when
continuous: a dash of cold water, or of cold air, produces a
reaction; but a continued chilliness will produce disease. There
is a danger in wet feet, but this danger, as every one knows, does

* WATSON: *Practice of Physic,* I. 91.

not reach the sportsman, or the pedestrian, unless he sit still with
wet feet; it is the chilliness which comes on when evaporation is
not compensated by production of warmth, that causes the evil.
Again, it is dangerous to drink cold water after violent exercise;
but not at all dangerous to drink it during the exercise, before
the body has begun to cool. The organism can withstand the
most sudden alternations of heat and cold, but they must be
sudden, and the organism must be in vigour. A Russian heats
himself in a vapour bath and immediately plunges into snow.
But if he were to wait some minutes after quitting the vapour
bath, and allow his body to begin cooling, the snow bath would
probably kill him.

THEORY OF ANIMAL HEAT. — It will be necessary to devote a
few paragraphs to that theory of "Why we are warm, and how
we keep so," which has obtained general acceptance. There is
indeed a powerful and ever-increasing minority which rejects
that theory, and as this minority seems to me to have the best of
the argument, I will first state what the theory is, and then briefly
criticise it.

Animal Heat, it is said, is the effect of which Respiration is
the cause. In Respiration, oxygen is absorbed, which burns the
carbon of the food into carbonic acid, and the hydrogen into
water; in these acts of oxidation, heat is generated, for no combination of a combustible substance with oxygen can take place
without disengaging heat. No matter whether such oxidations
take place in the body or out of it, rapidly or slowly, at a low
temperature or at a high one, the amount of heat set free by the
combination of a given quantity of oxygen with a given quantity
of carbon or hydrogen, is always and everywhere the same. The
oxidation of the carbon of the food will liberate precisely as much
heat as if, instead of being spread over a long time, the combustion had taken place in a vessel of pure oxygen. Chemistry
assures us of these facts. Physiology assures us that oxygen is
incessantly absorbed in the lungs, and that carbonic acid and
water are as incessantly exhaled; and further assures us that,
concurrently with this absorption of oxygen and exhalation of
carbonic acid and water, there is an amount of heat generated

which would be generated by an equivalent combustion of carbon and hydrogen out of the organism. "It is obvious," says Liebig, "that the amount of heat liberated must increase or diminish with the quantity of oxygen introduced in equal times by respiration. Those animals, therefore, which respire frequently, and consequently consume much oxygen, possess a higher temperature than others, which, with a body of equal size to be heated, take into the system less oxygen."

Such is the so-called "chemical theory of Animal Heat." We have already seen how little confidence is to be given to the notion of the food being burnt in the organism; and when, therefore, we hear "the carbon of the food" spoken of as passing into carbonic acid, and disengaging heat, we must, if we accept the theory, declare that what is burnt is the carbon of the tissues made from that food. The oxygen which is absorbed in the lungs does not then and there combine with carbon in the blood, and generate its due amount of heat; this, which was formerly believed, is now given up by all competent physiologists. In giving up this idea, we must follow the course of the oxygen in the blood, until we detect it, *flagrante delicto*, in the act of burning the carbon; but this has hitherto escaped all research. *We are in utter ignorance as to the origin of carbonic acid in the organism.* We have many plausible explanations as to how it *may* arise, but how it *does* arise we do not know. It is extremely doubtful, according to Robin and Verdeil, whether *any* direct oxidation of carbon takes place at all, and is quite certain that much of the carbonic acid is not so produced. *  Without venturing further on ground so delicate, we will sum up in the words of the distinguished chemist Regnault, who has specially studied this question: "It was long believed (and many chemists still believe it) that the heat produced by an animal in a given time is precisely equal to that which would be produced by the burning in oxygen of the same amount of carbon and hydrogen which is found in the carbonic acid and water exhaled in that time. It is very probable that animal heat is entirely produced

---

* ROBIN et VERDEIL: *Traité de Chimie Anatomique*, II. 58 seq., 67, 168, 462, and III. 185 seq. Compare also BERNARD: *Liquides de l'Organisme*, I. 441 seq., on the absence of proof that water is formed in the organism.

by *the chemical actions which take place in the organism*, but the phenomenon is too complex to admit of our calculating it according to the quantity of oxygen consumed."[*] The simple fact that the carbonic acid exhaled, at times, contains *more* oxygen than has been absorbed, although perfectly intelligible when we remember the influence of food on the exhalation of carbonic acid, is of itself enough to destroy all confidence in such calculations.

As an example of the heat which is formed in the organism by the processes of life, not reducible to mere oxidations, let us consider the simple fact of muscular contraction. That heat is liberated every time a muscle contracts is well known, and the experiments of Matteucci and Helmboltz show that this heat is quite independent of any circulation of the blood. The former placed several frogs' legs in a glass and surrounded a thermometer with them; on irritating their nerves so as to produce muscular contractions, the temperature rose in the glass. Now unless it be maintained that oxidation necessarily precedes or accompanies every contraction of a muscle, it will be obvious that oxidation is not the sole source of Animal Heat; and when we reflect on the enormous amount of muscular contractions of all kinds which take place within the organism, we shall see that from this source alone a large amount of heat must arise. The same is true of all organic processes.

While, therefore, it is still undecided whether carbonic acid and water arise in the organism by a process of direct oxidation, the theory of Animal Heat, which is based on such an assumption, must necessarily be held questionable. Meanwhile we may look a little closer into the evidence which declares that Animal Heat is the direct product of Respiration, rising and falling with it, dependent on it, as effect upon cause. That a mass of evidence can be adduced is perfectly true, because, whatever theory we may form, we must still perceive that *an* intimate relation necessarily exists between Respiration and Animal Heat; if only on the ground that all vital processes are intimately related, and in the organism one function is necessarily dependent on another. The question, however, is not whether *an* intimate relation exists; but whether *the* causal relation exists, whether the two pheno-

* REGNAULT: *Cours Élémentaire de Chimie*, II. 868.

mena are in invariable correspondence, the one never feeble when the other is energetic — the one never acting after the other has ceased.

Disregarding the mass of evidence which may be adduced in favour of the correspondence, let us here fix our attention solely on some striking exceptions. The cases are by no means very rare in which a corpse has preserved a high temperature for many hours; and as Respiration must altogether have ceased, these cases have great significance for us. Dr. Livingstone mentions a case which came under his own eye, of a Portuguese lady, who died of fever at three o'clock in the morning of the 26th April. "The heat of the body continued unabated till six o'clock, when I was called in, and I found her bosom as warm as ever I did in a living case of fever. This continued for three hours more. As I had never seen such a case in which fever-heat continued so long after death, I delayed the funeral till unmistakable symptoms of dissolution occurred." Mr. George Redford informed me of a case which he had under his own eye. A soldier, given to drink, died, I forget from what cause, and the next day Mr. Redford was quite startled at finding the body still warm. Dr. Bennett Dowler, of New Orleans, has likewise observed that, in many cases, the temperature *rises* after death; and as these observations are cited by so eminent an authority as Professor Dunglison, we must give them a credit which might perhaps be refused to the cases previously mentioned. Dr. Dowler found that where the highest temperature during life was 104° under the armpit, it rose to 109° in ten minutes after death; fifteen minutes afterwards it was 113° in an incision in the thigh; in one hour forty minutes, it. was 109° in the heart. Three hours after all the viscera had been removed, an incision in the thigh showed the temperature to be 110°.

When we remember that, even after death, processes of growth and secretion have been observed to take place, there is nothing incredible in these examples of continued heat after death; but we cannot see how the advocates of the Respiration theory reconcile such facts as the complete absence of Respiration during several hours, with no diminution of Animal Heat. According to theory, the two phenomena are in immediate dependence, the intensity of heat corresponding with the energy of respiration; but here there is no respiration, nor has there been any for some hours, yet the heat continues to be produced. If it is said that the oxygen breathed during life suffices to keep up the oxidation after death; the answer is, that on this reasoning *all* bodies should continue warm many hours after death.

There are, moreover, numerous facts which show a similar want of correspondence between the energy of respiration and the intensity of heat. In tetanus, for example, the temperature has been known to rise to 110⁰ — an amazing height; yet no corresponding increase of respiration is noted. In women the energy of Respiration is strikingly inferior to that in men; according to Barral, 40 per cent less. Yet, although they "burn" so much less carbon than men, their temperature is scarcely lower, if lower at all. We lay more stress on this fact, because it is the expression of the normal condition of the organism. In all cases of disease there is a possibility of some totally new conditions which render our inferences inapplicable; but in the natural breathing of ordinary men and women we may expect to see the unobstructed action of the law which connects Respiration with Animal Heat. According to theory, women ought to have a very much lower temperature than men, for they exhale very much less carbonic acid in respiration, and must therefore "burn" less carbon. According to fact, women have as high a temperature as men. It looks plausible when we read that the amount of heat liberated must increase or diminish with the quantity of oxygen introduced in equal times by respiration; yet this plausibility becomes troubled when we find Animal Heat sometimes bearing no such relation to the amount of inspired oxygen. The woman is as warm as the man, with feebler respiration.

When we take a general survey of the animal kingdom, the correspondence between energetic respiration and high temperature is very striking, and affords that evidence to which allusion was made just now in favour of the current theory. The cold-blooded animals are all feeble breathers, and the most energetic breathers are the warmest-blooded. A mollusc, a fish, a frog, a quadruped, and a bird, represent the various stages of this correspondence. The absorption of oxygen is smallest in the mollusc, and greatest in the bird. The mollusc has the temperature of the medium in which it lives, or is so slightly raised above it that our ordinary instruments detect no elevation. The bird keeps a constant temperature of 110°.

So long as we content ourselves with such generalities, the evidence is ample. Indeed, we might, *a priori*, conclude that a general correspondence would necessarily be observed, because of the general connection which two organic functions always exhibit; but no sooner do we descend from generals to particulars — no sooner do we compare animals with each other, than the correspondence suddenly ceases to lend its aid to the theory. It is true, as a general fact, that birds have a higher temperature and more energetic respiration than quadrupeds. It is true, moreover, as a general fact, that in birds the highest temperature is found in those of the most energetic respiration, the active hawk or swallow being warmer than the barndoor fowl; but this is true only as a general fact: and if we continue comparing birds together, we shall find that the active predatory petrel has uniformly a much *lower* temperature than the domestic duck. Here the correspondence suddenly fails. "If we bear in mind the current ideas respecting the production of animal heat," says Brown-Séquard, parenthetically, "there is assuredly something strange in the fact that the class of birds to which the petrel belongs has not a higher temperature than we find to be the case. The active life of these birds, their extreme vigour, the rapidity of their flight, their food, so rich in fatty principles, and the warm climate in which many of them live, are so many circumstances which ought to give them a high temperature." As M. Brown-Séquard does not doubt the current theory, he is inclined to attribute this discrepancy to the occasional fasts which these birds are subject to. Being, on the whole, less well fed than domestic ducks, they are therefore, he thinks, lower in temperature. This will doubtless have its influence; yet differences in the temperature of birds cannot be wholly attributed to it: for, as M. Martins finds, ducks have a higher temperature than geese. Now, inasmuch as the goose is as well fed as the duck, as well covered with feathers, and as energetic in respiration, we should, *a priori*, expect it to have a higher temperature than the duck, because it is a general law that the smaller the animal the greater the rapidity with which it parts with its heat; yet the inexorable thermometer shows the duck to have a higher temperature than the goose.

A mouse eats eight times as much food, in proportion to its size, as a man, and its respiration is, according to Valentin,* eighteen times more energetic; yet its temperature is little higher than that of man', and its power of resistance to cold is incomparably lower. Birds eat six to ten times as much as a man, in proportion to weight, respire much more vigorously, and lose less heat by evaporation; nevertheless, they are only a few degrees higher, and their power of resistance to cold is in general much less. Valentin says that a dog consumes twice as much oxygen as a man, in proportion; yet the difference in their temperature is very slight.

These illustrations suffice to show that no invariable constancy can be found between Respiration and Animal Heat: even should the theory we are criticising ultimately turn out to be correct, the objections we have urged will still retain their force, not, indeed, against the truth of the theory, but against its inconsiderate interpretation; they will retain their value as indications of the presence of *physiological conditions*, and will show how varieties in the organism modify the operation of the general physical laws; thus removing the question of Animal Heat from the hands of the Chemist, and replacing it in the hands of the Physiologist. Treating the question as a physiological one, we are forced to consider Animal Heat as determined by the energy of two processes, one of production and another of radiation. Some organisms produce heat more rapidly than others, and some part with it more rapidly. The temperature of the organism will be determined by a balance of these processes. Insects produce heat with great rapidity; but they part with it so rapidly that their temperature is as low as that of the reptile, which produces heat slowly. The hybernating animals part with their heat more rapidly than other warm-blooded classes —

* VALENTIN: *Text-Book of Physiology* (translated by W. BRINTON), p. 351.

part with it too rapidly for the maintenance of their necessary warmth when the external temperature falls, and thus, the balance being destroyed, they sink into the condition of cold-blooded animals. If a young bird and an adult of the same species be exposed to the same degree of cold, although they have both the same temperature at starting, the young bird will in a short period be found to have a much *lower* temperature than the adult, because its production of heat has not been sufficiently rapid to keep pace with the loss.   The physiological causes which determine this rapid loss in the insect, the hedgehog, and the young bird, have yet to be investigated, and may at once be surmised to be different in each case. In the insect, the rapid loss is probably owing to the smallness of its size, and the free penetration of the air through its body. In the hedgehog and young bird, the actual loss may not be greater than in other animals of the same size; but the effect of cold on their organisms may be such as to materially retard those processes on which the production of heat depends. So clearly is the production of heat regulated by the general condition of the organism, that, at different seasons of the year, the same organism will produce different amounts of heat at the same temperature. In winter, the organism is in its greatest heat-producing condition; in summer at its lowest. If subjected in summer to a temperature of zero, its power of resistance will be found very inadequate to such a degree of cold; whereas in winter its power of resistance is so great as to make this degree of cold perfectly endurable. The usual explanation is, that there is a greater amount of oxygen contained in a similar volume of air in winter than in summer, so that at each inspiration a greater amount of combustion is rendered possible. But this is unsatisfactory. In the first place, in winter as in summer, the temperature of the mouth and lungs is constant, and the cold air entering would be warmed before the oxygen reached the blood; so that, unless the oxygen is in a different condition in winter than in summer (as some maintain), no solid argument can rest on the difference of the temperature of the air. In the second place, the experiments of W. Edwards do not admit of being thus explained. He placed sparrows in a glass vase, the air of which was maintained at freezing-point, in the months of February and July. This air, consequently, contained the same amount of oxygen in each case: and as the apparatus was in each case the same, and the birds the same, every variation in the result would be owing to the temporary condition of the organisms. In February the temperature of the birds only fell one degree centigrade during the first hour, remaining stationary there during the two succeeding hours; whereas in July it fell more than three degrees in the first hour, and continued to fall till the close of the third hour, when it had lost as much as six degrees. This experiment by no means tallies with the proposition laid down by Liebig, that "in different climates the quantity of oxygen introduced into the system by respiration, varies according to the temperature of the external air; the quantity of oxygen inspired increases with the loss of heat by external cooling; and the quantity of carbon or hydrogen necessary to combine with this oxygen must be increased in the same ratio;" for, on the contrary, we see here that the same temperature of the external air will at different seasons lower the temperature of the same bird *one* degree or *six* degrees. The cause cannot lie in the external air and its amount of oxygen, but in the organism, and its different conditions in winter and summer.

Has it never occurred to you, when standing beside a pond in early spring, that there was something paradoxical in the fact of frogs and toads crawling at the bottom, and never once rising to the surface to breathe? They are animals with lungs,' and in summer live mostly on land, perishing, indeed, if unable to get out of the water from time to time; yet during the whole winter, late autumn, and early spring, they pass their time under water. Puzzled by this fact, we applied to a zoologist for an explanation, and received in reply one of those explanations with which the majority of mankind are willing to be content, namely, a restatement of the fact in different language. Our own experiments and observations gave no explanation. We found, for instance, the two species of newt — land and water newts — behave very differently. Both have gills when young, and lungs in a more developed condition. When the gills of the land-newt disappear, the possibility of living under water dis-

314 WHY WE ARE WARM, AND HOW WE KEEP SO.

appears: the animal quits the water for ever, and you meet him
on your staircase, while his companion the water-newt is still
in the aquarium, and only occasionally thrusting his head above
water. As the season advances, the water-newt also feels the
need of occasionally quitting the water, and he will lie basking
on the bit of stone or wood for hours together, descending into the water as the coolness of evening descends. To
keep him under water for many hours in the hot weather, is to
kill him. It is the same with frogs and toads; and the reason
was made clear to us by the experiments of W. Edwards. He
found that as long as the temperature of the water is no more
than fifteen or sixteen degrees above freezing-point (47°-48°),
frogs will live the whole year round without once rising to the
surface. In this condition they *breathe only by the skin.* He
has shown the relation which surface-respiration bears to pulmonary respiration in these animals; and he finds that the skin
exhales sufficient carbonic acid, and absorbs sufficient oxygen,
to supply all their needs of languid life at this temperature. No
sooner does the temperature of the water rise, than the vital activity of the frog increases; and with this increase there is a
greater need of oxygen, a greater production of carbonic acid
— in other words, a greater energy of Respiration, for which
the skin no longer suffices, the lungs are called upon to do their
work; they cannot do this work in the water; and if the frog be
prevented from rising to the surface, it is prevented from breathing, and it perishes. We see this in spring. The frog, or newt,
occasionally rises to expire carbonic acid, and absorb oxygen by
its lungs. It then dives under the surface again. As the season
advances, the risings become more frequent, till in the hot
weather the frog lives chiefly on land, and the newt also is forced
to expose itself to the air.

    These facts do not accord with the hypothesis of Animal Heat
being the direct effect of Respiration; for we do not see the frogs
get warmer because their Respiration has become more extensive,
but their Respiration becomes more extensive because they are
warmer: warmth has increased the activity of their vital functions, and has increased Respiration, which is one of these.
We know how intimately dependent the vital functions are on

temperature, and in Chap. VI. we saw how Respiration in the cold-blooded animals uniformly increases in energy as the external warmth increases, up to a certain point; and we are therefore able to understand how it is that a low degree of vital activity will be found coincident with a feeble respiration and low temperature, while a high degree of vital activity is coincident with energetic Respiration and a high temperature, without our being forced to admit that this coincidence implies a direct causal relation between energy of Respiration and Animal Heat.

In conclusion, we may say that the hypothesis generally adopted respecting the production of Animal Heat is very far from possessing the evidence demanded by science. It may be true; we do not think It is true; and we are persuaded that it is not proven. It rests on two pillars, the very foundations of which are insecure. The first of these is the chemical hypothesis of direct oxidation of the carbon and hydrogen. The second is the assumed invariableness of the relation between intensity of heat and energy of respiration. We are not warranted in affirming either of these propositions; all we are warranted in affirming is this: Animal Heat is evolved in various chemical and physical changes which occur in the processes of life, and is consequently in direct correspondence with their energy, rising in intensity as they become more active, and falling as they fall. We have every reason to believe that oxygen is the great *inciter* of such changes, the indispensable condition of vital activity; but we have no direct evidence that these changes are all oxidations; we have direct evidence that some of them are not oxidations, but are dependent on Respiration only as one organic process is dependent on another, and as Respiration itself is dependent on them.

END OF VOL. I.